MW01592596

SOUL STORM

THE EDEN HUNTER TRILOGY (BOOK 1)

D.N. ERIKSON

Copyright © 2018 D.N. Erikson. All rights reserved.

Published by Watchfire Press.

This book is a work of fiction. Similarities to actual events, places, persons or other entities are coincidental.

Watchfire Press

www.watchfirepress.com

www.dnerikson.com

Cover design by James T. Egan of Bookfly Design

www.bookflydesign.com

Soul Storm/D.N. Erikson. – 1st ed.

ALSO BY D.N. ERIKSON

THE HALF-DEMON ROGUE TRILOGY

Half-demon Kalos Aeon lives by a simple code. But saving the world might force him to break it.

Demon Rogue (Book 1)

Blood Frost (Book 2)

Moon Burn (Book 3)

The Half-Demon Rogue: The Complete Trilogy

THE RUBY CALLAWAY TRILOGY

After twenty years in lockup, supernatural bounty hunter Ruby Callaway is conditionally released to help the FBI catch a killer.

Lightning Blade (Book 1)

Shadow Flare (Book 2)

Blood River (Book 3)

Ruby Callaway: The Complete Collection (The Complete Trilogy and All Four Side Stories)

THE EDEN HUNTER TRILOGY

Eden Hunter reluctantly reaps souls for a vampire warlord in the island city she calls home. Until an old enemy frames her for murder.

Soul Storm (Book 1)

Soul Fire (Book 2)

Soul Bite (Book 3)

Eden Hunter: The Complete Collection

1

I tossed and turned on the worn leather couch, staring out the living room window at the gentle ocean as I waited for sleep to take me.

It did not oblige.

Tonight felt like the exact kind of night where everything seemed okay, but where, somewhere deep in your soul, you knew everything was about to go wrong. I shifted my gaze toward the slanted ceiling that stretched twenty feet above my bare living room.

Sleep still refused to come—just like most nights.

Dying once will do that.

But, like most people, I'd also been dealing with a little work-related stress. Granted, my issues were more unusual than the standard nine-to-five annoyances.

There'd been a shortage of souls available to harvest on the island over the last couple months.

I'd gotten lucky last week, carving out my fifth soul just before my quota was due.

And my employer didn't take missed quotas lightly.

With my cheek smooshed against the armrest, I

surveyed the room. Other than my sofa, a lamp, and all the clothing I owned—some worn jeans, a few vintage t-shirts, a couple pairs of low-top sneakers—the living room was as empty as a grave-robbed tomb.

Just how I liked it.

A girl doesn't buy herself beachfront property at the jungle's edge for no damn reason.

A *scritch-scratch* on the stairs outside made my arm hair stand on end.

Live on the precipice of the known world alone for too long and every small noise got the imagination churning.

Killer warlocks, coming to learn my secrets with mind control magic.

Vampires ready to slit my throat to gain access to what only I knew.

Or maybe just an ambitious and morally bankrupt alchemist, coming to see if the island's only Reaper had a stash of souls hidden under her floorboards.

They'd all be out of luck. The only things I had on hand other than the couch were whiskey and black coffee—and the souls were locked safely away. But the scratching outside didn't stop.

Instead, it got louder.

I swung my feet off the couch and peered out the window, seeing little in the moonlit darkness beyond the winding marble staircase leading up from the beach. I reached beneath the couch for my Reaper's Switch—a four-inch switchblade that was my only weapon—feeling its cool plastic handle touch my fingertips.

The scratching grew closer.

It's just a monkey, Eden. Or a tree sloth bumbling in from the jungle.

But then I heard the unmistakable, guttural howl of a beast answering the call of the moon.

A werewolf was outside my door.

As quietly as possible, I rose from the couch, clutching the Reaper's Switch. Stiff denim chafed my thighs. These jeans needed to be washed, badly.

After slipping my sneakers on, I stole across the bamboo hardwood into the adjacent foyer. The living room merged into the villa's entrance almost seamlessly, with only the stubbiest of walls sticking out to delineate the two areas. I pressed myself against the hearty oak doors, the cool wood brushing my cheek as I stared out the peephole.

The werewolf's scarred face wore a wild-eyed stare. His clothing hung in tatters around his semi-naked body. No one I recognized. His transformation wasn't yet complete, but he was already grunting and shaking in a manner no human—other than a meth-head—ever did. Thick, knotty veins circling his forearms hinted at the rough, primal strength wolves were legendary for.

Werewolves were one of the oldest species of magical creatures on Earth—a brand of creature classified by arcana archeologists as primordial beasts. Being of rather archaic lineage, their instincts tended to be of a baser nature, and they still possessed the raw genetic physical skills necessary to survive in a nasty and brutish world.

The ugly, scarred man howled at the moon again. Coarse brown hair sprouted on his face. His nose twitched feverishly as his head swiveled through the warm night air.

Shit. He could smell me.

His full weight smashed against the front doors.

The thick oak cracked at the hinges, buckling inward and slamming against my forehead.

I stumbled backward.

Blood pumping, head spinning, my instincts told me to run.

But I had nowhere to go.

The door caved in after a second effort from the wolf.

The half-transformed beast hurled the cracked wood aside like cheap plastic.

"Eden Hunter." His eyes blazed with a fierce red glow. Thick brown hair now covered most of his body, and his jaw had taken on a snout-like shape. He had a strong, musky odor, like he'd spent the night rolling in his own pee.

A few minutes more and his feral nature would take over.

Then I'd be screwed.

"I don't remember inviting company." I stood my ground, wearing a confident smile as the words drifted into silent nothingness.

The wolf stalked forward, but I resisted the urge to run. Fleeing would trigger his primal instincts. I'd need to slow him down before I could escape.

Seeing his markings up close, I could see this wasn't just any wolf, either.

This was an alpha—one who had killed many times before.

His soul tasted blackened and corrupt, like a poorly grilled steak combined with a nuclear winter. I tried to spit the taste out, but it lingered, my tongue dry as desert bone.

Sometimes I hated being a Reaper. Tasting people's life stories sucked.

"To what do I owe this astounding pleasure?" I asked with a defiant smirk.

It was all bluster. My stomach felt like it was filled with molten jelly.

"Consider this notice of your early termination, Eden

Hunter," he said, delivering the message like a process server. His fur-covered hands hung by his sides. I watched his nails grow into yellow, talon-like claws as the seconds ticked by. "Questions?"

How nice of an assassin to ask. But he'd clearly been given orders by someone who outranked him—and, as such, he was obliged to obey their commands.

I guess one of those instructions had been to grant me a few last words.

"Now that you mention it..." I brought my head up to meet his gaze. A jagged scar raked through his matted fur, zig-zagging from his half-formed snout to the corner of his left eye. "I do have one question."

"Which is?"

"Would you like something to drink?"

Confusion washed over his remaining human features, and he looked away, staring at my picture-less walls for an explanation.

It wasn't an unexpected reaction.

The brain has trouble processing unexpected requests.

We expect the world—and conversation—to follow certain rules. I was supposed to scream or beg for my life or tell him to fuck off. But posing a trivial question made no sense. Which forced him to stop and think.

Not much of an opening, but it was enough.

The Reaper's Switch deployed with a snap.

I slashed him deep in his right leg.

Blood sprayed against the bare white wall.

He reeled backward, a whine slipping from his furry lips.

But I didn't stop to see how injured he was.

I just sprinted toward the glass staircase hugging the living room wall, hoping my second life wasn't about to end.

2

I took the clear glass steps two at a time and cut a hard right into what would've been the guest bedroom—if I'd ever bothered to have guests. I could still smell the drywall and paint from when I'd fixed the empty room up four years ago.

I threw the large oceanside window open and glanced outside. Two-story drop, plenty of rocks to hit if I missed the sand. But staying inside wasn't more appealing. Downstairs, the wolf roared, his transformation accelerated by my attack.

I tossed the Reaper's Switch out first. It hit a rock with a sharp *crack* and bounced into the foliage ringing the villa.

Great. Well, at least I knew where *not* to jump. With a deep breath—and a silent prayer to my goddess—I took the plunge.

The wind streamed through my hair. I landed in a dense grove of bushes and rolled toward the black sand, breaking my fall without injury. Inside, the werewolf unleashed a final roiling howl. After scrambling for the

Reaper's Switch—which I mercifully found without too much effort—I began running like hell up the dark beach.

The switchblade's broken plastic handle cut into my palm as my feet pounded over the moonlit black sand. Slivers of starry light glinted off the four-inch stainless steel magical blade. The beachy aroma of sea salt drifted through the late summer air, carrying the squawks of monkeys and toucans.

So, you know, just your average romantic night in paradise. Add a couple candles, an expensive red from a great year, and you'd have the perfect setup for a slow-burn kiss. The kind from a romance paperback.

Luckily, I read thrillers.

Unluckily, when I turned around, I saw a snarling were-wolf charging down the villa's marble stairs, determined to separate my head from my neck.

Not happening, buddy.

I'd died once already, and I'd seen nothing but black— until I hadn't. And I had little intention of visiting the Elysian Fields—and its *Dante's Inferno* inspired worlds of hierarchical hell—ever again.

My stiff jeans rubbed my thighs raw as I sprinted toward the service road.

I just needed to make it to my bike.

But, even with a wounded leg, the would-be assassin ate up a yard of beach with each loping stride, his paws thundering across the dark sand with the ferocity of a post-typhoon tide.

My sneakers sank into the wet sand, further slowing my escape. The service road was still a half-mile off—too far away. With the endless Pacific stretching out to my left, and the darkness of the feral jungle bounding me in on the right, I saw only one option remaining.

And it sure as hell wasn't escape.

I exhaled sharply and turned around, brandishing the knife in a defensive stance.

"Who the hell sent you?" I yelled, trying my best to sound fearsome. But when you're under five-six, and your attacker is six and a half feet of primal sinew and bone, bluffing rarely gets you very far.

The wolf howled in response as the moon reached its apex over the perfect aquamarine waters. It wasn't a full moon, but a single razor-sharp claw to the jugular would cut my borrowed life short all the same. I silently cursed the magical bonds forbidding me from wielding weapons—my pitiful Reaper's Switch excluded.

The knife had all the stopping power of a flyswatter against a full-grown alpha werewolf.

Saliva dangled from his bared fangs. No trace of the man remained—only beast.

Out of options, I pulled out the final proverbial rabbit remaining in my hat: the light show, as I liked to call it. The lantern sigil on my right wrist glowed as I called upon the only spell in my arsenal.

"Last chance, asshole." Light streamed from my wrist, forming a manic ball of fury around my fingers. The colors jumped from an apocalyptic orange to the greenish-blue of a mid-Pacific storm, then back again.

I held the glowing ball of energy, expecting him to recoil in fear. But he didn't move, despite being only twelve paces away.

Instead, he laughed.

The bastard knew it was all a trick—like a venomless snake adopting the markings of its far deadlier brethren. The light show made me *look* like a powerful sorceress, but it didn't give me real fangs.

The gambit almost always worked, though, because few knew about my sigil.

In fact, no one knew—outside of my current employer and the ink master who had done the work four years ago.

A tingle rushed over my skin like an electrical charge. *Early termination.* Points to the wolf for making a clever, double-edged pun: my employer was giving me the axe in literal fashion. So I had the *who* responsible.

But I still lacked a *why*: why would Aldric try to kill his only Reaper?

I'd hit last week's deadline by the skin of my teeth, but I'd still delivered five souls.

Just as agreed.

I'd be sure to ask what the hell was going on, assuming I survived the next two minutes.

I wasn't much of a fighter, nor had I ever been, even in the past—you know, in those halcyon days when holding a weapon *didn't* result in a horrible, festering blister burn only a talented apothecarial sorceress could heal.

Fortunately, however, I also had a backup plan to Plans A and B.

With a spine-tingling yell, I unleashed the Molotov of useless light at the wolf's scarred face. He roared, shielding his blood-red eyes from the glowing ball as it zoomed past.

I dropped to one knee, planting the Reaper's Switch blade-up in the dark sand three steps away.

The temporarily blinded wolf charged.

A second later, his full weight came down—straight through my knife.

Due to the light, his usually keen eyes had been unable to spot the blade in the dark sand.

He unleashed a spine-cracking howl.

Twelve feet away. One-yard gait.

Simple math—like the odds in blackjack.

Unfortunately, I hadn't factored inertia into the equation.

His momentum carried his thick body straight into my legs, and we crashed into the frothing low tide.

The wolf whimpered as he tried to claw at me. I dodged the half-speed blows and rolled further into the pleasantly cool water. Heart pounding like an unhinged freight train, I slowly rose and limped back to the wolf, who was clawing at the blade. The point glistened with blood, sticking from the top of his foot like a flagpole claiming a summit.

It had gone straight through the bottom.

Not bad for a backup plan.

"Silver and obsidian studded," I said. "Cuts through anything. But Aldric probably mentioned that."

I pressed my wet sneaker against his wounded leg.

The assassin's eyes flashed a deep, feral red. He swiped again, but his reflexes were dulled by the silver. I avoided the wolf's punch-drunk slashes as I reclaimed my Reaper's Switch from his ruined paw. Blood streamed across the dark sand when I removed the knife.

"Tell Aldric he made his point." I wagged the blade at the alpha's sharp snout in warning.

I still wasn't sure what point that was, exactly. But I was hoping the wolf would get the message and dutifully relay it to our mutual employer. I wasn't a killer—and besides, I couldn't kill him even if I had wanted to.

Yet another rule courtesy of the rain goddess who had also barred me from properly arming myself. This goddamn island was overrun by annoying red tape, contracts, and rules.

But I'd signed the contracts and made the agreements.

Unfortunately, my new acquaintance didn't care.

And he was a fast son of a bitch without the silver in him.

I was pinned to the shore before I could tell him to give up again. The Reaper's Switch tumbled into the foaming tide.

My elbows scraped over broken shells.

Slobbery strands dripped from the wolf's sharp snout as he snapped at my face.

I bobbed left and he came up with a mouthful of sand. Taking the opening, I bashed my wrist into his nose. His lips curled in a manic snarl—more annoyed than hurt.

His soul called to me, bloodlust consuming every aspect of his being. I'd learned how to read people when I was a teenager, but glimpsing into the soul was like seeing their poker hand.

And right now, I was seeing an intense desire for him to wear me as a hat.

My fingers blindly searched for the blade.

My pulse thumped out a staccato, off-kilter rhythm.

The wolf stared at my jugular with those blood-red eyes.

I snared the wet Reaper's Switch between my index and middle fingers just as he reared back again. This time, however, he aimed lower.

The fangs sliced through my shoulder.

I yelped. His jaw tightened, driving his teeth deeper.

But I clung to the Reaper's Switch like a life preserver in a roiling sea.

Then I plunged the glittering, blood-soaked blade right into his sinewy neck, shitty employers, goddesses, and unbreakable agreements be damned.

His jaw released from my shoulder like I'd smashed a

button. I yanked the Reaper's Switch out from the mountain of dense fur and stabbed his neck again.

And again, one last time.

Then I pushed with all my strength, squirming from beneath the hairy body. My adversary rasped out a convulsing breath and then went still, snout down in the dark, damp sand.

My shoulder throbbed from the bite. Nothing moved in the still night.

I whispered, "Damnit."

Breaking the no-kill rule would have serious consequences. You didn't screw with the gods. Lucille would reclaim my sister's life—or worse—for breaking our agreement. So, as the water lapped against my stiff, tired body, I figured there was only one way to avoid paying for my sins.

Bury them.

I'd been a con artist once. A master of the grift.

I'd have to conjure up all my dormant skills to make this illusion stick.

To think, twenty minutes before, I'd been concerned about my soul quota.

Now, that seemed as menial as any other nine-to-five deadline.

My forearms quivered as I dragged the furry body into the ocean. The water lapped over my aching feet, soaking my sneakers as I worked. My fingers lingered on the corpse, which bobbed in the gentle surf. Finally, I took out my Reaper's Switch and slid the blade in right above his heart, where every being's soul resided.

The wolf's looked exactly like it had tasted: like the remnants of a terrible fire. I cradled the tiny chunk of matter in my palm, no larger than a pack of gum.

That made one.

Another week in paradise, another quota to fulfill.

But I had a feeling this week was going to be just a *little* different.

Because, for one thing, it looked like I no longer had a job.

I waded back to shore, my jeans clinging to my thighs like crackly cellophane.

A light wind picked up from the horizon, chilling my damp skin.

Far up the beach, I heard thunder in the cloudless night. Maybe I was already screwed. Deities had a way of knowing things before anyone else. I couldn't keep a secret this big tucked away from a rain goddess for long.

Bang.

An uneasy shiver racked my wet body.

That wasn't thunder.

That was a gun.

And it was coming from the direction of my villa. Right next to it, in fact.

Another muzzle flash lit up the horizon, and then another.

Which is when I heard a different noise.

A scream—the kind of scream I'd have made earlier if I'd had any breath to spare.

Fear chilled my spine as the shots cascaded into the starry blackness. Aldric wasn't done.

My last remaining adrenaline reserves kicked in, and I sprinted toward the service road as the shooter emptied their gun into the otherwise silent night.

3

I RAN THROUGH ALL THE POSSIBLE NEXT MOVES AS THE wind streamed through my hair. The import bike's 4-stroke engine growled as the speedometer raced past sixty. I leaned into the sharp turn, the road almost touching my soaked jeans. What had started as a sleepless night had quickly turned into a literal existential crisis. As in, if things progressed down the rabbit hole further, it wouldn't be long before I ceased to exist.

If I'd just been handed my pink slip, I'd have been thrilled. I liked harvesting souls for Aldric about as much as I liked poking needles through my fingers.

But Aldric had tried to kill me instead.

And then he'd sent backup to finish the job.

Worst part was, I couldn't just quit. We had a soul-binding agreement.

And I'd held up my end of the deal for the last four years, hating every minute.

Ultimately, every choice ran to one inevitable end: heading into the city to face him.

Maybe my judgement was clouded by the werewolf's bite—or maybe I was just pissed enough at Aldric to confront him.

Regardless of motive, it was an insane plan. No plan at all, really, unless my goal was to die. I'd survived my clash with the werewolf assassin, but that was blind luck—like hitting on twenty in blackjack and being gifted an ace.

Going toe-to-toe with a 2,400-year-old vampire? That wouldn't end well.

But I couldn't return home, since my villa had suddenly become murder central. There was no place I could hide on Atheas if he wanted me dead. Aldric had discovered the island back in 552 A.D., which meant he owned it, ran it, and ruled it with an iron fist. And seeing as how my indentured contract lasted another three years—during which time I couldn't leave the island's borders—going on the lam elsewhere wasn't viable.

Fleeing wouldn't have been an option anyway. Aldric had infinite time and resources to extract his pound of flesh. A vampire warlord who had helped Alaric the Visigoth sack Rome—and adopted a variant of his former master's name in tribute—wasn't someone you ran from.

So, maybe I wasn't crazy.

Maybe I was thinking straight.

One thing bothered me as the city lights approached: I still couldn't understand why I was being terminated. I was his only Reaper. We were rare, and we sure as hell weren't free. He'd paid a hefty price in souls and favors to have me revived me from the Elysian Fields, minted as a harvester of souls, and then finally returned to the land of the living.

None of it added up.

I eased off the throttle, allowing the bike to coast down a

short hill as Black Sea Holdings' headquarters came into view. You couldn't miss it if you ventured into the city. It was a bland, corporate-looking structure, the kind all illegitimate crime lords dream of owning one day to launder their money and sponsor youth softball leagues. The glass and steel skyscraper stretched about thirty stories into the starry night. Barely noticeable in a place like Chicago, but here it dominated the skyline. All the lights were out, except for the massive penthouse office, which took up a third of the building's height. It glowed like a beacon, urging me closer. Or maybe it was a warning flare, screaming at me to run like hell.

Either way, I'd made up my mind.

I'd just have to live—or die—with the consequences.

I killed the bike's engine and left it parked in the executive lot. My soaked sneakers squished on the smooth asphalt as I headed toward the immaculate sandstone sidewalk. I passed the logo-emblazoned stone sign sitting next to a flower bed. The clean logo was so nondescript—not even an image to go with the text—that it was impossible to tell what Black Sea Holdings did. Which was the point.

Were they a shipping magnate?

A law firm?

Some sort of import-export operation?

Even looking at their balance sheet wouldn't have told you a damn thing.

After all, there wasn't a double-entry bookkeeping system with a "souls harvested" column. Not that my small role in the organization was what kept it from being fully transparent—I was merely a tiny, scythe-carrying cog in a sordid supernatural machine.

The automatic glass doors slid open when I punched in

my access code. Good to know I still worked here—or maybe Aldric hadn't expected me to ever return. No need to waste time disabling a soon-to-be deprecated code.

I dragged my aching body inside, footsteps echoing across the unlit, sparsely furnished lobby. My right shoulder throbbed from the werewolf bite. The wound was already seeping brackish slime through the torn black fabric. Foul fluid dripped all the way down to the crook of my elbow.

I'd have to get the wound examined, and soon. Leave a werewolf bite go untreated for too long and the results got ugly. Well, it was already ugly, but I meant *wake up without make-up after raiding the Jim Beam distillery* level ugly. As I headed toward the glittering elevators, I made a mental note to visit Jack's Apothecary Shack before amputation became a necessity.

I called the penthouse elevator. It promptly dinged, inviting me in. A little voice—the one of reason, perhaps—whispered that I could still turn around, that everything could be forgotten.

But then I thought about the gunshots near the villa, and that horrible scream, and I stepped inside, knowing that, if I didn't face Aldric now, that would be me.

Sooner, rather than later.

Better to die bravely than live in fear, right? I'm sure some smart person wrote that down in a book for posterity, but as the elevator doors opened, I wanted to reach through time, shake them, and scream that they were full of shit.

I stepped into a dimly lit hallway where everything gleamed. This was where the vampire worked, slept, and fed. The dueling scents of bleach and ammonia hung in the midnight quiet. My sneakers left behind little pools of water as I walked across the polished black granite, the soggy soles emitting squeaking echoes with each step in the cathedral-like hall. The ceiling stretched a hundred feet in the air, money being no object when intimidation was the name of the game. Much to my eternal chagrin, my knees wobbled as I braved the gauntlet. There was only one set of doors at the end of the hall, but Aldric made you sweat it out for a good two hundred feet.

Two massive doors, crafted from petrified oak trees imported from the Eurasian Steppes, were embedded within a wall resembling a sheer, smooth cliff face. Black granite soared into a ceiling of glass that segued seamlessly into the starry night. A chestnut leather sofa, probably costing more than my villa, sat outside the office doors, matched with a conservative but elegant glass table. There was a single book on the table—Aldric's favorite, impossible to forget—a first edition, ready for visitors to read.

Despite being a classic, it had already made my never-in-an-infinite-lifetime reading list. Which, when you dealt with magical creatures, was a real possibility. The immortality thing—not reading *The Lord of the Flies*. Leave it to ancient vampires to shit all over the good classics. Why couldn't he have picked the kind of crap that had made me drop out of high school, like *The Scarlet Letter*? Not even the try-hard study bees enjoyed that Puritan mess.

I dug my Reaper's Switch out and tightened my fingers around the broken handle. A futile gesture if there ever was one, but it made me feel like I had a little chance—like when you buy a Powerball ticket and start dreaming of all the yachts you're about to buy. Never gonna happen, but hope is a powerful drug.

Slightly emboldened, I banged against the solid doors. No answer came, so I waited, feeling smaller and more inconsequential by the second. My pulse thumped in my ears, and the little voice in my head returned to whisper *run, run, run*.

But I'd already crossed the Rubicon.

A voice came from the office, its icy edge well-cultivated from years of pillaging.

"Come in, Eden Hunter."

It's said that people can't get enough of hearing their own name. But that was the second time that night when hearing it had been a markedly unpleasant experience. The solid door opened on its own, controlled by an invisible mechanism. I slipped inside, finding myself in the same room I'd visited almost every Friday for the past four years. As always, Aldric's office was utilitarian and spartan. Behind the desk, I could see his close-cropped black hair and the hint of a well-maintained beard. He'd been turned as a young man, so his appearance offered no hint of his true age—other than the titanic, room-enveloping presence of his long-lived soul. The effect was so overwhelming that I suspected everyone could sense it, even if they didn't know exactly how to describe it. They might refer to it as an aura, or some brand of talismanic charisma.

The vampire warlord often had his soul obscured by cloaking wards. Which suggested that he'd been expecting me, and was trying to drive home a point.

He didn't turn to greet me, but I could feel his hawkish green eyes studying my reflection in the immaculate window pane. I could also see my face wrought with fear, lips trembling, legs about to collapse in a damp heap. Guess I wasn't ready to die again. Maybe I should've listened to that little whisper.

Oh, well. Too damn late now.

"If it isn't my favorite Reaper."

"You're like my third favorite vampire."

"Sit."

I looked at the chairs like they'd been plucked from a dumpster fire. "I'll stand if it's all the same to you."

"I should have selected a more pliable individual." He snapped his fingers, which had no effect on me. I'd seen humans willing to throw themselves off high-rises after such a gesture. Training at Black Sea Holdings was...a little different, let's say. "One of my few regrets."

"I believe the way you described me was a diamond in the rough." Or something to that effect. My initiation into the supernatural world had been fraught with fear and confusion. Being suddenly revived from the dead will do that.

"Sometimes diamonds are merely cubic zirconia." Aldric sighed, his lean muscles tensing beneath his sharp suit. My heart beat faster. If he so chose, he could rip my throat out and feed it to me before I even realized his chair was empty. But he remained seated, albeit in restrained annoyance.

"Is that why you tried to kill me?"

He rubbed his bearded chin and ignored my question. "There is no going back, as the people of this country say. There is only forward."

"You sure we're really a part of America?" Not that I needed to be correcting him, but I'd never considered Atheas an American territory. Maybe, after all these years, my mother's pleas to "be proper" had finally rubbed off. That was almost more horrifying than the thought of my voice box lying in bloody tatters on the teak hardwood.

"The FBI seems to believe they have jurisdiction in my territory."

Under normal circumstances, that would have rated as

interesting news. Given the situation, however, I was focused on more selfish concerns.

Like whether I was going to walk out of here alive.

And, if I did, what it was going to cost me.

Aldric spun around slowly, the chair's bearings creaking. His eyes reflected the passage of more than two thousand years, and even though I was immune to any of his vampiric tricks, they were still powerful enough to make me almost freeze in place. His entire body was as lean and sharp as a well-tempered blade, down to his high cheekbones and strong chin. It wasn't the angularity that made him ugly. If I didn't know better, I would share a whiskey with him. But once the curtain came up, blood dripped from all those sharp edges. Death clung to his skin like his perfectly-tailored custom suit, lurking in each perfectly pressed fold.

"The FBI, huh?" I managed to say, having nothing clever prepared.

"But truth be told, I could not care what the American government thinks at all."

That was a lie, and a bad one. Their presence ate at him. This was one of the last places on Earth ruled by a single man. An island kingdom with its vampire warlord—a place that, due to weather features and vagaries of science no one understood, was invisible from the air and impossible to find without the assistance of a knowledgeable navigator. Some might call that magic, others a strange quirk of chemistry and physics. But the reality remained the same, either way: no accurate maps to Atheas existed, and in a world smothered by satellites and selfies, it lay uncharted and left to its own devices some hundred miles south of Hawaii.

But we were getting off track. I stepped toward his desk, and Aldric raised his hand.

"What happened to your Reaper's Switch?"

I glanced at the broken handle, which I still clutched tightly. "You know what happened."

"Give it to me." He held out a smooth hand, the perfect cuff of his collared shirt peeking out from his suit jacket. I hesitated and glared. "Or I can take it from you."

"You wouldn't—" But it was out of my hands before I could finish my sentence. He propped his Italian loafers on his desk as he tossed the blade back and forth.

"You should treat your gifts better." He caught the knife with a final flourish and shot me an icy stare. "Otherwise, the gift-giver might get the wrong impression."

"Is that why you tried to kill me? Wrong impressions?"

"Wake-up calls are mere warnings, Eden." Aldric stroked his beard and kicked an open manila folder toward me with his heel. "Although, I must admit, the odds were not in your favor."

"Glad I could surprise you."

"You have never failed in that regard."

I squinted to examine the files. It looked like it had come from a CIA typewriter circa-1960—no doubt written by one of Moreland's goons. Like all the best criminal masterminds, Aldric had a network of spies and informants running around the island that could challenge the best intelligence agencies.

My stomach flopped when I got to the second paragraph.

That soul shortage keeping me up late at night?

Turns out I had a little Reaping rival on the island.

"You said I was the only one."

"You can see how this development leaves my—is it, they say, hands bound?"

"Close enough," I said, not bothering to correct the idiom. "You still get your souls either way. What do you care?"

"Because." Aldric's expensive shoes slid slowly off the desk—far more terrifying a gesture than putting a knife to my throat. "It means that a competitor has arrived."

Warlords didn't do competitors. Souls were like gold—a currency valued for both their relative rarity and myriad of uses. Other than a medium of exchange, they could be used to create magical items, grant someone powers—like my lantern sigil—who otherwise had none, and a host of other useful things. This was why Aldric had gone to such great lengths to acquire a Reaper of his own: I provided steady access to the most valuable commodity in the supernatural world.

He'd enjoyed a monopoly over that sliver of the island's supernatural economy. But if someone else had their very own Reaper, that meant his stranglehold on that particular black market revenue stream was in danger of deteriorating. *No muy bueno.* The massive penthouse office suddenly felt very claustrophobic indeed.

I'd thought I was the only Reaper on the island.

But, apparently, I was wrong.

I finally stepped forward and flipped through the rest of the papers. Things didn't get better. Judging from the estimated harvesting totals on the other documents, I now also ranked as the *second*-best Reaper on Atheas.

Upon reaching the end, I found no photographs or information on my competition, other than the fact that she existed and was good at her job. Even her gender was merely conjecture.

"Wouldn't killing your own Reaper strengthen your competition?"

"And yet, you survived."

"Two assassins are pretty tough odds to beat."

This got Aldric's attention. His head cocked sharply, like a predator hearing something it didn't like. "The wolf was the only one."

"Then explain why someone was firing off a six shooter in front of my house," I said.

"That individual was not doing my bidding."

"Forgive me if I don't believe you."

"What you believe changes nothing." Aldric's muscles relaxed as he leaned back in his executive chair. "You should be more concerned about how you might improve your professional performance going forward."

Ah. The real reason for my attempted early termination.

Poor performance. Being second best just wouldn't do.

And, after all this, it sure sounded like *I* was going to have to make things up to *him*. Like it was my fault someone else had gone through the Reaper making song and dance, then set up shop in his backyard. I wasn't security or enforcement; I just delivered the goods and went home.

"This is bullshit," I said in a soft voice.

"Such is life, Eden."

I rubbed my soggy sneaker against the slick hardwood and waited for the words to come—the silver-tongued phrase that would free me from the proverbial noose tightening around my neck. But I could sense, from the way Aldric had chosen to impart his little lesson on performance —and how his green eyes now cut into me from across the heavy desk—that nothing I could say would change his mind.

So I just said, "What do you want me to do?"

"That's simple, Eden." Here, a normal person might've smiled—maliciously, perhaps, to establish their dominance, or with a sneer, to indicate that incompetence wouldn't be tolerated. But Aldric didn't need to resort to petty displays of power. His expression remained etched in stone: cold and unfeeling. "Seven souls a week."

I swallowed the urge to scream. Five had been hard enough. Creatures had to *die* for me to harvest their souls. Since I wasn't a serial killer, that meant I had to keep on the flatlined pulse of every dead thing across this massive floating land mass.

"Okay," I finally said, seeing no other option.

"And you must remove your competition."

"Remove as in what?" I asked.

Aldric didn't respond. Oh, Lucille would love that. Not one, but *two* murders. That would go over real smoothly.

"You wouldn't perhaps know *who* this other Reaper might be?" I tapped the closed file.

"I trust you'll be resourceful," Aldric said, offering no additional cache of information. "After returning from the dead, such a task should be simple."

His opinion of simple and mine were apparently different. I waited in the vain hope that he would elaborate—maybe give me a lead beyond *there's someone who's doing a better job at this than you and I do not approve*. But I must've been wishing for too much, because he simply stared back in stony silence. After a moment, I turned to leave, and he cleared his throat.

"Forgetting something?"

"What?" I glanced back, just in time to see the open Reaper's Switch hurtling through the air. I barely caught the handle before the blade would have cleaved off my ear. The smashed plastic was now wrapped in thick tape.

"Duct tape is one of the few signs of progress in this modern world," Aldric said, his icy expression not changing. "Don't waste this gift, Eden."

I looked at the knife and then retracted the blade, swallowing hard. His "gift" wasn't the slap-dash fix for the Reaper's Switch.

The vampire warlord meant my second chance, which, in my book, wasn't really much of a second chance at all.

4

WELL, WONDERFUL.

I had nearly been killed for being outperformed by a fellow Reaper who, until ten minutes ago, I hadn't even known existed. That seemed unfair, but then again, fairness was for fifth graders. The real world was just relentless buckets of ice water. If you were lucky, whoever was tossing them in your face didn't leave an ice pick at the bottom.

Not wanting to go home, I went for a midnight ride to clear my head.

Threats to my life aside, I now needed to deliver seven souls to Aldric come Friday.

So I put in a late-night call to Edgar, the local funeral director.

As luck would have it, he was awake and had something "impressive" in stock.

I headed over to Atheas Acres Funeral Parlor and parked out front. The door was locked this late at night, but a quick jimmy from my switchblade and I was inside.

I took in the faded furniture as I pushed into the casket showroom.

I sensed Edgar before I saw him.

His soul tasted bitter, like a vodka tonic made with too much lime and bottom-shelf liquor. I tried to shake the sensation from my tongue as I paced around the plain-carpeted showroom floor densely packed with gleaming caskets and obscenely priced urns.

Low volume classical music flowed from small in-ceiling speakers to set an appropriately somber tone. The lack of windows made me feel like I was the one who had died. I brushed my fingers over an expensive casket allegedly crafted from mahogany. Furniture polish hovered around the coffin in thick, smog-like clouds. The rich wood was banded by a gold inlay, and its plush interior was a rich, royal shade of purple velvet. It was either destined for a king or a pimp. Depending on how snarky you wanted to get, you might ask, *what's the historical difference, Eden?*

To which I'd have a bulletproof answer ready: respectability. It might have been an illusion, but it forgave almost all misdeeds. The oldest of cons.

I did a second lap around the funeral home's showroom and sighed. Getting rid of the soul's taste was futile, same as always. I'd have to wait for it to fade. Just one of the amazing perks of being a Reaper—a soul radar granting me involuntary free samples of everyone's life story, 'til perpetuity.

Some stories sucked worse than others. At least Edgar's wasn't as bad the werewolf assassin's.

Returning to the garish pimp-king casket, I touched the handles, which were also—what else—gold. But a quick scrape from my fingernail revealed that the precious metal was nothing but stainless steel coated in a couple layers of cheap spray paint. It made me wonder, when Mom went to bury Dad, whether the funeral director back in Chicago had ripped her off, too. I'd never gotten along with her—nor was I the type to get all sentimental about funeral theater—but for some reason the thought made me sad.

"Must you always do this, Eden?"

"Maybe if your fakes weren't crap, I wouldn't have to." I turned toward Edgar's reedy voice. The short, pudgy man was obscured by a marble table covered in sample flower arrangements. I hoped that, for a couple hundred bucks, you'd at least get real flowers to pair with your counterfeit coffin.

These were the sort of people I did business with. I'd have claimed this was a new thing, but there comes a time in a girl's life when she has to level with herself. A decade of criminality wasn't indication of a passing phase, but a career choice.

"Well, you've looked better," Edgar said.

"You haven't," I replied.

Edgar coughed, a chronic condition from inhaling too much formaldehyde over the embalming table when he was younger. The funeral director shuffled forward, his cheap slacks and even cheaper dress shirt hanging loosely over his wide frame. He limped from the silver bullet fragment permanently lodged in his left leg. Too close to an artery to remove. Yes, apparently vampires could bleed to death—an ironic fate that Edgar wasn't willing to tempt with risky surgery. A wispy attempt at facial hair crying out for a razor's aid dotted his formless cheekbones. His skin was tanned an awful shade of orange-bronze to hide the fact that he was a vampire.

A good, if somewhat uninspired, career choice for a bloodsucker: late hours, easy access to blood, and no casual visitors. Plus, if you were an enterprising fellow like Edgar, then a respectable, quiet business afforded ample cover for more lucrative side endeavors.

The only evidence of his more sordid activities was an expensive, limited edition digital watch hiding in plain sight on his wrist, easily running into the six figures. He'd talked to me about it once—it was a piece of film memorabilia or something, hence the price—like I'd be impressed, but I'd almost died of boredom. Even when they were dead—or undead, I guess—guys still tried to run the same bogus game. Like a trinket slapped around his forearm would make me overlook the rest of the screaming red flags.

The music shifted to Bach, which I took as my cue to hurry things up.

"You mentioned something impressive on the phone."

"One quality soul for my favorite Reaper." Edgar reached into his floppy slacks and handed me a prescription bottle.

"What the fuck is this?" I held the amber plastic up to the soft light. The contents looked like a two-week-old pasta bowl that had been left uncovered in the fridge. More science experiment than something I could hand to Aldric.

"Professional gambler." Edgar's beady eyes gauged my reaction. "I thought you'd appreciate that."

"I could give a shit." The former owner's morality, or lack thereof, wasn't the problem—often, in fact, evil creatures had souls containing room-shaking power.

Nope—the main problem was this soul wasn't intact. Because, as I'd told Edgar repeatedly, harvesting souls without a Reaper's Switch almost always resulted in an unusable mess. And that was if the wannabe Reaper managed to survive the extraction at all.

"You need to stop using Reaper's Willow." I glared at the pudgy vampire. Here I was, out on a Sunday, trying to get a jump on my recently increased quota. And this idiot was wasting my time with his hobby experiments.

A sigil—a crude tattoo facsimile of a Reaper's Switch—glowed lightly on the back of Edgar's right hand. Normally, if any creature other than a Reaper tried to harvest a soul, it resulted in unpleasant consequences. Escaping with scalding third-degree burns was a victory. The magic now coursing through his sigil allowed him to play Reaper without fear of losing his hand entirely.

After a long standoff, I tossed the ruined soul back to Edgar. A sad look fell over his formless cheeks. Whether that was because I'd insulted his shoddy handiwork or because he'd just missed out on a thousand bucks was anyone's guess.

"I need to get going." It was getting late, and I didn't want to hang out in the overly perfumed funeral home any longer than necessary. The music alone was about to drive me insane.

"There is one other thing, Reaper." Edgar slipped the prescription bottle back into his slacks and unleashed a phlegmy cough. After the fit subsided, he mopped his lips with a handkerchief. "A big score."

"I'm listening," I said. How could I resist, given the circumstances?

"It's off-site."

"I got that much," I said. "Am I gonna have to play twenty questions for you to tell me the rest?"

Edgar returned the blood-spackled handkerchief to his front shirt pocket and affixed his beady gaze to me. Normally, a vampire had some sway, able to persuade others with their eyes. I had little doubt that the funeral director used this to his advantage when shilling his counterfeit wares to grieving spouses. But, as a Reaper, I was immune.

All I saw was a slimy, over-tanned, pudgy scammer. One who, regrettably, was an important ally. That didn't mean I had to respect him, though, and I always made sure that I took that small sliver of freedom straight to heart.

Edgar finally said, "You are quite rude sometimes, Eden."

"Whine to someone who gives a shit." Most vampires could skin me and wear me as next season's fashion, but the silver fragments slowed him down enough to make him a containable non-threat.

"Fine." Edgar removed a small piece of paper from his vast pockets. "But the price is two thousand."

"How many souls?"

"Could be none, could be a lot." A salesman's grin leaked across his lips.

The gambler in me liked the sound of *a lot*. What was it about uncertainty and bad odds that got the human mind racing with the delusion of pure possibility?

"Let me see that." I reached for the paper, but the vampire dodged my fingers. Even with the silver leeching into his bloodstream from the bullet fragment, he was still quick.

"Payment, then the paper."

Now it was my turn to reach into my pockets. I pulled out a thick money clip and whipped off the right number of hundreds. Part of my generous salary. I refused to spend it on anything other than work expenses. The rest I donated to the local food kitchen. No need to spend blood money to enrich myself when I only wanted things that money couldn't buy, like my freedom from the soul-harvesting grind. Besides, I had a sizable rainy-day fund stashed away.

The bills were crinkly, and somewhat soggy, but that didn't matter.

They were still good.

"I'm not paying you without seeing that paper."

His pudgy cheeks rippled as he cocked his head to consider my proposal. "You won't tell anyone else, if you don't buy the information?"

"Who else would buy it?"

The vampire gave me a shifty look and dodged the question. "Okay." He held out the mysterious paper.

I grabbed it much too eagerly and unfolded it from the tattered corners. Just an address in the city with 2:00 AM written underneath. I pulled out my phone and checked the time. It was already past one.

If memory served, the address was in a shady part of town, near the nightclub district.

"There's a magical buy," Edgar said. "Seller will be waiting in the back of the abandoned antiques shop."

"You said souls."

"No," he said, still wearing that slimy grin, "*you* said souls."

"Who's the seller?" I asked.

"Rumor has it, she's someone just like you."

Aldric's imperative rang in my ears.

The seller could be the Reaper.

Or Edgar could be lying. Still, that gambler's urge whispered in my ear.

The sensible voice in my head told the adventurous one to slow down.

It didn't listen. A big haul could fulfill my quota for a couple weeks. And if my new rival was there...

Well, I wasn't sure what I'd do.

I wasn't a killer.

But after tonight, the game had changed.

I handed Edgar the bills and said, "If you're ripping me off..."

The beady eyes snapped up for a moment. "No one rips Aldric off and lives."

Truer words had never been spoken.

5

THE ABANDONED ANTIQUES SHOP'S EXTERIOR LOOKED as vintage as the wares it had once housed. A sun-faded FOR RENT poster hung in the window of the empty ice cream parlor next door.

A warm island breeze blew past as I cut the bike's engine about a block up. Other than a few stray streetlights clinging to life, the street was dark, and I didn't want to attract attention. There were no cars save for the beat-up jalopy parked right in front of the antiques shop, and, near the corner, a Mercedes luxury sedan trying—but failing—to hide in the shadows.

I kept my head low as I approached the shop. Aldric's headquarters loomed over me about a mile away—watching over the city like a lighthouse. Or a malicious sentinel, depending on how much you knew about the vampire.

I peered through the grime-streaked windows, but I might as well have been trying to spot a boat thirty miles from shore in a San Francisco fog. The inside of the shop was dark.

But I could hear a low conversation. I pressed my ear to the dusty glass, catching snatches of the exchange.

"You're running a dangerous game," a man said.

A muffled female voice answered.

"Hell if I care about you taking the risk. That bastard Aldric won't sell me shit."

Another muted response.

"If these souls are as good as you say, then I'll be back for plenty more."

Jackpot. This had to be the Reaper.

And she'd brought souls.

This was like killing two birds with one stone: cutting off the rival soul pipeline *and* filling my quota. Maybe Aldric would give me a couple days off as a bonus.

I stifled a snort. A girl could dream, but that didn't mean her dreams would come true.

Taking a step back, I weighed my options. Charging in blind was silly. Despite my earlier victory over the wolf, I didn't want to risk a head-to-head battle. Better if I just figured out this Reaper's identity, then let Aldric's goons take care of the rest.

And if I were the seller, I wouldn't keep magical wares on site during a transaction, anyway. They were far too valuable—and the supernatural black market far too treacherous—to simply trust the other party to play nice.

Souls first. Then I'd deal with the competition.

The first spot to check was the trunk. I headed to the junker parked out front, flipping out the Reaper's Switch. The four-inch stainless steel blade glinted in the murky streetlights. I normally kept a hairpin in the plastic handle, but it had been lost during the collision with the rocks. After a couple seconds on my hands and knees, I found a thin, rusted nail that would suffice.

I jammed the blade and nail into the lock. I'd never had my sister's prodigious lock picking skills, but this rusted mess didn't pose much of a challenge. After a quick pop from the sharp blade, I was inside.

Other than a battered tire iron and a rubber hose probably used for siphoning gas, there was nothing. I patted the worn shag interior, searching for hidden compartments, but didn't find any secrets. After breaking into the car itself, I struck out in similar fashion: a few loose coins, a fast food bag, and a couple bent, unsmoked cigarettes.

No souls.

I let the door click shut quietly and considered my next move. The Mercedes sat at least a hundred yards away, all the way at the end of the empty street, near the corner. Judging by its sleek lines, it was a recent model. Jamming a knife in the lock would send the expensive sedan into a screaming shitfit.

Not a bad way to draw the buyer and seller out.

An old door groaned.

I glanced over the car's rusted top, finding a pair of eyes glaring at me from the antiques shop.

"The hell you doin'?" the man asked, followed by the distinct ratcheting of a shotgun.

I sprinted toward the Mercedes.

The man cursed loudly.

The door slammed shut as he ran out of the shop.

Then he fired.

The force of the boom shook the window panes. I pushed harder, willing myself from all my late-night runs on the beach. His footsteps faded as I raced past the Mercedes and knifed around the corner.

I ran up to a crumbling bar with a half-open door. The entrance smelled thickly of stale beer and smoke, even though the property had long ago been abandoned. I peered through a porthole window, waiting for the man to come around the corner.

He didn't.

Instead, he cursed at the woman, demanding to know who had been hanging out by his car.

A low voice calmly addressed his concerns, and the bloodthirsty shouting stopped.

A minute later, the crimson glare of the junker's headlights streaked across the intersection. Then everything was silent—my throbbing pulse notwithstanding.

A figure wearing a hoodie rounded the corner and came into view. She wore sunglasses, even at night, and dark jeans that acted as camouflage on the shadowy street. The hoodie was drawn tight around her face, making her impossible to identify. After a quick glance down an alley—and some cursory looks at the surrounding buildings—she headed into the narrow space.

That was my cue.

I slipped out of the bar and jogged across the street. I tried to sense the Reaper's soul.

But I got nothing. Maybe she was just human.

Or perhaps she was a demoness, with no soul at all.

I stepped into the alley's oil-stained mouth. The dueling scents of rotting fruit and pee accosted me. The narrow space dead-ended into a cement wall, where the hooded woman was leaning into a paint-stripped dumpster. The bright white glow of her smartphone's flash illuminated the otherwise dark area.

I plunged into the alley, trash rustling beneath my sneakers.

The clanging stopped. Her feet flailed as she tried to find the ground.

I hit her square in the back. She spiraled face-first into the dumpster with a squishy bang.

She groaned, face down in a trash bag. Next to her was a cardboard box with fresh, clean edges. That had to be the souls.

"Who are you?" I asked, jerking the hoodie.

I reached for the box with my other hand and she bit me.

"Damnit!" I recoiled, then charged back in, belly pressed against the dumpster's lip.

I pinned her hooded head against the trash and grabbed the cardboard box.

"Who do you work for?"

Muffled speaking.

I heard the sound of a car engine coming by.

Unsure whether it was the buyer returning, I yanked the box out of the dumpster and sprinted like hell back around the corner.

Headlights rolled past. Just a mom in her Accord.

When I jogged back to the dumpster, the woman was gone.

"Damnit." I trudged out of the dim alley and glanced in the Mercedes as I walked past.

Clean interior. Nothing of value on display. A temporary sticker on the back windshield indicated the car was brand new.

I popped my Reaper's Switch out and set the box down.

When I touched the tip of the blade to the trunk's lock, the car shocked me.

"Ow." I shook out my fingers.

Some sort of magic.

Then I heard a pistol cock in the night.

I turned around, where, coming around the corner, the hooded figure brandished a gun.

I grabbed the box and dropped into a dead sprint back to the bike.

The tires screamed as I peeled out and raced away. But no shots followed.

At a stoplight a few blocks over, I took the liberty of looking inside the box. Four glass jars glinted in the moonlight, each containing a creature's soul. They were carefully labeled with masking tape—WOLF, WARLOCK, and so forth—just like Mom had done with my elementary school lunches. None of that mush Edgar had tried to peddle earlier.

The light turned green, and I closed the box's flaps.

I now had five souls in my possession.

Assassins aside, not a bad way to start the week.

6

I TUCKED MY BIKE UNDERNEATH ITS FLORAL camouflage on the service road and headed back up the beach. It'd been a few hours since I'd heard the gunshots, so if the shooter was still lurking around, that made him an idiot. Aldric had claimed that the second guy hadn't been his, but I remained skeptical. Then again, I might not have trusted the vampire, but there was little reason to lie. If he'd wanted me dead, he could've killed me in the penthouse office. No one would have ever found my body. One old-school warning was enough for a warlord to make his point.

After passing where I'd killed the wolf—no trace of our life-and-death struggle remaining in the dark sand beyond a few raggedy footprints—I headed back to the villa. Weariness seeped through every sinew of my being. Where had this fatigue been a few hours before, when I'd been tossing on the couch? I guess the fact that it hadn't come on then was a hidden blessing: if I'd been asleep, it would have been me floating in the South Pacific instead of Aldric's would-be assassin.

With some trepidation, I approached my villa. While

the word villa conjures up ostentatious overtones of jet-setting millionaires drinking champagne in their pastel polo shirts, I worked hard to buck such clichés. No one had visited me in four years, and I aimed to keep it that way. The last person who had been inside other than me had been the real estate agent.

And that wolf. But he hadn't been on the guest list.

In any event, the place was the only residence around for a couple miles, enjoying its own little pocket of idyllic isolation on the southwest tip of the island. Its exterior drew on multiple schools of influence, as if the designer had flipped through a few ancient architectural books for inspiration and then decided to create his own modern Greco-Roman motif. Moonlight glinted off the moss-dappled red-tiled roof and orchid-covered stucco exterior, accenting the modern silver trim on the doorknobs and window frames. Little modern touches like those melded classical elegance with the twenty-first century. The windows, too, were wide and sweeping, a fact I was now thankful for, having been forced to unceremoniously flee through one of them.

If anyone had ever come out to visit, they'd probably have wondered how a twenty-eight-year-old could afford a spread like this, all purchased in cash. The answer was simple: unlike what those PSAs blared, crime did pay. Handsomely. Until I died. But, when you get a second bite of the apple, you can also get someone to retrieve your rainy-day fund, even when you're confined to an uncharted island.

Aldric might've paid me well, but I didn't spend a dime of his money on anything other than business expenses. Ripping off scamming Wall Street assholes and narcissistic Silicon Valley sociopaths had a certain Robin Hood appeal, but his blood money made me feel ill. Besides, I had about three million in cash, gold, and bearer bonds stashed in a weatherproof steel box in the nearby jungle, in case of financial emergency.

I paused at the bottom of the winding marble staircase, listening to the chatter of the jungle. Nothing sounded unusual, so after a deep breath, I headed up.

I reached the top of the stairs and stared ruefully at the wreckage of the thick oak doors. I could see all the way to the kitchen's polished limestone countertops. All I really wanted to do was flop down on the couch. But the unsolved mystery of who had been shooting—and screaming—next to the villa overrode my immediate fatigue.

I didn't know what I'd find—a body, blood, a few shell casings, or even the shooter.

But sleep could wait until I investigated.

So I wound my way back down the staircase and headed toward the shoreline. I didn't have to go far to get my answer. A body lay next to the bushes, right below the guest room window. I shoved my hand into my still damp jeans, touching the Reaper's Switch just in case. But the two bullets in the back of his head suggested he wouldn't be walking around again any time soon.

The dead guy was lying face down in the sandy grass. There was a small burn that looked like an ink stain or a powder burn on his right arm. Maybe from the gun's hot barrel pressing against his skin. The man was young, judging by the color of his hair and how thick it was. The clothes were nice, but the style was bland—chosen by a sales associate at a department store, maybe. Scanning the surrounding area, I spied six spent casings scattered in the black sand. I nudged one with my sneaker. It looked like a .45, but I couldn't be sure in the pre-dawn darkness.

A thought pierced my fatigued mind like a flaming arrow: this body was next to my house.

That was not good. Not good at all.

The opposite of good, in fact. As in, I would have a lot of people up in my shit if they found this dead guy taking a permanent dirt nap in my bushes.

So I did the only practical thing that came to mind, rattled and exhausted as I was: I reached down and tugged on his damp collared shirt to start pulling him toward the ocean.

I heard a metallic *ting* as something slipped from his pocket and bounced off the rocks.

The gold bar glinted, even in the darkness.

Shouts came from up the beach, accompanied by flashing lights that meant only one thing.

Cops.

"Damnit." I let go of the shirt and darted up the front stairs. After dodging the wreckage that was now my front doors, I yanked a trash bag from the deep, dusty recesses of an otherwise empty cabinet. With no small degree of manic urgency, I rushed back to the ruined doors.

Searchlights crisscrossed the black sand beach. Someone had called in the body. But seeing as how I was the only one living out here, I had to wonder who that might've been. It would've been silly for the killer to dime himself out. Maybe Aldric was testing me again—he was the only one who knew about the shooter, since I'd told him.

But I think he'd gotten his money's worth out of his dead werewolf assassin. I was safe from any more wake-up calls—at least until my fellow Reaper made me look bad again.

I hung the trash bag over the splintered doorframe. The right door was still semi-intact and upright, so I closed it as best I could. I hoped that a trash bag would be enough of a legal barrier to prevent the cops from entering.

Then, with the cavalry closing in, I heard an unmistakable creak.

Footsteps pattered upstairs in the abandoned master bedroom.

Not this crap again.

I flicked out the Reaper's Switch, the blade still sticky with the wolf's blood.

No time to scrub that clean. Not being a gun, it wasn't *the* murder weapon, but it was *a* murder weapon. Chucking the blade into the jungle wasn't an option, though, seeing as how I couldn't harvest souls without it.

Plus, it was the only weapon I *could* wield.

There was a loud crash upstairs, and the intruder uttered a string of breathy expletives. Using the noise as cover, I slunk into the untouched living room, everything exactly as I'd left it.

Not that there was much to take.

Moonlight slipped through the circular second-floor windows. Against my better judgement, I crept up the clear glass stairs, damp shoes squeaking. Their transparent nature made it feel like I was walking on pure air. A cool trick that had lost its luster within the first week of home ownership.

I glanced inside the guest room. But the illusion magic cloaking the hidden safe embedded in the wall beneath the open window was undisturbed and the room was empty.

Outside, sirens wailed as off-road tires chewed up the beach.

The rustling stopped.

I glanced at the bloody blade. Was I ready to double down? Lucille was certain to revoke our agreement for one death—that much was certain. But two? That was going to be a kind of hell I didn't want to imagine.

Lacking better options, I said, "I know you're in there, you son of a bitch." My knuckles were white from gripping the knife so tight.

Multiple loud thumps echoed from the master bedroom, followed by the splintering crash of broken glass. I rushed inside just in time to see a well-polished men's dress shoe disappearing through the high window.

I slashed with the Reaper's Switch, but missed.

The intruder crashed into the sand below.

I put my hand on the jagged sill, ready to vault out in pursuit. But the man—young, brown haired, wearing a suit —was already vanishing into the jungle. I hadn't seen his face. When I brought my hand away, blood dripped from my cut hand.

A cursory examination of the room revealed no clues.

Nothing was missing, because there had been nothing to take.

Which begged the obvious question: what the hell had the intruder been doing up here?

I would've torn the room apart for answers. But I didn't get the opportunity to even organize my thoughts before the thumping knocks at my half of a front door announced a new problem.

The cops had arrived.

And they wanted answers about the body lying face down on my beachfront property.

7

IF THERE WAS A SILVER LINING TO THE POLICE SHOWING up on my marble doorstep, it was this: I'd finally found a bulletproof cure for exhaustion. Because any lingering fatigue had been replaced by a primal, shit-your-pants fear.

What was that old saying? Out of the werewolf's jaws, onto the vampire's shitlist, and into the police's cuffs? As long as Aldric could create his own interpretation of old clichés, so could I. And this one fit.

The cops pounded at the damaged door like they were determined to make it cave in. I gave the master bedroom a final cursory glance but couldn't find anything out of place. It dawned on me, with a sinking feeling of dread, that the thief—or killer—might have brought something *inside,* instead.

I stashed the five souls and money clip in the wall safe cloaked by illusion magic that I'd had specially installed in the guest bedroom. Then I tried to push the worry from my mind as I took the glass stairs three at a time.

Hushed voices—belonging to a man and a woman— filtered through the flapping, dusty trash bag. The woman was arguing in favor of charging through. Her partner, by contrast, was more interested in a measured approach that respected small matters like Constitutional rights.

That made me furrow my brow. The police force on the island had always practiced its own brand of selective, Wild West style law enforcement—a vestige of an age when the lawmen were as crooked as the criminals. While regular cops no longer practiced that style of law enforcement anymore due to pesky cell phones, the local police force was largely immune to such nuisances. Word didn't leak out from Atheas like it tended to on the mainland, at least where the police department was concerned.

The woman didn't seem to care about going viral, though. She was ready to storm the Bastille and take my head. I kind of dug her style, but I didn't like being at the end of her bayonet.

As I passed the large bay window—and saw the law enforcement ant colony combing the beach—I realized that these weren't cops at all. The people about to find a body on what amounted to my front lawn were the same folks who Aldric was very, very pissed about having as guests on the island.

"FBI." The man's rich, mellow baritone floated through the pre-dawn air like a gentle breeze. "Anyone home?"

"I'm making coffee," I called back, even though I was about three steps from the flapping trash bag.

"Is that an invitation?" the woman replied, sounding eager to have me in cuffs.

"It is not," I said.

"The door's missing," the woman said. "That's a clear sign of forced—"

"Remodeling." My brain kicked in. Sooner or later, the FBI was going to enter, and I needed to look semi-presentable when that happened. Expecting them to pack up and leave was wishful thinking. I rushed back into the living room and grabbed a semi-clean t-shirt from the single, sad lamp standing guard over the leather couch. The print said, *fuck you, you'll do what I tell you*, a play on a rebel anthem that I used to blast from Mom's Honda Civic, like any good teenage anarchist. I immediately ruined the tee with a smear of blood from my wounded palm. So, instead of a change of clothes, I got a makeshift bandage.

Since they'd stopped knocking, I took that as an invitation to actually make coffee. As the water heated, and I stared at the waving black trash bag from the kitchen, I considered my next move. The first faint trickles of dawn seeped around the edges of the bag, but no great answer to my rapidly multiplying problems presented itself. I did, however, take the opportunity to scrub the blood from the Reaper's Switch. I also examined the wound on my palm, which wasn't deep, but was bleeding at a prodigious rate.

I cleaned it in the sink and then tied the shirt around it. Not perfect, but it'd have to do for now. As for my right shoulder, well, that looked like a biohazard. A burnt-looking crust was beginning to form where the wolf's teeth had crunched into my shoulder—and the less said about the smell, the better. The sleeve was in tatters, like I'd put it through a cheese grater. My jeans and shoes were still slightly damp, but they were more scratchy-stiff from the ocean water than anything else.

"Ma'am?" The man sounded genuinely concerned about me, whereas his partner wanted to throw me in the Gulag as soon as possible so she could beat the answers out of my simpering body.

"I told you, I'm making coffee," I said.

"Could you perhaps let us in?"

"I could," I said. "But I won't."

"We can get a warrant," the woman said. It was a good cop, bad cop riff, but I got the impression that it hadn't been planned. Their natural personalities were just on display in the early morning hours.

"Then get a warrant," I replied. I dumped the instant coffee into the mug, watching it dissolve into something that resembled black tar heroin. "What the hell is the FBI doing out here, anyway?"

"We're asking the questions here," the woman said.

"Suit yourself." Lacking spoons—or silverware of any kind—I shook the plain cup until the liquid looked safe to drink. I took a sip to test it out. Strong enough to use as off-label paint thinner. Perfect.

I took the steaming mug toward the broken door, the smell of crappy generic roast drifting behind me. The remnants of the other half of the door still lay just inside the foyer, where the wolf had tossed it. Even if I'd wanted to move it, the thick oak would've been too heavy to deal with on my own. Guess I'd be getting some more visitors out here later to fix this mess. At least they'd be invited.

I glanced in the mirror hanging by the door. If I felt like shit, I looked about five times worse. I brushed the visible sand from my clumped up brown hair, pinched my cheeks so they didn't look pale from fright and fatigue and then angled my body to the left to hide the bite.

The woman said, "Come on, Hunter, I hear you beyond this—what the hell *is* this, a tarp? I don't have all—"

"Day," I replied, swinging the door wide open with a bright smile. An attractive, broad-shouldered FBI agent blocked much of my view. The scene behind him had gotten more serious since I'd last checked, with the colony of agents setting up work lamps and mobile workstations.

My stomach tightened into a knot as the blackish-gray light beat into my tired eyes, dissolving my plastic smile into a scowl.

The female agent cut in front of her partner, which only further dampened my mood. Up close, I could tell she was slightly older—maybe mid-thirties. She struck an imposing figure. Tall, pretty, and in control. The perfectly tapered jeans and blazer with the sleeves rolled up gave the illusion that she was casual. She perched like a bird of prey on her stylish stiletto boots, waiting to strike.

"We were out here for three minutes." She checked her gold-trimmed wristwatch. "*Four* minutes."

"Sounds like a crime," I said. "Better call the cops."

Neither agent smiled. The three of us stood in an awkward silence. I took the opportunity to take a sip of coffee, trying to maintain an air of disinterested nonchalance. Behind them, I counted four vehicles parked right on the beach, and at least eight additional agents. The FBI was making a splash on the island with their first investigation. What a lucky girl I was to have it all unfold right in my backyard.

I rubbed my tongue over my teeth, feeling a day's worth of film and grime on their surface. A cold shower and a quick sleep didn't sound all that far from heaven. Too bad I wouldn't be getting any sleep with this fire threatening to burn down what remained of my shitty life.

"What happened to your door, Miss Hunter?" the man asked from behind his stern-looking partner.

"Storm." I stood on my tiptoes, looking past the female agent to address him directly.

"And your wall?"

I glanced at the blood spatter, from when I'd slashed the wolf in the leg. "Cut myself."

With my best bashful smile, I held up my bloody hand. "Doing what?"

Damn. This guy was persistent. "On a broken window."

"Is there something you're not telling me, Miss Hunter?"

"I don't remember telling you my name, that's for sure."

"We looked up the property records on the ride." The man gestured toward the jungle and the ocean with his large arms. His long black hair flowed over a casual, form-fitting oxford cloth shirt. Apparently this branch of FBI didn't have a dress code; their looks were more *Hawaii Five-o* than *X-Files*. An entire sleeve of tattoos spiraled up his right arm, starting just beyond the powerful wrist. I spotted a spear on the inside of his forearm, rendered in traditional Polynesian style.

"What island are you from originally?" I nodded toward the tattoo.

His eyebrows arched almost imperceptibly. "Oahu."

"Pretty bold call to dub yourself a warrior."

"It was given to me by another," the man said. "Family tradition."

That was much better. It was annoying to see some twenty-year-old douche with kanji or tribal ink declaring himself brave or strong. That wasn't the kind of attribution one bestowed upon themselves. At least not without looking like a moron.

The mysterious agent seemed to possess a wisdom beyond his years. His very presence was calming, even though it shouldn't have been. After all, this was the FBI, and they were investigating a murder approximately two feet from my house.

"I have a lantern." I turned my wrist up so he could see

the sigil. "If I were to get a tattoo like yours, what would the artist choose?"

I smiled at him, genuinely curious at what the answer might be.

He brushed his long hair over his shoulders. "I cannot say."

"All right, all right." The woman threw up her hands like she'd had enough. "You're not batting your eyelashes out of this shitstorm, Hunter."

She leaned on my name like it was the most important piece of evidence she had. Joke was on her, since it wasn't even my real name, although my license and paperwork would all claim otherwise. Besides, flirting had never gotten me all that far. Back when I was running cons and had my own crew, my role hadn't been to look doe-eyed and pretty. My sister Sierra had always been the seductress. Nope—I'd always been the one with the marker and the white board, drawing up the plan, organizing the chessboard *just so*. Assessing the risks, and occasionally rolling the dice big.

Too bad this board was looking stacked against me.

"We're gonna get inside, Hunter. With or without a warrant."

"I'll take the former." I felt the smile melt from my face. "If you don't mind, I have some more shitty coffee I need to burn."

I went to drop the trash bag curtain.

"Stingray," the man said, catching the bag before it could fully close. "You'd be a stingray."

"Interesting choice," I said. "Why?"

"Because a stingray uses its wits to survive the ocean. But it is also willing to emerge from the sand to defend those things that matter."

If he hadn't been so earnest, I'd have thought he was

running a line on me. It was the type of thing you'd say to win a mark's heart. Build rapport, give them compliments— try to make them feel understood. But, even in that moment, with the other agents milling over the beach, and the searchlights bleaching the black sand with their high-powered beams, it seemed genuine.

I narrowed my eyes at the broad-shouldered agent. Was he some sort of creature? No—he was human. But, strangely, I could sense a warmth emanating from this guy's being, almost magical, even though he was human as the day was long. I couldn't quite feel his soul, but I could feel the sincerity in his words. He was a good man—or at least he appeared to be.

That's where everyone goes wrong, right?

But I said, "Don't you two need to announce yourselves or something?"

The man reached into his back pocket and draped his badge over his partner's shoulder. "Agent Kai Taylor."

His partner begrudgingly reached into the pocket of her expensive jeans. With a theatrical sweep of her wavy blonde hair—clearly not her original color—she gave me an authoritative smile and said, "Agent Rayna Denton. *Now,* if you wouldn't mind."

Against my better judgement, I let them come inside. They'd get their warrant within a few hours, and cooperating would buy me some goodwill. Rayna immediately headed toward the living room, and I whistled at her like a wandering dog.

"Really like what you've done with the place." She dismissed the spare living room with a derisive nod.

"In here." I nodded toward the large kitchen a few steps away. "Just a couple people having shitty coffee. If I'd known I was having company, I'd have bought a fruit plate."

"I love shitty coffee." Rayna's sour expression suggested she didn't like anything at all. "But you know what I really enjoy, Hunter?"

"We all can't wait to find out." I put the water on to boil.

"Honesty. So just do us all a favor and—"

"Is this the part where you say 96% of murders that happen near a home are committed by the person inside, or some other statistic you make up on the spot?" Steam jetted from the electric kettle. "Or maybe that you can cut me a deal if I just admit to killing the poor guy."

Silence overtook the kitchen. I glanced up from the stovetop to find them both staring at me.

"Is there something on my face?"

"We didn't mention a murder," Kai said. His brow was furrowed, like he was trying to figure me out. Rayna was having no such trouble, however. After being temporarily caught off guard by my slip of the tongue, she now wore a smug, self-satisfied expression—the victorious grin of a triumphant apex predator.

"That, Hunter, is what we call probable cause." Rayna reached out for the cup of coffee I'd just finished making. I dumped it down the drain in the middle of the kitchen island. Unperturbed, she reached for the dregs of mine and drank the rest with a catty glare. "You're right about one thing, though."

"What's that?" I asked, even though I didn't want to hear the answer.

"This is some awful coffee." Rayna left out the front door. Her partner lingered.

"If you know what happened outside..." Kai said, giving me space to fill in the blanks. I didn't take his baited hook, though, and silence settled over the modern kitchen. Rayna returned a minute later with three more agents in tow. She told them to tear the place apart. I would've protested, but I wasn't really in a position to do so. I'd just given her probable cause.

Fucking sleepless nights.

"I need to search you, too." Kai gestured for me to hold out my arms.

"That must be how you get all the girls."

Kai looked embarrassed but didn't respond. With graceful movements, he made his way around the limestone island. Close, now, I could tell he was well over six feet. He seemed big enough to swallow me whole, or shield me from harm. Except he was the harm about to crush my life.

"What happened to your shoulder, Miss Hunter?"

"Eden," I said.

"Okay, Eden. The shoulder?"

"Ran into a door," I said.

He grinned with minor amusement as his strong fingers glided over the stiff denim. They stopped at my pockets, where he extracted my phone, keyring, and the Reaper's Switch. After checking my ankles, he examined my belongings and then flicked out the Reaper's Switch.

"And why does a nice woman need to carry a bloody knife like that, Eden?"

"And me what now?" My words failed me as I processed what he was saying. Blood? I'd washed it off in the sink. I turned to the knife, and my heart sank. The duct tape had caught some of the run-off, and its dirtied edges now carried a light crimson tint.

Aldric. The vampire gift that kept on giving.

Kai gave me a funny look and said, "That wasn't English."

"There are bears and things out here," I mumbled, giving no explanation at all for the blood. Further conversation was cut short by a triumphant screech from upstairs. Somewhere that sounded suspiciously like the master bedroom.

I gave Kai a look, and we seemed to share a psychic understanding that Rayna was insane. But she was also the one with the badge, the gun, and all the cards, while I was just the "nice woman" with a broken door, a bloody knife, and a whole lot of explaining to do.

I heard Rayna before I saw her, those stiletto boots pounding out an ominous sonata as she came down the stairs. Once she was in the living room, I saw that she bore the smirk of someone who had found *exactly* what they were looking for. Behind her, the forensics team filtered out, perhaps to gather more evidence.

But it didn't look like they'd need much more. She dropped a plastic evidence bag with a .45 revolver inside on the polished limestone counter. I rubbed my nose and tried to maintain an even expression.

"That's not mine," I said. "The guy—a young guy, brown hair, a suit, he planted it up there."

"Points for the extra creative details," Rayna replied, not buying it for a second. She tossed her wavy blonde hair over her shoulder. "Eden Hunter, you're under arrest for the murder of Roan Kelly. You have the right to remain—"

I almost fell over. "Wait, what'd you say?"

Rayna bristled at the interruption. "It would be wise to keep your mouth shut, Hunter. But if you want to confess to stashing the murder weapon beneath the floorboards, no one's stopping you."

"The victim's name," I said as I felt Kai snap the cold metal cuffs around my wrists. "What'd you say his damn name was?"

"Roan—"

But that was all I needed to hear. I knew Roan Kelly well. One might say intimately. Because, once upon a time, he'd been part of my old crew. We'd been in love. My first love, you could say. And now, he'd turned up dead on the beach next to my house.

If I didn't know any better, I'd have said someone was trying to frame me.

And, if I didn't know any better, I'd have said they'd damn well succeeded.

8

THIS WASN'T THE BEST MONDAY MORNING I'D EVER had, all things considered.

From the looks of the holding cell, the FBI had set up their Atheas shop in a hurry. In fact, this wasn't really a holding cell at all, but an old, semi-converted hotel room. There was an outline on the wallpaper where a king bed had once shielded the wall from the outside light. The rest of the wall was a faded and sun-bleached tan. A pilling black carpet rounded out the budget aesthetic. The table at which I sat was merely the old room's desk. The FBI's main addition was a single, cheap security camera blinking in the corner. A thin door placed next to a bathroom separated me from freedom.

Without anyone else in the room, I decided to check out the view. I walked to the drawn blinds, where the rising sun was creeping in. Peeking through the cracked and fraying plastic, I found myself five stories up. There was no balcony. I could see Black Sea Holdings' headquarters four blocks away.

The FBI had set up shop in the heart of the city, not far

from Aldric's base of operations. That couldn't have been a mistake. Atheas was a massive island, seventy-six miles across at its widest point. The southwestern portion was dominated by the city, its population nudging closer to six figures every day. In the northwest were the suburbs— where, if the FBI had been at least pretending to lie low, they could have stationed their field office. The eastern sections of the island were a little bit more...wild and sparsely populated. That would have been my choice for establishing a clandestine outpost. But setting up shop in Aldric's backyard sent a clear message: the Feds were coming in hot, sirens blazing and bureaucratic dicks swinging, ready to take the vampire warlord head on.

The battered door creaked, and I turned to find Rayna Denton entering the room wearing a smug little smirk. She held up the clear plastic evidence bag that contained the revolver as if to say *we got you*.

I walked to the worn desk and sat down. She dangled the bag in front of my face. I batted it away.

She placed her French-manicured fingers on her service weapon and said, "Don't do that."

"Funny, I was about to say the same thing to you."

"Have anything you'd like to tell me?" Rayna asked, showing a row of too-perfect white teeth that had to be veneers. Good ones, but still. They were as phony as her friendly question.

"Besides fuck off?" I beamed back at her from ear to ear.

"You're a handful." The evidence bag crumpled slightly as her hand tightened into a fist. "Don't go anywhere."

As if I were liable to go *poof* and teleport away. No risk of that. That wasn't even a thing, anyway. Magic, like all properties in the universe, had laws that I'd come to learn— vaguely—over the past four years. So it was time to get cozy.

From my previous brushes with the law, I knew damn well I was going to be here for a little while. Unlike those occasions, however, I wasn't sure I'd be leaving quickly—or at all. Roan had been our little crew's systems expert, finding backdoors and unpatched ports into mainframes. Evidence would disappear on technicalities, reports would be doctored to make chain of custody fuzzy. Little hiccups and inconsistencies would appear that would inevitably give the local district attorney cold feet. Not that I'd made a habit of getting caught, but on the two occasions when it *had* happened, the charges had been tossed long before trial. Unfortunately for me, Roan was dead, and if the events of the past twelve hours were anything to go by, allies were in short supply.

There was a knock at the thin door. Well, here it was: the part where Rayna and Kai went on a fishing expedition. Maybe they'd offer me a deal they weren't authorized to make and that would never hold up when it crossed the prosecutor's swamped desk. That sort of bullshit dog-and-pony show.

The hinges groaned, crying out for oil. Much to my surprise, in walked a short, gray-haired woman wearing a permanently severe expression. She carried a crocodile skin briefcase. I couldn't tell if it was a fashion statement or an intimidation tactic. Either way, it threw me off guard, and I sat up straight in the folding chair.

The woman's suit and briefcase were far too nice to purchase on a government salary. I hoped that meant she was here to help, but my optimism was tempered by the fact that she looked like she hadn't smiled in the past twenty years. Even across the room, she stank of nicotine and stale perfume. She shuffled over, the thick cigarette smog coming with her, and grunted as she set down the briefcase. The light splashing over the leather made the briefcase look alive, like it was lurking in a swamp and waiting for the right moment to strike.

"And you are?" I asked.

The woman extracted a pair of reading glasses from a hidden flap in the case. She thumbed through a thin folder of documents without glancing at me. "Agnes Willsprout."

"Is that supposed to mean something?"

"Our mutual employer sent me," the woman said in a flat tone that somehow still managed to be condescending. "It seems, Miss Hunter, that you have gotten yourself in quite the little jam."

I disagreed with the insinuation that I was somehow at fault. Then again, I'd spilled that I knew about the murder without much prodding.

"We fought them for years. Yet here they are." She set the file down on the pockmarked desk and looked around the cheap room disdainfully. "The Supreme Court vote barely passed. Almost half a decade of billable hours, all for naught."

Not sure why she cared. That sounded like a win for her and a loss for Aldric.

"I don't follow."

"The Feds, honey." She gestured at the outline of the missing bed. "And now they've set up in this hooker flop-house." Agnes snorted. "The Golden Hind. An apt name, if there ever was one."

I knew what she was talking about—both the hotel, and its namesake. The hotel had been closed by the time I'd arrived on Atheas, long since abandoned to a seedy low-level criminal element. But the ship it had been named after —that, well, that was a more interesting tale. Sir Francis Drake's fabled ship, laden with treasure. There were those who believed he had wrecked it on this island—despite the clear historical record indicating it had made it back to England—and used the magical resources at his disposal to protect his prodigious hoard from fellow treasure seekers. In the centuries hence, the legend had attracted a fair number of would-be adventurers to the island. And no shortage of souls, since said adventurers would often die in absurdly stupid ways. A human soul wasn't worth quite as much as a magical creature's, but it still filled my quota in a pinch. Aldric usually got grouchy if I gave him too many, so I tended to keep them to a minimum.

I said, "So how bad does it look?"

"Miss Hunter," she began, like she was dictating a letter to her stenographer, "how bad things look is not the question. What we can do to make them look better is the order of the day."

"I see."

"Did you do it?" She gave me a severe look and then waved a wrinkled hand. "Don't answer that. It doesn't make a damn difference to me."

Good to know my counsel had a loose—or, more specifically, no—moral code. Hopefully her legalese and bullshit would weave its own sort of magic, able to twist the meaning of justice into something grossly misrepresentative of the spirit of the law. Normally, I'd be against such miscarriages of justice. But, sitting here in this hotel-turned-flop-house-turned-FBI interrogation room, all I cared about was getting the hell out of there.

Agnes snapped her wrinkled fingers and the camera light in the corner went off. Her hands disappeared into the folds of the crocodile skin briefcase, emerging with a sizable stack of papers. From this stack, she selected a single sheet from the middle, like a magician choosing a card. With a red pen, she circled a section at the bottom. She slid the paper across the worn wood and then tented her fingers together.

"You recall your original agreement with Aldric, do you not?" Agnes finally called him by name now that the camera was off.

"How could I forget?" That had been an eventful night. I'd been slightly delirious—being revived and unceremoniously dragged from the Elysian Fields will do that—but I did remember signing it. After all, the alternative—a return to the land of the dead—hadn't been all that appealing.

I skimmed the document. All the terms were there. Seven years of indentured service to Aldric, during which I couldn't leave the boundaries of the island. Five souls per week, to be delivered each Friday, regardless of weather, health, or other concerns. And, at the very bottom, a freshly circled clause I didn't recall: that, should my performance flag behind some unspecified "market standard," the terms were renegotiable.

A tight ball of angry fear hardened in my stomach. I twisted my lips into a scowl and said, "This is a load of crap."

"Is that not your signature, Miss Hunter?"

"Yes," I said, growling through gritted teeth.

"And your mark?" She tapped my bloody thumbprint at the bottom.

"That's mine, too."

"And does it not seem that, given the shifts in the marketplace, your performance no longer meets the terms specified in your contract?"

"I don't agree with that."

"But we can agree on one point, Miss Hunter." Agnes plucked another paper from her mountain of legal documents. She pushed her glasses up her nose, and gave me a stern look. "You would very much like to get out of this place."

Her fingers crept across the table, pushing the new sheet with it. Another contract. The language was much like the last one—a one-page agreement stipulating the terms of my employment. But this one had a couple key differences. One I was already aware of: the unreasonable weekly quota bump to seven souls. That would be a pain in the ass, but it was manageable.

What was untenable was the second change.

"Indefinite servitude," I said, the words sounding bizarre and horrible when uttered aloud.

"Aldric has made a significant investment in your training and development," Agnes said. "It would be a shame for all that to be wasted."

"You bitch."

"Did you know the Persians used to reward those messengers who brought tidings of victory from the battle-front?" Agnes squared the bottom of the papers against the table before returning them to her briefcase. "But they killed those who returned bearing messages of defeat."

"Thanks for the history lesson," I said, still staring in disbelief at the new contract. *Indefinite.* That was just a bullshit way of saying *forever.* The three remaining years were already a tough enough pill to swallow. I would rather die than work for Aldric until the end of time.

"The lesson, Miss Hunter, is simple." Agnes pushed a pen across the table. "The Persian empire crumbled long ago. For if you shoot the messenger, people tend to only tell you what you wish to hear. Not what you need to."

"And what do I need to hear?"

"The Federal Bureau of Investigation has the murder weapon, which they found hidden in your residence. They have motive, in your romantic relationship to Mr. Kelly. They have your skin fragments on Mr. Kelly's shirt. And they have a clear story that will sway a jury. An eccentric woman who vanished from the grid, changed her name, and now lives alone on an uncharted island went crazy and killed her ex-boyfriend. And for that, you will hang."

I would've asked how she knew Roan was my ex-boyfriend, but Aldric knew my old name and everything about my past.

"But that story isn't true."

"It will become truth soon enough." Agnes folded her wrinkled hands together. "And you, better than anyone, should know how malleable the truth can become."

"Unless I sign," I said.

"Now you're beginning to understand."

"I understand."

"Then would you please sign the goddamn sheet so we can both leave this forsaken trash pile?"

That was the rational move. Everything Agnes had said was true: the Feds had a slam-dunk case. The ex-lover taking revenge, stashing the murder weapon in the house where she'd fled to survive a catastrophic breakup. One small hitch in that story, of course: I hadn't fled, and there'd been no traditional breakup. I'd died. Technically, we'd never even broken up. Not that I still loved him, of course. Too much time and space had passed for those feelings to be much more than memories. But whether anyone would believe the truth—that I'd returned from the dead like Lazarus—well...

Still, I heard myself say, "Fuck the contract," and then I made a show of tearing the old one up. Or trying to, at least. The enchanted paper resisted my attempts. If only severing magical bonds were so easy. After a few moments of futile struggle, I gave up and started on the new one, the result being much the same.

Agnes sighed and brushed away a strand of errant gray hair from her over powdered cheeks. "If you are done with your tantrum, then perhaps we can both leave."

Soul-binds. What a pain in the ass. Unbreakable, other than through extraordinary and unreasonable methods beyond my comprehension and resources. At the bottom of the first contract, my bloody thumbprint stared back at me, mocking my desperate naiveté.

Should've taken your chances in the afterlife, dumbass.

I glowered at the crinkled face, the gray hair, the power suit. "How did a human lawyer get caught up with Aldric, anyway?"

"Money." Her weathered hand tapped the new contract. "He has more of it than the gods. Now if you would, Miss Hunter."

I could only imagine how fun Agnes Willsprout was at parties. But one thing couldn't be denied: she was damn good at her job. Aldric only employed the best. Well, besides me. I was apparently second best, and paying a rapidly escalating price for my failures.

With nowhere left to turn, I clicked the pen. After signing my name at the bottom of the new contract, I turned a dial, and a small blade replaced the pen's tip. I raked it across my thumb and pressed the bloody digit to the paper. A faint magical thrum passed through my skin, binding my soul to the agreement. Aldric had already added his own thumbprint and signature, making our pact complete. The old contract shriveled and dissolved into a burst of ash after being replaced by the new terms. After a moment, I removed my thumb and glared at the lawyer.

"Is that all?"

Agnes brushed the dust from the desk's surface and, after examining the completed contract, gave a perfunctory nod. My attorney placed the enchanted document back into her crocodile skin briefcase and then snapped her fingers. The camera light sprung back on. "Our mutual employer would like you to understand one thing very clearly, Miss Hunter."

"Which is?"

"Your current career trajectory will no longer be tolerated."

I didn't like the sound of that, but I tried to keep it cool with a flippant, "Oh?"

"There will be consequences if you don't live up to these new terms." Her tone suggested she also knew about the unwritten terms: how I needed to get rid of the Reaping competition.

Damnit.

"Tell our mutual employer there's nothing to worry about."

Agnes rose from the table and headed for the thin door. Before reaching for the handle, she looked back. "Coming?"

"Now?"

"No time like the present, Miss Hunter." She patted the briefcase. "I have your bail money."

"I thought you were clearing my name."

"Honey," Agnes said, with what almost looked like pity, "a word of advice."

"I'm all ears."

"No one's going to look out for you but you."

Which shouted one thing loud and clear.

After I got out of jail, I was on my own.

9

So I was free—except not really. Still, it felt good to be out of jail, even if it came with leaden strings. Agnes putting up a million of Aldric's bucks in bail meant I could leave the converted hotel without a police escort.

But I hadn't been cleared. And, if the disgusted looks of the agents gathered in the cramped lobby were any indication, the Feds weren't going to sit down while a murderer walked free. They'd hunt like hell to find enough evidence to lock me up forever. Between now and then, I'd have to clear my name.

"Don't leave town," Rayna said, waiting like a hawk in those stiletto boots by the single door exit.

"Wouldn't dream of it." I gave her a jovial little wave as I walked into the light. It was full-on morning now, the pleasant, blue-skied type of island morning that people believe will make them happy forever. But people in warm climes are no happier than those hacking it on the tundra. Just another con. Misery lurks even in the shadows of the sunshine, same as everywhere else.

My sea-salt stiffened jeans scraped against my tired

thighs as I walked up the trash-strewn sidewalk to hail a cab. While my new lawyer hadn't booked me a ride home, she had gotten my cell phone, keys, and Reaper's Switch returned, and handed me a little walking around money to get myself "sorted out," as she had derisively put it.

I was happiest about the blade, since that meant it had been deemed unrelated to the Roan Kelly case—or any other deaths that might one day crop up on the FBI's radar. That was good news for me, since my livelihood—quite liter-ally—depended on my little scythe.

About a block away from the FBI field office, I posi-tioned myself on the corner beside a sun-faded stoplight. As I waited for a cab, I reflected on the eventful day.

If there was an island to be framed for murder on, this wasn't the worst one, I guess. I might not have had many staunch allies, but there were resources and contacts I could exploit to my advantage. A supernatural latticework snaked through the jungles and tributaries, up the snowy peaks, down into the hearts of the volcanoes, into the city, past the suburbs and beyond. It was everywhere, and I'd need to tap all that knowledge to uncover the truth.

My ex-boyfriend was dead. Someone had tried to pin the rap on me.

There was a new Reaper in town. And she was beating me at my own game.

And the FBI had shown up to shake some branches.

That would've been an eventful year. Right now, that was just what I called Monday.

I was thankful Agnes had arrived before the Feds could grill me with questions, because, quite frankly, I didn't know how well I'd have stood up. I'd basically screwed myself by telling them I knew about the murder. Between fatigue and the injuries, my mouth was only liable to get me in trouble.

My right shoulder throbbed, begging for relief. Leaving the bite untreated for almost twelve hours hadn't done me any favors. The black, brackish blood caked to my skin like swamp mud made me nauseous. While a Reaper couldn't be turned by a werewolf's bite, that didn't mean I wouldn't experience plenty of fun side effects. Another day or two, and I'd be seriously up the river.

If I ever wanted to find out who'd set me up for the fall, first I'd just need to *survive*.

I saw a cab racing toward the corner and brought up my fingers to hail it down. Time to visit Jack's Apothecary Shack and get patched up. As I raised my tired arm, I felt fingers brush lightly against my jeans—a lift, and a good one. Something I wouldn't have noticed had I not swiped my fair share of wallets.

I spun around and caught sight of a small red-haired woman sprinting nimbly across the street.

"Hey!" I stepped out into the wide road, but a blaring honk made me jump back. The cab, as if summoned from the depths of time and space, flashed its lights in irritation. I took one last glance at the escaping thief, and then sighed, considering my priorities.

First, survival.

Then, answers.

I climbed into the cab. The cabbie gave me a funny look, but I waved a couple twenties in his face, and he was more than happy to take me where I needed to go. Tentatively, I reached into my other pocket. But nothing was missing.

Instead, the thief had given me something.

A lot of that was going around today, it seemed.

I pulled out a small piece of shiny red paper and began

to unfold its edges. Much to my surprise, it popped open and transformed into a flapping bird.

"Meet me at The Loaded Gun at midnight, Hunter." The paper bird's beak jawed at me. "And come alone."

Then the enchanted paper crumbled, dusting my jeans in ash. I was familiar with The Loaded Gun. I'd drank there a couple times when I was out of whiskey and the liquor stores had been closed for the night. A hipster dive, the kind of manufactured shit show where your feet were glued to the floor in twenty-dollar beer. It was only a couple blocks from the new FBI field office—where things started to get *really* seedy, and the nice part of town became just a memory.

"Hey, you gonna clean that up?" the cab driver asked, his stubble-coated jaw twisted in an annoyed grimace. Apparently, he hadn't seen the more interesting part of the program, where a bunch of ground up dead tree matter had spoken to me. That was probably for the best.

"No." I fed another twenty through the glass divide, and we enjoyed a blissful silence the rest of the way to the apothecary shop. The wind picked up outside the taxi's closed windows as we headed up an incline, toward the bluff where the store sat alone. While it was technically on the northwest part of the island, in the suburbs, most of the surrounding half-mile or so hadn't been developed. That meant a lot of sparse shrubs and fragmented rocks lying about like a giant had gotten bored of playing with them and simply left his earthly toys scattered in random places.

Most people didn't want to be exposed to the elements right out on the cliff. But Jack wasn't most people, and Jack's Apothecary Shack wasn't a traditional store. Well known among the supernatural element on the island, to a human —or anyone not in the know—it merely looked like your basic ramshackle ranch house painted a rather garish shade of teal. Home to a few surfers and stoners, maybe the occasional late-night party.

But the rest of us knew better. While not an apothecarial warlock himself, Jack had procured the best collection of herbs, magical augments, creatures, and other oddities this side of Chicago—or maybe even Chicago itself. And that was saying a lot, because Chicago was practically supernatural Mecca. Had I known that when I lived there, maybe I would have found the place more interesting.

"Wait here," I said as the taxi slowed.

The cabbie kept the meter running as he parked up the street. "You gotta pay by the minute if you want me to stick around, lady."

"This won't take long."

"As long as you pay." He got out with me and lit a cigarette as he leaned on the hood. "You pay, we ain't got no problems."

How refreshingly simple capitalism made matters. I could dig this guy's attitude. If I still had any real friends, they'd probably tell me that was an indication of deeper issues. Whatever. Lone wolves can't lose their pack. I'd ran with a crew before, and it'd cost me everything. Better just to work alone and avoid collateral damage.

I approached the ranch home's front walk with caution, following the map I'd memorized. Two steps over by the rose bush, four to the palm tree, a spin around the rock circle a few yards from the front door. Not that anything bad would happen if I just waltzed up—Jack couldn't just drop a lightning bolt on the mailman, after all—but the silly hoops would deactivate the wards to let Jack know I was on the right list.

I mean, we knew each other, but the guy was like eighty

going on a million, and his memory wasn't the greatest. Plus, I suspected that, in addition to his apothecarial supplies, he was growing some high grade hydroponic weed and shrooms somewhere in the basement. Most likely magically augmented. You think the regular stuff gets you paranoid, well, let me tell you, you're in for a very unpleasant surprise if someone at a party ever tricks you into smoking that shit.

I completed the little song-and-dance by rubbing a tortoise shell on the concrete porch. Except, unlike the other times I'd been there, I didn't sense the wards release. Usually there was a little magical chime to let you know you'd passed the trial.

I furrowed my eyebrows and rubbed the tortoise shell once more for luck.

Still nothing.

After throwing a glance back at the driver—who had apparently been watching the whole charade, and was now looking at me like I'd just escaped from the asylum—I decided there was really nothing else to do but knock. After wiping some stray red dust—a vestige of the reverse-pick-pocket's cryptic message—from my tattered shirt, I banged on the unpainted, wind-beaten aluminum door.

"Who's there?" The voice buzzed through an intercom that hadn't been previously installed. Given the crackling low-fidelity of the transmission, it was hard to tell who was on the other end.

"Jack? It's me." When I didn't get a response, I added, "Eden."

"Last name?"

I clenched my fist and resisted the urge to say something snarky. "It's Eden Hunter."

"Fascinating." There was a long silence. "Did your parents name you that, or—"

"Let's skip the twenty questions, Jack," I said. Maybe he was stoned. "I really need to come inside."

"The place is kind of a mess. Renovations."

"I'm not picky."

"Then enter at your own peril." The lock clicked, and the weathered door popped slightly ajar. I nudged it open with my low-top sneaker, expecting Jack to be waiting at the entrance. But all I saw past the bare front room was the kitchen, where there used to be a solid wall. A plaster-covered sledgehammer lay on the floor by the broken wall. The kitchen was also empty, save for the box of cereal on the dusty countertop. He hadn't been kidding about the renovations.

A slender man wearing no shirt glanced over, half his body hidden by an exposed beam.

"Hello, Eden." The half-naked man had a smooth British accent.

"You're not Jack."

"I'd have to agree with that observation." He brought the bowl of cereal closer to his handsome face and took a few bites. Milk dribbled down the blond stubble gracing his jaw. He wiped it away casually and kept chewing. His golden-flecked brown eyes examined me with a strange combination of detachment and intense curiosity. They glittered in the late morning light.

I took another step into the house, and the door shut on its own behind me. Jumpy from the day's previous escapades, I let out a small yelp. My cheeks flushed almost immediately.

The slender man stared, eyebrow half-raised like a zoologist studying a strange new breed of chimpanzee. His skin was the sort of deep bronze one could only attain by completely ignoring the perils of sun exposure. Thick sandy brown hair, bleached by the sun, sat in a pleasant mess on his head. Upon closer inspection, the stubble gracing his strong jaw was the type that pretended to be uncultivated, but took a razor to maintain.

I knew a bullshitter when I saw one.

The man finished half his cereal before saying, "You're staring, Eden."

Like a third grader, I said, "Am not."

Which only made my skin feel hotter. Suddenly, wearing pants on a tropical island seemed like a horrible move. I was thrown off, but not by his charm—which, admittedly, he had in spades. When I finally took a deep breath, tasting the little flecks of his soul that danced around the house like confetti in a snow globe, I understood.

This guy was *old*—and complicated.

Feeling his soul made me shiver as I processed the various layers. Time had a way of sanding away certain features of the soul and rendering others in stark relief. Human, but with a strong magical current running through his core.

"You're a Reaper." He took another bite of Cocoa Puffs. His taste in cereal was amusing, given the depth of his life experience.

Finally regaining my wits, instead of saying *how'd you know*, I said, "So you must've bought Jack's place."

"Actually, the old man kicked it." He made a kind of clicking sound with his mouth and shrugged, but his eyes glowed with an empathetic unspoken epitaph. "And I inherited the business."

"So what, you're his son?"

This elicited a wry smile. The man dumped another mountain of breakfast cereal into his bowl and said, "More like an old friend."

"And he just gave you the place."

"I helped him through a rough spot once."

"Not sure I follow."

"You're a little uptight, you know that?" The man set down his cereal and placed his slender elbows on the dusty countertop. "You gotta relax a little."

I glared at him. The worst thing you can possibly tell a woman is she looks grouchy. Or needs to relax. That's a one-way trip to wearing a drink.

"How about you sell me something for this," I said, pointing at my infected shoulder, "and then I'll go relax somewhere else."

"That's pretty nasty. Wolf?"

"You a healer or something?"

"Been around awhile, Eden, and no one's accused me of that yet." He emerged from behind the countertop. A pair of loose sweatpants hung below his bare v-shaped torso. The man moved with the deliberate ease of someone who had seen many years slip through time's hourglass—a man with no place to be in a hurry. The old floorboards creaked as he extended his hand.

"Dante Cross."

I clasped his hand, and he shook it firmly, for just the right amount of time. Our hands drifted apart, and I looked at his abs.

"So, is this your move?"

"Only when there's an attractive woman around." He held my gaze and took a bite of cereal. This time, however, I didn't blush or blink. Nope. My shoulder hurt way too bad for that, and his devil-may-care debonair was starting to feel a little forced. Not that most girls would have noticed. But most girls couldn't sense the blood and the gold and the cannon shot that swirled around the fractured shards of his old soul.

"Nice one, Romeo. You must say that to all the girls."

"Only the—"

"Attractive ones. Got it."

"Hasn't failed me before now." He raised one eyebrow ever so slightly. "So, Reaper, why have you been battling creatures outside your weight class?"

"Never needed an explanation to shop here before."

"Hey, I'm not trying to pry." Cross held his hands up in surrender. "We all need a few secrets."

I craned my neck to better assess my surroundings. The wide entrance room branched off three ways—straight ahead, into the kitchen; to the left, which looked like an old library; and to the right, where there were a couple of bedrooms, one of which contained a hidden fireplace heading into the basement. It didn't look like anything had changed, other than the missing wall to the kitchen. But the idle plaster-covered sledgehammer was clearly responsible for that.

"Werewolves are an occupational hazard," I said, trying to push past the subject as I stared into library. The musty aroma of vintage books wafted by. Jack's many rare volumes were still stacked floor to ceiling in thick, tall bookcases, the overflow almost covering the bare hardwood floor. A faded leather chair sat in the corner, the upholstery frayed to its wooden frame.

"See anything you like?" Cross asked, tone playful.

"How'd the old man die?" I looked at the ceiling, which was water warped by the harsh elements. Atheas was notorious for its wild weather swings, even in the regions with mostly stable climates. In the northwest, the temperature didn't drop to freezing, but ferocious storms were an omnipresent possibility. Most people blamed it on geography, but I knew better: we had our own little fickle rain goddess in Lucille.

"You think I killed him." A statement, not a question—one with a little bit of an edge.

I slipped my hand into my pocket, gripping the Reaper's Switch just in case. "I'm just trying to get all the facts."

Cross headed into the library and extended his long arm to grab a small paperback on a high shelf. Before I could read the title, he flipped it open, and two folded sheets of paper came out. One was Jack's last will and testament. Sure enough, the old man had left his home and the assets within to none other than Dante Cross. The other was a photocopy of an MRI.

"Stage four throat cancer," I said. "Damn."

"Med school?" Cross asked.

"Played a doctor once or twice."

Cross looked unsure what that meant, exactly.

"Tough bastard until the end. But the abyss comes for us all, one way or another." The darkness writ across his face indicated that Cross understood this reality of life better than most.

Suddenly, I felt bad for pressing the matter at all. An awkward silence settled over the room after I handed him back the papers.

"Was there a cat in the will?" I asked, suddenly recalling Jack's pet. He was all black, except for a big white streak running down from the center of his head to his tail. Which made the ornery creature look like a skunk.

"No cat," Cross replied. "Just the house and whatever was inside."

The awkward silence returned.

Finally, Cross said, "Don't Reapers usually hunt, I don't know, dead things?"

So much for leaving the werewolf topic alone. But Cross was the kind of guy who attacked a problem from multiple angles, getting his answers any way he could.

"It's a long story." My shoulder pounded, reminding me that I needed to get this show on the road. "I brought cash."

"Well, about that." Cross leaned against the arching doorway that led to the library. "The shop isn't quite what it once was."

"You didn't maintain the storeroom?"

"Not really my thing, Eden." Panic flooded my veins, and I briefly considered heading back to the taxi—the meter was running, after all—and finding a different method of treatment. I was burning valuable time here if this shirtless immortal surf bum didn't have a poultice or a wound compress. True, the available alternatives would likely cost me more than money, but this was looking like a dead end. Besides, while Cross might have inherited the business, I still didn't trust him. He was a slick talker, ready with a clever quip or line to distract you from his true agenda.

I didn't buy the *laissez-faire* attitude for a second. I knew the type well. I'd hung out with Cross-types for years.

"What the hell have you been doing besides eating and running around with your shirt off?"

"Wouldn't you like to know?" Cross replied with a masterful wink, which—despite my best intentions and resistance—made my mind briefly venture to places I didn't really need to visit right then. I stuck my tongue out, but the rest of my body language had already given me away.

"I *would* like to know," I said. "That's why I asked."

"Business isn't really my thing."

"Too many big numbers?"

"Too ephemeral." Cross disappeared into the kitchen to root through a drawer. With a big smile, he showed me his find: a keyring. The metal jangled as he approached. He nodded toward the first bedroom. I followed him to the fake fireplace—the most obvious of hidden entrances, since no one in their right fucking mind would need a fireplace in this part of Atheas, but whatever.

"I'm not sure you're going to be happy with the state of affairs." Cross inserted the key into a hidden notch in the brick. A gear clicked, and the transformation began. "But you're welcome to look."

"With that ringing endorsement, I can hardly wait."

The bricks groaned as they shifted to reveal a steep set of stairs leading down into the basement shop. From the smell alone, I already knew everything was wrong. The shop had always been fresh and eclectic—maybe not quite pleasant, but *alive*. Now, it just smelled musty and kind of rotten, like moldy cardboard after a rainstorm.

Cross knelt and flicked the light switch along the baseboard next to the fireplace. The stairs were covered in a thin layer of dust.

"What have your other customers said about this disaster?" I stared into the abyss, dread churning in my stomach like curdled milk. There were other apothecaries and potion vendors on the island, sure, but they tended to want things other than money.

Souls, mainly.

I needed to check this out, even if it looked like a complete bust.

"I wouldn't know." Cross stepped forward so that he was next to me. His words were even and casual. Like even if everything wasn't going to be okay, in the grand cosmic scheme of things, everything would still be cool. "You're the first person I've allowed down here since I moved in a month ago."

So, naturally, I said, "*Why*?"

And he responded, without looking over, "Because you're hot." Then he winked. "And I had a good feeling about you."

Then Cross disappeared into the basement store as I thought to myself, *well, that was probably your first mistake*.

10

As the first customer to see Jack's Apothecary Shack post-inheritance, I feel obligated to state in no uncertain terms that the shop—or, rather, its feral fragmented remnants—was an unmitigated disaster. Any lingering hope of finding anything useful vanished into the musty air once I was midway down the steep steps.

The aisles had never been organized, but now they were overtaken by the magical wilderness that had thrived in the unmonitored subterranean darkness. Even the cash register had moss—or, more likely, poisonous lichen—crawling over its yellowed plastic. And that was about as good as it got. The odor was evocative of a backwoods swamp in the middle of a heatwave, suggesting that the remaining stock hadn't exactly kept fresh.

Cross reached the bottom of the stairs and waited for me to join him. Our presence made the already tight basement feel even more claustrophobic. While the single bulb over the stairwell was still going strong, the ones lining the basement ceiling had shattered or burned out. Something hissed in aisle five, lurking where the light couldn't reach.

"A little rough around the edges, but it has its charms," Cross said. "But whatever you find is yours. No charge."

"Gee, how generous."

"I aim to please."

I slipped around him, crunching something beneath my sneaker. I lifted my low-top, finding that I'd mushed a large magical spider into the ground. Its blood was a royal shade of purple. While I wasn't a pansy around bugs, the fact that critters like this had full run of the basement didn't fill me with confidence. Jack had always kept some weird things in stock. Things that could've grown...out of control in the past few weeks.

I reached into my pocket and took out the Reaper's Switch. A loud mewing answered the blade's snap. Aisle five, same place as the hissing.

"Thought there was no cat in the will."

"There wasn't," Cross said.

I made my way slowly toward aisle five. The mewing intensified. "I think you got more than you bargained for."

"Life is full of wonderful surprises." Cross didn't sound thrilled about the possibility of inheriting a furry friend. Especially one who had been surviving in this mess for the past month—or longer.

I held the knife out in front of me as I turned down the aisle. Already densely packed—the basement was small, and five aisles was pushing things—the ensuing months of disrepair had transformed the apothecary into a cramped grotto. Magical vines dangled from the ceiling. A strange fuzz graced the shelves. The ground was dotted with mushrooms and stalks of exotic plants ranging from hemlock to sorcerer's wheatgrass, which was like that awful "superfood" people took for cleanses, but instead of terrible diarrhea, this variant offered enhanced spellcasting ability. And, as a bonus, it tasted twice as nasty.

"How you doin' back there, Eden?" Cross's voice seemed like it was coming from a distant planet.

"Making progress." I'd been attacked by an alpha wolf and threatened by a 2,400-year-old vampire, but *this* might have been the freakiest thing I'd experienced in the past twelve hours. Or maybe I was just delirious from exhaustion. Either way, I felt like an explorer marching through uncharted territory, unsure what might lunge out from the indigenous plants.

I wondered if this was how Aldric had felt when he had sailed here in the sixth century. None of Atheas had existed. However strange the island was now, it had to have once been an unfriendly and unfathomable expanse.

A black blur roared out from beneath a tattered box. Much to my embarrassment, I let out an ear piercing shriek, tumbling into the fuzzy shelf to my right. A jar shattered, spraying my shoes with glass as a serpent snapped, narrowly missing my ear. Meanwhile, the cat was attached to my leg, clawing its way up my stiff, torn jeans.

Thinking only of escape, I swung my arm into the snake shelf. The aisles crumpled on top of one another in a screeching cacophony of breaking glass and crackling vegetation.

The cat, for his part, was determined to make a summit of Mount Eden. I grabbed him by the nape of the neck to get his claws out of my skin, but the bastard clung tight, his cool blue eyes glaring back at me.

Were a cat's eyes supposed to be this blue? We shared a moment, his claws still digging into my leg, until, very firmly, the cat said, "Release me, human."

Which was about the time I fainted.

11

NIGHTFALL HAD SWEPT ACROSS THE ISLAND BY THE time I awoke in the second bedroom. A fresh bandage wrapped my arm, from where I had smacked into the glass. The wound on my palm had also been redressed. When I rolled over on the bed, I felt another mass of fabric bundled around my ear.

"Sandstorm viper," Cross said, rising from a chair in the corner of the small room. He leaned over to check my pulse. I noted that he'd seen fit to put on a shirt. "Couple more minutes and you'd have been dead."

So the snake had actually nipped me in the ear. I hadn't noticed, since my heart had been about ready to leap out of my chest between the hissing and the cat trying to scale my pants. At least I hadn't fainted from seeing a stray cat and a few bugs. That would have been too humiliating to live down. Much better to almost die and escape with my dignity intact.

I tried to sit up, but found my muscles uncooperative due to the snake venom. On second thought, maybe my

pride could have taken this particular hit. With an exaggerated groan, I allowed myself to sink back into the soft bed.
My eyesight blurred back into a vague semblance of focus,
and I noticed Cross had a bandage of his own along his wrist.

"The snake got you too?"

"No," he said with a wry smile. "That was Khan."

"Khan?"

"You never read *The Jungle Book*? My god, when that
came out in England..." He trailed off, looking out the
window. This side of the ranch house overlooked a sheer
drop into the ocean. Waves broke on the horizon, out by the
moon. Cross turned away from the window and winked,
revealing that the old man reminiscing bit was just an act.
"It's an appropriate name, suffice to say."

"Well, he's your cat." My mouth felt like it was stuffed
with sandpaper and cotton balls. I tried to reach for the
water on the nearby nightstand, but my muscles still weren't
on board.

"We'll cross that bridge when we get to it," Cross said.

"Did he talk to you, too?"

Cross's golden-flecked brown eyes lit up with concern.
He ran his hand through his messy sun-bleached hair.
"Talk? I must say, Eden—"

"Cut the shit, buddy. You're not as good a liar as you
think." My eyes were half-open, but I wasn't buying it.

"I was right about that feeling." Cross returned to his
chair, which put him mostly out of my line of sight. I could
just barely see his leg if I strained my right eye. Which
made it a little like talking to a spirit. That could have just
been the venom and antidote running through my
veins, too.

"How do you figure that happened?"

"The feeling? You learn to read people after five hundred years. Give or take."

"I meant the talking cat."

"Oh, that." I heard Cross rap his fingers against the worn plaster. The room smelled slightly damp, like the sea had come inside for a visit long ago, but never quite left. "Probably got trapped. Ate the right cocktail and gave himself the gift of speech."

"Just like that."

"Well, he created the antidote that saved you."

"Really?"

"And called you *stupid human* a lot. Among other things you probably don't need repeated."

"Lovely." I stared at the water-damaged ceiling. Jack had really let this place deteriorate over the last few years. It wasn't even worth claiming as inheritance. That made me wonder why Dante Cross had even bothered to show up. "Seen a lot of talking animals in your travels?"

"He would be the first."

"You're taking this remarkably well." I groaned, suddenly remembering I was on the clock. I had that midnight meeting at The Loaded Gun. Not like I could call up the short, red-haired woman to reschedule.

Struggling mightily, I finally managed to prop myself up in an L position against the creaky headboard. My head swam with what had to be the worst hangover I'd ever encountered. I rubbed my legs gingerly, coming across new tears in my jeans and some fresh scratches.

Frigging wildlife.

"No comment, then?" I asked, finally turning my head —slowly, to avoid any sudden bursts of pain—to look at Cross. For the first time, I noticed he had a shotgun sitting next to him in the corner. "Something I need to be aware of?"

"When you live this long, you expect the impossible," he replied, answering both questions and yet answering neither.

"You're like talking to a fucking Ouija board." I bent my arm at an angle to pull out my phone. The display read 10:32. I needed to get out of here, but that didn't look possible in my current condition. At least I'd gotten a few hours of much needed sleep. "Help me up, would you?"

He smiled. "I think you can do it yourself."

"When did chivalry die?" I muttered, straining to wrestle free from the thick covers. Finally, I managed to haul my legs over the side of the bed. My feet touched the cool hardwood.

"See?" Cross nodded, like he'd known all along. "Didn't need my help."

"What'd you do with the rest of downstairs?"

"Couldn't be saved. Everything was consumed by darkness."

For the first time, I noticed the faint scent of woodchips. As if to answer my unspoken question, Cross pointed out the door, toward the front of the house. Guess there was a bonfire blazing on the front lawn. At least he didn't have any close neighbors.

"Jack wasn't a connoisseur of the dark arts, though."

"No." A world-weariness crept into Cross's normally carefree tone. "But when anarchy festers for too long, creatures lose their way. Especially those with poison already in their veins."

Couldn't say I was going to pour one out for that snake. "And Khan?"

"Alive, but taking an extended nap." Cross rubbed his

scratched arm ruefully. "I'm afraid he might be beyond saving."

"That what the shotgun is for?"

"No." Cross didn't elaborate.

"Khan was always an asshole, even when he couldn't talk." I tested my balance by gingerly putting weight on my right foot. A sudden bout of vertigo forced me back down to the bed. "I'll take him."

"He's all yours, Reaper."

I almost choked after a few seconds passed, realizing that I, Eden Hunter, had just volunteered to rescue a living creature—and care for it. One who was, quite possibly, a bigger jackass than me. A match made in heaven.

I was so going to die alone, and it was all my fault.

"He did seem to like you." Cross grinned, warmth flowing from the corner. The smile snapped off his face when there was a creak at the house's entrance. He stood quickly, moving with the caution of someone who had seen death before. "Stay here and be quiet."

"Maybe it's the taxi driver." God, that was going to be a big bill.

"I paid him hours ago."

Maybe chivalry wasn't dead—only dormant. There was another crack, this one sharp enough to clearly indicate that someone else was inside. I reached for the Reaper's Switch —the only damn thing that could protect me—and about had a heart attack when it was missing. Then I saw it on the nightstand. With a trembling arm, I grabbed the blade and clutched it to my chest like a familiar teddy bear.

Cross racked the shotgun and said, "Be right back."

Before I could say anything, he slipped out of the room like a wraith, leaving me alone. Hopefully the noises were just Khan escaping from his cage and causing a ruckus.

My hopes were quickly dashed when the shotgun unleashed an enormous, booming roar. Cross yelled—the kind of sound a man makes only when he's injured.

After much trial and tribulation, I squeezed my bare feet into my sneakers and limped to the bedroom door. An amber light from the fire outside cast a dancing shadow against the plain hallway. I crept out of the room and snuck toward the foyer. The faint tendrils of wood smoke that had come inside had turned royal purple.

"Idiot," I said.

Cross was neither a businessman nor a student of magic. Mixing that many magical ingredients together would emit an easily traceable signature. To a human, it probably looked like an illicit fireworks display. But to the supernatural community, it was like a homing beacon that screamed *here lies rare things*. Ones worth taking by force— or worth investigating by the island's bureaucracy.

I wasn't talking about the Atheas PD or the FBI. The Department of Supernatural Affairs was a far bigger bureaucratic nightmare, and just the kind of organization that would investigate this type of disturbance.

Cross, naturally, was nowhere to be found. I swung into the entrance room, glancing in the library and kitchen. Both empty. The front door stood slightly ajar, a humid summer breeze bringing the acrid aroma of torched magical objects through the crack. My head pounded with each halting step, my body still recovering from the snake bite.

Then I saw it.

Blood, glistening right near the welcome mat. Fresh. And no small amount, either. A yell came from outside, followed by a massive growl. I wanted to dart out and help, but I was useless in my current state. Goddamn Lucille and her silly rules. Even under the best of circumstances, I was a grasshopper in a magical world of sharks and lions—and, right now, I couldn't even jump.

A glass window broke and two bodies crashed into the dark library across from me. I limped toward the noise, Reaper's Switch extended.

A purplish bolt sizzled like a solar flare. Cross rolled away just in time, but the spell left a scorch mark in the hardwood and devoured a stack of old books for good measure. He winked at me, like he had everything under control. But his chest was bleeding badly—and it was easy to tell why when his demonic adversary rose from the shredded glass.

The demon stood well over six feet, its hideous muscles tensing. It barked and snapped, which wasn't particularly interesting. Of greater concern were its glowing claws, which had been equipped with magical castings normally reserved for warlocks or sorceresses.

The soulless monster swiped at Cross's head. Cross deftly ducked, countering with a glancing blow from the shotgun stock. Cross might have been immortal and in good shape, but a demon was born in the molten depths of the Elysian Fields—the worst tiers, where no one wanted to be sent. Demons had no souls at all, which meant they possessed an unquenchable thirst to fill the limitless void within. That meant a lot of bodies and a wake of destruction.

Cross glanced at me quickly and shook his head ever so slightly, imploring me to run. But I'd never been a good listener—and I wasn't turning over a new leaf now. I limped into the library, ready to join the fray. The demon whipped its horned, scarred face toward me, unleashing a primal scream from its jagged-toothed lips.

A glowing claw raked down Cross's wounded chest,

and he buckled, gasping for air as the shotgun clattered away. The demon roared in victory, gloating about its victory before delivering the final blow.

"Hey," I said. "Over here."

The demon cocked its hideous head and narrowed its yellow eyes. It was unusual for someone to challenge a demon directly, mainly because doing so was suicidal. Best case scenario, you emerged looking like you'd had a head-on collision with a bullet train. Worst case, he devoured your soul, which complicated your afterlife prospects.

Cold sweat trickled down my cheek as I held out the Reaper's Switch. We stared one another down, locked in a silent standoff as Cross tried to recover. From the corner of my eye, I saw him reaching for the shotgun. But from the way he was moving, he wasn't going to get there in time.

There was another option, though.

"The books!" A towering, precarious stack lurked behind the demon. Cross swung his legs out, sending the old volumes toppling over. The demon roared in displeasure, throwing its bumpy, hairless arms up in confusion.

That was the only opening I needed. I tossed the Reaper's Switch to Cross while the beast was distracted. He plunged the blade into the demon's shin. A room-rocking scream I never wanted to hear again filled the library. Then Cross rolled over, pumped the shotgun once, and fired.

A geyser of blood erupted from the demon's ruined neck. His headless torso crashed against the bookshelves, sending more musty volumes flying as the dying creature repainted the walls crimson in a final act of demonic destruction. Finally, it stumbled forward and landed on top of Cross, who let out a mighty groan.

I traversed the smoldering, bloody sea of ruined books

and demon giblets and kicked the warm corpse. Definitely dead.

"Man, they're gonna be pissed at you." Cross's voice was muted by a mountain of rotting flesh.

"Why's that?" A foreboding, rumbling sense of existential doom cascaded through my empty stomach. No way this day could get any worse. That had to be statistically impossible. After all, I'd come here for a healing potion, only to instead be bitten by a snake, adopt an ornery cat, and battle a demon.

Cross emerged from beneath the headless body wearing a bright smile on his tan face.

"Because no one messes with the DSA. Or Lucille." He wiped skull fragments off his wounded chest, wincing as he touched the large gash. "Except for me. And now, well, you."

I glowered and stomped out of the ruined library.

Goddamn, did it suck being right.

12

I didn't help Cross dress his wounds. I was too furious to even look at him, no matter how much of his immortal British charm he tried to pour on. Instead, I vigorously scrubbed the demon guts off my bare skin in his cramped shower, wincing as the hot water sluiced over my wounds. To ignore the pain, I reflected on my rapidly deteriorating situation.

I wasn't sure that was a strong enough descriptor for the total shit show my life had become. Twenty-four hours ago, I'd been employed by a vicious vampire warlord. Now, that time seemed like a distant, fond memory.

I knew one thing for sure—Lucille didn't need another reason to be pissed at me.

A little background: other than being goddess of rain, she was also the head of the DSA—otherwise known as the Department of Supernatural Affairs. As its name might have suggested, it was a government bureaucracy. What its name might not have immediately suggested, however, was this: it was run by the gods and goddesses who had abandoned Earth for the Elysian Fields. Since they no longer wanted to watch over mortal affairs, they'd created an agency to do the job for them.

Lucille had been the lucky goddess who had gotten to stay behind and run the agency. Not by choice. Her options had been execution—the gods favored disembowelment—or a permanent banishment to Earth, and a role as Director of the DSA. I suppose gods didn't take kindly to the murder of other gods in a jealous rage. She'd caught her husband with the harvest goddess, things had gotten ugly, and, suffice to say, Eros had emerged from the ordeal very dead.

Where I entered this little equation was simple: the DSA was a well-known entity on the island. No one particularly liked them, since they were pricks the likes of which even the bought-and-paid for police force couldn't aspire to be. Everyone knew Lucille was a royal bitch, too, and ruthless in her interpretation of the letter of the supernatural law.

What they didn't know, unlike yours truly, was that she was a rain goddess. Everyone else believed there had never been any gods—or those who had once watched over humanity had all left. That was the secret she and I alone shared, and which she made clear—in no uncertain terms—would result in my entire family's demise, should it ever leak out. I'd have claimed that I would have preferred she kept such celestial secrets to herself, but that would've been a lie. I hadn't been the only one to die in that alley in Bourbon Street, but I had been the only one to be revived by Aldric.

My sister, however, had stayed dead. And I'd fixed that the only way I'd known how: by making a deal with a goddess—who, as a growing mountain of evidence suggested, was closer to a devil. After all, you don't get tossed from the Elysian Fields for being a peach. Not that this should have been surprising—even her name bore more than a passing resemblance to Lucifer. The old scriptures and myths got a few things right, but often got the details and genders wrong.

I got out of the shower and wrung out my wet hair. The bruises and wounds I'd accumulated over the past day gave my skin a sickly appearance. Deep bags pulled at the bottom of my eyelids. I turned away and finished toweling off.

There was a knock at the bathroom door. I glowered in the thick steam, refusing to answer. But Cross was relentless, and finally I said, "Go away."

"I'm sorry, Eden."

"I have somewhere to be in an hour."

"Classy or low-key?"

"What?" It took me a minute to process. "I don't know. Classy." Better to catch my mystery note-giver off guard than show up like I'd emerged from beneath a pile of demon guts. The latter was closer to the truth, but the truth could get you killed. Even if The Loaded Gun was a dive, there was no reason I couldn't wear something nice.

Besides, after getting covered in demon guts and rooting around in dumpsters, a little break wouldn't be the worst thing in the world.

"Come see me in the kitchen when you're finished." Cross's footsteps trailed off down the hall, leaving me alone. There was no sign of a limp, no grunts of pain. Guess that explained his rather complex soul.

There were two flavors of immortality: standard and deluxe, if you will. With standard immortality came an infinite lifespan and freedom from all disease and sundry infections that would fell a mortal. However, one remained rather vulnerable to violent demises—bullets, stab wounds, and other dangers were still very much in play. As such, these immortals had a very intense motivation to keep their blood within the confines of their body.

This flavor of immortality didn't come cheap, but it was relatively attainable for the enterprising and morally ambiguous individual: a sliver of your beloved's soul, or that of a blood relative's, would suffice. Of course, you had to find the proper vita warlock or sorceress to perform the casting.

On the other hand, you had the deluxe package, which Cross had clearly sprung for. Rapid healing, like you might see in a creature like a wolf or vampire. Almost complete immunity to deadly wounds.

And the deluxe package cost extra.

A lot extra—as in, the entire soul of a lover or a blood relative.

The realization didn't make me nervous.

I'd just have to be wary around him.

I wrapped the rough towel around my chest and slipped out of the bathroom at the end of the hallway. As I padded to the archway, I could smell burnt plants in the entrance area. A quick glance across to the library revealed that Cross had removed the demon's body. Streaks of blood still coated the bookshelves like an avant-garde painter had gotten loose inside.

I turned toward the kitchen, where I could see Cross munching on a bowl of cereal through the hole in the wall.

"Have you no modesty?" He shielded his eyes in mock horror, pretending to be offended by my towel-only garb.

"You're one to talk," I said. "When do you think the DSA will send an investigatory team?"

"Oh, you know, a day. Maybe two." He seemed decidedly nonchalant for someone who had just murdered what amounted to a bureaucratic official. I know, I know—it was technically a demon. Weren't they all?

Bad—but true—jokes aside, the fact remained that we had just offed a cog in the DSA's machine. Imagine how the Feds responded to killing an FBI agent, and you kind of had an idea regarding the maelstrom of retribution liable to swarm the house like a locust plague.

"Glad you're so chipper."

"We're both alive, aren't we?" He scratched at his designer stubble. The wound on his bare chest was a light shade of bright pink, like it'd been healing for days instead of hours. If I'd had any lingering doubts about how he'd acquired his immortality, they were now completely gone.

"What does Lucille want with you?"

"You know Lucille?" Cross replied, answering my question with one of his own.

"Everyone knows her," I said, sidestepping that potential land-mine. "She's the law around here."

"Some might argue that Aldric of Scythia is the law in these parts."

Now there was a moniker I hadn't heard in some time. Only older creatures called him that—and then, only those who hadn't visited in some time. Either Cross was putting on a show for my benefit or he'd been telling the truth and had really only been around for a month.

"The FBI is tossing their hat into the ring, too."

"How does a Reaper know so much about law enforcement?" Cross chewed thoughtfully, his golden-flecked brown eyes holding my gaze. For how hot he'd claimed I was, it was almost disappointing that he was only staring at my face.

"How does a- what the fuck are you, anyway?"

Cross finished chewing and said, "Depends on who you

ask." He set the bowl down and gestured toward the lone chair in the kitchen. "There you go. Classy."

"What the hell is *this*?" I tiptoed over the cold floor and touched the little black dress. It was imported silk—high quality, designer made.

"Someone left it here," he said, like it wasn't unusual. When he caught my questioning gaze, he shrugged. "If there's something you'd like to know—"

"I think you've said enough. Turn around, buddy."

Cross gave me a sly pouty face, but did as he was told. I dropped the towel and slid into the soft fabric. Tonight was looking like a no underwear type of night. I wasn't going to borrow *that*. I adjusted the straps and wriggled my butt a little bit. Perfect fit. Whoever Cross's one-night stand was, she was a dead ringer for my body.

I poked the black clutch sitting on the chair, and found it already weighted down with my cell phone, Reaper's Switch, and cash. How nice of him to pack me a to-go bag.

I tucked it under my arm, and posed, unsure exactly how to hold it for maximum seductive effect. Personally, I was a big fan of pockets, hence the jeans and general avoidance of purse-like objects.

"So?"

Cross kept turned. "I'm just staring at the wall. It's a nice wall. Could use some spackling—"

"Just turn around, dumbass."

He did as he was told. He didn't do anything like whistle. Just nodded.

"No smart comments?" I asked.

"That needs to be redressed." He pointed at my bandages, which had been bloodied by demon guts. "Let me see if I can help."

He turned to the plastic countertop. Much to my

surprise, the cabinets contained more than sugary cereal. There was a roll of bandages on one of the shelves. With gentle, well-practiced fingers, he dressed my wounded shoulder and then wrapped a clean, white bandage around it. He repeated the process with my injured palm. The snake bite on my ear had gone down enough from the hot shower and Khan's antidote that it no longer required additional care.

Cross stepped back to survey his handiwork. "Perfect."

"I don't suppose you could give me a ride," I asked, checking my watch. Twenty minutes until showtime with my secret pen pal.

"Leaving so soon?"

"I wouldn't call it *that* soon."

"Would if I could, but someone has to keep us from getting caught around here." Cross disappeared from the kitchen. To my eternal chagrin, I found my heart jackhammering beneath the luxurious fabric. Silent pleas for it to stop proved unsuccessful. I pretended it was because of the near-death experience and held my breath. Which only made things worse.

Cross returned, and I exhaled loudly. He shot me a strange look, but said nothing. Instead, he tossed me a set of keys, which I snagged out of the air.

"It's up the street."

"What is?"

"You can't miss it." He turned around and walked out of the kitchen. "Just be careful."

"Yes, Mom."

"I meant of what lurks in the darkness."

I shivered as I caught my reflection in the mirror on the way out the door.

Cross had a point.

Because, for the first time in a while, I looked scared.

CROSS WASN'T KIDDING THAT I'D NOTICE HIS CAR. EVEN in the starry night, it made a hell of a first impression. His ride was a glistening white Porsche Boxster, recent, judging by the impressive navigation system and slick black leather interior. The two-door roadster growled to life when I pressed the starter. I put the top down and popped the clutch. Then I was tearing off to meet the mystery woman with the long red hair.

I racked my brain, trying to match the small figure with people from my past. There were enough pissed off marks lurking in the recesses of my life that it wouldn't surprise me if one had returned for their pound of flesh. They'd have to take a number. It'd been a busy Monday, and I wasn't sure my schedule could accommodate any more disgruntled people.

I screeched into a narrow spot in The Loaded Gun's parking lot, almost taking out a row of compact cars. Fortunately, Dad had insisted that I'd learned to drive a stick—even as he'd been dying—otherwise all those cars would have been screwed. I snatched the clutch purse off the passenger's seat and smoothed down the black dress. When I tried to get out, though, I found that I couldn't actually open the door. With an extended sigh, I vaulted over the convertible's side, making sure to keep my little black dress down. Wishful thinking at its best. Maybe I should've borrowed panties.

A quick glance at my phone indicated I was two minutes late. Hopefully my mystery date would forgive the minor tardiness given the extenuating circumstances. I hurried across the lot, beat up sneakers not matching the dress.

To call The Loaded Gun unlike any place else on Atheas would be an understatement. It was what I called an "artisanal" dive—shitty, loud, and rough, but wildly over-priced, like it had been created in a weird hipster craft beer lab. There were few places where supernatural creatures congregated, even on the island, let alone public watering holes where they were brash enough to let loose. I mean, in the basement, there was a dueling arena where bets were placed. Kind of like cockfighting, except between, say, a warlock and vampire. It rarely ended well.

An assault of aggressive heavy metal mashed up with hip hop floated through the crisp night air as a couple exited the bar. They gave me sideways glances, but were largely too interested in getting in one another's pants to look me over too closely. I caught the roughhewn wooden door, which resembled a medieval tavern's, and slipped inside, heading down the stairs.

I should've been clearer: the dueling arena was in the *sub*-basement. Because this entire place was already under-ground, scraping precariously close to sea level. As I reached the bottom, the metal mash-up began to meld with the roar of drunken conversation, revelry, and singing. Despite the medieval pub aesthetic—lots of unfinished wood, which resulted in pleasant splinters, and pewter plates—the place drew a surprisingly hip crowd. Probably because this was the only place where most creatures could be themselves.

The metal song dissolved into the ether, followed by a terrible remix of "I Love Rock and Roll" crossed with the DJ's unfortunate beat. Some classics didn't demand improvement. Certainly not by some idiot who didn't know which way to wear his hat. I'd have begged for someone to kill me, but death was a narrowly worse fate than the scratching bass bastardizing Joan Jett's iconic vocals. To be fair, her version was a cover itself, but it was *the* cover.

All the boys in school loved old Emma's classic rock pedantry. And by all, I meant zero.

Heads turned as I wound through the wooden tables and throngs of creatures willingly drinking fifteen-dollar shots from what looked like dirty glasses. Hand blown, by the owner himself. Only in 2018 were even ancient vampires and wolves willing to pay a premium for faux-authenticity. No small feat, considering at least a handful of the creatures in this place had experienced the real Middle Ages firsthand.

A tapestry of Sir Francis Drake in all his privateering glory dangled behind the bar, next to a detailed model of his fabled ship, exposing the proprietor as one of the many who believed the real ship had been left in Atheas by Drake for safekeeping. Like most stupid rumors, that didn't really track, considering the actual ship had been on public display until around 1650, at which point it had been broken up due to wood rot. But it was just one idiotic legend among many attempting to explain the fate of Drake's famed inheritance. A variant on the tale was that, on one of his voyages, the famed captain—or pirate, depending on whose side of history you landed on—had discovered Atheas, and found it possessed all the character-istics of a perfect hiding spot.

I still had my doubts. It had all the marks of a con cooked up by a commerce board trying to attract investment and interest. The kind of underground "secret" that would attract people with deep pockets—but not too many. None-theless, being an intrepid little snoop and stepping on people's toes about the treasure could get you killed right quick. Rule number one: keep your hands to yourself, and you tended to keep them. So I stayed away from the gold rush.

I scanned to the right side of the curved bar, doing a double-take when I saw Rayna Denton. She waved me over with a manicured hand. The path to her was blocked by dancing idiots and chanting fools, so I did a little stepping stone jig from table-to-table, which received a few *oohs* and *ahs*. I slid onto the stool next to her and slammed my clutch on the sticky bar.

"Don't tell me it was you," I said. "Neat trick. *Meet me at The Loaded Gun at midnight, Hunter.*"

I made sure my rendition of the enchanted paper's voice was suitably sarcastic.

"Well, I couldn't exactly run out there and schedule a meeting myself, now could I?"

"If you're looking for a confession, then we can cut straight through the shit right now."

"Just having a friendly drink is all," Rayna said, her gaze telling me her intentions were anything but friendly.

"Double vodka tonic with extra ice, then," I called to the bartender, and jerked my thumb at Rayna. "On her tab."

The bartender gave her a look, and Rayna nodded, her wavy blonde hair bobbing over her shoulders. The cut was stylish, but not overwhelmingly so—perfect for professional and personal matters. She looked hip and fresh, wearing a slim cut blazer with the sleeves rolled up. Beneath that was a tight black tank top, and rounding out the outfit was a pair of low riding dark jeans that revealed a flat midriff. I could see the start of wrinkles beginning to form lines around her eyes.

We waited in silence until my drink arrived a couple

minutes later. I sniffed the dirty glass with suspicion, but beneath the scalding scent of rubbing alcohol, the lip just smelled like dish soap. In fact, The Loaded Gun smelled remarkably fresh, given the grungy interior.

I stirred the drink with the tiny black straw as the crowd launched into another ear-searing butchering of a classic rock track.

Rayna shot me a sly glance, but didn't say anything. Her eyes sized me up. It was hard to sort out the clashing souls in here, but concentrating the brunt of my attention on her presence told me all I needed to know.

"You're half-shifter," I said, furrowing my brow, slightly surprised I hadn't noticed before. "How—how'd you hide that?"

"It's hard to find what you're not looking for." The agent took a sip of her beer. I could tell from the lack of condensation she'd been sitting here a while. That made sense; she struck me as the kind of woman who always wanted to be in control of a situation. Didn't do well with surprises. Wanted to catch her suspects off guard, like she'd done to me this morning. I resisted the urge to keep talking, keep asking questions. The trick to acquiring intel was listening. The trick to giving it all away was trying to fill awkward silences.

An entire song played on the jukebox before Rayna spoke again. It was a far cry from the full-court press she'd put on this morning. All part of some invisible plan, no doubt.

"Do you know how long I've been watching you, Hunter?"

"I'm sure you'll tell me." I gulped the vodka tonic through the straw, momentarily forgetting my drink order. The double burned like I'd poured gasoline down my throat. I stifled a cough, chucked the straw, downed the rest, and flagged the bartender for a refill.

"Since that little scam you were running in New Orleans." The agent ran her finger along the rim of her glass. "I'm sure you have no problem doing that math."

Four years. I brought my new drink up to my lips, then set it down. Better not get too hammered. "Here you know so much about me, and I know nothing about you."

"You said that this morning," Rayna replied, her tone suggesting she had no reason to share.

"But I'm sure your story is interesting."

"Is that what you think, Hunter?" The agent's eyes suddenly blazed with anger. "That you can run a grift on me? Build rapport, maybe get me to admit my mother was difficult, say that yours was the same, and then, *bam*, we're girlfriends for life?" She sipped her beer. "You're a murderer."

Her gaze chilled my blood. All sensible thoughts were screaming to hit *eject* and bail from the situation. Agnes Willsprout would no doubt have a stroke if she caught wind of this off-the-books meeting. But my curiosity was enough to keep me rooted to the rough stool. If Rayna had wanted to jerk my chain in an official capacity, she'd have dragged me back to the field office on some thin bullshit.

So, I sat still. But I took a long drink while I waited for her to continue. Rayna's eyes didn't leave me. It was like being watched by a vengeful servant of justice.

"Well, can you at least tell me what the hell you want?" I flashed a weak smile, which was about all I could muster. The vodka was beginning to take effect, creating a pleasant blanket of warmth that dulled my throbbing shoulder.

Instead of answering, she reached into her blazer pocket and pulled out an evidence photo. I briefly saw her service weapon in its holster before it disappeared back beneath the jacket. She placed the photo on the counter, in the middle of the drink residue and crumbled bar peanuts.

I gave her a funny look. "Is this another trick?" I asked.

"Look at the photo, Hunter."

I wanted to resist, but my curiosity—and buzz—got the better of me. So I pulled the glossy picture toward me. If I'd been feeling less than glib before, the contents of the photo made me feel positively nauseous.

Seeing your own dead body will do that.

"I saw you die four years ago, Hunter." Rayna snapped her fingers to pull my attention back to her. I guess we were done with the awkward silences. She had her interrogation techniques down cold, and now that she had me off guard, she was mashing the accelerator through the floor. "Not many people return from the Elysian Fields. Especially with new names."

I would've asked her how she knew about that, but the half-shifter lineage explained that away—maybe. Most creatures were still in the dark about the mystical world at large. However she'd uncovered the knowledge, one thing was certain: she'd done her homework.

"Why were you watching me in the first place?"

"Because we were building a case against you morons."

I shivered, despite the packed bar being about a hundred degrees. "What is this, a threat?" As secrets went, my coming back to life wasn't really one of them. It was a prerequisite to becoming a Reaper. One of those *you have to learn how the sausage is made* training scenarios. In this case, the trip through the factory was dying and experiencing the misery of the afterlife. After that, you had a better idea of a Reaper's cosmic significance.

"Please." Rayna took the evidence photo and crumpled

it in her manicured hands. "This is old news. Unexciting news."

That wasn't just empty talk. She reached back into her blazer and took out an evidence bag containing something that made me almost fall over. The gold bar that had fallen out of Roan's pocket. This one she didn't offer to me.

"Isn't it illegal to show evidence to suspects?"

"I know you killed your boyfriend, Hunter." The gold bar waved in front of me like a hypnotist's metronome. "All I need to know now is where you stashed your cut."

I laughed in her face. I couldn't help it. The whole thing was ludicrous. Roan had shown up, running some grift or scam, and somehow—one way or another—his antics had bought him two bullets in the back of the skull. Clearly, whoever didn't like him very much also didn't like me much, either, since they'd seen fit to rope me into this crap.

"Does that actually work?" I sipped the vodka and giggled. Here I'd thought Rayna had been a master manipulator. Luckily, it was all a smoke show. "Like, on anyone, *ever*?"

"If the gold is not in my possession by Friday, then I'll match up Eden Hunter's file with Emma Miller's." She drummed her fingers on the rough bar top. "Your connection with Roan Kelly is what I believe they call motive."

"I'll get right on retrieving the gold." I tapped on the counter along to the rap-rock remix playing on the loudspeaker, despite my disdain for the music. Blame the vodka tonics. "Right after you go fuck yourself."

With a wink, I yanked my clutch off the beer-battered bar and slid off the chair. Her fingers dug into the bandage on my shoulder, those manicured nails pressing into the wound. I winced, my knees buckling a little.

Her lips came up to my ear, tongue almost pressed

inside my earlobe. "There's no escaping from me, Emma Miller. *Ever.*"

I tried to shake loose from her grip, but she held fast.

Which is when the vodka tonics took over and I punched Rayna Denton right in her pretty face.

13

Unleashing a punch in The Loaded Gun—as its name might suggest—was like microwaving ten tons of dynamite. To call the results explosive would be the understatement of the century. No sooner had I landed my right hook on Rayna's cheek did the music stop. It was a unique magical feature, a warning against violence.

Rayna didn't take it in stride, though, and she retaliated with a leg sweep from some martial art I wasn't acquainted with. I dropped the clutch as we kicked and grappled to the dirty ground, surrounded by the bar's stunned patrons. The problem with starting a fight with no training whatsoever quickly became apparent: I couldn't finish. Rayna might've been caught off guard by the brashness, but now I was losing. She had my good shoulder twisted at a bad angle as her knee dug into my ribs.

A disquiet settled over the bar as I tried to claw at Rayna's eyes. I missed, although I succeeded in smearing her eyeliner. Unfortunately, I didn't get points for making her uglier.

I gasped for air as her crazed eyes bore into me with all the fire of a solar eclipse.

"You think you can just say *no* and walk on—" Before she could finish her screaming tirade, Rayna's body shook like it'd been hit by a lightning bolt. I smelled burning hair, and felt the sharp tingle of electricity course over my own skin. The FBI agent crumpled, landing face first on the floor.

The bar erupted in a raucous cheer. For a brief moment of vodka-inspired delusion, I thought perhaps I'd awakened some latent power that had lain dormant within me until now. But that hope was soon crushed when I heard a thunderous clap that silenced the room.

"There is no fighting upstairs, morons!" The man's deep voice seemed to shake the very foundations of the basement itself, like a sudden seismic event. But I knew from experience that this was no earthquake or act of God. It was the owner, who I might have had a little history with.

As in, not allowed back.

Ever.

But what were rules *really* for, other than breaking?

The mishmash of souls vying for attention suddenly parted like the sea, overridden by one extremely strong—and old—soul that could belong only to Magnus. His presence brought about an uneasy calm—the kind one might expect before one hell of a storm.

I used a nearby table to drag myself upright, brushing splinters from my legs. Rayna babbled on the ground, still recovering from the lightning blast. The floor rumbled as the tree trunk of a man rumbled toward us. My eyes wandered to the bar, wondering if I could get to my vodka glass before the dwarf Jötun arrived.

Not for any defensive purposes.

Just to make the next few minutes more pleasant.

Before I could take a step, however, a massive hand enveloped my unwounded shoulder.

"You are not allowed here, Eden." His voice rippled over my skin.

"Must've slipped my mind."

He cleared his throat, and I finally turned. I got a full view of the bottom part of his burly torso and the baggy canvas sack-like fabric that covered it. His entire backstory was fuzzy, but Magnus wasn't from around here—and he was old, with his own customs. Rumor was, he'd been expelled from his people for being the runt of the litter. Him being tiny in comparison to anything was hard to fathom. You could've put two of me next to each other, and I still wouldn't have been as broad as his shoulders.

My eyes traced up his bare, scarred arms. I had to crane my neck at an uncomfortable angle just to see his face. He had at least two feet on me. A dwarf Jötun—or giant, for those unfamiliar with the Old Norse terminology—was kind of like a dwarf polar bear. Scrawny only in comparison to its brethren.

I finally managed to meet his crystal-blue gaze, nearly having to stand on my tiptoes to do so. His thick blond hair was shaved into a mohawk. Two sigils, supposedly bestowed by ancient Viking shamanic practitioners of *seidhr*, glowed on his neck. Under normal circumstances, the bolt and hammer looked like ill-fated stylistic decisions. These were not normal circumstances, however, and the sigils now glowed with enchanted energy—the bolt an electric white, the hammer more amber than the hottest forge.

No one else in The Loaded Gun moved.

"This is the *second* fight you have caused here."

"You know what I think, Magnus?" I glanced around at the crowd.

"I care not what you think, Reaper." His thick arms folded like a stern guardian ordering someone away. "You are not welcome here."

"I think it's fucking weird that a giant runs a hipster dive bar." The vodka was getting to me. But whatever. He could ban me again. Woo, scary.

"Never provoke a creature's baser nature," the dwarf giant said. When he loosened his shoulders, I saw a necklace of teeth caught in the flowing fabric around his neck. They looked like they belonged to werewolves. Fresh trophies accompanied ancient kills. A faint sense of dread churning in my stomach. Then the vodka took control again, and I smirked at the ancient giant.

"Words you should live by, my Viking friend." I gave him a buddy tap on the muscular shoulder and found my clutch on the floor next to some spilled fries, feeling everyone's eyes on my back. No one said anything. They couldn't believe I'd openly disrespected him.

No one did that to Magnus, because he was right.

Provoking any creature of magic was a dangerous game.

But it'd just been that kind of day where, quite frankly, I didn't give a shit anymore.

14

I RUBBED MY JAW IN THE BAR'S DARK PARKING LOT, trying to coax feeling back into my numb cheeks. Even through the alcohol jacket, I could feel my right shoulder. Blood seeped through the bandage on my palm, the cut reopened during my tussle with Rayna.

I shook off the fog and grabbed a coffee from a twenty-four-hour diner. Then I napped in the convertible to sober up. By the time I awoke a couple hours later, most of the cars had cleared out from the lot. Even then, the sun wouldn't be up for another few hours.

Sipping the cold coffee—noting its distinct lack of improvement with age—I contemplated my next move. Rayna had thrown an unwelcome monkey wrench into the proceedings. I almost blew the coffee through my nose when it dawned on me that, should the FBI link old Emma with the new Eden, they'd likely revoke my bail. I'd be flagged as a flight risk and career criminal. Do not pass go, do not collect two hundred dollars. At that point, all I'd have to look forward to was the executioner's needle.

It looked like every piece of my past was turning up on Atheas: first my old flame Roan, now the ghostly trail of scams and deceit I'd left behind. All I needed was for Sierra to show up, and the whole band would be right back together.

Although the general picture remained fuzzy, there was one thing I knew for certain: Rayna was a relentless bitch. And her obsession with the gold made her a prime suspect. Killing Roan and framing me in the process? I made for a good fall girl. She'd known about my previous activities, which meant she would've known about my relationship with Roan. I'd gotten a glance at her sidearm in the bar—not surprising, since Atheas doesn't exactly have strict gun control laws—and it'd been a .45.

Not one of those lady versions, either—if there was such a .45, which to my knowledge, there wasn't. Her sidearm was something a sheriff in a western would carry during the drawdown, complete with a six-inch barrel. Loud enough to sound like thunder, even at a couple hundred yards. And plenty of stopping power to put down a full-grown man cold.

Not FBI issue, but Rayna clearly did what she wanted. Otherwise she wouldn't have met me in a bar to shake me down.

Realizing I was still too buzzed to drive, I chewed over her not-so-veiled threat. She could bury me, and she wasn't going to stop unless I handed over the gold. I didn't know if it was sheer greed, or if there were other factors at play. It didn't really matter. Friday was now a hard deadline, and it was already, technically speaking, Tuesday morning.

That made solving the murder my priority. Even if I didn't find the evidence necessary to convict Roan's killer, learning the truth would lead me to the gold cache. After that, I could decide whether to hand it over to Rayna or shove it right up her tight, well-maintained butt.

I propped my sneakers on the dash, then remembered I wasn't wearing underwear. Even comfort was too much to ask for today. So I put the seat back as far as it would go, staring at the stars as I ran through other possible suspects.

Aldric had seemed genuinely surprised to hear about the other gunshots. But he was a sociopath and well-seasoned warlord who had survived for centuries. Lying would be old hat. On the other hand, Aldric's goal hadn't been to put me six feet under. Plus, he could have guillotined me with my own snapped femur in his penthouse office. No, he just wanted me to collect more souls to feed his criminal enterprise.

Which led me to another obvious suspect: this mysterious rival Reaper. She'd already cut in on my territory and made me look bad. Maybe her freelancing ambitions had grown, and now she coveted the entire pie. Framing me for murder would mean no future competition for souls.

But she'd also had an open shot at me in the darkness, and hadn't pulled the trigger. Maybe it hadn't been the Reaper out near the antiques shop—but if it was, why hadn't she tried to put a bullet in my head?

Caveats aside, that still made three decent suspects. No doubt more were lurking in the wings.

I bit my tongue and watched a taxi pick up a stumbling drunk. About those other, as-yet-unidentified suspects: I needed a more robust list, and information on my competition.

That meant going home was out of the question.

Buzzed or not, I didn't really feel like driving at this

hour. Which is how I found myself in a cab, speeding toward the one person you didn't want to visit late at night on Atheas.

Meaning the mayor, of course.

15

THE MAYOR WAS A WARLOCK WITH A FOOT FETISH—AN all-around creepy, creepy dude.

Not because of the foot thing. Just the vibe.

But the mayor was also a well-connected creepy dude. The FBI had its databases, Aldric had his paid spies, and the DSA had their little demonic bureaucrats. What I had, though, was a carefully cultivated web of contacts.

Right now, I was headed straight to the man who had his pulse on everything important—and probably unimportant—that occurred on Atheas. If someone's gold stash had been ripped off and they were trying to make a sale, the mayor would know.

And the thieves would be prime suspects in the murder of Roan Kelly.

The modest city's lights dwindled in the rearview, giving way to the suburbs that covered the northwest quarter of the island. You had to hand it to Aldric: for an uncharted island overrun with beasties and magic, he'd done a remarkable job getting the word out about real estate opportunities. This wasn't some land of misfit toys, where wolves and vamps and warlocks lurked in every house. There were honest-to-goodness families living out here, with humans outstripping the supernatural presence by a factor of ten to one.

The cab cut down an idle cul-de-sac that terminated in an ostentatious pink mansion. All the lights were out inside.

The driver said, "I wouldn't fight with this guy, lady."

I caught my reflection in the rearview. A minor cut leaked blood over my right eye. Thanks, Rayna. "You know the mayor?"

"This is the mayor's house?" The thick guy in the front seat shrugged. "I was just sayin' that 'cause the house is huge."

"Which means?"

"He's got a lotta lawyers." The cabbie held his hand out for payment, and I obliged. Indeed, I had little doubt the mayor of our fine little island had plenty of lawyers lurking in the shadows of this Miami Beach-style monstrosity. But I wasn't concerned about that minor detail.

He and I were friends. Of sorts. We enjoyed that vague sort of Russia-US "alliance," where an uneasy truce existed because the alternative was bad for everyone's health. The night I'd arrived, he'd been the only one to discover my secret—that I knew Lucille was a goddess. And she would answer my call. One time, at least.

And that gave him power. But it also gave me power, because hey, I had a (drunken) goddess's ear. Mutually assured destruction, if there ever was such a thing. I was rather skeptical Lucille would drop everything to help me. After all, she and I shared an uneasy alliance of our own that was now teetering in a rather precarious state.

I approached the sprawling neon mansion, winding my way up the carefully designed cobblestone walkway toward the wide stairs at the house's front. I was about halfway there when I saw something glistening on the marble front stairs. It was unmistakable, even at more than fifty yards.

Blood.

I reached into the clutch and flicked out the Reaper's Switch. A pragmatic little voice, the one that made all the plans, told me to get the hell out of there. But all the planning in the world hadn't saved me from this inferno of bullshit about to swallow me whole. For the foreseeable future, I was a gambling girl. So, without a plan—or much of anything besides morbid curiosity—I made my way up the polished concrete stairs.

I knelt by the blood, which coated at least four steps. That meant a sizable wound. I touched the crimson pool and found it slightly tacky. Fresh, but not immediately so. It was impossible to tell given the humidity, but it had to have been an hour or two old, at the least. Hopefully it wasn't the mayor's, although I had little doubt the warlock could hold his own in combat.

I wiped my finger on the stairs and rose. The tall, two-story bright turquoise front doors beckoned me inside. The voice of pragmatism told me the attacker could still be on the premises. Perhaps ransacking the mayor's office, or holding him at knifepoint as part of some demand. Or the mayor had gotten himself in trouble—maybe some girl hadn't shown him her feet. Either way, entering the house was not the move.

So I headed to the door and placed my hand on the massive brass knob.

To my surprise, it was unlocked. I pushed on the giant

door, and it glided open effortlessly. A looming, shadowy foyer greeted me. Two curved staircases headed up to a second floor. Straight ahead was the sprawling backyard, a pool visible through the perfect glass. The foyer split into east and west wings of the house—from past experience, I knew his offices were to the right, and the living quarters to the left.

Business and pleasure, all under one roof.

I jumped as the door slammed shut behind me. To the right of the tall front doors, hanging next to an oil portrait of the mayor, a security camera swiveled to greet my gaze.

The back lights came on full blast, glinting off the perfect aquamarine pool. Toward the back fence, far enough from the glow to be a shadow, stood a man with a shovel.

I walked slowly toward the backyard. An invisible sensor noted my presence, parting the glass doors.

The moonlit night made the mayor's backyard look even more impressive. A few steps from the ceramic-tiled pool was a complete bar that would have required a liquor license to operate in most jurisdictions. Behind that was a sprawling cabana sporting multiple flat screen televisions, wood grain speakers, and variety of seating options, from lounge chairs to massage tables.

But I was less concerned about that than I was about the blood. It coated the concrete surrounding the pool, leaving a thick trail of red breadcrumbs to the shadowy figure hard at work in the grass. It didn't take a genius to put the pieces together.

The rhythmic scratch of the shovel cutting into the dirt scored my cautious approach.

I stopped ten yards away. His back was turned to me. A wave of nerves dynamited their way through my stomach.

"Hello?" I asked.

In response, the man held an object up in the air. It, quite clearly, was a human head.

"What'd you do to the mayor?"

"Nothing at all, Eden."

The voice was as clear and featureless as glass. It was a smooth voice, a radio voice, the kind with the right lulls and rhythm that could trick the undiscerning—other than the fact that the flat tonality made it resemble a robot's impersonation of human speech. Like Mayor Stefan Cambridge's, but without the *aww shucks* accent I'd always suspected was a little bit of a put-on.

A wind danced through the yard, carrying the killer's soul with it—blacker than a torched village, but like devil's food cake, all that heart-stopping destruction was studded in a razor-sharp sweetness. Despite the darkness, he was genuinely happy and pleased with his station in life.

And he also liked feet.

I gagged, realizing that the mayor had been far grosser than I could have imagined.

"What do you see?"

I shook the sensation off like a bad dream and said, "Nothing but an asshole wasting my time."

Stefan jabbed the shovel into the pile of soil with a decisive motion. I shivered, but didn't step back. He turned around and winked. "All dressed up tonight for me?"

I said, "What the fuck?" The blade came up reflexively, offering the thinnest of protections. So much for trying to play it cool. But the creepy wink had been too much. He'd cast some considerable cloaking wards over his soul to hide from me before.

Stefan was covered in mud and blood. His bald head

gleamed, and a big smile graced his toothy mouth. He looked like a murderous pig in shit.

"You wanna know what the problem with politics is, Eden?" The grin widened as he slipped into the rhythms of his slightly twangy speech. The *aww shucks* thing really convinced people that he could be trusted. If only they knew. The Reaper's Switch shook in my hand. I ground my teeth and gripped it tighter, holding the clutch in my other hand.

"Jesus Christ, man." I glanced in the hole, immediately regretting my decision.

"It's a damn dirty business." Stefan jerked a thumb toward his garden shed. "And sometimes there are actual bodies to bury. Grab a shovel."

"I'm not grabbing shit."

Stefan mopped his face with his ruined collared shirt. The whites of his eyes stared out from his dirty face. It made me squeak.

Just a little, but it might as well have been a gunshot. I put the clutch over my mouth, irritated by my tired brain's betrayal.

"I guess that settles it."

"Settles what?" I asked.

"Eden Hunter can be rattled after all."

"I didn't know that was an open question." I regained my composure and added, "Bury him yourself."

Some great leads I was getting here.

Really wonderful stuff. I'd have the case cracked in no time at this rate.

"But when one doesn't have skin in the game, that can lead to a paranoid counterparty." He leaned against the shovel, still wearing that friendly grin. But it seemed more like staring into the jaws of a Mako shark than anything else.

"I'll take my chances."

"You know exactly where that path ends."

Well, that put things into perspective. This wasn't a request. I stared at the blood dotting the concrete by the pool, and concluded that burying the body was a better alternative to running. After all, he was a warlock. I'd be ash before I reached the cabana. With a deep sigh to communicate that I was participating under protest, I tossed the clutch and Reaper's Switch into the grass, then headed toward the shed. There was a biometric lock on the small building's exterior.

Like a wraith, Stefan appeared behind me and pressed his thumb to the reader. It glowed green, and an automatic door slid open, disappearing into the shed's walls. I saw the spare shovel. There were quite a few of them hanging from a rack along the back wall.

But I was more focused on the row of jewel-studded skulls lining the top shelf.

Without a word, I grabbed a shovel and walked back to the hole. The neck—or what was left of it, after Stefan's hatchet job—peeked out from beneath a layer of dirt. As for the head, that sat perched atop a dirt pile. From the hair and the eyes, it was definitely male. At least Stefan wasn't the rape-and-kill brand of murderer. I hoped. I quickly covered the lifeless stump with a thick mound of dirt.

"You can reap his soul before we bury him."

I grunted to indicate *no*.

"I heard your quota went up. You really should consider it. My gift."

Goddamnit, he had a point. Swallowing my pride—and morals—I jumped into the grave.

"Give me the blade," I said.

"Why yes, certainly." He searched in the grass and then handed the open blade to me. "Partner."

"Don't call me that." I plunged the blade into the dirt, right above where the dead man's heart should have been. The silver-and-obsidian studded edge cut through the dead skin effortlessly. Then I reached into the moist soil and extracted the soul. It was hard to see in the dark, but I could feel that it was misshapen and bore the slight odor of despair. Not a good man, by any stretch of the imagination.

Stefan offered a hand, but I pushed myself out of the grave. With no pockets, I placed the dirty knife and soul in the clutch before silently returning to work. I shoveled twice as fast, dumping soil into the hole as the mayor tossed in chopped up pieces.

"So, why did you come to my door in the middle of the night, Eden?"

I didn't answer, choosing to focus on the work. It was amazing how quickly a six-foot hole could fill up. I tried to figure out why they only buried people six feet deep. It probably was so they could spend as little time with serial killers as possible.

"You're thrown by the truth of who I am."

I patted down the final bit of soil with the flat end of the shovel and said, "Is that it?"

"It has to be re-sodded." I saw his pale finger point toward the shed.

"Get it yourself."

"Eden." His voice was laced with the hint of a threat.

"The only way I'm going back in there is if you add me to your collection."

I saw his lips curl into a smile-like expression. But I now knew that, whatever I had thought of Stefan before, it had all been an act. Not just a kiss-the-baby, glad-handing campaign trail act, but a stone-cold, sociopath emulation of something human.

He walked by, chilling the warm air. It was probably an illusion, but it still felt like a frost had briefly passed through.

I stared at the patch of fresh soil. It was uniform and rectangular, about the size of a funeral plot. Running my gaze over the rest of the vast yard, to the fence, I did a quick calculation and promptly felt ill. Well, I'd done one thing right: I had yet another suspect. Stefan's motive for framing me was an open question, since he clearly liked taking all the credit for his kills—and keeping the bodies right outside his bedroom window. But if he needed me out of the picture and wanted someone dead, he certainly possessed the stunning lack of morals necessary to execute such a plan.

Stefan returned with a rolled-up clump of sod. I didn't offer to help, and he didn't ask again. I just watched as he scrubbed the evidence of the kill from the face of the earth.

"They're all bad men and women, Eden."

"I didn't ask."

"But your entire posture judges." He stopped patting the grass and cocked his head at me like a dog. "And I've heard you're in some trouble of your own."

"Bad news travels fast." I reached down to grab the clutch and get the hell out of there. "Don't go thinking we're alike."

"I would never dream of it."

"Can I go, now?"

"I would offer to step in and assure the FBI of your bulletproof character." Stefan performed a final smooth-down of the fresh grass. Satisfied, he gave it a last, almost loving tap before standing. "But here you are, burying bodies in the dead of night."

"Funny."

"Yes, I suppose life is funny." Stefan extended his hand. I looked at him like he'd just pulled down his pants. "If we can't trust each other, then we have larger problems."

"I shouldn't have come," I muttered.

"That would've been better for us both. Yet here we are, beneath a cloudless sky, sharing the night."

His speech was switching between the *aww shucks* fraud and his smooth-as-glass voice, like he couldn't decide which to use with me anymore. I shook his hand as quickly as I could. After what I'd witnessed, it felt like shaking hands with the abyss itself. The plasticine smile stayed in place as his predatory eyes scanned my face.

I'd say it was something in the island's water that got him elected, but let's be real: this could happen anywhere. I knew as well as anyone how easily people could be deceived. Everyone wanted to believe. All anyone had to do was give them a little nudge.

"It would be a shame to leave without getting what you came for," Stefan said. I took a final glance at the grave, which seamlessly merged with the yard.

Might as well. This was no time to take a moral stand.

"Heard anything about a gold heist?"

Stefan scratched his clean-shaven face and said, "Nothing."

"I need whatever you can find on Roan Kelly."

"Hoping to solve a murder, are we?" His mouth widened into that toothy smile. "The irony is delicious, wouldn't you say?"

"Yes, yes, serial killer helps catch the bad guy." I rolled my eyes. "You didn't kill him, did you?"

"Was he missing his skull?"

I wondered if he'd killed so many people that he legitimately couldn't remember, or whether he was yanking my chain. Normally, I could tell when people were lying or fucking with me. But here I'd thought he was just your usual ladder-climbing slimeball, and it turned out he was the island's biggest health threat since the Europeans introduced tobacco in the sixteenth century.

"Roan's head still had two .45 rounds lodged in it."

"That would ruin my shelf's aesthetic."

The unpleasant image flashed through my memory bank and I bit my tongue. "Just get me the fucking information."

"And you'll forget about this?"

"About what?" I asked, staring at him blankly, and his eyes alit with the knowledge that his secret was safe, and that yes, we had an understanding. I turned and hurried away, feeling the fake grin crawling up my back as I avoided the blood pools.

"Lionhawk Ink." Stefan's voice shot across the night like an arrow.

I stopped. "Why?"

"The FBI report said you claimed the gun was planted by a young man in a suit. Sounds like just the place such a man would frequent."

"No it doesn't."

"There might have been a fingerprint left on the broken sill in your house that confirms my suspicion."

"What, are you stalking me, now?" I asked.

"Keep your allies close and your enemies closer, Eden," he called back. "And your partners closest of all."

I felt bile well up in my throat, and I had to shut my mouth to keep from vomiting. If he was the killer, it would almost be worth taking the fall never to return. But I had the feeling I'd be back here, sooner or later. Because in my line of work, crossing paths with bad people wasn't just an occupational hazard.

It was the only way to stay alive.

16

I DIALED CROSS—I COULD USE THE COMPANY, AND HE was the closest thing I had to an ally. But he responded with a text. He was busy taking care of a few things—and besides, I had his Porsche. He asked me for my location; when I told him the mayor's, he said that was too far out of the way, since he was on the eastern part of the island, but he'd meet up with me when I got downtown.

I wondered what the hell he was doing on the other half of Atheas at this hour. The conclusion was obvious: he didn't want his activities to crop up on anyone's radar. I was as brave as the next girl, but I tried to stick on this side of the island when I could. Unfortunately, reaping souls was a dangerous business, and I found myself in the east pretty damn often.

The taxi stopped at the end of the cul-de-sac, where I'd been waiting alone for twenty minutes, covered in dirt, wishing I had a cigarette. And I had never liked smoking one damn bit. But right then seemed like the perfect time to start.

The ride back to the city was quiet. I was beginning to

feel fatigue shout in my ears, but I couldn't rest yet. What-ever Khan had whipped up to counteract the sandstorm viper venom had slowed the side effects of the bite, too, buying me more time. But the top part of my shoulder was now gray—something I *definitely* needed to address before my arm fell off.

But right now, I needed to follow up on the mayor's lead at Lionhawk Ink more. Who knew how long my unwanted visitor would hang around the island?

So, back to The Loaded Gun I went. The taxi driver dropped me off at the corner, and I paid him. I made my way past the drunken stragglers enjoying mediocre late-night pizza they would regret in the morning. I approached the parking lot, which was now empty save for the borrowed Porsche—and the dwarf Jötun who had banned me from his bar.

Twice, now. An impressive record.

I tried keeping to the shadows, but Magnus thundered, "You dare return, Eden?"

I waved at him, acting like he'd been happy to see me. "Just getting my car."

"Tell me, something, Reaper." He pushed off from the brick façade, which had been worn away from years of abuse from cigarettes, beer, and urine. I don't know about anyone else, but having a towering man with neck tattoos come at you in a dark, dirty parking lot at four in the morning will get the old blood pumping. Discombobulated, I almost dropped the clutch into a pool of oil.

He stopped a few paces away. The sigils on his neck glowed slightly in the darkness. Someone was still angry.

I swallowed hard and tried to maintain my smile. "Look, I'm really not trying to come back. Ever. Your place sucks too hard."

Magnus didn't answer. The faint amber glow of the hammer sigil stared at me like a harbinger of doom. Not that he needed to cast any of his ancient Norse spells to kill me. He could just reach out and snap my neck with one of those bear paw sized hands.

"How did the FBI arrive on our island?" Magnus asked.

I breathed an audible sigh of relief. He just wanted to know about Rayna. "So you saw her badge, huh?"

"While we were dragging her outside, yes." He folded his arms. "Are you one of them?"

"Why, you got something to hide?"

His lips folded into a scowl. Wrong tact. Bad Eden. But it was hard to bullshit when you were sick and tired and getting framed for murders you didn't commit. Which, ironically enough, was the *exact* time when quality bullshitting skills were most critical.

"I have business interests the Americans would frown upon."

"You mean your underground fight nights?"

The dwarf giant's crystal blue eyes flooded with suspicion. Instead of answering the question, Magnus said, "What does Aldric think about these developments?"

"Unhappy," I said.

"I see. And he can do nothing about their presence?"

"Even overly controlling assholes have limits to their powers." I shrugged, immediately regretting it when my shoulder barked in pain. "Death, taxes, the government, and all that good stuff."

A vein in Magnus's neck bulged, making the hammer look ready to strike. I shifted my weight from foot to foot, trying to communicate my desire to return to the Porsche.

Finally, I said, "Quit being a pussy and just ask your real question."

This caught Magnus off guard. Women two feet shorter than him didn't openly confront him. But I wanted to follow up on the mayor's lead at Lionhawk Ink tonight.

"A man attempted to spend this tonight." Magnus extracted a gold bar from his rough shirt. Same size and weight as the one from Roan's pocket. "I believe it belongs to your employer."

He handed it to me and I held it up to the dim light. The insignia was unmistakable—a cloaked rider atop a galloping horse. The Scythians had been talented horsemen, striking terror in the Eurasian Steppes for hundreds of years with their innovative battle tactics. This was Aldric's way of honoring the past—and delineating his revenue streams. For this logo only appeared on his ill-gotten gains and other illegitimate enterprises.

"Why are you giving me this?"

"Because there is word that someone has stolen from Aldric." Magnus crossed his arms. "And I do not wish to be viewed as a suspect in that particular matter."

"Any idea what this man might have looked like?" I asked.

"British. Slender. Charming—you know, chatting with the ladies." Magnus looked up at the stars, as if thinking. "And my bartender said he was asking about someone."

"Anyone in particular?"

"You." Magnus pointed at the gold bar I now held in my hands. "He tried to buy information."

"Interesting." I nodded toward the lonely convertible. "If that's all."

"Just ensure Aldric knows."

"I'll do that," I said, and headed to the sports car without a goodbye. After tossing the gold bar and dirty clutch on the passenger's seat, I hopped over the side and glanced in the mirror. Magnus was staring at the car. He looked worried.

He should've been.

Like hell was I putting in a good word for him. He could suck it. But this development was interesting—because it meant Roan had ripped off Aldric. And he'd had a partner help him do it.

A partner who sounded very much like Dante Cross.

17

I SPUN OUT OF THE PARKING LOT IN A CLOUD OF DUST, and gunned the convertible toward Lionhawk Ink. The pleasant breeze streamed through my hair, almost making me forget that I was covered in sweaty dirt.

As I drove, I considered the new evidence implicating Cross.

It was compelling.

But I had questions.

Why had he saved me from dying in the basement if he was trying to frame me? My death would close the book on Roan Kelly's murder—the Feds would stop investigating, notch a win, and move on.

I didn't have answers for those questions.

But I intended to find them before the Tuesday sun came up.

Late night visits to tattoo shops were rarely a good call. In this case, that advice went double. I could be stepping into a hostile environment, since the guy who had planted a gun beneath my floorboards was allegedly on the premises. But that seemed about par for the course these days. If I didn't risk my neck, I had no shot of clearing my name. As Agnes had said, no one was gonna look out for Eden besides Eden.

It was past four when I pulled into the lot and cut the engine. I took the Reaper's Switch and gold bar out of the clutch, then crammed the small black bag into the glovebox. As I walked across the parking lot at the city's outskirts, I cracked my knuckles. Lionhawk Ink's sign cast a neon glow across the empty, fading asphalt. The nail salon and laundromat next door were closed for the night. Or maybe they were never open at all. But Lionhawk Ink's interior glowed, and people moved within. Even this late, they remained open and ready for business.

Of course, they didn't deal in tattoos. Okay, they did your normal stuff—your tramp stamps, the regrettable boyfriend's name inked under a side boob. Speaking from experience, what you think is forever usually lasts less time than a value-size bottle of shampoo. But that type of ink wasn't their bread and butter. It was just a money-laundering front for what they couldn't put on the books: magic. For the right price, Mick could brand you with a sigil. Sure, a sigil looked like a tattoo to the undiscerning eye. The non-magically inclined would be none the wiser. But, depending on what abilities the purchaser desired—and how much they could pay—it would do a lot more.

Wanted to make James Bond or Casanova look like amateurs? The Heartbreaker was a good choice. What about sing like Freddy Mercury? Golden Voice might be a little more up your alley.

But, as the old saying went, everything had its price. And mere currency wouldn't grant you the otherworldly powers you desired. Imbuing someone with magical energy where there was none before demanded a powerful fuel source. A sigil could only be created using souls. A shred, perhaps, would suffice for something as materialistic and shallow as the Heartbreaker. But work like Magnus's, which resulted in a Zeusian display of thunder and lightning, demanded many souls. Of course, he had received his brands in a time when human life was nasty, brutish, and short.

These days, there were pesky ethics and laws. Which made this type of operation a more clandestine affair. And operating in the darkness brought with it the holy trinity of danger: desperation, narcissism, and greed.

So, under normal circumstances, I stayed clear of places fueled by souls. Entering them as a Reaper was like coming to a dog shelter covered in steaks. The outcome was not good—everyone salivated at your presence, eager to eat you up and spit you out. If I wasn't Aldric's Reaper, more than a few people would have tried to forcibly enlist me in their own employ. Even with Aldric's looming, unspoken guillotine waiting in the shadows, certain creatures were too excited by the possibility of having their own little soul generator to resist fucking with me.

So maybe I was overplaying my hand. But the walls were closing in around me. Which meant going it alone to this dingy, neon-bathed shit shack was the best option on the table. Because, if the Feds kept digging, they were going to find out I could speak with Lucille. That one god still remained on Earth. And, maybe, that meant the others would return. The anarchy that would cause—no, that was untenable.

It was one thing to light a couple candles and pray.

It was another for those prayers to be answered.

More importantly, if that secret came out, Sierra would reap the consequences. I wasn't keen on dying again—but

I'd do anything to keep my sister from going back to the Elysian Fields.

A bell jingled in the warm air as I yanked the door open. The tall clerk turned—too quick to be human—and gave me a quick inspection. I recognized him as a wolf named Darius from the last time I'd been here.

"We're closing soon," he said. Another wolf in the corner pretended to push a mop. They were really security. When you dealt in souls, and kept some on hand, it was like having a vault full of gold on the premises. Eighties hair metal blared from the speakers. Four vinyl chairs were lined up in parallel. Behind the chairs was a wall of designs—everything from script to flaming skulls.

One of the chairs was taken by a teenager who didn't look like she could even buy a pack of smokes. Not that I was judging; I would've pulled the same shit at her age, had I liked the idea of permanence.

I now had one permanent sigil, of course, courtesy of Aldric. Cheap, at least as sigils went. I'd had the work done at Lionhawk four years ago.

I hadn't returned since.

"Take a pitcha, why don't ya?" The girl laid on her snarling East Coast accent thick, like it made her tough. Her eyes told me she wanted to be, probably because something had happened that had made her feel small and afraid. I could relate.

But I didn't have time to indulge teenage angst. Tonight's circumstances were different. Because, tonight, the guy who had broken into my house and tried to frame me was hiding in here. Was he the actual killer? I was tempted to say yes out of spite, even if all the answers ended up pointing to no.

"I'll pass," I said.

The wolf in the corner stopped mopping and cast a wary eye over his sinewy shoulder. It didn't take good instincts to taste the tension in the room. But it wasn't between me and the girl, who was a human and non-threat.

It was between me and the man doing her work.

Seated on a stool, his weathered fingers clutching a buzzing pen, was Mick Anderson. His sun-beaten skin was remarkably free of tattoos. The only ones visible were on his knuckles—each joint bearing an intricate design. To a regular client, they were merely a personal expression of his art—a choice to place his ink where it was most meaningful.

But I knew better. The placement was to maximize the magical power his hands could channel. I wasn't apprised of all the nuances of sigils, but suffice to say, the location mattered. A skilled artisan could double or triple the effectiveness of a spell by placing it in the correct location. Mick was what was known as an ink master. That was why my lantern sigil was close to my hand—it allowed the energy to flow up through my fingers.

He didn't turn around. His pen continued tracing across the girl's ankle.

"I have to hand it to you, Eden."

"Hand what?"

"It takes real courage to visit a man whose eye you took." The buzzing pen punctuated the silence. I could feel both wolves tense. Last night had been lucky. I wasn't ready to gamble on myself again so soon, especially outnumbered two to one. But I wasn't leaving, either, because I needed answers about whoever had planted the gun in my villa.

"Or real stupidity," I said.

He snorted. "Courage and stupidity are dangerously close on the continuum."

"You tried to *kill* him?" the girl whispered, her accent

disappearing, suddenly realizing she was in over her head. She tried to jerk her ankle away, but Mick's strong, practiced hands held it steady. "Let me go."

"You don't want half the words, do you?" Mick pressed his reading glasses up his craggy nose. I could just see his good side from this angle, the one that still had an eye. What was left of his hair splayed out at graying, odd angles, like an aging bad boy's.

"I just want to go home." Her voice was small.

"Darius." Mick nodded toward the mop-holding wolf. "Get this young lady's money from the register."

What happened next surprised even me. Mick's right hand glowed bright blue, dousing the linoleum tile in an effusive glow. The girl squealed. Mick paid her cries no heed. His hand—still clutching the tattoo needle—moved in a blur, too fast to see. The work was finished before Darius had returned with the girl's crumpled bills. The light dissipated, ceding luminescent duties back to the musty box-store style fluorescents humming in the particle-board ceiling.

Mick let the girl's ankle go and gently placed the money in her hand. She said nothing, and sprinted out the door without looking back. The ink master ran through the supplies in his metal case, cleaning up after the job. Despite the speed, there were no ink spills or stains. Everything was perfect.

"Where is he, Mick?"

"Do you know how many stitches it takes to close a four-inch gash?"

"A lot, I'd presume." I glared at Darius, who had his thick arms crossed. The wolf stood next to his boss like the old man needed his help. But Mick could handle himself.

"A hundred and thirty-four." He took final stock of the

instruments in his tattoo case, then snapped the metal clasps shut. "And two pints of blood."

"I would've guessed two hundred. You made it out ahead."

Mick turned for the first time. The scar ran from the middle of his cheek to his eyebrow. Even in the craggy wrinkles, the raised white flesh was clear as day. The hollow socket stared back at me, as if searching for guilt. But I had a good poker face.

That, and I could give a shit about slashing up his face. No, I wasn't a sociopath. But you try coming back from the dead, waking up on a strange island, then being dragged to a tattoo parlor in a basically abandoned strip mall. Your fight-or-flight instincts would be ringing all sorts of alarm bells, too.

I said, "If we're done rehashing ancient history, I heard someone hangs out here."

"I don't recall having any visitors."

"Young guy. Well dressed, business suit. Brown hair," I said, gauging his reaction. From the way his good pupil dilated, I knew he recognized the description. But Mick was a pretty good liar himself, and could keep secrets.

"Doesn't sound like anyone I know."

I opened my hand—the one clutching the gold bar.

Mick's good eye grew wide in his craggy face.

"That belongs to Aldric," Mick said.

"More than you know," I replied.

"It's true about the heist, then."

"Don't believe everything you hear."

"She lives alone. Runs at night, up the beach and through the forest. Leaves no soul untouched." Mick took a step forward, the metal case containing his equipment banging against his leg. "Aldric's Reaper is totally insane."

I guess he assumed I'd ripped my own boss off.

"If you're done with the armchair psychology, maybe we can get down to business."

"I won't accept that." Mick nodded toward his security. I watched the second wolf prop the mop against the wall to join Darius. "I'd rather stay alive."

The old man shuffled past me without looking me in the eye. His two hired hands closed in. Their desire to avenge their boss and rip me to shreds flashed in their eyes. I'd done something bad to their master, and they wanted me to atone.

"I wasn't offering to pay you," I said. "I was offering you a chance to stay off Aldric's shitlist."

"Aldric and I have no problems," Mick replied, slipping into a back room behind the counter covered by a dark curtain.

"Until he hears you refused to help me get his gold back." I gave Darius and the other wolf a big smirk, standing my ground even though every instinct told me to run. I could sense their primitive desire to run free in the night, my intestines dangling from their sharp jaws.

A long silence settled over the dingy shop.

"It's my son, James," Mick called from the back room.

The curtain rustled, but instead of Mick, the young man came out wearing a sullen expression. His father didn't step out with him. Offering him up as a sacrifice wouldn't win Mick any father of the year awards, but it was the prudent call when the threat of a vampire warlord's wrath loomed over your head.

A boot briefly emerged from behind the curtain, giving the young man a literal kick in the ass. James shuffled forward, still wearing the suit I'd seen him in last night. His hair was well-coiffed, and he looked every bit the antithesis of his father—a well-heeled corporate lackey.

The young man stopped near the register and leaned against the stickered counter.

"I don't hafta tell you shit." His voice and tone didn't match the clean-cut demeanor. Not a corporate lackey—not by a long shot. He was a thug in a nice a suit.

"Why'd you kill Roan Kelly?" I asked, my mind finally registering the fact that Roan was actually dead as the words came from my mouth. Strange to think that someone I'd spent so much time with was just gone. No time for sentimentality, though.

"Oh, you know." He shrugged, his nondescript features twisting into a smirk. "Money, jealousy, revenge. Take your pick, lady."

I went to take a step forward, but Darius and his fellow wolf blocked my path. He knew what happened when I was angry and got close to someone holding my Reaper's Switch. James would be lucky if all he lost was an eye.

I scowled at the two werewolves and held up the gold brick. "Tell me what you know about this."

"I don't know nothin'." But he was a bad liar, too inexperienced to sell the bullshit. After all, he was used to just fading away into the background, never being seen again. Tell the cops *it was a white guy in a suit* and they'd have to arrest half of the continental United States. But the cops didn't have connections like mine.

I stifled a scowl as I recalled the intel's price. The murdered man's soul was in the glovebox, like a sordid memento.

"I'm sending the FBI to your doorstep, then, and you can explain why your prints were on my window sill."

"I do installations," he said, still cocky.

"And then I'll tell Aldric."

The young man bit his lip and gave me a mean glare. It didn't scare me much. I'd seen far worse over the past day. After a long pause he said, "Fine."

"You want me to tell him?"

"No, I meant some guy gave me a call. Told me if I came down to the beach quick, put the gun in the lady's house, he'd give me fifty grand."

"Sounds like bullshit."

"Pops?" James looked pleadingly over his shoulder toward the curtain. The old man didn't emerge, but a small duffel bag flew through the fabric and bounced off the counter. A couple stacks of banded twenty-dollar bills spilled out of the open top, skittering next to Darius's boots.

James gave me a look like *you satisfied?*

Nope. Not by a longshot.

"This guy have a name?"

"Yeah, we're Facebook friends." James yanked the bag off the floor and stuffed the errant bills back inside. "The fuck you think, lady?"

"I think you're a dumbass who stuck his nose where it doesn't belong."

"I ain't the one with the wolves 'bout to kill me."

"You touch me, you all burn." I glanced up at Darius, who despite standing a head taller than me, looked concerned about the prospect of Aldric showing up. At least there was one person in the room who wasn't a complete moron.

"I told you all I know," James said.

"What'd the guy on the phone sound like?" I asked.

"I dunno. Knew you, though."

"Knew me?"

"Called you Eden Hunter. That's you, right? The chick

who slashed up my pops?"

"Something like that," I said. "Anything else?" I recalled Magnus's description of the man who had tried to buy information on me at The Loaded Gun with the gold brick I now held in my hand. "Did he sound charming?"

"What, I look like some sorta fag to you?"

"I'm sure you're quite the ladykiller," I said. "Just answer the question."

A pained look crept over his face, and then he kind of mumbled, "Guess he was a smooth talker, you know?"

"British?"

"Yeah, you know him?"

I did know him—and I was beginning to get a very clear picture of who had set me up. I gave James a wicked wink and headed toward the glass door. The three men didn't move, like they'd been stunned by a tornado that had just run roughshod through the shop.

Stepping into the warm, sweet night, a wave of satisfaction rushed over me. I'd have this case wrapped up in twenty-four hours, tied up neatly with a bow on the FBI's desk. Then Rayna could shove her blackmail scheme, and the Feds would have no reason to burrow further into my past.

And that good feeling lasted all of thirty seconds until I saw who was leaning against the sports car. Tall, slender. Most definitely charming.

And, judging by tonight's revelations, almost definitely a murderer.

"It's not downtown, but I figured it was close enough," Dante Cross said with a casual wave. "Want a ride home?"

I did not. But I mustered up a smile from the depths and said, "That'd be lovely," as I walked straight across the lot, right into the belly of the beast.

18

CROSS SLIPPED INTO THE SPORTS CAR AND OPENED THE passenger side door from within. I slid inside, feeling the cool leather caress my dirty skin. Before I could shut my door, we were spinning smoothly out of Lionhawk Ink's empty parking lot, headed the other way. A cool wind passed over the open convertible as I fumbled with the glovebox and removed the clutch. With my suddenly damp fingers, I jimmied the zipper and put the gold bar back inside.

Cross didn't acknowledge its presence.

I tossed the clutch on the floor, but kept the Reaper's Switch on my dirt-stained lap.

Cross finally broke the silence as we turned onto the cliffside drive back into the city.

"So, you know the mayor."

"Better than I'd like."

"That sounds ominous."

"Not like that," I said.

"I wasn't saying anything." He gave me a friendly smile, but given the circumstances, it felt like an illusion had been lifted. I couldn't trust anyone. Paranoia was never conducive to productivity, but in my case, it was justified.

I fiddled with the radio, but couldn't find anything to my liking. A rock song cut off mid-solo as I tapped the power button, plunging the ride back into silence. The sports car's engine growled in the night, as the tires devoured the narrow road. Over the cliff, only feet to our left, sat the endless ocean. A black abyss if I ever saw one.

Cross's smile disappeared, and he said, "You're not thinking about yanking the wheel, right?"

"That's pretty dark, man."

"You have that look, Eden."

"And what look would that be?"

"Like your house burned down with your dog inside."

"Sounds better than the night I've had."

"Now who's being dark?" Cross slowed the car at the stoplight, which was red despite there being no cars around for miles.

"Go through," I said.

Instead of moving, Cross cut the engine. The light flashed to green, and then back to red as we waited. Neither of us spoke. Nothing moved in the brush that now lined the road, the cliff being little more than a distant roadside memory.

I tried to focus on the rational side of things. But I'd been having a hard time doing that since yesterday. Roan's death had been like a sucker punch to the gut, and the most annoying thing about the whole situation wasn't the frame job, or the FBI, or Rayna Denton breathing down my neck.

Nope.

It was that, no matter how much I shoved it down, I cared. Not in that lovelorn teenager kind of way that I used to look at him, but still, I cared. Seven years, off and on, from seventeen to when I'd died at twenty-four. That was a long time, but it still seemed like weakness. My old life was nothing but ash and faded photographs. Time to move on. But I hadn't, which might've been why I'd thrown any semblance of rationality to the wind. I mean, shit, I'd basically shown up at Lionhawk Ink and accused Mick's son of murder.

"That's quite a story," Cross said, and I jumped.

I gave him a look, and then realized from the dryness of my lips that I'd been speaking to myself the whole time. A rush of blood flooded my ears, and heat swam in my cheeks. Then I got angry.

"How the fuck did you know where I was, anyway?"

"Oh, that's easy," Cross said, pulling out his phone. "Car dealership installed a tracking app. Pretty cool, right?"

"If you're a stalker."

"Maybe I wanted to make sure no demons were going to come eat your face." Cross tried to look serious.

I wasn't buying it.

"You can track me if you want," Cross said. "Give me your phone."

"What? No." I hugged my couch tight.

"It might come in handy."

I rolled my eyes and gave him my phone. The car slowed down as he tapped the screen.

"Done." He handed the device back a minute later.

I checked for anything extra he might have installed. "Awesome. Now I won't need to hunt you down to ask why you're trying to bribe bartenders for info about me."

"Always good to know who your new friends are."

"But you already knew. Because you were Roan's partner."

Cross sighed. "You know what?"

"What?"

"I just wanted to know why a guy like Roan decided to sell you out for a couple bucks. Didn't make sense after I met you."

"Sold me out?"

"Back in New Orleans." Cross waved his hand in the air, like none of it mattered. "No one told me anything good, in case you were wondering."

"Let me out."

"There aren't any cabs this late, Eden. I'll take you home."

I didn't want him to take me home, but I also didn't want to tip him off that I *knew*. No use confronting a murderer and then getting added to his victim list. Time to build a case, find some evidence, and get his ass locked up.

Or have Aldric take care of it. That was always an option.

"Fine," I said. "As long as you shut up."

Cross obliged, and silence descended on the sports car as we wound along the tropical road.

Tires screeched.

Two vans—the kind children are forever warned to avoid—burst out of nowhere, their lights slicing through the darkness like apex predators. They quickly blocked our path forward.

Cross slammed on the brakes. Scorched rubber filled the quiet air as the convertible stopped on a dime.

A trail car boxed us in from the back.

"Well, shit." Cross opened the glovebox. A chrome pistol flashed in the moonlight.

I watched the goons in perfect import suits and dress shoes filter from the van. Most of them were the faceless lackey types that are soon forgotten, but one of the men I was familiar with: Moreland, Aldric's Head of Intelligence Operations—or as I liked to call him, the Marauder in Chief. Aldric's right-hand man and most trusted adviser.

I wrapped my fingers around Cross's tan wrist and said, "No, be cool."

"They don't look cool, Eden."

"Trust me."

Moreland was an insanely powerful warlock. No idea how old, but that didn't really matter. What did matter was simple: he could toast Cross's little import convertible into the next century with a sneeze. I placed both hands on the dashboard like I'd been pulled over for a traffic stop as Moreland approached.

"Remember what I told you," I said under my breath. Cross didn't respond, but he put the gun back into the glovebox and shut it. I took that as a promising sign.

Much like his underlings, the warlock was dressed like a stockbroker trying to peddle worthless junk bonds. His well-starched clothing vibed well with the stern face that suggested he'd had a few too many sticks surgically implanted in his butt.

He leaned over the door into my personal space and brought his face about two inches from mine. As usual, he didn't smile. A pale patch of hair clung to the middle of his head, dangling before my nose. "My dear girl."

"The ladies must love you," I said.

"Your kind has never done it for me, alas."

"I should hook you up with my friend, then," I said, nodding toward Cross.

Moreland gave a dismissive snort. "I do not like the surfer look. Or the debonair adventurers."

"That wasn't a real offer."

"If you're me, then you don't wait for offers."

Ah, how liberating it must've felt to be shackled only by the scantiest of eleventh-century laws. If you're the king, it wasn't rape or murder, it was simply divined by the gods. Admittedly, such a judicial system had its appeals, provided you were at the top 0.1% of the food chain—and a fucking sociopath.

I didn't back down from Moreland's dead eyes, a show of defiance he didn't appreciate. As a display of power, he made the Porsche rock back and forth. Cross—cool and collected as ever—said nothing.

I said, "Quit the dick-waving, Moreland, and tell me what you want."

"It's not what I want, dear girl."

"I'm pretty sure we're on a first-name basis by now."

"It is *who* Master Aldric wants." Moreland stood up straight and the car stopped rocking. The clutch purse clattered off the windshield and bounced to the floor between my feet with a metallic ting.

"What is it the two of you have here?" The warlock reached over the side and plucked the dirt-streaked clutch off the floormat. Upon unzipping it and seeing the gold bar, his dead eyes almost lit up. "Oh, you have been a naughty girl."

"Magnus gave it to me at The Loaded Gun."

"Always with the silver tongue, dear girl."

"Yeah, check the trunk for the rest of the haul, asshole," I said. "Brilliant plan, ripping off Aldric. I'll just spend it all on the island I can't leave."

Moreland backed away from the door and gestured for one of his faceless lackeys to pop the sports car's small trunk. I turned around to watch the production, which I knew from experience would be ridiculous and unnecessary. Suffice to say, I wasn't disappointed. Instead of asking for the keys, one of them unlocked it with dark magic and then lifted the trunk with a different spell. Overkill, but the message came across loud and clear about who was in control.

Hint: it wasn't the people seated in the vehicle.

"What do you see?" Moreland asked with semi-restrained curiosity.

His fellow warlock shook his head and said, "It's empty."

"*What?*" Moreland stomped over, his willowy, long limbs a blur of confused fury. He stuck his head inside the trunk and looked around, as if certain we'd hidden *something* inside. Finally, after much huffing and puffing, he emerged and glared at me.

"You are hiding something."

"If that's all—"

"It is *not* all!" Moreland's voice cracked as he shrieked at me. I didn't know whether to laugh or pee my pants. All told, he wouldn't do anything without Aldric giving the go ahead. But I didn't relish the thought of being out here at night with an angry Moreland. "Master Aldric does not like to be kept waiting."

The subtext wasn't exactly hidden: I was to come for a late-night—or early morning, depending on your vantage point—chat with my boss.

Non-optional.

"Very well." I turned to Cross. "I'll see you later." I grabbed the Reaper's Switch and prepared to get out of the car.

"Wait," Moreland said. "Perhaps *he's* the thief, stealing Master Aldric's gold."

I stifled the urge to say *more than you know* and instead said, "I'm not getting out of this damn car if you hurt him."

"Adorable. Like a kitten baring its teeth." Moreland walked up alongside the sports car and leaned over the door again. "But a kitten should not mess with a lion, lest it wishes to get—"

I pushed the door open as hard as I could, taking the ancient warlock out at the knees. Moreland gasped and buckled, writhing on the pavement. His goons immediately closed around the car, but he waved them off as I stepped over him and then knelt to pick up my clutch, which he'd dropped.

I offered him my other hand. Surprise registered in his dead eyes, but he attempted to take me up on my offer. Unfortunately for the warlock, I rescinded it at the last minute. He crashed ass-first against the asphalt.

That was too much insolence for his ancient tastes, and he unleashed a wind spell that blasted me against the side of one of the vans. The world spun, and I groaned.

"Forever taking it a step too far, Eden."

"Don't...don't hurt him." Not sure why I cared, since I was convinced Cross was the murderer. He'd been Roan's partner. He'd called up James to plant the evidence. What more did I need to know? Still, I felt like it was important he didn't die.

Moreland's pale face loomed into fuzzy view. He displayed a row of jagged yellow teeth crying out for the gentle touch of a toothbrush.

"A deal is a deal, as they say in this wretched language." Then his goons hurled me into the van and tossed my belongings in behind me.

And then away we went to meet Master Aldric.

Or, as I liked to call him these days, my asshole boss.

19

MUCH TO MY CHAGRIN—AND CONCERN, SINCE I'D rarely met Aldric outside his office—we weren't going to Black Sea Holdings' headquarters. Instead, the van veered east, which, given my altercation with Moreland, didn't make me feel warm and fuzzy. I watched civilization disappear through the grime-streaked square windows, my heart sinking further with each bump and jolt. This had all the trappings of an execution, where I'd be taken to a secluded part of the jungle and buried where no one would ever find the remains.

Or maybe exhaustion was just making me paranoid. It was early Tuesday morning, and I'd slept all of about six hours out of the last forty-eight. The dirt-streaked dress was beginning to make me feel like a girl on an endless walk of shame. I tried catching Moreland's attention with a smirk, but he was busy phoning in our arrival.

"Hey, Moreland, what's unfuckable and going to die alone?"

Moreland finally finished whispering into the phone and ended the call with, "We'll bring her up right away, sir."

He finally glared at me and crossed his thin arms. "Let me guess."

"Never took you for having low self-esteem." I made a pouty face and smirked. "Because I was going to say the last person in the apocalypse."

He looked ready to strangle me for walking into that one, but he managed to say through clenched yellow teeth, "You have jokes, now, dear girl, but we shall see what you think after the hour has tolled."

"Hey, Moreland."

"Don't push it."

"Get a dictionary from this fucking century. Dipshit."

In response, I felt a minor burn in the seat of my dress. Smelling smoke, I rubbed my ass against the van's rubber mats to extinguish the embers. Moreland looked extra satisfied with his little bit of wizardry.

"A thousand years and you can light my ass on fire. Impressive."

"It is the only way I would touch your dirty ass, my dear girl."

Ooh. Point Moreland. Apparently, there was more going on in that old pale head than fantasies of torturing people with black magic and owning his own galley of loyal sex slaves.

The last one was just an assumption.

Just seemed like the type of dream he'd have.

I peered out the dirty windows as the van slowed down. We had arrived at what could best be described as a secluded resort at the edge of the ocean. An elaborate wooden boardwalk with a shoulder-high handrail wound its way into the sea, where a three-story property stood almost suspended over the water. Judging by the snowcapped mountains looming nearby, we were on the northeast part of the island. I rarely ventured out this way—mainly because the roads sucked, and the low population meant it was hardly a hotbed for souls.

"What, is this his bang pad or something?" I tapped on the small glass divider to the front seat.

Moreland looked horrified. "Master Aldric would never bring *you* to such a place, would such a place exist."

We all got out of the van.

I followed Moreland up the boardwalk. Over the horizon, the sun was beginning to creep up. Another day and another mostly sleepless night. I really needed some rest in an actual bed.

Moreland opened the home's glass door and stood aside. "Master Aldric has been waiting. I would pretend to hurry."

"You're not invited?"

"I have matters to attend to. Murders are bad for business." He waved one finger at a time as the door shut and locked. I felt a shiver snake up my spine. A metal spiral staircase wound its way up through the heart of the house. Aldric wasn't on the first floor, which had a modern stainless steel and light hardwood aesthetic going on. I glanced toward the kitchen, which had a fruit basket on the counter. Kind of like it had been furnished for a magazine shoot. Seemed like a waste of a nice property, but then, I was one to talk with my one couch and electric kettle existence.

I traipsed up the stairs, wondering what this pre-dawn abduction was all about. Wondering how I'd bullshit my way out of it. My brain wanted to shut down, but I couldn't afford any more sloppy missteps.

Aldric wasn't on the second floor, either, which shared the first floor's taste in décor. There was no kitchen on this level, its spot claimed by another bedroom. But that was about it for differences, so I continued my journey upward.

The third floor was different—a single wide room with no walls. Steel cables ran from the ceiling to the floor. The cables had been covered by wooden columns on the floors below, but up here, Aldric was going for an industrial look. Or maybe he hadn't finished the interior yet.

The ancient vampire stood staring at the imminent sunrise at the east window. The windows doubled as the room's walls. As always, he wore a perfectly tailored suit. The first strains of the sun glinted off his polished Italian loafers. A blazing ball peeked over the distant mountains, its warm glow shimmering off the icy peaks. The light near the house remained a purplish-black, just starting to brighten.

"Cutting it a little close, don't you think?" I said as I approached. There was a single desk in the back of the large room, furnished with three chairs. All told, it was remarkably similar to his downtown office.

"It is always nice to see the morning sun." Aldric tapped a remote hidden in his hand, and the shades darkened, plunging the room into utter blackness. After another click, a couple overhead lights flickered on, restoring light to the space.

He'd also taken the liberty of coming closer during the brief blackout, so that we were face-to-face. I was too tired to be startled.

"Cool party trick," I said.

He looked at me and said, "You look like you've been having a good time."

I stared at the rumpled, dirty dress and said, "Not as good as you might think."

"Moreland tells me you have my gold."

Sure. The sooner we got down to business, the sooner I could rest my eyes. I unzipped the clutch. All my belongings remained—the Reaper's Switch, my phone, what was left of the cash Agnes had given me, the dead man's soul from the mayor's backyard, and, of course, what Aldric wanted most.

The ancient vampire's hawkish emerald gaze latched onto his gold bar, his cold eyes stoked by the obsessive fires of greed. I'd have claimed it was unhealthy, but the guy had survived twenty-five centuries, whereas I'd died before I'd made it two and a half decades, so what the hell did I really know?

He didn't say anything, but I took his hint. All out of witty banter, and not wanting to stay longer than necessary, I said, "It's yours."

"Moreland explained the details. Is it true?"

"Guy came into The Loaded Gun trying to pay with it. Magnus said no way, gave it to me for safekeeping." I offered it to the ancient vampire, but he made no move to take it.

"What did this man look like?"

"Oh, you know, shitty description," I said. "Besides, he was trying to buy information about me."

"*You?*"

I was a little insulted by Aldric's shock, but I kept it together. "Apparently, I'm a more valuable commodity than certain individuals think."

Aldric's smooth hand ran over his well-maintained beard. Finally, he dropped his hand and took the golden bar.

"I'll have Moreland run fingerprint analysis."

I'd already wiped it down, so I said, "Definitely a good call."

The thought of wasting Moreland's time warmed my little heart.

"Have you any useful information on Mr. Kelly's

accomplice?" Aldric stared deep into my eyes, probing me with his vampire powers.

While I was almost convinced that Cross was the killer, I wasn't about to share that information with Aldric. Because if Cross disappeared into the jungle vines, I'd never clear my name.

I shrugged and said, "Not really. Magnus didn't remember that much."

Aldric didn't look entirely convinced, but he let the matter die for the time being. "Your shoulder is looking worse."

I must have winced when I'd shrugged. Quite frankly, it was surprising I was still upright. Whatever Khan had whipped up from the dregs of Jack's remaining supplies had been surprisingly effective. But it had been a temporary panacea. It'd been almost thirty hours since the wolf had sunk his teeth into my skin. That was longer than I could've hoped for.

Aldric placed two fingers in his mouth and let loose a shrill whistle. No more than fifteen seconds later, an elevator within the office dinged, a hidden panel in the floor opening to reveal a buxom assistant in a clear box. Because of course you needed an elevator in a three-story house. I mean, why not?

His assistant wasn't human, from the way she moved, or by how the shards of her soul carried by the wind tasted on my tongue. A shifter of some sort, but more dangerous than your typical fox, coyote or small animal. A species I hadn't encountered.

She shot me a predatory glare as she placed a silver tray in Aldric's hands. Then she disappeared without a word, leaving the two of us alone to discuss my fate. Aldric trotted over to the desk and placed the silver tray on its surface. I stared at the black pouch tied with a blue ribbon.

"What is it?" I asked.

"A gift."

"A gift," I repeated, certain I had misheard. Unlike the other gifts I'd gotten lately, this one actually looked promising. Maybe my wound had gone septic, and I was actually in the dying hallucinatory throes of my final seconds in a swampy ditch. That seemed infinitely more likely than Aldric showing mercy—or *rewarding* me.

"You have clearly failed to live up to our original performance contract." Aldric's eyes refused to blink. "But you will have no chance of redeeming yourself should you prematurely expire."

"Redeem myself." I somehow corralled my tongue and avoided screaming, *this is a big load of bullshit.* I'd already told him that yesterday. No need to revisit that point. "Is *that* why you called me here?"

Call was a generous word for Moreland's shenanigans, but unleashing my unfiltered thoughts regarding the matter seemed unwise.

"A small reason, yes," Aldric said. "One must keep their investments in peak working condition." His emerald eyes skimmed over the empty room. Glad I ranked on the same level as this random property on the edge of nowhere.

"Fantastic," I said, barely suppressing my immense irritation. "If that's all—"

"I don't expend such resources on favors." His tone was sharp. He turned and flashed a quick, mirthless smile, revealing his razor-like fangs. That was a warning.

"So this comes with strings." I stared at the black pouch, which now looked like a morbid life preserver. "I already signed your new contract."

162   D.N. ERIKSON

"And yet, you bring me only vague news of accomplices." He rolled up the sleeves of his dress shirt in that calculated, perfectly creased way investment bankers do after work. "That is disappointing, considering the time that has transpired since last night."

To my eye, the ensuing hours had been quite eventful: I'd discovered the mayor was a serial killer, tracked a key cog in my frame to Lionhawk Ink, been threatened by Rayna, had been almost killed by a snake—and demons—in Cross's inherited house, and, oh yeah, discovered that guy, Cross, had been an accomplice of Roan, and together they'd robbed Aldric.

But, since I'd kept most of that to myself, I guess it could be misconstrued that I'd spent most of that time getting drunk or trying to get laid in this little black number.

"Explain how I can get my performance up, then," I said, frowning when I realized it sounded like I was making some weird sexual innuendo.

Aldric either ignored it or didn't notice. "That is simple." He walked slowly to the bag and tossed it from one hand to the other. "I will give you this."

"I like where this is going."

"And you will deliver the following things to me come Friday." Aldric paused and looked me dead in the eye, to ensure I was listening. He needn't have worried. His serious tone had my rapt attention, even though I knew I would hate what came next. "Your seven soul quota. Your rival Reaper. And the party responsible for stealing thirteen million dollars in gold bullion from my vault."

I almost said, *damn, Cross.* Thirteen million was impressive. But I kept that to myself, and instead said, "That's kind of a full plate."

"You're going to earn every dollar I've invested in you, Eden."

"Can't Moreland track down your gold?"

"Moreland has his own tasks."

"Fine." I mean, what else was I going to do? Debate the finer points of his strategy? I had my marching orders, and now I'd just have to figure out a way to make everyone happy. That seemed unlikely, which meant one thing: I was going to wind up extremely unhappy, whatever the final result.

"Take your gift."

"Happy to." I willed my leaden feet forward to the desk. One step away, I caught the faintest wisp of his soul. He had it cloaked and warded out the ass right now, so it was just the smallest of shards. But I still didn't like what I felt. Not one damn bit.

I grabbed the black pouch and tripped as I tried to get away.

"Come, now, Eden." Aldric's emerald eyes glittered like corrupted jewels. "I don't bite."

"That's not what I've heard."

"Genghis Khan didn't conquer the steppes by burning everything in his path. He conquered it through propaganda and planning."

"I guess everyone needs heroes." Aldric didn't look amused by my commentary. Time to get the hell out of there. "Anything else?"

"Do you require more tasks? You are more ambitious than I believed."

I swallowed, but my throat was dry. "I'm good."

"I can rustle up a few more." Aldric's sharp features tightened into a hawkish smile, like he was toying with me.

"Said I'm good, asshole." Whoops. Couldn't help

myself.

"Now why would you say something so hurtful during an otherwise pleasant meeting?"

"You're right, completely ridiculous."

"I sense sarcasm."

I refrained from speaking further, lest my employment offer suddenly found itself amended once more. It dawned on me that the ancient vampire had never intended to allow me out of our original contract. The rug would have been pulled out from under me on the last day. This whole "other Reaper" business had just offered him a prime excuse to cloak the con in the thinnest veil of legitimacy. After all, he'd bailed me out from jail—didn't I owe him? The notion, of course, was laughable, considering he was almost inevitably connected to my predicament.

Since the conversation appeared to be over, I walked to the spiral staircase to begin my descent.

"Do stay safe, Eden."

"When am I not?"

"Are you not going to open your gift?"

"Of course," I said through gritted teeth, staring at the blue ribbon. I tugged on it, and it drifted to the polished hardwood. With tentative fingers—because, let's be serious, this had a serious Trojan Horse vibe—I undid the velvet folds and peered inside. The scent of mint and a pungent lemon aroma hit my nostrils. My aching arm felt better just from that.

"Friday, remember."

I started down the stairs and called up, "Wouldn't miss it for anything."

"And one more thing."

"Yes?"

"It is important that those responsible are punished." I

heard Aldric's knuckles crack. Or maybe it was his neck, or fangs. God, vampires were frigging scary. "Because there must be justice meted out to those who willfully cross me."

Great. I'd just have to rent one of Moreland's vans and toss Cross in the back, then cruise around the city until I found the other Reaper. How could anything go wrong?

Four years of solid work, and this was the thanks I got.

And you thought your boss was a dick.

Moreland was there to greet me outside. The morning light stung my eyes after the shaded third floor room. I squinted at the warlock, watching his tuft of hair wave in the gentle wind.

"It is time to go home." Moreland pointed toward the overgrown road. Didn't get much traffic out here, I guess.

"What, I don't get a ride?"

"Do you not have friends to pick you up?"

"And here I thought you couldn't suck any harder." I was short on allies, and between all the taxis, I had about six bucks left in my clutch.

That wasn't going to get me home.

Things were not coming up Eden right now.

"Enjoy your little vacation in the east," Moreland said, gesturing for his goons to take me away. They stalked forward, even though the warlock could have easily led me off the boardwalk on his own. Just an extra display of power to hammer home exactly who was in charge.

Spoiler: it wasn't me.

I shook off their grip and headed toward the worn, empty road, flipping them the bird.

At this rate, the rest of the week was going to be way worse than Monday.

But you know what they say.

It's important to have something to look forward to.

20

I COULD GET CELL SERVICE, JUST BARELY, BUT THE TAXI companies were either not answering or the lines were busy. Regretting my resistance to downloading app-based transportation prior to being stranded in a place where mobile internet ran at the speed of a snail running a salt gauntlet, I trekked up the empty road alone in the early morning. The gray dawn haze was starting to give way to the brightness of the actual day. After the past thirty hours, all I wanted to do was curl up on the side of the road and sleep. Given the throaty roars coming from the jungle that ran along both sides of the derelict road, however, that seemed like a poor idea.

My phone beeped, indicating I'd received a text message. Cross.

The guy had some serious balls, I had to give him that.

"We need to talk," I said, reading the message aloud as I chewed on the lemon-mint healing mixture. The relief flooding through my shoulder and palm almost made me forget the indignities I'd suffered over the past day. Almost, but not quite.

I was about to put my phone away, but the clutch slipped from my sweaty fingers. That extra half-second of indecision spawned a new idea. I tapped the screen and checked the car location app Cross had installed on my phone.

As it turned out, he was parked just four miles up the road.

Either he was coming to save me from Moreland, or he was finishing whatever he'd started before he'd tracked me to the Lionhawk Ink parking lot last night. My money was on the latter. Time to figure out what he'd been doing on the eastern part of the island.

I took a final glance at the dot, which seemed to be solidly stationed at the Happy Paws Vet Clinic. Then I bashed the phone into a pulp of circuitry and glass against a nearby rock and hurled the ruined plastic into the jungle. If anyone was tracking me, they'd be shit out of luck.

A panther roared in response.

"I know how you feel, bud." I was sick of being ambushed, too. With a surprisingly light step, I headed up the road, velvet bag swinging from its drawstring in one hand, the dirt-streaked clutch in my other. I could only imagine how I looked—probably like I'd just woken up from the most epic cocaine binge on historical record. But my appearance didn't matter, since not a single car passed me on the way to the clinic.

My feet howled in protest as I rounded a curve in the road. Sweat soaked the tight dress through, making it feel more like a damp towel. But, when I saw what lay around the curve, I felt like I'd stumbled upon El Dorado itself.

If El Dorado had been a vet clinic with a burnt-out sign, half-collapsed roof, and two beaters sitting in what one might generously call parking spaces. Others might simply say that the cars were parked in the thick of the jungle. Right in front of the cracked concrete steps, however, was the real reason for my excitement: Cross's Porsche—bright and shiny as the day it had come off the lot—indicated he was still inside.

Of course, there was the minor detail that I was out here alone, without backup, about to confront a murderer while I was totally running on fumes.

You can take the gambler out of the casino, but you can't take the gambler out of the girl.

Nothing moved inside the clinic, but the blinds were drawn, and the windows were plastered over with old, yellowing newspapers. If this place had ever produced any happy paws, it hadn't been in the last decade.

I crept to the first car—an old sedan nearly reclaimed by rust—and slid down against the back wheel. The lush grass felt like a luxury mattress.

Hearing the deep rumble of an engine, I peeked out from behind the sedan's trunk. A beat-up red pickup truck fishtailed around the bend like it was being chased by a demonic plague. Nothing followed, however, and the truck veered into an open spot in front of the clinic as I dived back behind the sedan.

The driver stumbled out of the truck's cab. From his groaning and the cadence of his steps, he wasn't doing so good. I wriggled on my belly along the grass and peeked out behind the bumper. Fresh blood covered the stalks of grass where he'd stumbled out.

More interestingly, I recognized the massive guy: it was Magnus.

The dwarf Jötun crashed through the clinic's doors. Surprised yells came from inside.

I kept myself plastered to the plush grass, listening as

the voices—there were at least three of them—discussed the situation. I wasn't sure if Cross was one of them. Ultimately, they dragged the giant out of the ruined doorway—I could tell from their exaggerated groans and his cries of pain. Then the voices grew fainter.

I took the opportunity to break into Magnus's truck. That was a generous way of putting it; the injured dwarf giant hadn't locked the doors, which was basically inviting a free-for-all on his belongings. Blood dripped down the driver's seat, all the way to the pedals. The engine was still running.

I opted to get in the other side.

"Not the cleanest guy, are we?" I brushed a mountain of crumpled hamburger wrappers off the worn seat, the scent of stale beef suggesting they were well over a week old. Rummaging around in the glovebox, I discovered nothing but an expired registration and a few sticks of unwrapped gum that crumbled in my fingers like chalk.

Through the front windshield, I saw a short, red-haired woman emerge from the clinic, nimbly bounding down the concrete steps toward Cross's sports car. I ducked, disappearing onto the truck's floor with the stale wrappers.

Beneath the seat, I saw gold.

More specifically, gold bars. A dozen of them, glinting like they'd just been stolen from a casino vault. They were the same size as the one Magnus had offered me earlier to prove his loyalty to Aldric. That, of course, was bullshit: judging by this stash, Magnus had been in on the thirteen-million-dollar heist, too.

All kilobars, containing a little over 32 ounces of gold.

A back of the envelope calculation suggested I was staring at about half a million dollars.

I flipped it over, and sure enough found a cloaked rider stamped into the cold metal.

The truck's passenger door opened, and a short, red-haired woman screamed.

I recognized her. She was the reverse pickpocket who had slipped me Rayna's note.

"Quiet," I said, still clutching the gold bar.

"Thief!"

I pushed the short woman away and slammed the door.

Cross raced out the clinic's broken doors. His latex gloved hands were bright red.

I slid into the driver's seat, feeling the blood stick against my bare legs, and threw the truck into reverse. The bald tires screamed in protest as the cab filled with the thick scent of diesel.

I spun onto the poorly maintained road and shifted.

The old truck jackknifed like it had hit a patch of ice, bursting toward the sharp corner like a spooked horse. When I tried to course correct, the passenger side wheels elevated.

I jerked the wheel right, tipping the vehicle's weight back to solid ground.

And sending me straight for an almond tree.

The fragile trunk snapped in two as the truck came to a decisive halt.

With nothing to stop my momentum, I slammed head-first into the steering wheel, sending the entire world into darkness.

21

THERE ARE INFINITE WAYS TO RUN A CON.

The classic "pretty girl in a bar milking you for free drinks" is one—if a bit cliché. Gambits like three-card Monte or a corner shell game take more skill than a smile and a tight dress, but they're still in the minor leagues. The hot tip or inside information scheme are classics, but harder to pull off. And then, of course, you have your ambitious scams: the Spanish Prisoner, maybe, or a Ponzi scheme.

Or you could just go to Wall Street and become a banker.

An attractive option if jail's not your thing.

As I said, there are plenty of ways to run a successful con. What you decide on is based on your skills and personality. Some people like walking the tight rope, no net, above a blazing inferno.

Thus, it was with a mixture of adrenaline-pumping curiosity and stomach-clenching horror that I watched the disaster currently unfolding in the dingy Bourbon Street dive bar. A nearby mutt growled on the chipped concrete floor, its red-rimmed eyes and mange warning me not to come closer. No magic, no special circumstances—just a dog in the bar, because we were in one of the last places in America that got along just fine without rules, thanks. The dog's gutter punk owner was passed out in a sea of vomit, crust mingling with the guy's face tattoos. He was definitely not helping the smell, which was a perpetual mixture of piss, stale beer, and centuries of poor decisions.

I dug my heels into the wobbly barstool, watching two months of hard work circle the drain.

Roan whispered in my ear, "Didn't think anyone could resist little sis's charms."

I swatted him away like an annoying fly. "It's all going to shit."

"Maybe you should swap." He winked at me in that way nerds who think they're slick do. He had long brown hair and a nice smile. I'd even sent him to Nordstrom's, where the sales associates had somehow tricked him into wearing something other than gym shorts. But what had gotten me was his intelligence. Definitely not the bad jokes.

I wrinkled my nose. "Not for all the gold in the world."

"I'm just saying, Smith has a thing for you."

"That's not the plan."

"You could make it work. Head over." He handed me his vodka double. I chewed on the straw and then downed it for courage, tipping the decision-making scales toward intervention.

We'd pitched the Silicon Valley whiz kid our vaporware app. He'd shook on the deal, but paperwork hadn't been forthcoming yet. After all, we'd come out of nowhere, with an idea that sounded too good to be true: instant virtual currency transfers that interfaced with all existing bank accounts, payment platforms, and card processors. Sure, there'd been the "demo" Roan had whipped up, but it was all smoke and mirrors. Turn down the wrong digital corridor and you'd bang into the glass. My role in this scheme was playing the CFO to Roan's brilliant programmer, trying to broker a deal between two future kings of Silicon Valley. I'd done my part, but handshake deals were ephemeral—especially when there was no corresponding app to sell for seven figures.

We were now executing the plan's final phase—solidifying trust. Like the man who steals your wallet and then pretends to give it back to enter your good graces, this was where Maxwell Smith would wire the funds over on the spot in gratitude for us saving him.

The plan was simple: the pretty girl—that'd be my sister —would seduce him in the bar. Maxwell hadn't met her before, by design. They'd make the journey back to the hotel around the corner, on one of those side streets in the French Quarter where you fell into the oblivion the hurricane had left behind. She'd pull a gun and hold him up. Then, Roan and I would bravely intervene. As for her avoiding armed robbery charges, that was easy: she'd drop a year's supply of condoms, clearly identifying her as a hooker. And Maxwell Smith, patron saint of Silicon Valley, didn't need *that* kind of publicity. The whole thing would die, and we'd abscond with our funds.

As I said, easy.

Except for one tiny hitch: Maxwell was leaving. *Without* Sierra.

No one resisted my sister's advances. Boys trailed behind her like she was the Pied Piper, marching to their inevitable heartbreak with puppy-like naiveté. But Maxwell was already on the hazy dance floor, heading toward me.

All told, it was time to bail. But that's the problem with ambition: it demands risk.

And risk is a monster you cannot control.

Roan was right: if I wanted to salvage this situation, I had no choice.

I'd have to step in and play the charmer.

I took a final sip of lukewarm vodka, adjusted the suit pants, and untucked my shirt. The attire made me look older than twenty-four—old enough to be look trustworthy, like someone old enough to have her shit together. People respond to the trappings of authority and power, even when they don't have a goddamn reason to.

My hands shook, and I stuffed the one not holding the vodka into my business casual blazer. The cool metal of a small pistol greeted me—for protection, not coercion.

My mind scrambled to lay down a jazz-like improvisation over the plan we'd honed for months. Casually allowing the vodka to sway with devil-may-care swagger, I made my way through the late-night revelers.

I glanced through the sea of undulating bodies back at the bar, where Roan had been only a moment before. But he had vanished, seemingly into thin air.

Odd.

Maintaining my loose cool, shoulders swinging to the dub-step remix blaring over the shitty speakers, I got closer to Maxwell, catching his eye in the throng.

He hurried over once he noticed me and blinked twice behind his Buddy Holly glasses and said, "I want to get out of here." He threw a glance over his shoulder like he was being pursued by angry bees.

"You were hitting it off with that hottie, man." I playfully punched his shoulder.

"I—I don't know." He whispered into my ear. "She seems kind of desperate."

I looked past our mark and gave an imperceptible headshake to Sierra. She'd love that assessment come tomorrow morning. But for now, this was in my court, and I needed to focus. Sierra gave me a look like I'd grown three heads. Her brown hair, tied back in a conservative ponytail, swished as she shook her head. My sister smacked her ruby red lips before disappearing into the crowd.

We'd engineered her look to mesh with Maxwell's tastes —carefully gleaned from press clippings and social media. But social engineering was more art than science. He rubbed his hand through his gelled, short businessman's cut and blinked again—a nervous affectation.

And Roan was right—it happened a lot in my presence. I should've been flattered, I suppose. Sierra had always dominated the boys' attention, even when we were younger. Which wasn't to say I was homely by any stretch, merely that I was a little strange, and she was the outgoing, bubbly girl everyone fell in love with. If you really wanted to dive into my brain, the genesis of this whole scheme—ripping people off, drifting from city-to-city—started right there. I'd studied hard to know which buttons to press at just the right time. What my sister did naturally, I did through study.

Of course, she still did it in the field. I was usually like a coach calling plays from the sidelines. Tonight, however, I had been thrust into a starring role. My body pulsed with the limitless possibility.

Maxwell looked at me hopefully, and I gave him an easy smile. "She's gone. You wanna get out of here?"

This was the simplest con of all, called *pretty girl relieves you of your money and then breaks your heart*. An old classic, practiced in endless permutations the world over. When the Earth is nothing but dust, there will still be some poor bastard trapped in a trophy wife honeypot without a prenup.

I latched my fingers between his. He gave me a look—the kind of happy relief someone feels when things finally work out—and I felt a wave of guilt crash over me. Then again, this same guy had screwed over all his original investors and kicked his partner out of the company—the lead programmer of the app, no less—with nothing. So I might've been an asshole, but I was also a karmic boomerang coming back to whip him in the ass.

Maxwell stumbled forward, a little drunker than I expected. The pleasant expression on his face twisted into a grimace.

"What's wrong?" I asked.

"It...it hurts." His hand slipped out of mine and clutched his stomach. I looked down in the kaleidoscopic lights and saw blood soaking through his baggy dress shirt. Whirling around frantically, I couldn't see who—or what—had hurt him. I dropped the vodka glass as the blood spread up to his chest. Then he crumbled to the ground. I yelled for help, but the bass was too loud, and everyone was too drunk.

I knelt to the dirty concrete and pressed my fingers against Maxwell's neck.

Dead as a post.

A singular thought roared like a battle cry: *I needed to find Sierra. Now.*

The rest of the bar didn't even notice that he was down for the count. I wouldn't be sticking around for the police report. I elbowed my way through the crowd, receiving a few sour glances for my trouble. The faded orange EXIT sign beckoned me like a beacon into the marshland city of rusty patinas, crumbling concrete and faded colonial structures. I walked out the door-less exit into the humid and thick early morning air. Bourbon Street was still populated, albeit sporadically. Keeping my head down, I hurried to our emergency meeting spot. Roan and Sierra might not have seen what happened, but they would show up eventually.

I cut down the tight alley, looking for my sister and boyfriend. Sierra was nowhere to be found amid the paint-stripped dumpsters and spent plastic cups. I craned my neck back toward the street, hoping to catch a glimpse of her brunette wig. But there was nothing but faded people making decisions they would regret come afternoon.

Heart stammering, I looked at my blood-stained fingers. This had gone catastrophically wrong. Who would have wanted to kill Maxwell Smith? I scanned the alley again—which was when I saw *it* lying in a muddy puddle by a pair of battered trash cans. Fake strands of hair glinted in the early dawn light. Red stained the fibers, and I hurried over and leaned in, close enough to see if it was—

"Blood, my dear girl." The slightly foreign voice spoke crisp, lifeless English. Despite the swampy heat cloaking the city like a shroud, my core temperature dropped a few degrees. "Your sister, correct?"

I heard a whimper, which could only be Sierra. My cheeks flushed with white-hot anger as a pale man stepped out from behind a battered dumpster. The shadows cloaked his face, but my sister's terrified expression was clear as day.

"We have money," I said, the words unsteady.

The mystery man touched Sierra's heart-shaped chin. Blood flowed from an open wound at her temple, staining her platinum blonde hair brackish brown.

"What are you doing?" I asked, voice quivering. Even though he was cloaked in shadow, I could see that his eyes were completely dead. Devoid of life in a totally inhuman way. He leaned forward, revealing a row of jagged yellow teeth with a menacing glare. Then he receded into the shadows once more, featureless and deadly. My legs almost gave out, but I managed to stay standing.

"Do you know what I am?" the man responded, uninterested in answering my offer.

"A dick." I rubbed my hand along the blazer's fabric. There was a Glock 26 hidden inside the pocket, just small enough to be out of sight. Yeah, plenty of the bars around here had no firearms signs, but fuck them. An unarmed grifter becomes a dead one, sooner or later.

A sudden bolt of annoyance pierced his dead eyes, and he snarled. "I have watched you children long enough."

"I'm not a child." I was twenty-four, and a student of anarchy, always above the law, until that moment, when I found myself desperately hoping that the entire police force would come haul us away.

"It is all relative." The pale man stroked Sierra's chin as a realization dawned on me.

This man wasn't human.

I willed my frozen hand toward the pistol as Sierra silently cried, the tears streaking her perfect mascara. The man shoved her away, down to the dirty pavement just as I got my hand on the pistol's tacky grip. I slid it out and pulled the trigger, but there was nothing there when the bullet smacked against the wall.

"For that, my dear girl, your sister will die, too." His voice was a caustic whisper in my ear. I turned, but he was gone. "But, alas, unlike you, she shall not return."

A knife plunged deep into my chest. My legs buckled and I collapsed next to the bloody wig. Blood cascaded from the wound as the pale man loomed over me. I still couldn't make out his features, beyond the dead eyes. Almost like a magical spell obscured his face, making you forget it the instant you caught a glimpse.

The raucous sounds of Bourbon Street faded into blackness, and instead of screaming, my dying words were, "We just wanted a new life."

"Then you shall get what you always desired."

His eyebrows rose as he watched me take my final, shuddering breath. All I could manage to mouth was the word *where?*

"Where else, dear girl?" He offered me a disinterested shrug, then turned back toward Bourbon Street. "Paradise."

22

I awoke with a shuddering start on a small cot. My ribs hurt, and I had a massive headache. The cramped exam room smelled like ammonia and wet fur. I was still wearing the dirt-streaked dress. Old, yellowing newspaper covered the room's sole window.

I'd realized something, too, while I'd been sleeping.

The son of a bitch who had killed me four years ago? That had been Moreland. The memory hadn't returned until now, either from shock or whatever magic he might have cast to make me forget. But crashing into the almond tree had shaken the truth loose.

And Moreland's involvement meant one thing: Aldric had orchestrated my death.

I swung my bare feet onto the cool linoleum floor and tried to stand. Instead, I collapsed in a heap, barely saving myself from faceplanting by clutching a rickety metal tray table. It kept me from falling, but couldn't hold my weight for long. The table tipped over and I smacked into the hard ground. I curled into a ball, listening to the voices in the hall grow louder as they approached.

The door swung open. Dante Cross stood inside the frame. His cuticles were stained with blood. Magnus's, presumably. I briefly wondered whether the dwarf giant had made it before promptly concluding that I didn't give a shit.

"Well, you certainly have a knack for hurting yourself." He took a step inside, but I recoiled, scraping at the peeling floor like a dog terrified of what was about to happen next. "The hell is up with you?"

"Stay away from me." All I could think was, *Cross is the murderer. He's the goddamn murderer.* My fingers searched for anything I could defend myself with. But the metal tray table had been empty for years, and the clutch containing my Reaper's Switch was nowhere in the immediate vicinity. I might as well have been a mackerel beached on shore, curling its hooked lip in futile defiance at the fisherman.

An apt metaphor, considering I'd been captured.

I finally managed to push myself up from the floor by my knuckles. The room spun just from the effort of standing. I probably had a minor concussion from totaling the truck, along with whatever had happened to my ribs.

We stared at one another in silence until the short, red-haired woman came up behind Cross.

Up close, I could see she was youngish—maybe thirty-five, or forty—and clearly a fox shifter. She might as well have had a sign hanging from her neck. Although her long, straight red hair did that pretty well on its own. Her eyes trusted nothing, least of all me. The woman stood on her tiptoes to whisper in Cross's ear.

"Zoe here says we should get rid of you." Cross looked amused, the golden flecks in his brown eyes glittering. "That bringing you here was a mistake."

"Interesting proposition," I said. I didn't know what he meant by *bringing me here*.

Zoe, for her part, glared icy daggers of death at Cross before nimbly stalking out.

I spotted the dirty—and now, thanks to the wreck, torn —clutch by the green-tinted steel sink, and willed myself over by sheer determination. Opening the zipper was a trial. I felt Cross's hand touch mine and I shrieked.

"All right, all right." He backed away and leaned against a faded red biohazard bin in the corner. "You don't want my help. Noted."

I finally got the clasp open and searched for the herbs. The pouch wasn't on the counter, which meant it had to be inside the clutch—right?

Wrong. All I found was the Reaper's Switch, the dead man's soul, and a couple stray dollars. Fists tightening into little balls of fury, I turned slowly.

"Where the hell is it?"

"You should rest," Cross said with a cool toss of his sun-bleached, messy hair.

I flicked out the blade. "You know exactly what I'm talking about."

Cross rolled his eyes. "Put that away."

"I'll put it right through your chest if you don't bring me back the pouch." I narrowed my eyes into the tiniest of slits. "And you know what happens to an immortal when their soul is stolen."

That registered the slightest bit of concern. "Warlock's Lemonmint, was it?" He gestured toward the exam room's door. "May I, or are you going to—"

"Two minutes before I hunt your ass down."

"Duly noted, Eden." Cross slipped into the hall, leaving me alone in the cold room. I stared at a faded poster on the cracked wall that featured a smiling woman with a plastic smile imploring everyone to spay and neuter.

Multiple pairs of footsteps drew my attention toward the hall. Much to my chagrin, it wasn't Cross returning with the velvet bag, but Zoe and a second party—a middle-aged, mousy looking librarian. I had no idea how she'd gotten caught up in this mess, but suffice to say, Aldric would relish the opportunity to remove her head from her body. She was at least a head taller than Zoe, who barely scraped five feet.

I glanced between them, still holding the knife. "I'm not getting the herbs, am I?"

"Magnus needs them." From the way Zoe's voice shook, she cared deeply about the giant. I wasn't sure how that worked, physically, since he looked liable to crush her, but good for them. Nonetheless, true love was getting in the way of my own healing process.

I jerked my head at the librarian, immediately regretting it as the room exploded in a muted sea of fuzzy color. "What's your deal?" My words sounded like they were coming from underwater.

The woman didn't respond. Zoe spoke for her. "Doris took a vow of silence."

"How quaint." The world settled into some semblance of stability. "What does she do?"

"She's our security."

"Does she bore people to death?" I looked at Doris, who blankly returned my gaze.

A dagger zoomed by my head, lodging itself in the cabinet behind my ear.

Her hand disappeared back into her sensible pants as my pulse rose a few notches.

"That should be enough of a demonstration," Zoe said with a smirking grin.

Zoe glided across the cold floor like a figure skater over ice. She didn't even come up to my chin, but she struck an imposing presence nonetheless.

"You're either on board, or you're in the jungle."

That sounded ominous.

"What happened to Magnus?" I asked, instead of acknowledging Zoe's threat. "Aldric get him?"

"That's none of your concern." The shifter's voice was snippy, like she was barely holding back a dam of emotion. "Until you tell us what side you're on."

Her shirt was touching the tip of the Reaper's Switch. Had to say, I appreciated the moxie. But I wasn't really interested in forming a suicide pact with these idiots. Especially when all the current evidence suggested there was a murderer among them who liked eliminating team members.

I smiled. "You know Aldric's going to pick you off one by one, right?"

Doris's blade removed itself from the cupboard and circled around my head. I'd heard of this type of sorcery before, but never seen it in person. The gleaming point touched my nose gently, *just* pressing into my soft skin.

"An answer, Reaper," Zoe said.

"Why'd you kill Roan Kelly?" Saying his name hurt a little, even though Cross had claimed Roan had sold me out in New Orleans. That could've been just another lie, though, to throw me off Cross's trail.

The knife pricked into my nose, drawing blood. I bit my lip to avoid crying out. That wouldn't be a good look. My nose itched as I felt the warm blood trickle down to my nostril.

"Don't believe everything you hear," Zoe said, looking genuinely hurt by the accusation.

"I'll have to remember that."

Before Zoe could reply, or Doris could carve me up with her flying knife, Cross returned to the doorway. His eyes widened when he saw the situation.

"You have a real gift for making friends, Eden."

"My sister got all that talent," I said, speaking the truth for the first time in a while. You had to sprinkle it in like seasoning. The truth had a certain consistency that, when mixed with lies, gave falsehoods a believable ring.

"Oh, she couldn't have gotten everything." Cross smiled, but I didn't reciprocate, and the grin quickly faded. He clasped his tan hands together. "Well, it looks like the big guy is gonna pull through."

"Then I'd like to go home, if it's all the same to you."

Cross shared a quick glance with his two allies and said, "That depends on if you're in or out."

Without any other choice, I told one more lie. "Of course I'm fucking in."

And then I gave Cross, Zoe, and Doris the biggest shit eating grin I'd ever mustered in my life.

23

Except, of course, I wasn't in. I had reservations about turning them over to Aldric—that was a lot of blood for one person's hands—but I had no plans of joining their suicide pact, either.

Cross drove me back to the villa. I wanted to confront Cross about the murder. Tell him I knew about James, knew about the call to plant the gun in my master bedroom. But I kept it all to myself. Maybe it was fear—or maybe it was the nagging sensation that everything wasn't as it seemed.

Instead, we rode in silence—except for Khan, who screeched and complained in his cat carrier the whole ride home. He'd been living at the vet clinic for the past day, treated by Zoe for whatever he'd eaten in Jack's dark basement. The grumbling tirades weren't exactly endearing my new pet to me.

"Here," Cross said as he pulled up to the service road a mile from my villa. My dress smelled like sweat and fear, and I wanted nothing more than to get the hell away from him. But I turned anyway, and saw that he had a large pinch of Warlock's Lemonmint in his palm.

I planted it in my cheek without a thank you—it was mine, after all, and those pricks had stolen it.

Khan hissed in the backseat. "Stupid human, it is more effective as a tea."

I smacked the dented carrier, and the cat unleashed a stream of curses about the indignity of being caged. With a tired arm, I pushed against the car door, straining against the modest weight.

I glanced back at Cross. "Who carved Magnus up?"

"Aldric was looking to see what the big guy knew about the gold bar."

"And what did the 'big guy' tell him?"

"Nothing. All part of the plan." Cross winked, but I could tell he was shaken.

Luckily, the dwarf Jötun was a tough bastard. Otherwise their plan could have turned into tragedy pretty damn quick.

Cross handed me Khan's carrier. "Eden—"

"You said Roan sold me out in New Orleans." I stared at him. "How?"

"It's a long story."

"Well, I've got until Friday, so whenever you're ready."

Cross shrugged and stretched. "He got an offer for a couple million. Sell out your location, your emergency meetup spot. Times, everything."

"How nice." I rubbed my sneaker against the dirty asphalt. "He tell you why someone would offer him that sort of cash?"

"Something about your special skills. Rare. Had to have you on his team. Roan thought it was a recruiting thing. Military or law enforcement."

"Or kidnapping." Aldric—or Moreland, on behalf of his master—had paid my ex-boyfriend to sell me down the river. Sierra and I had been dead the instant we'd stepped out of that Bourbon Street dive.

"Probably that," Cross said, his messy sun-bleached hair waving as he nodded. "He didn't think they'd—well, you know how it went down."

"Kill me?"

"That."

"What's your deal, anyway?" The carrier twisted my shoulder as Khan petulantly adjusted all his weight toward the back.

"Now that *is* a long story, Eden Hunter." Cross offered me a grin stained by the darkness of events long past. There was that taste of his soul on my dry lips again, still fractured and tinged with blood, gold, and cannon shot. "One, perhaps, you will hear in time."

"Give me the executive summary."

"I'm a treasure hunter with a nomad's soul."

The words didn't sound romantic or charming.

They sounded wistful and sad.

I turned away from the car without answering. Cross peeled out and raced away.

Sighing, I began the impossibly long journey home. My arm started killing me about halfway up the beach. I set the carrier down and unlatched its gate.

"Welcome to my house," I said.

Yes, the acres of black sand were mine as well.

Perks of living where no one else wants to.

The cat poked his head out like he was seeing the outside world for the first time.

"What the hell are you doing, human?" His nose twitched in agitation. Khan had a white stripe running from the tip of his nose to his tail that made him resemble a skunk. Which was also reflective of his less than sunny disposition. "You expect me to walk on this—this *dirt*?"

With great trepidation and his head held high with indignation, the cat ventured into the sunlight and glared at me with his ice blue eyes. I kicked the battered carrier into the dense underbrush, and he arched his back with no small amount of annoyance.

"What if I preferred for you to carry me, human?"

"It's Eden," I said. "And I could give a shit about your preferences."

"I saved your life, human."

"It could be argued that I saved yours first," I said. "Since you'd still be down in that cellar if I hadn't come knocking."

I walked away. The dirt-streaked dress was clammy, smelling like sweat and dried blood. Khan screamed as loud as his little cat vocal cords allowed, "How far is your domicile?"

"About a mile."

"These terms are unacceptable."

"That's the way this island is." I stared out at the breaking waves. "The terms are rarely in your favor."

And you never really learned to accept them.

You just learned how to survive.

24

Given my gauntlet of trials, it wasn't a surprise when I slept until Wednesday morning. After sixteen hours, I awoke refreshed and no worse for wear—relatively speaking, at least. If I breathed deeply, there was a dull ache in my ribs from the crash. But, otherwise, my shoulder, palm, and head all seemed to be in good shape.

If only I could've said the same about the rest of my life.

Despite my best efforts, the rest of the day was a total bust—both on the case and souls front—and so the calendar flipped over to Thursday without much progress. Cross remained my prime suspect, but I had neither the evidence nor a plan to confront him. I'd been avoiding his messages since he'd dropped me off.

I rose from the worn leather sofa, back slightly stiff, and dodged a sleeping Khan. The electric kettle sang as the water boiled. I rubbed my fingertips over the polished limestone island, staring at the new front doors. At least I'd gotten one thing crossed off the to-do list yesterday. Three grand later, and it was like the werewolf assassin had never been here at all—slash of blood on the nearby wall notwithstanding.

I'd also gotten a new burner phone.

Otherwise, fresh developments were sparse indeed.

After dumping a hefty tablespoon of instant coffee into the steaming water, I walked into the living room to get dressed. A pair of jeans and a black tank top won out by default, being the only remotely clean articles of clothing to my name. I wedged my feet into my low-top sneakers and sipped the bitter brew as another Friday quota loomed.

Fortunately, I'd ripped off what was probably Reaper rival on Sunday night, acquiring four souls for my trouble. They were still stashed in the guest room safe—along with the werewolf assassin's and the mayor's unfortunate victim.

Unfortunately, that still left me one short. Which, in Aldric's book, would be as good as having none. There was, of course, the small matter of bringing the ancient vampire those responsible for the heist, as well as my Reaping competition. At least Rayna no longer needed the gold by Friday, seeing as how she was part of the crew.

I'd figured out she was involved via the Zoe link: the fox shifter had slipped me Rayna's note to meet at The Loaded Gun.

It had also dawned on me, during Wednesday's fruitless workday, that they had run an elaborate con to bring me to their doorstep. Any part of a good con is *allowing* the mark to arrive at their own conclusions—with the grifter's helpful guidance, of course. The magical note, Rayna's ultimatum to find the gold, Magnus waiting outside The Loaded Gun with the gold bar, Cross conveniently installing the car locator app—all details leading me straight to Happy Paws.

The only thing I didn't know was *why*.

Why did they need my help *after* a thirteen-million-dollar heist?

Satisfying my curiosity could wait. Aside from Aldric's unreasonable demands, I still had a murder charge hanging over my head. Fully rested, and no longer frantically scrambling to figure out what was going on, I had a plan.

First, I'd finish up with the souls. Maybe Aldric would give me an extension on the other two tasks if I completed my main job. Wishful thinking, but Cross's words stuck with me—Aldric had tracked me to New Orleans because I was special. Reapers didn't grow on Reaping trees. They were difficult and costly to create.

Above all else, Aldric was a businessman. Destroying your investments didn't make sense.

I hoped.

After sending out a few feelers to my network, I spent most of the day waiting by the phone. Outside the living room's large bay window, the perfect blue sky gave way to a dusky navy night. I finally got a hit back from Edgar at around eight. There was a fresh body on his embalming table with a soul I could reap. Some type of sorceress.

I texted him back and told him in no uncertain terms that he was to keep his wannabe Reaper's hands off the soul. He replied with a sad face emoji.

Vampires now expressed their emotions with crudely drawn, low-resolution faces.

What a time to be alive.

After finishing another cup of terrible coffee for a nighttime boost, I rode the bike out to Edgar's. The cheery Atheas Acres Funeral Parlor sign greeted me as I pulled in between an SUV and a compact sedan parallel parked out front. Business must've been booming today.

I jogged up the three stone steps and entered through the glass door.

The familiar wave of overpowering perfume slapped me in the face. A grieving widow clutched an empty box of tissues in the corner of the waiting area. She barely looked up. The small, red-haired woman pacing around the coffee table strewn with old magazines, however, looked straight at me.

"Zoe?" I'd have called this a pleasant surprise, but that would've been a huge lie. Since I liked having my limbs attached to my body, steering clear of Cross and his insane crew seemed like the best option. Otherwise I was liable to get caught in the buzzsaw when Aldric inevitably caught them.

Her eyes narrowed in extreme suspicion. "What are you doing here?"

"I know the owner," I said, heading toward the showroom, which was separated by a thin, fading curtain. The small woman agilely blocked my path.

"There's only one reason a Reaper visits a funeral home." Her glare could have curdled milk.

I threw a glance at the crying old woman in the corner. "Would you like to announce that to *everyone*?"

I gave her a small smile, like we were all on the same side.

I'd joined their crew, remember?

She wasn't buying it. "No."

"I didn't say anything."

"You're not reaping Doris's soul."

When Edgar had mentioned sorceress, my first thought had been terminal illness. Car accident. Maybe a hit and run victim, or a spellcaster with an inter-clan dispute.

Definitely not the mousy-looking librarian assassin who had tossed knives at my head.

Her death could mean only one thing: the heist's inevitable aftermath was starting to play out. And it seemed my unavoidable cosmic destiny to be sucked into its spinning vortex of bullshit.

"I didn't come for Doris," I said. "Different body." I slipped past, but the fox shifter was nimble, grabbing my arm to stop me.

"I'll accompany you."

"Be my guest."

Damnit, damnit, damnit.

The chemical scent of harsh preservatives and shitty taste of Edgar's bitter soul greeted me as I headed down to the embalming room. Zoe followed me down the steep stairwell, maintaining a watchful eye.

The pudgy vampire held a scalpel over a corpse. Before I could react, Zoe darted forward and collided with him. Edgar grunted as the scalpel clattered to the concrete floor, near the built-in drain.

When I got closer, I knew why she'd charged.

The body on the slab was Doris.

A gooey compound seeped through the white sheet covering her body. It was right above her heart. I glared at Edgar, who was massaging his bad leg on the ground as Doris perched over him like a coiled predator.

"What did I tell you about the damn Reaper's Willow?" I examined the body. No incisions had been made. Of course, that didn't solve the other problem—the tiny, terrier-like watchdog guarding her friend's departed soul.

"But my skills are improving, Eden," Edgar said in protest.

"Since Sunday?" I shook my head at the mere thought of the unusable slop he'd tried to sell me then. I wasn't big on crying for the dead, but that hatchet-job bordered on desecration.

Edgar unleashed a riotous cough into his blood-spackled handkerchief. After he recovered, he teetered to his feet, eying Zoe with trepidation.

"Before I was rudely interrupted, I was preparing your latest soul." Edgar limped to the metal slab and stood over the sorceress's corpse. "Top quality. Aldric will be most pleased—"

"You touch her, you die." Zoe's voice didn't waver. She brandished the scalpel at him.

"Who is this barnacle that has attached herself to you?" Edgar's lips were puckered so tightly in annoyance that his formless cheekbones almost had definition.

"This barnacle," Zoe said, circling the slab with the knife still outstretched, "is telling you to keep your slimy hands off."

It crossed my mind that I could grab Doris's soul and then make a break for it—paying Edgar the tab later—but I'd probably have to fight Zoe to the death when she caught up with me. I figured my odds in that match-up were fifty-fifty, but a victory would likely cause more problems than dying.

What did Doris need her soul for, anyway? It'd be better if she just winked out of existence, rather than the rung of the Elysian Fields where she was likely headed. Yes, yes, spare the sanctimony—when I reaped a soul, it barred most mortal creatures from the eternal afterlife. They simply dissolved out of existence and consciousness. For most, however, that proved to be an unrequested blessing. Most people and creatures just weren't as morally solid as they thought. A woman like Doris certainly hadn't gotten that good with knives by playing smiling homemaker.

Despite the temptation, I decided against rash action.

"Guess that concludes our business." I turned toward the stairs. If I wasn't going to get my last soul here, then I needed to hit the old dusty trail to knock on some doors.

"There are other options," Edgar said with overeager used car-salesman enthusiasm. "I heard the last information I sold you bore interesting fruit."

"It wasn't bad," I said, playing it cool as a negotiating tactic.

Edgar limped to the wall of stainless steel subzero cold lockers and threw one open. A gust of icy air rushed across the embalming room like a winter storm. The pudgy vampire dug into the darkened frozen recesses of the chamber.

Edgar cursed and then crawled inside the cold locker.

Zoe nodded me over to the table.

Without anything better to do, I shuffled over.

"I think Doris was poisoned," she said.

"Poisoned?"

"Look." Zoe flicked on the autopsy lamp and gently lifted her fallen friend's right eyelid. I couldn't recall what color Doris's eyes had been in life, but they certainly hadn't been this striking shade of radioactive purple.

"Contact lens?"

"No," the small woman replied, her tone studded with thorny annoyance. "Alchemist's hemlock. Capable of killing even highly resilient—or even immortal —creatures."

"What are you, a doctor?"

"If you must know, Reaper, yes." Zoe shot me a heated

glare. "Of sorts. A five-year apprenticeship to an apothe-carial sorceress."

"Didn't make it all ten years, huh?" Maybe not the time to be busting chops. But I seemed to recall her voting to kill me.

Zoe's fists balled up, and she took a step around the slab, ready to make me eat my words—and maybe a few teeth.

Edgar stumbled out of the cold chamber just in time. After a magnificent, room-quaking coughing fit, he limped between us and set his find on top of Doris's body. The sheet shifted slightly, revealing a dull gash around her neck.

Like someone had tried to remove it for a trophy.

I had a sickening feeling that I knew exactly who had done this, but I didn't share my thoughts.

"I found this earlier today," Edgar said, like he was Sher-lock Holmes. "Impressive, yes?"

"What am I looking at?" I asked.

That wasn't snark or sarcasm. I really had no idea. To me, it was just a boring syringe.

"It's a pre-packaged spell known as an arcana kit." Zoe turned the syringe over. "Like a frozen dinner. Just follow the instructions, jam in your leg, and boom."

"So that means it has—"

"Soul fragments within," Edgar said, unable to keep himself from interjecting. "I got it...well, that's not important."

"Thought you found it." The truth clicked together. The crappy Reaper's Switch sigil on his right hand was one of these do-it-yourself jobs.

If people were shooting themselves up with back alley magic, it wasn't really my problem. This stuff no doubt had side effects and potential risks, but I wasn't the soul police.

People could waste their souls making whatever dumb products they wanted.

But I asked anyway, "Why should I care?"

"That's easy." Edgar clenched his pudgy fingers in uncontained glee. "Because the seller must be getting his supply of souls from the other Reaper. And I know where he lives. And his name."

"Who's my competition?" I flicked the Reaper's Switch out, acid dripping from my voice.

The vampire stumbled toward Zoe. "I just know the dealer."

"We'll see what you say when I jam this right above your heart."

His fangs snapped out. Fight or flight will do that.

"I can tell you where the seller—where *Renard* is." Edgar's formless cheeks rolled into a gelatinous half-smile. "And the rest is up to you."

With a long, tired sigh, I said, "How much is this gonna cost me?"

"Cheap. Three thousand."

I peeled off the bills from my money clip. In a low voice, Edgar told me the address. It was in the northwest—the suburbs, to be exact. As I went to leave, Zoe tagged along like we are attached at the hip, no doubt concerned that I'd double back for Doris's soul.

I stopped on the stairwell and said, "I'm not the only Reaper in town you have to worry about these days."

"You're the only one I can keep track of." The diminutive fox shifter folded her arms.

"If you take the body, then you won't have to keep track of either of us." I raised my eyebrows, as if to say *wouldn't that be better?* But it was doubtful she could even see me in the dim light.

After a long pause, she said, "I'll call Magnus."

Her feet glided silently down the thin stairs. She'd keep a watchful eye on Edgar until her dwarf Jötun beau arrived, just to make sure the funeral director didn't pull any quick stunts.

That worked for me.

Because I had a spell peddler to visit.

One who would hopefully lead me to this competitor causing me so much damn grief.

25

I KILLED THE BIKE HALFWAY UP THE SUBURBAN STREET, glancing at the rows of cookie-cutter houses. Moonlight sliced over the identical semi-green lawns, puke-yellow paint jobs, and two-car garages. White picket fences were conspicuously missing, but perhaps only because the uninspired architect had forgotten. The only differences between the homes were the yards, where some people had kids' toys, a few had flags—including an American one—and one guy had a car in about six hundred pieces scattered across the dying grass.

It had to be a guy, because no suburban housewife would put up with that.

The neighborhood association was no doubt having a conniption.

If only they knew someone was slinging get-magic-quick syringes from his heavily mortgaged dream home.

I skimmed the mailbox numbers, finding 357—which seemed foreboding, given the circumstances—emblazoned with the name Martin in peeling rainbow-colored stickers. While there were no toys—or anything else, for that matter

—in the yard, that was a clear sign there were children inside.

Thanks for the heads up, Edgar.

But the funeral director could have called ahead and just scheduled a meeting for me. Instead, I'd wanted to come out here and catch Renard Martin off guard. Give someone too much time to prepare, and they spend it concocting layers of bullshit so thick that it was impossible to uncover the truth. This way, I'd get him on his heels quick. That gave me the best shot at pilfering any souls he might have stashed—and, just maybe, getting the name of his contact.

I approached the bland black door and glanced in the window. A middle-aged man sat reading quietly in the living room. That had to be Renard. The man didn't look particularly intimidating. He looked like the cool teacher at school, with his well-maintained goatee, kind face, and carefully trimmed afro.

But appearances could be deceiving.

Instead of knocking on the door, I rapped on the glass. His head turned away from the dense book to look at me. Then he rose.

Good. No need to get the kids involved in this.

The door unlatched, and the man took off his reading glasses. "Can I help you?" The man spoke with a thick accent. The book clutched in his hands had a French title. He was also very clearly human, and, if my shoddy translation of the title was any indication—*A Brief History of Scientific Rationality*—not a big believer in magic.

Or he was trying to cover up a lucrative side business.

"Renard Martin?"

His body tensed in defense. "Why do you wish to speak with my son?"

So much for leaving the kids out of it. I resisted the natural impulse to ask, *your son?*, and said, "It's about school. May I come in?"

"Renard isn't home right now," the father replied, the ragged edges of his voice suggesting he was at the end of his rope. "I'm sorry, are you a teacher of his?"

"Miss Miller." I extended my hand, hoping he'd buy it with me dressed in jeans and a tank top. "Advanced English."

From his initial reaction, I was betting that his kid had failed a couple of classes.

I was right, because Mr. Martin said, "My son isn't in Advanced English."

"That's why I'm here, Mr. Martin." I dusted off my widest *I care* smile from the attic. "I think he should be."

He looked surprised for a moment, then pride washed over his features. Yes, just as any good parent believed— their kid should be in the advanced courses, and they were getting a raw shake. Hell, Mom had thought the same about me until I was about sixteen. Then she'd seen the writing on the wall, scrawled in a string of incompletes and Fs in geometry and biology, accompanied by comments like *rude* and *refuses to listen to instructions* and *lights cigarettes during class, but doesn't smoke them*.

I was edgy like that.

I wondered what Renard's rap was as his father gestured for me to come inside the house. It smelled faintly of pot roast, but not fresh. More of the microwaved leftovers variety. I sat down on a comfortable cloth sofa in the living room, and the father returned to his recliner.

"I was really hoping to speak to you both," I said, still wearing my friendly smile. "Renard has such a gift."

"Sarah is out of town," the man said. "With our little

girl." He wiped his eyes and stared up at the ceiling. "A gift?"

I hoped I hadn't gone too far. If Renard was of the *pay someone else to write his term papers* persuasion, that dog wouldn't hunt. But Mr. Martin smiled wistfully to himself and nodded.

"My boy always did have a lyrical voice."

"Exactly the word I would use," I said as my gaze traced over the living room. A glass coffee table, a few framed pictures of the happy family. One recent, showing them at a restaurant. If I had to guess, Renard was anywhere from sixteen to eighteen. My eyes swept over the bookshelf, noting the French language titles as well as a myriad of English classics.

Recalling the reading list from my own truncated high school education, I said, "He wrote a fantastic paper on *Lord of the Flies*. The whole English department loved it."

I'd never read the book. But Aldric was at the forefront of my mind these days, so it made sense that his favorite novel would be stuck to my lips like glue.

"Isn't it a little odd, Miss Miller—"

"Emma," I said with an easy smile.

He leaned back in the chair for a moment. "My, I forgot to introduce myself. Victor."

"It's quite all right." I folded my hands over my torn jeans. "You were saying?"

"Oh—it's no bother."

"Please," I said, inviting him to speak with a warm wave of the hand.

"It's summer, Emma. School is not in session."

I hadn't considered that point, but I was quick to recover. Do this for long enough, and bullshit just flows through you like a monk channels Zen. With a short, almost embarrassed laugh, I said, "You got me, Victor. And yes, I understand it's quite late, too."

There was an easy silence where we both smiled. I could tell he was lonely, wondering where he'd gone wrong with his son. His wife and daughter weren't away on a trip. They'd left. My presence eased that existential angst, at least for a few minutes.

I continued, "You see, the paper was just that impressive. I told him that on the last day of school, and he promised he'd fill out the forms for my class next year."

"But he hasn't done it." Victor shook his head, finishing my thought for me. This was almost too easy, and I felt bad about it. But I needed to track down Renard. For all I knew, the kid was hanging out with my rival Reaper right now.

"I wanted to see if I could convince him to do it," I said. "It's rare you find a boy so bright."

"I suppose it is." Victor rubbed his well-groomed beard thoughtfully. "He's out."

"Can you reach him?"

"I don't think so, Emma." He slumped into the recliner like it was another defeat in a long-running war of parental attrition.

"I'd be happy to wait." I pulled out my phone and glanced at the time. Damn, it'd gotten later than I'd thought —almost eleven.

"I'm afraid you'd be waiting all night, unfortunately." Victor winced. I was losing him. Time to bail—but not without a little more searching.

"I'll come back another time, then." I stood and turned toward the entrance area. "Can I ask you one small favor?"

"Sure."

"May I use your bathroom?"

"Downstairs and to the right."

I slunk my shoulders down low. "I, um, it's—I prefer not to—"

"There's one upstairs, too. End of the hall, next to Renard's room."

Score. He'd clearly been worried I would say something regarding feminine needs or unleashing a hell-raising dump in his first-floor facilities. To spare us both the embarrassment of hearing that, he'd offered me an excuse to go exactly where I wanted.

I gave him a quick nod of thanks, then headed up the stairs and quickly went to the end of the second-floor hallway. After turning the water on and closing the door, I slipped into Renard's room.

If I was expecting a typical teenage boy's room, filled with car posters and girls in beach bikinis, I was in for a rude awakening. The room was bare, save for a bed, a small stack of books, and a desk with a gaming laptop—you know, the kind with the multicolored LED lights that make everything look like a disco—on top.

No notes or papers hinted at Renard's location. No phone, either, but that was to be expected—a teenager would be glued to that.

I could just call Edgar and have him set a meeting.

But that would eliminate the element of surprise, and surprise was often crucial for uncovering the truth. Where he kept his soul stash.

And, most critically of all, who his soul reaping supplier was.

I checked under the double bed, finding no arcana kits or souls. I pushed up off the carpet and headed to the small walk-in closet. Nothing but some branded t-shirts, gym shorts, and a few dust-collecting formal clothes on plastic hangers.

After examining his stack of books—mostly bestsellers and genre fare—I was about to give up when the dust jacket accidentally slipped from what I thought had been a copy of *The Hunger Games*. Instead of a young adult megaseller, however, the actual title within was called *Magical Arcana: A Practical Guide to Spellcrafting for Humans*.

I thumbed through the volume, which had crisp pages and surprisingly lively explanations on how to craft everything from a Reaper's Brand—which Edgar had clearly bought—to a Cuirass Shield, which protected the user from attacks to the torso.

There were some high-level spells in here. Ambitious kid. I could see why his old man had thought he was advanced class material. Frankly, he was probably too smart for school. But he was also playing a dangerous game.

I slid the dust jacket back over the book and checked on the laptop. To my surprise, it sprung to life without a password prompt. The computer, unlike his neat room, was an unorganized sea of files. I skimmed over the names, finding a lone spreadsheet named "grades" in all lower case.

It seemed pretty unlikely that a kid on the verge of failing out of school would be slicing and dicing his GPA in Excel to find an untapped edge, so I double clicked the file.

"Jackpot," I whispered, staring at the treasure trove glowing on screen. By the looks of it, Renard had been in business for six months—and making a hefty profit, too. This was despite sizable expenses that, while unlabeled, were likely a result of one important ingredient: souls. There was a master target, which was $100,000. He was already more than three quarters of the way there. I flipped between the sheets, clicking one labeled "schedule."

Bingo.

Tonight, he had a meeting with "Hot Delivery Girl" at

around midnight. That could only mean one thing: the other Reaper. The address was just over the middle of the island, about twenty miles east. That gave me less than an hour to get there.

I skimmed the rest of the schedule for any hints on the Reaper's identity, or where Renard might've been stashing his souls. But all the identifying information was purposely vague.

Smart, in case someone like me came snooping around.

Footsteps creaked in the hall.

I slammed the laptop shut and headed out of the room.

Victor stared at me from the stairwell.

"Emma?" His expression blended confusion and hurt. My first inclination was to dart into the bathroom and jump out the small window. But for some reason, I felt the need to keep the illusion intact, even if it was a dumb, losing effort.

I held up my hands and gave him a rueful grin. "I'm sorry, I know I shouldn't have—"

"That's my son's room."

"I was looking for the paper," I said. "I was...I was going to sign it myself." I looked up at the ceiling, trying to squeeze a few tears out. Nope. Not this time. Hopefully my fake expression of extreme shame would suffice. "I know, it's insane. I crossed the line."

"That's—"

"Unethical? Horrible? I know." I finally brought my gaze down to Victor's face, but then quickly glanced away, like I just couldn't handle his disappointment. "I'll resign. It was—I'm sorry."

Then Victor said somewhat hopefully, "Did you find it?"

I looked up and said in a small voice, "No."

"Well," the beleaguered father said, "you do whatever is necessary to get my boy into your class."

I nodded and started walking toward him, eager to leave.

"Just one thing."

I stopped in my tracks. "What?"

"Turn the water off before you go. It's been a dry summer." He smiled, then returned downstairs.

I cut the water, then left the Martins' house. Up the street, I checked my phone, finding I had about forty-three minutes to reach Renard before his "hot" delivery girl made an appearance.

Hopefully three wouldn't be too much of a crowd.

26

I'D LEFT THE CITY BEHIND MILES AGO, AND MOST OF the scattered country estates and farms had drifted long into the side mirror. I was crossing the line into the proper eastern part of the island, which didn't enjoy nearly the same population density. It was the kind of place to hide when you didn't want to be found.

The kind of place you bought and sold illegal magic.

The Department of Supernatural Affairs would have a shitfit if they found out Renard was selling do-it-yourself magical boosters. Kill him—maybe even his family.

An alarm buzzed on my phone, indicating midnight had arrived. I was still a couple miles from the meeting spot, but I eased off the throttle. Moonlight sliced through the thick forest canopy, painting jagged slivers across the two-lane road.

The trees parted ahead, revealing a small gas station nestled on the road's left-hand side. Rust coated the fifties-era crank pumps. The single-story service shop had more broken windows than visitors.

Of which there appeared to be two.

A silver family station wagon sat parked before one of the pumps. Nearby was a new pickup truck loaded with two wooden crates. A faint light glowed inside the abandoned service station.

I cut the bike's engine completely and guided it into the jungle. Safe from prying eyes, I crept toward the station—so small that it had no garage or parking lot—and glanced into the station wagon's backseat. A black plastic trash bag shaped like a thick stack of bills sat on the passenger's seat. Kid had watched too many gangster flicks.

I peered through the pumps, spotting two people inside the small building. No surprises. The delivery girl wore the same gray bunched up hoodie and sunglasses, making her unidentifiable. Well, not quite—I recognized her as the same person I'd ripped off back at the antiques shop.

The whole hoodie thing might've been a little bit on the nose, but I could dig the reference. Her soft, strained voice explained something to Renard. I stole toward the pickup truck and peeked into its bed. The wooden crates were about the size of the plastic storage bins one might pile up in the closet—no larger than a couple feet square. No logos or distinguishing features marked their exterior.

The conversation stopped, plunging the sticky jungle into silence.

I ducked behind the passenger side of the truck and peered toward the service station.

"Come on." Renard's surprisingly deep voice cut through the night. "I almost got the cash."

A low-pitched reply.

"The guy you work for, he has them. He has my—"

Another inaudible reply.

"Goddamn, you're an ice-cold bitch, you know that?"

A few seconds later, Renard burst through the door. He

was a tall, lanky kid with a well maintained high-top fade and walked with the confidence of someone who had dealt with tough people and come out the other side unscathed. The old station door rattled on its rusty hinges. I plunged behind the truck's wheel well and glanced out from beyond the brake lights.

He slammed his palm against the station wagon's chassis before opening the door. Then, without any transaction taking place, the kid drove away, his high beams tracing over the truck's lift gate.

I held my breath, but he didn't stop. His engine quickly became a distant memory.

I waited, listening to the chattering darkness.

The Reaper's Switch burned a hole in my pocket, begging to be used. It would be easy to solve my competition problem here. But that would just seal my fate with Lucille.

Self-defense I could justify. Maybe.

Murdering the competition over a turf war? That'd be an impossible sell.

No one had any rules against stealing, though.

I pushed myself into the truck's bed with a light metallic thud. The liner felt cool against my skin in the warm night. Wriggling on my belly to keep my head below the bed's walls, I quickly reached the wooden crates.

Up close, I could tell they were poorly constructed. That made my job easier—just flip out the knife and pop. The side of the crate opened, and I eased the wood panel to the bed.

I reached cautiously into the dark interior, feeling needles. Just like the arcana kit Edgar had shown me at the funeral parlor.

I found the second crate to be a similar bust.

Damnit. Tonight had been a failure, quota-wise.

I wondered if it was too late to take Doris's soul when I heard a door groan.

Shit.

The Reaper was returning to her truck.

Torn between making a break for it and staying put, I decided to roll the dice. It stood to reason she had a stash of her own souls. And I needed to know who I was dealing with—even if I had no intention of going through with Aldric's orders to eliminate her.

I pressed myself as flat as possible against the bed liner, my chin touching the cool rubber. I couldn't sense her soul. It must've still been warded.

The woman started the engine without double checking her cargo.

We were going for a little night ride.

27

AFTER DISCOVERING THAT LYING FACE DOWN IN THE truck bed meant absorbing a teeth-rattling shock every time there was a small bump in the road, I'd decided to turn over. My butt still begged for relief as the asphalt devolved into an unmaintained gauntlet of potholes.

The starry night glimmered above in the inky darkness. It was a newer truck, so at least it didn't vomit exhaust. The sweet scent of bananas and orchids drifted through the placid air.

We didn't pass a single car, which meant we were headed further east.

I would've tracked our position, but I had no reception.

Checking the time every few minutes didn't help the ride go quicker. But at least I knew the hour had ticked past one when the truck finally slowed to take a gentle turn.

This road was unpaved dirt, which was not an improvement.

I repeated *only a few more seconds, only a few more seconds* in my mind as the sky disappeared, devoured by the dense jungle canopy. A stifling, humid heat hovered around me as the truck wound its way up the backwoods trail.

Just when I was almost ready to bail, the truck settled to a bouncy stop. My head love-tapped against one of the wooden crates. I held my breath as the driver's side door opened. The bed—save for the two cargo crates—was empty. I wouldn't exactly blend in with the scenery. If my competition looked inside, she'd spot me.

I worked the Reaper's Switch out of my jeans and waited, still not breathing.

The blade snapped out quietly, and I looked at the glimmering edge.

The truck rocked as she jumped into what sounded like thick grass and slammed the door.

This was it.

My neck throbbed from my hammering pulse.

But her footsteps faded in the opposite direction. My breath silently streamed from my nostrils as I snuck a peek over the bed's edge. I caught a glimpse of a gray hoodie disappearing up a narrow foot trail.

Well, I'd come this far. No reason to waste a road trip.

I vaulted over the bed, landing in the soft, tall grass with a faint rustle. After a quick glance into the cab—empty and pristine—I hurried past the Mercedes I'd seen at the antiques shop.

Guess being the island's best Reaper netted you a small fleet of cars. No garage, though.

The dirt trail was well-maintained. She must've come out here often. The darkness made it difficult to see if additional footprints—from a partner or a boss—lined the ground.

After about five minutes of trailing fifty yards behind, I saw the trail open into a small clearing with a small building. One of those tiny homes that had somehow become a thing. The place couldn't have been much more than twelve feet square.

Me, I liked my space, even if I didn't do much with it.

She disappeared into the house without unlocking the door. Out here you didn't really need security. The home was mostly glass inlaid into stainless steel frames. Almost like a miniaturized version of the aesthetic at Black Sea Holdings' HQ. It didn't blend with the jungle, but I didn't think it was trying to.

A light came on, making the entire house glow like a lamp.

I plunged off the trail, firethorn bushes tugging at my bare arms.

What was a little more pain in the name of soul searching, though?

So I gritted my teeth, put my hands in front of my eyes, and cut an oblong path through the thick jungle.

With fifteen feet of brambly jungle still separating me from the structure, I stopped. I could now see that the tiny home was two stories, with a bed in a tall loft space at the top. The downstairs kitchen was littered in health foods, their labels legible through the window.

At the end opposite the entrance, there was what looked like a living room, with some colorfully girly pillows sitting on a small sofa that barely qualified as a loveseat. During my circuitous path through the surrounding jungle, my new friend had disappeared. But then she popped up from behind the cabinets and sink, her naked back turned. The hoodie was finally gone, and I could see that she had the type of platinum blonde hair cascading over her bare shoulders that you only saw in shampoo commercials.

Without turning, she headed to what looked like a small closet, then slipped inside.

It must've actually been a bathroom.

This was my chance.

I waded my way through the thorny mess and stole up the two wooden steps outside. The glass door opened without a sound.

Slipping inside, the smell hit me first. I'd know that hint of vanilla bean anywhere.

Sweet and seductive, like a bakery cake.

My sister's trademark.

28

When the pieces clicked, the truth was so obvious that it seemed like I'd been willfully deceiving myself over the past week.

I'd been killed because I possessed certain traits.

These traits allowed me to be brought back as a Reaper.

Four years ago, I'd begged a rain goddess to revive my sister. It stood to reason that she, too, possessed the same intangible traits that made for a good Reaper.

And it explained why she hadn't shot me in the back after I'd stolen her stash of souls out by the antiques shop.

Sierra clearly knew I lived on the island. Hence the wards and disguise to maintain a low profile.

The shower hummed, steam seeping from beneath the door. A gnawing panic burrowed deep in my gut as I picked up the discarded hoodie. Her car keys jingled inside the pouch, but otherwise nothing.

My fingers traced over the racks of vitamins and protein powders lining the bamboo counters. As obsessed as ever about looking good and staying in shape. But anyone would be, if they looked like Sierra. Ever wondered what it felt like being invisible? Head out to a bar with her in your tightest dress. Pair that experience with a few vodka tonics and watch your self-esteem plummet into oblivion.

I still couldn't sense her soul, so I fanned out over the small house to search for clues about how she'd spent the past four years. Had she come here immediately? Bided her time?

There were no pictures, no journals, not even a laptop for me to browse. Keeping secrets ran in the family, too. Then again, I'd taught my little sister how to skim and grift and cut out without attachment. So this place was straight out of the textbook I'd given her.

Renard had mentioned something about having the money and her employer having something of his. He'd called her an ice-cold bitch.

My gut told me I wouldn't like what Sierra had gotten herself into.

But I'd deal with her later.

I shook sentimentality from my mind and focused: I still needed to deliver the souls tomorrow. Sister or not, Sierra was responsible for my increased quota. The way I saw it, she could spare a couple to help me out of the jam she'd created.

I headed back to the kitchen and flung open the cabinet over the sink. Two neatly labeled jars stared back, with WOLF and DRAGON SHIFTER written on masking tape labels. I pocketed the two souls, feeling the faint shades of their history thrum through my fingertips.

After shutting the cabinet, I looked around for a pen.

The water shut off, so I improvised, grabbing the nearest jar of chocolate-vanilla hemp powder.

I dumped the greenish-brown substance on the counter.

In the mess, I wrote a very clear and concise message.

Fuck you.

The bathroom door opened. My sister's bare foot edged out.

I grabbed the gray hoodie, the keys jangling inside.

Then I ran, her shriek of surprise swallowed by the slamming glass door and the sweltering, humid chatter of the uncharted jungle.

29

You know what they say.

Those who visit glass houses shouldn't throw stones.

But I couldn't help being angry. Discovering that Sierra had caused much of my recent misery was like a haymaker right to an already bruised gut.

I tried to convince myself that she didn't know she'd been hurting me.

But it didn't help, because I didn't believe it.

After leaving her pickup truck at the abandoned gas station, I retrieved my bike. The two stolen souls—and an arcana kit from one of the crates—rattled in the hoodie's pouch all the way home. While I'd reached my elusive quota, I couldn't help but feel this week had cost me part of *my* soul.

A long, dreary trek up the beach and a quarter bottle of whiskey later, and I was mercifully out on the couch, wholly unequipped to handle the pressing issues in my life. And so, a brutal Friday morning rolled around with nothing in the way of concrete progress, as far as the case was concerned. I was rich in circumstantial evidence, rich in suspects—including Dante Cross, who still topped the list by a margin—but poor in verifiable proof.

That was a big problem, since my court date would rear its ugly head soon.

Khan woke me with a snarl.

It'd been a long night and a short sleep, and my body protested the unceremonious awakening.

"Go away," I said, eyes thick with crust. I tapped my phone.

The display indicated it was a little past seven.

"The dumb human is outside."

"That's incredibly unhelpful." Khan ranted about human stupidity all the time, from what I'd gathered since Tuesday. That, and the national debt, people trying to bring back communism, and the silliness of reality television.

"The fool you call Cross, who failed to ascertain the obvious fact I was alive in the cellar."

"Maybe he just didn't care."

"Then I will call animal services on him." The cat's ice blue eyes narrowed into fierce slits, the white fur on his nose bunching up.

"Just be sure to start with the fact you're a cat." I swung my feet onto the unfinished bamboo floor, which was already taking a beating from Khan's dagger-like claws. "They'll definitely take you more seriously after that."

Khan hissed before prancing away with his tail high in the air, lamenting his fate of having such a dunce for a master. The dislike was mutual.

I headed to the door in my underwear and let Cross inside.

"*Hey,*" he said, giving me a funny look, his British accent ever so slightly suggestive.

"Oh, like you haven't seen it before."

"Not looking that good."

"Spare me the pick-up lines and tell me why you came."

"You don't write. You don't call." Cross leaned against the doorframe, an easy smile on his lips. "So I figured I'd come see you."

"I'm busy." I went to close the door, but he didn't move.

"You'll want to hear this."

"I highly doubt that," I said. The last few days had been frustratingly devoid of good news.

I knew who had stolen Aldric's gold.

I knew who the rival Reaper was.

But I couldn't turn either of them over to Aldric.

And I still didn't know who had set me up. Other than the fact that all the evidence pointed to the confident jackass standing right in front of me.

Cross extracted a piece of folded parchment from his pocket. "This is good."

"Still don't care."

"What if I told you it might help with the case?"

"Unless you came to confess, I don't see how you could help."

Understanding flooded Cross's golden-flecked brown eyes, and he ran his fingers through his messy hair as he stepped back. His designer stubble glimmered as he smiled.

"I was wondering why you stopped talking to me." His slender shoulders loosened beneath his t-shirt. "Here I was thinking it was something I said."

"Nope," I said, eyes narrowed into deadly slits. "Just something you did."

"And tell me what you think I did, Eden."

"Killed Roan for his share of the gold. Then called James to plant the gun and frame me for it."

A look of surprise flashed across his handsome features.

He wasn't a great liar, so I was inclined to believe him.

Nonetheless, the available evidence suggested that I shouldn't.

"Interesting theory." Cross paced over the small marble porch. "And what's my motive?"

"Greed," I said.

"A timeless classic," Cross said. "And why would I allow the cat to save you from the snake's bite? Or battle the demon at my door alone?"

"You didn't battle him alone," I said.

"But I tried." Cross winked and smiled. "Let's say I have motive to kill Roan Kelly. Why pin it on you?"

"Opportunity," I said. "Convenience."

"Seems more...personal, doesn't it?"

"Maybe, maybe not."

"Tell me something, Eden." Cross stopped pacing and stood stock still. "Who the hell is James?"

"The guy who planted the gun."

"Oh, well, in that case." He gave me an easy, sarcastic shrug and reached into his pocket. He tossed his cell phone to me and I snagged the device out of the air. "Check it."

I scanned his call log. No calls to unknown numbers—a bunch of unanswered ones to me, some completed ones to the rest of the gold heist crew, including Roan prior to his death. Hardly conclusive, but not damning, either.

"You could've deleted the call. Called him from a payphone. Landline."

"Sounds like you have it all figured out." Cross looked genuinely annoyed, which I had thought was impossible. He glared at the gentle waves breaking offshore. "Of course, even if I did call this James to clean up my mess, there's another problem."

"That is?"

"I'd have to kill Doris, Magnus, Rayna, and Zoe, too. Cutting a score five ways isn't that much better than six, you know. And since I'm super greedy, I wouldn't stop at one murder."

"Well it's only four, since Doris bit it," I said. "Maybe you killed her, too, come to think of it."

Not sure what game I was playing. If he was the killer, I didn't exactly have backup waiting in the wings.

I suspected that the mayor had been responsible for Doris, anyway. Someone had tried to remove her head, but been interrupted. I only knew one sick jackass maintaining a trophy shelf of skulls.

"You shouldn't be so quick to accuse."

"I've sensed your soul."

Darkness flooded his pleasant face. "Then maybe you shouldn't jerk my chain."

"I'm right here, tough guy."

Cross shook his head, but didn't come after me.

"I had no reason to frame you, Eden Hunter." The immortal treasure hunter sighed bitterly. Who knew he could look so serious and angry? "Because we need you."

"For what?"

"For what I came here to show you." Cross waved the parchment and let out a mirthless laugh. "Roan was coming here to talk. Apologize. Ask for your help. But after he died, we all agreed that it would probably take a more roundabout approach to bring you into the group."

"Hence your little con," I said, recalling the sequence of events that had dumped me at Happy Paws' crumbling steps. Put the mark in a cage, offer her no way out, then corral her along the only path that felt safe.

"And if we still need you," Cross said, his golden-flecked eyes homing in on me, *through* me, focused with all the energy in his being, "why in the name of *fuck* would I want you in jail?"

"I don't know," I said, not ready to concede the point. "Why would Rayna be such a hardass?"

"Because that's Rayna," Cross said.

"I'd hate to see what she did to her enemies, then," I said under my breath.

"This was from Jack." Cross held out the parchment. "It's why we stole the thirteen million from Aldric. And it's why we need your help."

"What is it?" I asked, getting to the point. If I stood any longer in the doorway in my underwear, I was liable to get sunburned. Time to wrap this up or slam the door in his face.

"A glyph-cipher to Sir Francis Drake's greatest treasure." His sun-bleached brown hair rustled in the gentle sea breeze. "Decrypted by the world's best cipher-sorceress for a cool thirteen million in gold. Give or take."

There was Sir Francis Drake again. I had to admit to skepticism regarding the veracity of the rumors. But the presence of an actual treasure map piqued my curiosity.

"What do you need from me?" I asked.

"We need your help digging up the treasure."

"Get a shovel," I said.

"It's a little more complicated than that," Cross said with an easy smile.

I should have known better than to trust a treasure hunter's word. Especially someone who had taken the soul of a family member or lover in his quest for immortality— which Cross must have done to survive this long. But, somehow, his words seemed genuine.

At the very least, if I headed out with Cross, I could gather more information on him. Maybe find a piece of evidence that would definitively link him to Roan's shooting.

Not optimal, but I didn't exactly have good leads knocking down my door.

I said, "I need to get ready."

"No one would mind if you went out like that."

I rolled my eyes, nodded for him to come inside, then headed upstairs.

So this was what desperation looked like: Fresh out of leads and following my best suspect. Just great. After a quick shower, I scrambled into my jeans and a plain t-shirt. Downstairs, I could hear him giving Khan a hard time about the historical significance of tobacco farming. The cat was of the opinion that it was a blight on the planet, while Cross —I assumed humorously—was extolling its unmatched population-culling virtues.

As I padded down the clear glass steps, the cat leapt at Cross's face. The treasure hunter deftly sidestepped the attempted attack. The cat waltzed off, huffing to himself once more about imbecilic humans.

I headed to the kitchen and put on the electric kettle.

"Well, he's certainly charming," Cross said.

"You can always have him back."

"I couldn't bear to shatter the bond you two have developed."

I stuck out my tongue as the electric kettle ejected steam. After retrieving one of the few mugs I owned from the otherwise threadbare cupboard, I poured the hot water into the cup and pushed the plastic jar of instant coffee across the polished limestone.

"This would be considered cruel and unusual punishment on a pirate ship," Cross said.

"Suit yourself." I spooned out a large, heaping mound of

brown powder into the hot water. A quick stir later, and I was enjoying the burnt taste of battery acid.

"You can't possibly like this stuff."

"It does the trick," I said, not answering the actual question. "You mentioned something about Jack giving you Drake's map." I looked at him with suspicion over the steaming mug. "You have three minutes."

"I've already been here for half an—"

"Two minutes."

Cross's golden-flecked eyes twinkled. "Well, you know I've been around for a while."

"Clock's ticking." I took a long, bitter sip and glanced about the empty kitchen with feigned disinterest.

"Fine, Eden." Cross leaned his tanned elbows against the kitchen island, trying to catch my eye. I wouldn't let him. "As I said before, I located Drake's map and—"

"Good for you."

"The biggest find of the century, and that's all you can say?"

"Maybe you'll get your picture in the local paper." I finished the coffee, feeling the caffeine start to buzz through my body.

"I don't think you heard me."

"Nope, heard you fine. You're trying to turn thirteen million in gold into a few hundred million."

"That's not what Drake's treasure was," Cross said with a dismissive snort. "You think this is about money?" Realization flashed in his golden-flecked eyes. "You're still not convinced I didn't kill—"

"Treasure hunters tend to be greedy."

"It's never been about money. It's about the thrill."

Truer words had never been spoken.

Cross and I shared that primal, unquenchable thirst for

adrenaline. Sure, we went about it in different ways. I rolled the dice when the odds looked favorable—or so I told myself, at least. He dove into the swashbuckling fray.

But the end result was the same: living on the edge to chase that elusive feeling of being alive.

I stared at the brown puddle at the bottom of my cup, and decided it was now or never.

The dregs of the coffee lingered on my tongue as I considered how to frame the question.

"Who else knew Roan was going to be here to...patch things up?"

I was almost thankful he'd died. That conversation would've been awkward—*hey, babe, remember when you and your sister died? That was on me. Surprise! At least I banked a couple mil for it, though, right?*

And if that conversation *had* actually gone down, I might've wound up murdering him.

For real.

"The crew," Cross said. "But Zoe, Magnus, Rayna—they're all solid."

"Anyone else you can think of?"

"Roan had to make a stop beforehand."

"Where?"

"I figured he was getting a drink," Cross said. "Man sounded nervous. Considering...well, that made sense."

"You mean considering he basically killed me."

"If you want to look at it that way."

There wasn't really another way to look at it.

"Tell me what my role is." I walked around the kitchen island. "Otherwise you can leave."

"That's simple, Eden. You can talk to goddesses."

And my blood turned to ice as I realized my secret wasn't much of a secret at all.

Number of people I thought knew about me and the rain goddess at the start of the week: one extremely creepy mayor. Number of people who *actually* knew, circa Friday: unknown. Could've been damn near everyone. I envisioned people running roughshod through the streets, sacrificing small woodland creatures on car hoods as they implored the gods to answer their prayers.

Like everything else that had gone wrong over the past few days, I doubt the rain goddess would take *it wasn't my fault* as an explanation if she suddenly became a household name.

"Looking a little pale. Too fast?"

"Not the issue."

"Then why so sad, Eden Hunter?" Cross's messy sun-bleached hair streamed in the warm late summer breeze. "Treasure hunts are supposed to be fun."

"Will anyone else be joining us?"

"Just you and me, babe."

"It's a date, then."

Sun kissed off the car's bright white paint, which might

have made the excursion romantic under the right circumstances.

These were not the right circumstances, despite the breathtaking scenery and fresh smell of sea salt lingering on the clean air.

Cross accelerated along the winding road, oblivious to the dangers that might befall someone who hadn't made an immortal Faustian bargain.

Glad one of us felt comfortable enough to let loose.

Because, over here, I was shitting my pants.

Him knowing my secret was worse than him being the murderer. Much worse.

Plus, Cross had his own unspoken history with Lucille and the DSA, which made me even more nervous.

Did he want amnesty? A favor?

Too many unanswered questions bounced around in my skull, with not enough information to put the pieces together.

Time ran together in a blur of banana trees, orchids, and dense green foliage, and soon I realized the car was gliding to a gentle stop. The GPS beeped, indicating we'd reached our destination.

A humid heat settled over the car. We were in the deep rainforest, miles from civilization.

Birds chirped in the sunny jungle, making the dense forest seem almost inviting. Someone had tried to turn this place into a tourist attraction at some point.

What a con. At least the faded signs told me no one had bought it.

For good reason. The Boundless Jungle was a wilderness even Aldric's men avoided—and just the place for an explorer looking to hide a stash might go.

Cross cut the engine.

"Ready?" His hand snapped the chrome door handle.

"Not really." I remained glued to my seat, staring at the trees. The Boundless Jungle had been so named because the trees grew into the ocean for miles. No soil, no land—just an endless grove of tropical trees stretching into the aquamarine waters. Don't ask me how it was possible. Scientifically, it wasn't. But magic had funny ways of rendering science moot.

The Reaper's Switch dug into my leg next to the burner phone. Other than some cash, I was on my own out here. Then again, I'd chosen to come along.

Some plan, Eden.

Cross slipped out of the convertible and swung his head back over the side. His gold-flecked eyes sparkled. "If we're going to work together, you really need to trust me."

"It'd be easier to trust you if I knew just what the hell was going on out here."

"I told you," Cross said with an easy smile. "I inherited a glyph-cipher from Jack, and you can talk to goddesses."

"Allegedly."

The treasure hunter pulled out a piece of paper and offered it to me, much too white to be the ancient treasure map. I took the paper from him. Its touch and smell suggested it was modern.

"What's this?" From what I could tell, it was simply a plain white 8 x 11 sheet, same as you'd buy in five-hundred stack reams at your local Office Max.

"Just shake it so we can get moving."

I shook the sheet, and—like a novelty 8-ball—sharp text dissolved into focus. It was enchanted, albeit not identically to the message I'd received near FBI headquarters. This one was animated, with scrollable text. A magical iPad, of sorts. The text hovered over the white sheet, along with an image.

A young, brown haired woman stared back, her lips puckered in a frown.

This was my file.

The FBI's file on me, more specifically—everything they had. Which was *a lot* more than I'd anticipated. It was marked FOR EYES ONLY and stamped with the highest level of clearance. Didn't know I was that interesting.

Or that the FBI knew that much about magic. This file was some pretty high-level arcana.

"Why do you think the FBI came here, Eden?" Cross said.

"Aldric."

"You." Cross pointed a finger at me to drive the point home. "They found this place because they were looking for you."

I would have been flattered, but instead I couldn't breathe. Words popped out from the page: skilled con woman.

Pathological liar.

Believes herself Robin Hood.

Revived from the dead.

An image flashed by—the crime scene photo Rayna had shown me at The Loaded Gun. My body, lifeless and bloodied, lying in that Bourbon Street alley.

An audio recording was embedded on the next page, beneath a header that said ATHEAS. I tapped it. My voice, scared and shaky, crackled through the warm summer air.

"Mom? Mom, if you're there...I know it's been awhile. It's me, Mom. I'm sorry. I shouldn't have called—"

That was how the FBI had known I was alive. One call to my Mom back in Chicago, four years ago. She hadn't answered, but the phone must've been tapped.

I'd been a hot commodity even before I'd returned from the dead.

I swiped past, and more words flooded through. Reaper. Works for the local warlord. Lives alone. Highly effective. And then the next to last line: is the only one the gods have answered.

It was difficult to explain *why* word of Lucille's true identity and presence on Earth would be so bad. Everyone would rejoice, right? After all, it meant we weren't alone. Wrong. All the people who had their beliefs threatened would melt down. The pitchforks—or, more likely, the nukes—would come out. Civilization's illusory calm would break apart. And then we'd all be living underground, eating canned tuna and stale crackers until the end of days.

There was that other part, too. Remember what they did to Joan of Arc? Not that I was comparing myself to a legend—although according to the FBI's psycho-forensics, I had delusions of being Robin Hood. I'm just saying. She started hearing the voice of God, everyone rallied behind her, then they all decided she needed to check the fuck out. One large burning pyre later, and she was ash and bone.

No thanks.

My fingers were shaking, and I almost dropped the enchanted paper onto the floor mat as I swiped to the final page. This one was the stunner. Just two words, bold as anything.

Recruit immediately.

The spell dissolved from the paper, rendering it blank. I tried to breathe, but it was a slow, hitchy affair.

Finally, I said, "Who gave you this?"

"Rayna," Cross replied with an easy smile. "Lighten up. She was doing you a favor."

"Some favor. Why the hell would she work with someone like you anyway?"

I hadn't really figured that part of the puzzle out yet.

"Because Drake's treasure is important," the immortal man said cryptically. "Rayna knows what's at stake."

"And what's at stake?"

"It's best if I show you."

"No," I said. "You tell me now."

Cross leaned against the door and stretched. The sunlight glinted off his handsome stubble. "You're going to think it's crazy."

"Try me."

"We're going to kill Lucille."

I stared at him, waiting for the punchline.

It didn't come. After a long pause, I shrugged.

Why not? Dying a horrible death would solve all my problems immediately.

And death was a damn near certainty when one decided to take up arms against a vengeful rain goddess.

"What'd she do to you, anyway?" I finally asked.

"She made me the man I am today." His features darkened in the perfect light.

"Fine, I'll play," I said, stepping out of the convertible into the gravel lot.

Wildlife chattered in the background of the remote forest. A crisp waterfall crackled over rocks, hidden within the vast foliage. The noises swirled to crescendo as I took everything in.

As places to die went, I guess it wouldn't be bad.

Cross headed to the trunk and slid in the key. He tossed a shovel on the ground, followed by a rope. Hopefully he wasn't about to reveal himself as the mayor's accomplice.

Trying to kill a goddess? Sure, whatever.

Headhunting for a trophy shelf? Hard pass.

"Almost done," the treasure hunter said. A revolver tumbled to the ground next to the other supplies. The murder kit was capped off by a couple large bottles of water. Cross slammed glanced between the pile and me. "Looks a little suspicious, huh?"

"You're gonna kill a goddess with a couple lead bullets and a rope?" I kicked one of the water bottles. "Good plan."

"All will become clear." Without explanation, Cross flicked a coin at me.

The coin told its story in tarnished pockmarks and grime. Unlike a modern coin, its edges were misshapen and uneven, without the little ridges one takes for granted. This made the metal surprisingly smooth, despite its imperfectly circular shape. If I had to guess, it was pure gold, but the dirt made it difficult to tell. The figure once gracing its front had been worn away by the sands of time. It thrummed with a potent magical energy that I could feel but couldn't identify.

The centuries-old obsession with Drake's fortune made a lot more sense, now. Maybe I should've looked into the legends. But digging holes in the ground to look for wooden chests had never been my bag.

"What is this?" I held the gold up to the light. The sun knifing through the trees shone off it so brightly that I had to squint.

"Just a tiny slice of what lies within that jungle."

Cross froze as he stooped to gather the supplies. Not the way you do when you hear a sudden noise—the kind of freezing where your body shakes and your breathing slows.

No—he *stopped* in place, as if someone had pressed the pause button on his life.

I dropped behind the sports car and held my breath, listening to the sounds of the jungle.

"E-Eden." Cross's sounded like he was forcing the words out by sheer will. "The—the coin."

I stared at the small piece of treasure in my palm, unsure how it would help. Then I heard another voice—a melodious one that I hadn't heard in a long time.

"We finally meet again, Dante."

Lucille. The rain goddess. I felt the Reaper's Switch thrum in my pocket, which it only did when powerful beings were around.

That had happened only once before: when I had met Lucille on the black sand beach four years ago. I hadn't seen her since.

I wasn't excited about having a reunion.

I scrambled to the car's trunk, where Cross was half hunched over. His eyes slowly turned toward me. I placed the coin in his open palm, and he tumbled to the gravel like a sculpture.

"Is this about the dead demon?" I dove back to the passenger side for cover.

"Tell you later." Cross snatched the revolver off the ground. A wind spell buffeted the car as he joined me. "You'd think she'd let it go after four hundred years."

Then, before I could ask another question, the immortal treasure hunter sprinted into the jungle.

Leaving me no choice but to follow him into the wilderness.

31

Ah yes, precisely how I liked my Friday mornings: getting caught up in four-hundred-year-old feuds. I was in a similar boat, having also broken a promise to Lucille by killing that wolf. If the shaking forest around us and the blackening sky were any indication, she was what you might call volatile. There was no escaping her wrath. Period.

No matter. Being discovered was no longer the immediate concern. Mere survival was.

An animated tree root snaked at my legs as I sprinted up the scenic path. I leapt over it, narrowly missing its tentacle-like grasp. A bird dive bombed from the dense canopy, but Cross smoked it with a well-placed revolver shot.

Instead of blood, it disintegrated into a puff of black ash. Thunder and lightning crackled in the blustery air as we sprinted for the summit. The waterfall's pounding roar flooded my ears. I caught glimpses of the massive chasm separating us from the other side of the forest through the gaps in the trees. The river frothed hundreds of feet below.

"Duck!" Cross fired another shot. An inhuman howl of pain erupted behind us. With all the adrenaline, and the mélange of creatures trying to kill us, it was difficult to sense its soul.

I sprinted ahead of Cross, spurred onward by cold fear.

The thick forest hummed with a dark energy as we emerged at the incline's top. Calling it a mountain would have been generous, but the vantage point offered us a good view of the surrounding area. To the east, the Boundless Jungle stretched into the ocean for miles, the trees seemingly floating in the water. To the south, beyond the forest, was nothing but aquamarine water and ominous looking skies.

We were at the end of the island, and seemingly the world.

The rocky plateau terminated at a steep waterfall that dropped into a wide, churning river. No conveniently placed rope bridges offered us safe passage across. This was not a place for faint-hearted tourists. Precisely why Drake had hidden his treasure here.

I crept up to the plateau's edge and stared into the foaming water below. We had to be two or three hundred feet up at least. There would be no movie-esque leaps into the cascading falls to save ourselves. A rumbling growl shook the forest and the sky turned a darker shade of gray.

Lucille's voice rode on the wind. "I will collect what I am owed, Dante."

"I don't think she likes you very much," I said, trying to sound chipper in the face of certain death. When I turned around to see how Cross was taking things, however, I found him absent. As in, disappeared.

My heart promptly tried to escape through my throat. In a panic, I rushed back toward the forest, only to meet a shadowy creature emerging from the densely packed trees.

As it came into the light, I recognized it: a gorgon, snakes wriggling within her demonic hair.

The DSA would employ just about anyone, apparently.

The beast roared, trying to fix its stony gaze on me. Fortunately, it was a glacially slow creature, otherwise I'd have been toast. I darted back up the rocky plateau where I was trapped with nowhere to go. Now in full-blown shit-my-pants crisis mode, my first instinct was to sprint right into the waterfall. Better than being a lawn statue for the rest of my life.

The gorgon brayed behind me as I crept toward the edge again and closed my eyes tight. The sound of the churning sea washed over me, becoming part of my very being. It seemed to call to me.

"Eden. *Eden.*"

"I'm ready," I said to the crashing water.

"Jump, goddamnit."

It wasn't the waterfall.

It was Cross.

My eyes flashed open, and I saw his fingers waving out from the plunging water.

I didn't ask how. Today wasn't the day for that.

I just jumped, water surging around me as the forest behind me screamed.

32

I HIT THE SLICK GROUND AND ALMOST PITCHED FACE first into the rock face. Cross's strong forearm prevented me from sliding farther. I wanted to collapse into him, but my pride and annoyance both demanded that I push away immediately. As I caught my breath, I peered beyond the cascading water, into the air.

"Did the creatures see you, Eden?"

"I didn't see them reach the plateau."

"That doesn't mean they didn't see you."

"Let's assume they did," I said. "Then what?"

"Then we need to hurry." Cross scratched his head and narrowed his eyes, like he was calculating the best route forward. The revolver was tucked into his pants, its shiny finish coated by a fine mist. As for me, I was intact—although my jeans and low tops were soaked through.

He opened his hand, revealing a thin trickle of blood. The coin had made an indent in his flesh from gripping it too hard. For whatever reason, he'd clung to it the entire chase.

But that wasn't what concerned me.

"Why's it glowing?" And I didn't just mean the coin. An amber glow raced through his fingers, snaking up to his wrist before dying out. If our would-be killers in the forest had me concerned, this was on a whole different level.

"Incredible," Cross said, closing his fist and holding it up to his face in fascination.

"That's a matter of opinion." I watched as the light pulsed, casting a glow across the wall. There was an etching carved into the wet rock—unmistakably human. A treasure hunter's mark that was as clear a sign as any that Drake had been here long ago. Cross leaned in to examine the marking, but the light suddenly went out, plunging us into relative darkness.

"Seems like you have the magic touch," I said. "Congratulations."

Above the din of the waterfall came a furious burst of shouts and roars. Neither Lucille's minions—nor, presumably, the goddess herself—had given up the pursuit. It would be only a matter of time before they either found our hiding spot, or spread out in the jungle to surprise us when we emerged from hiding.

Cross snapped out of his awestruck state like a bell had been struck next to his ear. "Come with me."

His hand locked firmly around mine. I accepted his lead without question or snark, and we descended into the wet cave, wending our way through the narrow passages. Given the shadowy dimness, it was difficult to tell whether the passageway had been cut right into the cliff face, or if it was a natural formation. Either way, it made for a perfect hiding spot.

"What do you owe her, exactly?" I asked.

"You aren't the only one who has gained favors from goddesses, Eden."

"And here I thought I was special."

"But you're the only who she might still listen to." Cross pulled me a little harder around one corner. I was about to protest, but then I felt the *whoosh* of nothingness at my side, and realized that he'd guided me away from a black abyss.

"Why me?"

"Because you haven't crossed her yet."

"I wouldn't be so sure," I said.

"Then you'd better pray for forgiveness." Cross let the words die in the darkness before completing the thought. "Because she's more of a...devil."

"Like make a deal with the devil?" I pressed a little tighter against him, despite my ego's reservations. Pride could wait until after survival. His shoulders were taut, and his damp skin was cold from the churning falls. He didn't acknowledge the shift in our arrangement, just kept pressing on.

"That would be the one." I imagined him grinning with that devil-may-care cool in the darkness. "And you fail her trials at your own peril."

"What was your deal?"

"Can't tell you all my secrets," Cross said, his voice hinting at all the scary things his words left unsaid. "I need a few for myself."

"Don't we all?"

"Well, I know all yours."

Right. The FBI file. Here I'd been so concerned about my secrets getting out, and they'd all been lurking on some government mainframe for who knew how long.

"Probably not all of them," I said with a slight edge.

"Naughty girl." Cocky bastard. Five hundred years was plenty of time to cultivate a winning personality—or at least the outer appearance of one. "Stop here."

I rammed into his back, feeling his chest rise with mine in the darkness. It was so silent that I could hear the water droplets trickle off my hair onto the stone. I felt him raise his arm slowly, so as not to hit me. Then Cross snapped his fingers twice. A ring of lights instantly sprung on before us, illuminating a narrow walkway spanning a long chasm. On the other side, a room literally glittered.

"Thought this was your first time here," I said.

"Poetic license," Cross replied. "You think I'd crack the glyph-cipher and not check it out?"

"You could've just told me the truth."

"But the lie is more fun." I could hear the grin in his voice, even though his back was turned. "I hope you're not afraid of heights, Eden."

"Just don't fall, jackass. The directions out of this place are in your jeans."

He laughed, and I followed him over to the fortune lurking on the other side. Not falling to my death was a plus, although heights had never bothered me. The magical lanterns above the walkway snuffed themselves out as soon as we entered the treasure room. Drake's secret stash filled the large grotto. The room had to be at least twenty feet square—well, as square as a cave could get—and it was *covered* in treasure. It was like the archives of the most unbelievable museum on Earth. Glowing vases and glittering spoils were stacked right up to the rocky ceiling.

"Why the hell did we need shovels if everything's already here?" Not that we'd had the chance to bring them.

"Touch something." Cross had disappeared behind a row of golden spears taller than me.

I did so, feeling the cool metal. "It's gold."

"Exactly."

"Not sure I follow, buddy." My feet squished in the soft

dirt, as I walked around the glittering golden spears. They, like everything else in the room, were undeniably real: no illusion magic was turning lead into gold. The perfect spears seemed almost hypnotic, calling out from another age. The collection had to be worth hundreds of millions—if one were being conservative. I stared at Cross, who was digging a hole near the craggy wall.

"Gold is hardly worth the risk we took." Cross held an ancient piece of parchment high above his head. I realized he was holding the glyph-cipher out for me. "And to think, at one point, it was my only god."

"Had a religious conversion?"

"Not quite," Cross said cryptically. "But that's a story for another time."

So much for hunting down this treasure just for "thrills."

His shoulders tensed as voices snaked their way through the narrow rock hallways. The treasure hunter gestured silently with his head, imploring me to follow him. At the back of the room, which seemed to dead-end, he swept away the mounds of treasure—goblets, chains, even scrolls gilded in precious metals and jewels—and ran his hands methodically along the rough wall. The voices grew louder, mixing with the feral roars of creatures from the depths.

"Oh, dearest little Dante, you cannot escape your trial, try as you have all these centuries." The natural reverb of the caves granted Lucille's melodious voice a godly tenor, which made my already rampant nerves kick into overdrive.

Cross, for his part, remained unperturbed by her threats, continuing to trace over the rock with his fingers. Finally, there was a slight *click*, and the wall shifted. A small gap led to the center of the earth. On the other side was another passageway.

"Step over," Cross said, offering his hand.

"You know the way. You go first."

"It's easier if you do," Cross said. He tapped the parchment and handed me the magical coin. "Since you're good at keeping track of important things."

I stepped over the small hole and slipped into the crevice. A faint glow appeared on the wall above my head, an ancient enchantment lighting the way.

I turned back to Cross. "Let's go."

He smiled, but it was forced. His eyes were moving slowly, like he'd been frozen. I realized then, in horror, that the coin had been counteracting whatever spell Lucille had cast on him. "I'll see you in another life, Eden."

Then, with the last of his willpower, his fingers pressed the hidden switch, and the rock began to groan shut. He tossed the revolver in the narrow opening, and the gun bounced against my feet.

"Why?"

"Because four centuries is too long to run."

Then the rock face slammed shut, leaving me all alone.

33

SOMETIMES YOU FEEL SO TRAPPED YOU WANNA SCREAM.

Sometimes you are trapped, and you scream, and no one answers.

I was getting that feeling a lot this week.

I slammed my fists against the wall and screamed until my voice was raw, but nothing responded beyond my own frantic echoes. The false wall didn't open, nor could I get a response from the other side. Hands bruised, I finally abandoned my futile efforts. After examining Cross's glyph-cipher, I found that it was still uncracked. A glyph-cipher was just a magical enchantment—like password encryption for vellum and paper. That meant this one wasn't the map he'd inherited from Jack, but a new one he'd removed from the treasure vault.

Wherever it led, I was now its steward. I slipped it into my back pocket, then I reached down to grab the revolver. Upon checking the chamber in the dim light, I found it had one bullet remaining. Delightful.

It dawned on me, in the dark, that it was strange that I could touch *this* weapon. All others were off limits. Even some kitchen knives gave me trouble, blistering my hands like the utensils were hot coals mined from an active volcano. But I held the gun's damp rubber grip without any issue at all.

Then there was the magical coin. I stared at the small, misshapen piece of metal in the dim glow of the narrow tunnel. Nothing suggested that it was extraordinary, least of all its appearance. But it had allowed Cross to counteract Lucille's powerful magic. It must have been doing the same for me, allowing me to violate the terms of our agreement.

I put the coin in my pocket, but quickly discovered that the gun felt like hot lava in my fingers. It clattered to the ground at my feet, and I cursed. Apparently, I needed to be in contact with the metal. After waving my hand in the air for a few moments—luckily I hadn't held on long enough to get burned badly—I dug the coin out and picked up the revolver. I hadn't gotten a close look at it before Lucille had ambushed us, but I could see now that it was a .45.

So much for clearing Dante Cross as a suspect.

It would have been nice if I could've crossed *someone* off the damn list. No, it wasn't the murder weapon, but everyone in Cross's crew seemed to favor the exact same caliber of gun. Maybe that was pure coincidence, maybe not. Even though he'd saved my ass twice, now, I needed to keep my guard up. Everything could just be leading to a grand finale.

I slipped the revolver into my jeans along with the coin. The firearm didn't burn me through the denim, which worked for me. Then I yanked out the burner and turned it on.

No service, just as I'd expected.

Maybe if I got out of this passage, though, I could call for help.

After pocketing the phone, I headed the only way I could: forward. If our path through the caverns had been narrow before, here it was tight enough to feel my own breath deflected back at me off the wall.

The path had few curves. The magical light eventually sputtered into a faint flicker as the passage narrowed further. I had to shift my body horizontally to continue, my knees scraping the opposite wall as I crab walked to freedom. Faint sounds of nature—birds, rushing water, the wind—drifted past. I accelerated my sideways shuffle to its top speed, ankles awkwardly banging together as I sought to escape the claustrophobia.

I emerged at the hill's bottom, judging by the trickling rush of the river nearby. The crash of the waterfall was distant, further up the cliffs. Upon stumbling into a small clearing where the light sliced through the trees, a euphoric relief flooded through my veins. This *was* paradise. I took a few steps forward, into the unmarked jungle brush, then craned my neck backward. The entrance to the hidden tunnel looked like little more than a crag in a sheer cliff face. Impossible to spot unless you knew where it came out. Even then, utterly useless, since it was a one-way trip.

Before I could celebrate my daring escape, the Reaper's Switch thrummed against my leg.

Panic coursed through my body.

Lucille was lurking close by.

I swallowed, finding my throat drier than a Saharan drought, and swept my gaze over the dense foliage. There was no trail. While what Cross and I had sprinted up earlier hardly qualified, it looked positively tame compared to the dense overgrowth stretching out before me now.

A branch cracked.

I pulled out the Reaper's Switch and spun around,

heart pounding wildly. But I saw nothing in the infinite jungle.

I waited, but nothing moved in the dense foliage.

Still gripping the knife tightly, I glanced at the sun through the gaps in the branches, trying to estimate the time. From the position, it looked like it was a little before noon.

Aldric would be expecting delivery of his souls soon—that, and the rival Reaper. Oh, and the gold thieves, too. With no way out of the Boundless Jungle, though, I wouldn't have to worry about him skinning me alive for failing to perform. The burbling river gave me an idea, though. It likely flowed into the ocean. And if I found the ocean, that meant I'd find the coastline. And, where there was beach, there were inevitably people.

I oriented myself toward the sound of rushing water, took a deep breath, then plunged into the wilderness. Brambles tore at my jeans. I stifled a huge *fuck* as I tripped. Sweeping my hand out along the moist ground as far as I could, my knuckles touched something cool and smooth.

A skull grinned back at me, a fern growing between its missing front teeth.

Well, if I died out here, at least I'd have company.

I pushed myself up and ran toward the rushing water. The river wasn't far, now, from the sound. With any luck, I'd be out of this treasure hunter's hellhole and back in the city before sunset. What I'd tell Aldric at that point, I had no idea.

I emerged from the dense jungle and breathed a sigh of relief when I saw the wide river. It was short lived.

"Hello, Eden," Lucille called from across the river. "You are more predictable than I thought." My skin went cold despite the sweltering humidity. The Reaper's Switch vibrated like it was trying to squirm from my grip altogether. I watched as the colorful leaves parted and the goddess emerged alone. Her flowing see-through blouse was unaffected by the various sticks and prickly bushes. Enchanted with a demonic magic, no doubt. Last time I'd seen her, she'd just been naked. Without her minions lurking, I could taste Lucille's soul. Unlike our first meeting, she wasn't bothering to hide it in a semi-sweet veneer. It tasted like ash and the shittiest bourbon imaginable. Pure bitterness and destruction.

And more than enough power to knock me on my ass. Her strength exceeded even Aldric's. He'd never made the Switch so much as buzz.

I pretended to act casually as the tall woman prepared to sit on the mossy forest floor. Lucille could assume a more ethereal form, or so she claimed, but visited me in human form for "convenience's sake." Convenient for whom was anyone's guess.

The woman finally sat cross-legged near the edge of the river, sunlight slicing across the straight, straw-colored braid that hung to her waist. It swished back and forth like a jungle cat's tail. If she had been walking by in the supermarket, you wouldn't notice her, other than her height. Lucille was plain, her features instantly forgettable. Perhaps that was the point: to slip through humanity undetected.

She wore one piece of human jewelry: a small, simple silver stud in her nose. It made her look younger than her ageless years, like a college student going through a brief phase.

"Speak, child." I hadn't spoken to Lucille in four years. Not since she'd brought Sierra back.

"Hi?" What I'd hoped would be a confident greeting came out as more of a question.

The goddess rubbed the stud and flared her nostrils, but offered no reply, sitting still on the verdant forest floor. A macaw chirped deep within the trees as a sudden wave rose from the river. The tide surged over the edge, foam lapping over my sneakers before receding from whence it came.

"You're shaking, little Reaper." She stood sharply, like a dog unceremoniously awakened from a peaceful slumber. I suddenly was aware that my whole body was quaking like I was caught in the middle of a hurricane.

"Just a little cold," I replied.

She was silent. Amazingly, so was the jungle—as if every creature was holding its breath until this scourge disappeared.

"Tell me where Dante hides."

"I—I..."

"I have no time to talk to fawns. Tell me what I wish to know."

"That wasn't part of our deal."

In response, a rotting werewolf paw flew across the river and hit me in the chest. I stumbled back, more surprised than anything else. I felt the glyph-cipher slip out of my back pocket and fall to the ground. I was torn between picking it up and staying focused on the angry goddess before me.

I stayed still and said, "So you know."

"Did you not think I would find out?"

"Took you long enough." The revolver's tacky grip brushed against my sweaty fingers, hidden beneath the edge of my t-shirt. "Some goddess."

Guess I was feeling a little saucy with the river still separating us. Even Lucille was surprised by the insult, taking a step back.

Which was when I did something dumb.

Or smart, depending on the outcome.

Bravery, of course, was only a notch away from foolishness. But sometimes you just had to roll the dice. Best laid plans having the tendency to go to hell in a handbasket and all that.

I drew the .45 and fired the remaining bullet. The round grazed Lucille's cheek, but she looked more concerned about my renewed ability to use firearms. Exploiting the small opening, I plunged my hand into my other pocket and felt the warm glow of the coin against my fingers. With a quick flick of the wrist, I hurled the magical gold at her head. It blazed with burning energy like a little comet as it spiraled across the river.

The enchanted piece of treasure smashed against her cheek. Lucille screamed as her flesh burned like a lit cigarette. The magic, whatever the hell it was, briefly revealed her true nature.

Even the plain woman was just a façade. Her face and body were scarred by her less-than-noble deeds. Marks crisscrossed her face, as if someone had tied her to a post and lashed her until she bled.

Perhaps some god had.

That wasn't my concern. Survival was.

I hopped in the river and swam across. I flicked out the Reaper's Switch as I climbed to the mossy shore, its blade glinting in the slivers of light trickling through the treetops. Lucille was still grasping at her burning face. I charged forward, aiming the blade at her chest, right above the heart. She looked up just in time, her crazed eyes looking out from behind the scars and sinew.

She turned at the last second, and the Switch nicked off her shoulder, cleaving away a hunk of flesh and the slightest bit of her soul. I watched the physical soul pirouette through the leafy expanse, and dove to catch it. It landed safely in my palm.

"I will kill you, Reaper!" The goddess's screams shook the forest like a cyclone, turning the sky an apocalyptic shade of black.

I scrambled back to my feet and dove into the frothing river. Carried away by the now churning current, I struggled to keep my head above water as Lucille's threats crashed through the stormy air.

With the last of my energy, I shoved the Reaper's Switch and soul shard into my pockets.

Then I plunged beneath the surface and the world disappeared.

34

I CAME TO IN THE BACK OF A LUXURY SUV IN A delirious state of utter confusion, like life itself had been a lie, and I was suddenly seeing the world for the first time. Part of that was true: I was seeing *this* world for the first time. Through the tinted windows, I could see banana trees and orchids lining the road. Then the driver jerked the wheel around a tight corner, and I found myself tumbling against the hard plastic armrest.

The man next to me said, "Glad you're finally awake." His tone was slightly relieved, like it hadn't been a sure thing. He brushed a finger through his close-cropped black hair, making sure it was in place. A well-tailored import suit wrapped around his sharp, lean figure. He was no older than thirty.

Another man, this one older, leaned back from the front seat. He had a thin patch of hair attached to his pale head. My mind registered that he was familiar in some distant corner of my mind, but I couldn't quite place his face. His dead eyes barely skimmed me as he said, "Master Aldric, we'll be arriving at the destination in twenty minutes."

I tasted something foul and rancid in my mouth and tried to spit. The man in the front seat displayed a row of jagged teeth in a frowning sneer. It felt like the taste was somehow connected to him, but I couldn't be sure.

"Just in time." The man seated next to me—who was, apparently, 'Master Aldric,'—settled against the smooth leather. "Have you considered a name?"

A silence hung over the interior as the car bounced over the jungle road. Eventually, when no one answered, I realized he was speaking to me.

I glanced sideways at him, unsure whether I should look him in the eye. "A name?"

"Well, you can't be Emma Miller, now, can you?" Aldric peered down at a leather wallet I'd received for Christmas when I was sixteen, a couple months before I'd left home for good. I knew the picture inside well—I was beaming like the world couldn't stop me. The lady at the DMV had taken it multiple times, since you weren't supposed to smile, but I'd been adamant about keeping the toothy, shit-eating grin on my naïve face. Apparently, things had gone off the rails since that day, because the last thing I remembered was...

New Orleans. The faceless man's blade going through my chest. Telling me I'd wake up in paradise. The time between that moment and the present seemed like a bad dream, available in only snatches of images and fleeting memories.

I finally said, "But my name is Emma." My voice sounded timid and uncertain. Nothing like what I'd tried to cultivate over the last seven years. But any skills I'd had were on deep ice, disoriented and terrified as I was. Right now, I was just little old Emma, who never knew the right thing to say.

"You are trying my patience." Aldric mashed his finger against the window button and tossed the wallet out on the dark road. I heard the chatter of monkeys and exotic birds drift through the open window until he snapped it shut, returning the interior to its vacuum-like silence. "A name."

I blinked and sat upright, some reserve of stoicism telling me to pull it together. The words came together as if from a source of divine inspiration. "Eden Hunter."

"Interesting choice." Aldric tapped the pale man in the front seat and offered him a card. I could see that it was my driver's license. But I hadn't seen the man remove it from the wallet before chucking it out the window. Those were some quick hands—quicker than mine.

Too quick to be human, maybe.

I swallowed the thought and watched as the pale man in the front seat accepted the ID. He mumbled an incantation and removed a small pinch of a substance that smelled like melting plastic. After dumping the gray powder on the card, there was a small flash of blue light and a puff of smoke. Without comment, he handed the license back to Aldric, who then tossed it to me.

It landed in my lap. I stared at the picture. Gone was the smiling girl. In her stead was a woman who looked either stern or confused. I was going with the latter, since the woman was me, and the photograph had—somehow— been taken right then. With trembling fingers, I took the card and held it up to the window.

There was my new name. Eden Hunter. A new state that I'd never heard of, too.

"A-atheas?" I pronounced it like Athens.

"Atheas," Aldric said, pronouncing it so that it almost sounded like *atheist*. "Named after the greatest king who ever lived."

"I'll take your word for it."

"Feeling better, are we Eden?" Aldric smoothed out a nonexistent rumple in his perfectly tailored suit. His voice wasn't accented, but the English was too precise to be American. Almost like a person from Sweden. From his dark hair and beard, I doubted that was where he'd come from. While it was hard to nail down an exact origin, one thing was certain: he wasn't from around here. Then again, maybe he was. I'd never heard of Atheas.

Outside the tinted window, I noticed the jungle getting sparser, until it was merely a few trees lining the road. Up ahead, a small city loomed, with one building—perhaps three hundred feet tall—hovering over the rest, like it was keeping watch.

I drank in the environment, searching for clues.

How had I arrived here?

What had I been doing since New Orleans?

I asked, "What day is it?"

Aldric turned with a deliberate slowness, meeting my gaze. I could sense a strange sort of influence trying to win me over and control my mind. It took some effort to resist, but less than it felt should be necessary.

He smiled and said, "It seems my investment was not a waste."

I shook my head, feeling the sensation pass. "What the... what was that?"

"All things you will learn in time, Eden." Aldric leaned forward and removed a piece of paper from the passenger seat's back pocket. Without explanation, he handed it to me, along with a small pen that had seemingly materialized from the ether.

I was beginning to think there was magic afoot in the car. Of course, that was crazy. Magic was the stuff of Vegas illusionists and schizophrenic conspiracy theorists. No one actually believed in it.

I took the ice-cold pen from his outstretched palm and began reading the paper. It only took a few lines for me to realize it was a contract—one indenturing me to the man beside me for a period of seven years.

The words came out before I could stop them. "Fuck off."

"Finish reading before you comment, if you would be so kind." There was nothing kind about Aldric's body language. His hawkish emerald eyes bored into my very soul —if there was such a thing, which there wasn't—and I could sense a war-torn, bloodthirsty trail of tragedy stretching long into his past. I didn't know how I felt that, only that it felt as real as the strange rancid taste that refused to leave my tongue.

"Just tell me the date," I said, my voice wobbling only slightly. "I just want to know what goddamn day it is."

"July 26."

"You mean the second."

"Please, Eden, if you would just read the contract, it will alleviate your confusion."

From the front seat, the pale unpleasant man said, "Master Aldric, just force the dear girl to sign the contract."

"*Moreland.*" The rebuke was sharp and concise, and the man in the front seat stiffened like he'd been struck with a cattle prod. He offered no further comment as I examined the contract, reading the finer points.

Reaper. Five souls per week. To remain within the boundaries of Atheas until my duties had been fully discharged seven years hence.

It all sounded like a joke and I said, "This is ridiculous."

"I have indulged you, as I understand that...a reintroduction to the world can be stressful. And I realize that you are still like rough diamond, waiting for an artisan to hone your natural talents." His gaze cut through me like a knife. It looked, quite frankly, like he didn't understand *anything* about human life or emotions. But I was beginning to realize that he wasn't human—and neither was the creepy pale one called Moreland sitting up front.

I swallowed my fear and said, "I'm not signing this." With shaking fingers, I tried to hand him back his contract.

Aldric refused to take it. "That is not how this works." With great restraint, he added, "You would not like to wind up like your sister, would you?"

"What have you done with Sierra, you—"

"Parse your words carefully, Eden. I have never been known for mercy."

I kept my mouth open for a couple seconds longer, but quickly settled on the conclusion that this wasn't some idle threat. After rubbing my nose and pinching my cheeks to make sure I wasn't dreaming—sadly, I found that the situation was all too real—I slowly retracted the hand that still clutched the contract.

"What happened to my sister?"

"She remains in the Elysian Fields," Aldric said with slight annoyance.

From my dim grasp of Greek mythology, I realized that he was referring to the afterlife. The Elysian Fields didn't sound like a bad place. But the memories—or fragments of them—that I had of the past twenty-four days suggested that the myths weren't exactly reflective of the actual experience. Kind of like when you booked a room on the internet and it turned out to be a crack den. That level of false advertising.

A sort of bleak existential horror filled my chest like poison gas. Sierra was dead. My little sister was dead.

"If you would sign—"

"Fine." I scribbled over the bottom of the contract, still processing everything. When I tried to hand it to Aldric, he wouldn't take it.

I glanced at him and said, "Take the damn contract."

"It remains incomplete." Aldric plucked the pen from my hand and turned some imperceptible gear at its base. The tip disappeared, replaced by a tiny, glinting blade. "Your thumbprint."

Without protest, I pricked my thumb and then jammed it against the paper. I felt a tingle rush up through my arm. If I'd questioned magic's existence before, that about sealed it. Too much strange shit going on for this to be a product of science.

This time, Aldric took the paper with what qualified as eagerness, and quickly added his own signatures—ink and blood—to the bottom. A small charge wrapped around my heart when it was done, then everything went back to normal. I wasn't sure if that was adrenaline, or an indication that our deal was complete.

"Now, I can give you this." Aldric tucked the contract safely back into the passenger's seat pocket before fishing into his suit. His hand emerged with a black handled knife. "This is your tool."

"What am I supposed to do with this?" I asked, taking it from him. I flicked it out, revealing a stainless steel blade of about four inches. Without thinking much further, I knew *exactly* what I was going to do.

Jam it through his throat.

Before I could even cock my arm back, however, his cold fingers were wrapped around my wrist.

I strained against his coiled strength.

His arm didn't move.

"I am over twenty-four-hundred years old, Eden," Aldric said. "You will not kill me, nor should you try."

"Where's my sister?" I gritted my teeth and strained harder, to absolutely no avail.

"Gone. But you are still here. And I expect that you wish to remain so." Aldric's gaze settled on my face, his expression clearly conveying the futility of my resistance. Finally, I got the picture and stopped. "Good."

I retracted the switchblade and jammed it into my jeans.

"That is obsidian and silver studded steel," Aldric said, offering an explanation I hadn't asked for. "It will be crucial for harvesting souls."

"Always wanted my own personal scythe."

"You'll be getting more than that."

The car slowed, and I took a glance out the window. We were pulling into a time-battered strip mall, the kind just on the edge of the hellish suburban existence I had tried so hard to escape. A tattoo shop glowed in the night, its bright sign casting neon streaks across the worn asphalt. The SUV rumbled to a stop, and Aldric got out, indicating I should do the same. Moreland and the driver remained in the car.

"A little soon for matching tattoos, isn't it?"

"What did I say about respect?"

"I didn't read anything in the contract about that," I said. The gears in my head were already turning. I would get free of this creep by any means necessary. Then—if these Elysian Fields really existed, and he wasn't just feeding me some crap—I'd find Sierra. Roan, well, wherever he was, he'd call, or he wouldn't.

But I needed to save my sister. No matter the cost. I'd gotten her involved in this life.

Whatever had happened to her was on me.

I followed Aldric into a tattoo shop called Lionhawk Ink. The ancient man flung the door open with a flourish, wide enough that he didn't have to hold it for me. I just walked right in before it closed. There was a counter to our right, where a tall, muscular man stood behind a register. Behind that was a cloth curtain, light seeping out around the edges.

Dingy fluorescent bulbs—the kind you'd find in a big box store—flickered above a parallel row of four vinyl chairs. No customers were in the shop, because no one wanted a regrettable tattoo this late at night.

Aldric turned to the man working the counter and said, "Get your boss."

The man disappeared behind the black curtain and whispered a few things. Before long, he reappeared with an older man, with the kind of craggy looking face and sparse, wild hair that reminded me of a bad boy past his prime.

"Is this the one?" The older man wound his way from behind the counter and shook Aldric's hand. "I was beginning to think it couldn't be done, old friend."

"The right mix of genes, skill, and mental toughness is all it required." They were both looking at me like I was a specimen from a lab.

I glared and said, "I don't know what you're talking about—"

Aldric waved me off. "I do not normally take a hands-on role in employee training. This is costing me a great amount of capital."

"Sorry to be such a burden."

"One should express more gratitude for being saved from death's jaws."

I didn't have a response for that. So that was why I'd woken up in the backseat of his car. He was claiming that he—or one of his goons, since he seemed to have an extensive payroll of "old friends"—had dragged me back from the dead.

A little voice said, *go with it*. I needed to find out what had happened to Sierra.

"All right, let's do this," I said, heading over to the first chair and plopping down with a decisive *thud*. "Time is money, right?"

The tall, muscular clerk handed the weathered tattoo artist a metal case, which the older man took with both hands. He set it down near me on a metal table. As he prepared for whatever was coming next, he turned to Aldric.

"What were you thinking?"

"Oh, you know, Mick, nothing too elaborate."

"This is your first Reaper, though. Might pay to protect her."

"It'd fatten your account, maybe." Aldric rubbed the imported fabric of his custom suit. "She's a trickster. Give her a bag of tricks."

"You want it to have some bite?" Mick asked, sifting through the metal case. I could see inks and various needles, but could also *feel* the minor thrum of something else lurking inside. Something that called to me. The old man paused, resting his hands on the case's metal edge. I could see a tattoo on every knuckle, but nowhere else. Strange for a tattoo artist.

"I think she's got plenty of bite already," Aldric said, glancing at me. I glared back at him. We'd find out how true that was in short time. The switchblade pressed against my leg inside my jeans. It was my off hand, but if I got an opening...

"I can do something I call Fireworks." Mick extracted two vials of ink from the case, along with a small shard of a substance I didn't recognize. "It costs about an eighth of a soul."

"Can't beat the price."

"And two grand."

"Done," Aldric said, and extracted a silver money clip from his back pocket. He counted off the requisite cash and handed it to the tall man keeping watch at the counter. The cash register chimed merrily as Mick sterilized the needle.

"It'll be all show, though. No bite at all," the craggy faced man said.

"Hear that, Eden?" Aldric returned from the register and placed his hand on his well-groomed beard. "Be careful how you use your powers."

"I'll keep that in mind."

Mick glanced at me through the reading glasses perched atop his weathered nose. "This might sting a little."

I was about to fire off a witty retort when the needle touched my skin. Pain like I'd never felt before surged up my arm, and I tried to jerk free. A blue glow emanated from Mick's strong fingers as he worked. More concerningly, there was a glow transferring to my right wrist. His strong hands held me in place, his needle not missing a beat as the artwork came to life. After a moment, he paused and jammed the light-colored shard into the needle, which started to glow like a radioactive core.

Without warning, Mick pressed the hot point against my skin, and the pain doubled in intensity. Sweat trickled down my neck, soaking the thin t-shirt through. I ground my teeth in an effort not to scream, but I couldn't help it. A brief thought flashed through my mind: I needed to get out. They were doing something irreversible to me.

Mick took the needle away, and said, "Done." The roaring pain in my wrist subsided to about a seven, and I could see through the tears that he had etched a perfect lantern into my wrist. He nodded to his handiwork and said, "Want to try it out?"

This was my chance.

I'd only get one.

"This will probably sting a little." I dug the switch-blade out of my pocket and unsnapped it in a smooth motion. It caught him right across the face, raking him from cheek to eye. Now he was the one screaming, and I was sprinting toward the shop door, running toward free-dom, when I found myself hoisted off the ground, sneakers dangling over nothing but air. The bloody blade clattered to the ground.

Aldric's hawkish emerald eyes blazed with fury. "You cannot run from me Eden Hunter. You cannot escape. You cannot fight." His arm didn't move at all, but his grip got tighter around my neck, so tight that I couldn't even breathe. "So you will surrender. And you will do what I brought you here to do."

Aldric released his grip, and I tumbled to the floor in a defeated heap next to the crimson-stained blade. I heard, over Mick's moans, the sound of metal slam against the counter—Aldric's money clip one presumed, to pay for the inconvenience. Then the bell rang, and my new employer disappeared into the night, leaving me gasping on the floor.

After I regained my ability to breathe, I decided it was time to get the hell out of there. I grabbed the knife, plucked a few bills from the thick money clip on the counter, and darted out into the parking lot, rubbing feeling back into my sore throat. The SUV was nowhere to be found.

In its stead was a smartphone. I picked up the device, and found that it had been left for me, with a single message on the background.

Fulfill your quota.

I flicked through the settings and changed it to a picture of a blue sky, then I called a taxi. After grilling the driver about places to stay—I didn't have much money, and would need someone to retrieve my rainy-day stash for me—I settled on a black sand beach on the southwestern part of the island that he said was deserted. He dropped me off at an old service road. I handed him a couple of the bills, leaving me with twenty dollars, an apparently soul-stealing knife, and a smartphone to my new name.

The jungle murmured in the moonlit night as I walked along the warm, black sand. Despite the idyllic setting, I found my eyes welling up with tears. In a moment of despair, I dropped to my knees and said, "Please, if there's anyone listening..."

There was nothing but the chatter of monkeys and birds and the gentle sound of the low tide lapping against the shore. It was a stupid notion. I rose from the beach, brushing sand from my jeans, when I heard a voice.

"Hello." It was ethereal and melodious, carried by the wind itself. With apprehensive excitement, I turned around to find a naked woman with a long, waist-length braid standing in the sand. Her straw-colored hair didn't reflect the moonlight. She was the type of woman you immediately forgot. But I could sense something more, deep within my chest. Was it her soul?

I said, "Hi."

"You look troubled."

"Are you—are you a—" I couldn't get myself to form the word *goddess*, so I cut myself off.

"If there is something you desire, I can help." The braid swished like a panther's tail. "For a price."

Price contained the slightest hint of the devil's edge. I sensed something on my tongue—darkness, maybe a hint of whiskey, wrapped in a sweet package.

"Is my sister dead?"

"Is that what you are willing to pay for?"

"What's the cost?"

"No weapons, Reaper," the woman replied. "That will be your trial."

"Done."

"You should not be so quick to accept. Self-defense would be convenient in your new line of work." She flashed a smile that seemed either friendly or predatory, depending on how the moonlight hit it.

"Tell me."

"Her name?"

"Sierra Miller."

"So you are the one they call Emma." The woman nodded like my reputation preceded me.

"My sister," I said.

"She is dead, trapped in the sixth tier of the Elysian Fields." The woman shook her head. "That is not a good place to be. But you know that."

"I do?"

"Perhaps you have blocked out the memory. Smart girl."

"Who are you?"

"Lucille, goddess of rain." The woman procured a bottle of whiskey from nowhere, and drank heavily. I could tell, now, that she was quite drunk already. I wondered, briefly, if I was simply talking to a crazy person. "Ah, yes, you want a little demonstration."

She flicked her finger in the air like she was getting rid of a gnat. A thunderclap reverberated on the horizon, followed by a lightning bolt.

I stared at the ocean in a sort of stunned silence until she said, "Will that be all, Emma Miller?"

"I want her back," I said, the plea just a whisper.

"That is a tall order." The goddess paced back and forth, drinking from the bottle. "Most of my kind would decline. But they are not here, and you have caught me on a benevolent night."

She raised the bottle toward me and then took a long swig. "But such an endeavor demands a suitable trial."

"Whatever it takes." I could feel the dried tears on my cheeks. Sierra needed to come back. No matter the cost.

"You cannot kill another, whether creature or human," the goddess said. "Do you agree to this additional trial?"

I almost laughed. "Is that all?"

"You will find that to be most troublesome in your new circumstances, Reaper," Lucille said. "Especially when it comes to your own survival."

It sounded like a warning—or maybe even a prophetic threat. Either way, I had confidence that I would never, ever have the need to commit murder. "Just bring her back."

There was a slight buzz in my body, and I lost my balance, dropping to one knee. The goddess did a backflip, then screamed in an unknown tongue to the heavens. Then, the little ceremony ended, and she drank what whiskey hadn't spilled out before chucking the spent bottle into the suddenly silent jungle.

Wiping her lips, she looked at me with unsteady eyes. "Your sister lives."

"How do I know for sure?"

She rolled her eyes, like my questions were pedantic and unnecessary. "Hand me your phone, Reaper."

I tossed it to her, and she missed in her drunken stupor. Some goddess. Lucille punched in a number, then placed the device on speakerphone.

A confused voice answered. "H-hello?"

"Sierra?"

"Emma? Where are you?"

"I'm on an island. I'll come get you, just tell me where you—"

Lucille punched the end button and made a buzzer noise, like I'd failed to answer a question on a game show. It drowned out whatever I was going to say. She tapped a few keys and then tossed the device back. "Time's up, Reaper. Any last requests?"

I fumbled through the phone, but the call log had been deleted. There was no trace of Sierra.

"Bring her back."

"What trial are you willing to undertake for that?" Lucille swayed unsteadily on her feet with a sloppy, drunken grin. "Perhaps—no, I have indulged enough. We are not supposed to engage with humans in this way." She stumbled across the sand until she was toe-to-toe with me. Her energy seemed to swallow up the immediate area. "But you, you little Reaper, you are fascinating."

"How so?" I asked, avoiding her hot whiskey breath.

"I am sure everyone will find out soon enough." She brought her finger to her lips, her eyelids half-closed. The stud in her nose glinted in the soft moonlight. "But tell no one about our talk. For otherwise, you and your sister will return from whence you came."

Then, without so much as a goodbye, the goddess

sprinted into the jungle, leaving me alone on the empty beach. I sat and stared into the jungle, wondering what had just happened.

"And they say prayers aren't answered."

I sensed a disturbance on the warm air, and turned around to find a bald man wearing a politician's smile. "What do you want?"

"A goddess of my own wouldn't be the worst thing." He spoke with a down-home type of accent that had to be a put on.

"And who might you be?" I asked through gritted teeth.

"The mayor."

So much for keeping this a secret.

I could already tell that paradise wasn't going to be everything the brochures claimed.

Not by a long shot.

35

I COUGHED UP A MOUTHFUL OF SEAWATER AND vomited on the wet sand as water lapped against my salt-stiffened hair. Opening my eyes granted me a straight-shot view of the sun that burned my retinas, so I rolled over and pressed my face against the pleasantly warm ground.

I closed my eyes again, just wanting to sleep.

But I couldn't rest on the beach. I had a goddess to escape and a soul delivery to make.

I dragged myself upright and surveyed the empty landscape.

The churning river had dumped me into the ocean, which had taken me to the coast. Ominous storm clouds surrounded the island, like a barbarian horde threatening to siege the gates. The ocean itself remained calm, but from my trip down the swirling river, I knew how fast that could change if Lucille so chose. I checked my pockets, finding the goddess's soul shard, ruined cell phone, and Reaper's Switch still accounted for. I'd dropped the glyph-cipher in the forest. All I could do was hope it wasn't important.

But I knew that was wishful thinking. Cross had given it

to me for safekeeping. It held powerful information, and I'd simply left it in the flowers for Lucille to pluck up.

I felt sick thinking about how he was frozen down in the caves. With the crushing weight of reality pressing upon my shoulders, I launched into a dead sprint up the beach. My lungs begged me to stop, but I knew better than to give in.

Who knew how many minions Lucille had chasing my tail? I'd escaped her immediate wrath, but that was little comfort. She'd pursued Cross for over four hundred years. She'd find me again, sooner rather than later—and I didn't have a damn clue how I would survive when that hour came.

Plus, I still had my quota to deal with.

I glanced at the goddess's soul shard clutched in my hand.

If I could get this to Aldric, maybe he'd back off when it came to the rival Reaper and gold thieves.

Maybe.

I fumbled with the burner phone as I broke down into a shambling jog. The device was toast from my swim in the river. Time was running out. And unlike Visa, Aldric didn't accept late payments.

I slumped into the hot sand and dragged myself beneath a banyan tree. Its massive canopy provided shade from the harsh elements. In certain cultures, the banyan tree had sacred properties. I propped myself against the knotty bark and hoped, silently, that those myths were true, and someone would emerge from the jungle to save my ass.

But nothing happened. Waves just continued to crash against the deserted beach.

"Please help," I said, then cut myself off. Last time I'd done that, I'd summoned Lucille. Seeking divine help had proved to be the very definition of a double-edged sword. Of course, I wasn't the first one to appeal to the heavens. In times of drought, ancient cultures used to perform rain dances. An appeal to the gods for rain—but, on a more basic level, a call into the darkness hoping that they weren't alone. And if you've ever had your back against the wall and prayed for God, Yahweh, a spirit to come down and whisk away your problems, then you've performed a little rain dance, too. A ritual that wrests the teensiest bit of control from a confusing and sometimes cruel world.

The difference between those rain dances and mine was simple: I'd gotten a definitive answer.

Want to know the secret ingredient?

One part fear.

One part tears.

One part guilt.

Stirred, then garnished with a sudden awakening from the dead and an unforgiving vampire warlord boss. Served chilled, because life was a cruel, cold-hearted bitch.

I dug the phone out of my soggy jeans and tried it again.

Still dead, but a desperate plan formed.

After wiping the device dry—or as dry as it would get—I dug a small hole in the bone-dry sand. Then I put the phone inside and covered it up. My hope was that the sand would leech out the moisture, like a bag of rice, rendering the device usable again. It was a stab in the dark, but it wasn't like it was a high-risk gamble.

As I waited, I rifled through my mental files, trying to find something—*anything*—I'd missed in Roan's murder. Aldric's and Lucille's wrath aside, I was still on the hook for homicide. My chances didn't look good if the thing went to trial.

I ran over the evidence.

Roan Kelly had been coming to the villa that night to

apologize and make amends. His new crew needed my help with their goddess-killing scheme—*what* help, exactly, remained unclear. But they'd been confident enough that I was the final piece to rip off Aldric for thirteen million in gold bullion, then pay a cipher sorceress to break the code on one of Drake's ancient maps. Before Roan had been able to meet up, though, he'd been gunned down.

By someone who'd known he was coming.

That was a piece of the puzzle I hadn't considered before. I didn't know how it fit, yet. But it seemed important.

I continued going over what I knew.

We had James, Mick's son who had "gotten a call" and planted the gun in my villa. Cross had denied making that call.

I believed him. Dante Cross was a crappy liar.

Identifying the killer, then, hinged entirely on the primary motive.

Did this revolve around killing Roan?

Framing me?

Taking out the gold heist crew?

Whatever the motive, I still had a list of suspects longer than my arm.

Aldric remained a possibility, although his investment would plummet to zero if I sat in a jail cell for the rest of my life. Still, he'd tried to kill me twice already—succeeding once—so framing me for murder wasn't exactly a stretch.

Cross could have done it out of sheer greed, reducing the number of shares in Drake's boundless treasure stash. In that scenario, I would just be a convenient fall option, and he could get away scot-free. In fact, any of the crew—Rayna, Zoe, Doris, or Magnus—could've been responsible. But

James had singled out Cross as the one on the other end of the call.

It dawned on me, however, sitting there in the warm, pleasant heat, that I might have led James to that conclusion. *I* had asked if the caller was charming and British. After protests about his sexuality, James had begrudgingly agreed. That could have been a way of deflecting suspicion from himself. But James Anderson had no motive, no connection to Roan or me—other than my attack on his father four years ago. That motive seemed spurious at best, though.

Naturally, I had to add Lucille to the list. It was possible that a magical signal flare went up as soon as I'd violated the terms of our agreement. In that case, she would have instantly known—and could have unleashed her punishment mere minutes later. That would give her motive, and she had a history of being devious, stern, and unforgiving. All that made her a prime suspect, but as useless of one as Aldric. For legal purposes, they were untouchable. No jail could contain their power.

Finally, we had Mayor Stefan Cambridge, our disturbingly happy local serial killer. I didn't really see a motive, but serial killers didn't really need one. Roan's death didn't fit the MO, but maybe he'd gotten bored and branched out into more theatrical murders—complete with framing me as the coup de grâce.

There was also the small matter that I suspected the mayor was responsible for killing Doris. I wasn't sure how that fit in, or if it was merely a random occurrence unrelated to anything.

That left me with almost more suspects than I had fingers—and it didn't rule out the possibility that I had missed something entirely. After all, Rayna, Magnus, and

Cross had all led me by the nose into their little band, revealing layers of themselves as needed. Maybe my cold-reading skills had deteriorated over the past four years from disuse.

I shook the notion from my mind and brushed the sand away from the phone. With trepidation, I pushed the power button. The screen was a mess of distorted colors and glitchy symbols, but the dry sand had done the trick. Now, my only problem was the phonebook. I couldn't access the burner's contact list. But there was one number I'd called from enough payphones and backwater hangouts to know by heart.

My fingers lingered over the keypad, hesitating. But I had no choice.

The speaker buzzed with distortion. A female voice answered. "Aldric's office. Who's calling, please?"

"Eden."

"Do you have an appointment?" Clearly this woman was new, or jerking me around.

"Just put Aldric on the fucking phone now."

"Oh, he's pissed with you." Well, I had my answer. Just another asshole.

There was some cheery music as the call transferred, then Aldric said, "Eden." I could sense the anger, even over the tinny connection.

"I have your souls."

"Should I be impressed to hear that you are doing your job?"

"I have something else, too." I held out the soul shard. It caught the light, but not in a pretty way. Lucille had done some dark things. Maybe I should've chucked it into the sea, but it was my only bargaining chip. A slice of a goddess would be too delicious for him to ignore.

"Oh?" Aldric tried very hard to sound disinterested, but he wasn't as good of a liar as he thought. "You have found the thieves?"

"Better."

A growl came into his tone. "This is not a restaurant where you can make substitutions as you please, Eden."

"When I say better, I mean a lot better." I closed my hand around the twisted soul shard, feeling the powerful energy surge through up my arm like a current. "But I need a couple things from you."

"This conversation is growing tiresome, Eden."

"If one of your lackeys could check out my place, make sure no one's hiding in the bushes to kill me, that'd be great." Lucille obviously knew where I lived. But I still needed to head home and grab the rest of the souls from my safe.

"Any other requests I can accommodate?"

"Hold your sarcasm if you want me to give you what I found."

"*Eden—*"

"One other thing," I said. "I'm somewhere near the Boundless Jungle, on the beach. No one around for miles. Where should I meet your driver?"

An exasperated sigh knifed over the dodgy connection. I must say, pissing off Aldric felt good. Hey, if you couldn't irritate the vampire responsible for your first death, then what was the point of living? Actually, there were plenty of other reasons to keep living, but at the moment, needling him was what was keeping me *awake*.

Aldric said in his most measured tone, "On the northern part of the beach, there should be a small cabana. The Rum Shack or some such moronic nonsense. A car will meet you nearby."

"Good talk," I said, pushing myself to my feet with a huge groan. "And Aldric?"

"What?"

"If you send someone to kill me, you're never going to see what I got you." I ended the call and leaned against the banyan tree, feeling the knotty bark press into my spine. Then I got on my knees and started digging a small hole.

I buried the goddess's twisted soul shard inside.

"If you kill me, Aldric," I said to nothing but the wind, "you're not getting shit."

That was a small consolation, but right then, it made me feel confident enough to get up and start walking. And sometimes, all you could do was put one foot in front of the other and hope for the best.

36

AFTER FIFTEEN MINUTES—WHICH FELT MUCH CLOSER to fifteen hours—I came upon a small beachside cabana where some guy in board shorts and a fedora was slinging drinks. Aldric hadn't been too far off—the place had been dubbed the Rum Hut in askew, drunken script. The wicker chairs at the bar were empty. My spirits were lifted when I spotted a patch of road peeking out from the nearby jungle.

"You look like you had quite the party." A voice aged by too many cigarettes and years at sea floated out from behind the plastic bar.

"I hope not," I said, a bite in my tone. "Because if that was a party, parties have really started going downhill."

A man popped up from behind the counter, organizing his fishing supplies for the day's work. He slammed his tackle box on the bar next to a couple limes. A wad of tobacco the size of my hand was lodged in his sun-weath-ered cheek. His body had the general look of a piece of leather that had been cured for too long.

The man looked up from the tackle box and said, "Dale."

"Eden." I took a seat on one of the wicker stools, throwing a glance toward the road. My ride hadn't shown up. Without prompting, he poured two drinks—tequila on ice—and shoved one my way. The lip of the glass was rimmed with salt.

He raised his, tipped his fedora, and said, "Well, Eden, to another day in paradise."

I drank the gasoline-like mixture, chased it with a lime, then said, "I don't suppose paradise serves water."

He handed me a water bottle, and I heard a hidden fridge snap shut. I rubbed my temples and licked my chapped lips after taking a healthy sip.

"How's business out here?" I asked.

"I fish, I drink, get an occasional visitor." Dale threw a longing glance at the storm forming on the horizon. "And sometimes, shit, I just read when the breakers get too high. Looking like one of those days."

The clouds had edged closer to shore over the past hour.

A storm was coming.

"Yup," I said, and then polished off the water. He handed me another without asking. Who knew the world's best bartender was tucked away on a remote part of an uncharted island? Actually, that made perfect cosmic sense.

"So, Eden, are you searching for Drake's treasure?"

I almost spilled the second bottle of water. "Not sure I follow."

"Been hearing cars and trucks go by all day." Dale gave me a knowing nod, then turned the dial of a rusted, paint-stripped radio. After fiddling with a few of the knobs and extending the bent antenna, a broadcast crackled over the old speaker.

"Turn that up," I said, recognizing the voice. It was Magnus's slightly Nordic lilt.

"Drake's treasure is free for all to claim in the Boundless Jungle. Beware of supernatural forces, thieves, and those who would do you harm." Then it gave the coordinates before repeating on an endless loop.

Guess Cross has a contingency plan in case he went missing.

Dale turned the volume down and gave me a look, but didn't comment.

"So, did you go out and look for it?" I asked.

"The hell am I gonna do, fight with some bastard over a throne made of rubies?" Dale shook his weathered head and sipped straight from the tequila bottle. "Nah, I got everything I need right here."

"Wish I shared your philosophy."

"It ain't for everyone, that's for sure." Dale tipped the bottle too far back, and tequila dripped down his scraggly beard.

I nursed the water and made small talk until I heard the growl of what could only be one of Aldric's monstrous SUVs. A quick glance at the road confirmed that my ride had arrived.

"That's me," I said. "I'll get the driver to pay you."

Dale waved his sun-beaten hands. "Nah. There are things better than money."

"Such as?"

"I'll let you know when I find them," he said with a grin. Then Dale went back to drinking.

37

THANKFULLY, ONE OF MORELAND'S FACELESS GOONS had been sent to retrieve me, which meant I could nap on the hour-long ride back to the villa. I dreamed of nothing, which was preferable to any of the ghastly scenarios my imagination could no doubt conjure up from the depths of the shit show this week had been.

The driver beeped twice to wake me up and then said, "I'll be waiting here." The undertone was *don't keep me waiting*.

I checked the clock. Five past eleven.

I'd be delivering my quota just under the wire.

I got out of the vehicle and jogged up the black beach. Waves crashed and churned beneath a dark sky as thunder rumbled over the swirling ocean. Jungle critters voiced their displeasure about the impending storm.

Guess I was getting an answer to my rain dance.

And it was going to be a friggin' tsunami.

Two men in expensive suits—clearly from Moreland's security team—greeted me at the villa's marble stairs. That was a good sign: if Lucille's minions had paid a visit, both of these men would probably have had their decapitated heads stuffed up their own butts. As I went inside, however, I was still in for an unpleasant surprise.

"What the *hell* is this?" I stared at the couch, where a bloodied man sat gagged and bound with his shirt off. Next to him was Khan, who was not bound, but did have a muzzle on his striped face. The man looked up, and I recognized him as Kai Taylor, the FBI agent who had arrested me with Rayna Denton on Monday. He was shirtless, his thick muscles surprisingly relaxed given that he was in plastic cuffs. I traced my eyes up the tattoo sleeve on his right arm, remembering how he had said I was a stingray—willing to defend things that mattered.

Kai's calm eyes tracked me as I entered the living room, but the broad-shouldered man didn't move. The bamboo hardwood looked like a scratch pad. No doubt from Khan, who was growling—or trying to—and wriggling his head, trying to get free of the muzzle.

One of the guards strode up behind me and said, "We found this man searching your house." He glanced at the cat. "As for the cat, he was disagreeable and ornery."

"Sounds accurate." I went over to the couch and sat down next to Kai. He'd taken a sharp blow to the head, which was where the bruising and blood had come from. Otherwise, he looked largely uninjured. I worked at the cloth gag—which was actually one of my dirty t-shirts—and removed it from his mouth.

He looked at me with his calm eyes the whole time, but said nothing once the gag was removed.

"So, what were you doing here?"

"The search warrant is still valid." He wasn't defiant, merely explaining that he had been inside legally. With a nod of his head that made his shoulder-length black hair swish, he gestured toward his back pocket.

I worked my fingers into his pocket and removed the folded piece of paper.

"He said all this, ma'am," the talkative guard said. "But we didn't want him looking around."

"You know I'm out on bail, right?" I skimmed the warrant, which was indeed valid. At least one person in the FBI was continuing the investigation.

"All the more reason to get rid of this particular problem." A slide racked, and I looked up to see Moreland's goon raising his pistol. "If you'd just step aside, ma'am."

I got up and put my body between the gun and Kai. "What are you, drunk?"

The guard seemed taken aback. "Eliminating a threat."

"Yeah, we'll just bury a federal agent in my backyard." I put my hand over my eyes to convey my incredulous displeasure. "Just—just go outside."

"Ma'am?"

"Actually, go wait in the car. It's on the service road."

He gave me a confused look, like he couldn't process the orders correctly. "But..."

I dropped my hand and held up a finger. "Actually, you can save me a trip. Wait here." I glanced at Kai, giving him what I hoped was an *I'll free you once these idiots are gone* look, then hurried up the glass stairs two at a time. I cut into the guest bedroom next to the stairs and ran my hand along the small space beneath the window. Responding to my touch, the illusion magic disappeared, revealing a safe.

I punched in the code and grabbed the seven souls I'd collected over the week that were in a plastic bag on the top shelf. I left the eighth one for a rainy day and shut the door. After running my hand over the wall again, the illusion returned. I tapped the space beneath the window with my knuckle and felt plaster.

Satisfied everything was in order, I jogged back downstairs and handed the bag of souls to the guard. His confused expression deepened. "In front of—*him*, ma'am?"

"I'll sort things out with the agent." I gave the guard a shove toward the door. "Go and tell Aldric the good news."

"I'm not sure—"

"*Go*. And give me back Agent Taylor's service weapon, please."

The guard gave me a funny look, then removed the black, standard-issue Glock 22 from his waistband and handed it to me with a begrudging look of defeat. Good thing I was apparently higher on the totem pole than these two idiots. If I'd tried to get Moreland to give me back anything, the warlock would've laughed in my face.

I watched as the man scurried out of the villa, his partner hurrying from the kitchen to join the hasty escape. The front door slammed shut with a decisive *thud*. I looked out the living room window, watching them both hurrying up the beach. Satisfied they'd left, I turned to the couch.

Khan wriggled in disgust next to the FBI agent.

I removed the cat's muzzle.

"Finally, stupid human." He arched his back in disgust and bared his teeth. "It is as if you cannot take a hint."

The broad-shouldered FBI agent blinked twice and stared at the talking cat as if this experience had to be a hallucination. I knew the feeling. My whole life was starting to feel that way—and before this week, I'd been harvesting souls.

You think you've seen weird, and then an ill-mannered cat starts to insult you.

Khan glanced at our house guest and said, "Yes, stupid

man. I am capable of speech. It looks as if I have your tongue, though, do I not?"

The cat looked pleased with his bad pun. I was less amused, and showed it by snapping my fingers in front of his striped face. Khan hissed at me, but it was a half-hearted effort.

"Did the agent find anything before those two showed up?"

Khan flicked his striped tail. "I am not your butler."

"Jesus fucking Christ, I don't need you to be the concierge." I clenched both fists. "I just need to know if he found anything."

The cat's ears flattened against his skull as he slunk to the floor. I would've apologized for wounding his inflated ego, but the simmering rage—and desperation—coursing through my veins prevented me from making any peace offerings.

Khan wrinkled his nose. "The boy scout was waiting outside for you to arrive before executing the search."

I glanced at Kai, who still said nothing.

"All right." I nudged the ornery cat with my knee. "Go somewhere else."

"I will not."

"Then shut up." From the corner of my eye, I caught the glimmer of a smile spread across Kai's lips. It vanished once the agent knew I was looking. Without saying a word, I took out my Reaper's Switch and flicked out the blade. No fear registered in his gentle eyes. I reached behind him, pressing against his back to get him to move forward. I could feel the strong muscles shift as he adjusted his weight.

With a single swipe of the blade, I cut through the zip cuffs. He returned his hands to the front of his body, but didn't rub feeling back into them or have much of a reaction.

"If you could give me my shirt, that would be helpful, Miss Hunter."

"Eden." I didn't repeat the worn-out joke about Miss Hunter being my mother. After locating his torn shirt in the corner nearby, I returned, holding it out. "Why'd they try to strip you naked, anyway?"

He buttoned up the oxford shirt, leaving the top two unbuttoned. "They ripped it off in our fight."

"Not much of a fight, by the looks of it." I watched as he rolled up the sleeves, revealing his tattoos once more. "That how they got your Glock, too?"

"I didn't want to hurt them." It wasn't machismo, but truth.

"So you just like getting tied up?" I asked.

"Not so much in these circumstances," he said, matching my gaze. From hanging with Cross, I expected Kai to wink. But the agent just looked calm, which made it so I couldn't tell if it was a joke or not. After a minute, I gave up and sat down next to him on the couch.

"I didn't kill Roan Kelly," I said.

"The evidence doesn't support your claim." Kai didn't move. On the other part of the couch, Khan snorted, like trying to reason with this man he called the boy scout was futile. But while Kai might not have been corruptible through lies and illusions, I did have one thing going for me —for once.

The truth.

"Have you read my file?" I asked.

"Above my clearance," Kai said.

"Well, then you're in for a long story." With a deep breath, I launched into it all. I wasn't sure if this was the move, but I was out of allies, and there were too many suspects to investigate on my own. And the FBI might have been the only entity on the island powerful enough to save me from Lucille and Aldric.

Or maybe the Feds would just get swallowed in my vortex.

But they'd wanted to recruit me, so that was just part of the deal.

I left nothing out: the bargain I'd struck with Lucille my first night on the island to save my sister, my past with Roan, how Cross and his crew had ripped off the island's most powerful warlord in search of an ancient treasure. Everything except my sister's crimes, whatever they might have been. That, and the mayor's little...side hobby, since I didn't really feel like being charged as an accessory to murder after the fact. It felt odd unburdening myself to law enforcement, but Kai was a good listener.

Even Khan was silent, aside from the occasional *really* and *I can't believe you told him that.*

By the time I had finished, it was well past three in the afternoon. A gamble both in time and trust.

I bit my lip and said, "I feel like I've been talking for a while."

"You're a good storyteller." Kai scratched at his tattoo sleeve, right above the spear tattoo.

For some reason, this sounded like the highest compliment. I looked away and said, "Well, I've had a lot of practice."

"Might I see your—you call it a Reaper's Switch?"

I hesitated. The blade was part of me, now—and I hadn't realized it until that moment. Like a little extension of my physical being. I took it out of my jeans, feeling the duct-taped handle against my palm.

Then I placed it in the FBI agent's hand. He flicked it out. "You killed a werewolf with this." Kai held the blade up to the light, the obsidian and silver flecks glimmering.

"It wasn't easy," I said.

He snapped his wrist with a deft motion, and the blade closed seamlessly. The knife lingered for a moment in his palm, like he was trying to ascertain something from its weight. Then he offered it back to me, and my heart beat a little slower having it back in my possession.

What he did next surprised me.

Kai drew his service weapon.

Khan, who must've liked me far more than he let on, leapt at the FBI agent's head. The cat perched atop the man's flowing black hair like a bad hat. With a strong hand, Kai simply picked the cat up by the scruff of his neck, and placed Khan on the unfinished floor.

When the cat tried to scale his jeans, the agent said, "Stop."

Khan flicked his tail—and, apparently satisfied that he'd done all he could to save my life—pranced into the kitchen. I glanced warily at the pistol, wondering if I'd done the wrong thing by having it returned.

Kai said, "Take it."

"Another trial," I said. "I'm good at those."

I reached for the gun, grabbing it by the rubber grip. My skin began to sizzle, and I could feel a blister beginning to burn. But I hung on until I was certain it would leave a mark. It felt like I was clutching a pot of boiling water with my bare hands. Finally, the gun clattered to the floor and I stood up, cursing profusely. My hand was bright, scorched pink, white patches streaking through the burnt flesh.

Kai retrieved his service weapon from the bamboo hardwood and placed it on the leather sofa. "I'm sorry, Eden. I had to be sure."

"No hard feelings," I said as I shook out my hand. He disappeared from the living room, moving surprisingly quietly for cutting such a large figure. A minute later, he returned with an ice tray. Without a word, he took one of my shirts from the floor and wrapped the fabric around the ice. I took it with gratitude and pressed it against my palm, feeling cool relief rush over my skin.

"Too bad we don't have Warlock's Lemonmint."

I raised my eyebrow. "You really listened to *everything*."

"I'd be an idiot not to." Kai gave his service weapon a once over—as if checking to make sure it wouldn't burn him, too—then slid it back into the holster adorning his hip. "You briefly mentioned your sister."

"I did." In passing, at least.

"I think I might know her." Kai took out his phone and tapped a few buttons, pulling up a photo of a club taken from a stakeout vehicle. "Have you heard of Alkemy?"

I shook my head and said, "Haven't been there." I'd heard of it, naturally, but my work hadn't made it a necessity to swing by.

"There's a girl matching that description who works in the VIP lounge."

"And how would you know that?" I asked, suddenly suspicious of the boy scout. No one could be this clean. Maybe he blew off steam by snorting mountains of cocaine in nightclub bathrooms.

His calm gaze remained steady. "It's my job to know things."

"That's not an answer." I crossed my arms, still clutching the ice, which was beginning to melt through the fabric. "I told you everything."

"It's against protocol."

"Oh, well in that case." I got up in his face, so that my lips were only inches from his. "That's not how sharing works, buddy."

Kai didn't move, but his body tensed with a small amount of discomfort. Good to know he could be rattled. Here I was thinking that he was just an animated boulder. The tension mounted, neither of us breathing.

Finally, he said, "We think your sister might be a killer, Eden."

38

WORD TO THE WISE.

Whenever you think your week can't get any worse, here's a free tip: you're absolutely wrong. Be thankful for the shitty life you have, because unknown forces could always take you out at the knees and dance over your legless corpse.

Maybe that was an overdramatic way of looking at things. I didn't care. When you hear *oh, the FBI thinks your sister might be a murderer,* and then you match it with all the questionable things you've seen her do recently, you tend to have a lot of conflicting emotions. Some combination between *no way* and *oh my god, what if?* Then again, the Feds had thought the same about me and been wrong, so it was hardly open and shut.

Kai didn't slow down as the government sedan fishtailed into the downtown club district. I could practically smell the desperation, testosterone, and red-bottomed heels from here. He slammed on the brakes about three feet before we had to stop. I kept myself from going through the windshield with a well-timed hand against the dash.

He gave me a look. "You should really wear a seatbelt."

"I'll keep that in mind." He undid another button on his shirt, exposing more of his smooth, muscular chest. With the tattoos and shoulder-length hair, he looked more like a jet-setting rebel entrepreneur than an agent. The gentle, understanding stare gave the truth away, though.

I got out of the government sedan and looked at the glittering sign across the street.

"It's not love, it's Alkemy," I said, reading the club's tagline aloud. A line was wrapped around the block at before four in the afternoon. The bouncers at the street's other clubs looked sad and alone. "I don't think they're here because of the catchy slogan."

I'd been to more than a few clubs, and I'd never seen this kind of turnout before the sun went down. Unless they were giving out free handjobs inside, I couldn't explain this on a Friday afternoon.

My money was on the supernatural element. And if my Reaper sister worked at Alkemy, it had something to do with souls.

Wouldn't be the first time someone had used magic to bolster their business ventures. That usually backfired. Aldric already had established business interests here.

And he didn't like sharing.

"Been like this since it opened six months ago," Kai said, joining me at my side. His service weapon was clearly visible.

I pointed at his Glock. "Everyone's gonna love talking to you."

"I need my service weapon."

"Yeah, yeah, I get it." I reached around his back and snapped the waistband of his jeans. "Just tuck it beneath your shirt."

His expression indicated that deception—even the legal kind—didn't suit him. Luckily, he had me here to guide him away from any landmines that would blow our cover. Kai adjusted his shirttail to cover the service pistol, then started walking to the back of the line.

I yanked him back by the shirt cuff and said, "What the hell do you think you're doing?"

"If we're going undercover, that means we should wait in—"

"Like fuck that's what it means," I said. "Watch."

Dragging the large agent behind me like an unwilling dog on a leash, I marched right to the front. I wasn't exactly dressed in club-chic with my torn jeans, sneakers, and thrift store tee, but I also didn't really care, which was a big point in my column. Confidence made up for plenty of flaws. The bouncer didn't even glance at us as we approached. He was the kind of overweight, big-boned guy with a receding buzz cut and two diamond studs who thought that receiving the occasional blowjob from a drunk, coked out club chick made him cool. The guy stamped a trio of girls who were somehow already beyond faded at four in the afternoon, then checked out their asses as they disappeared into the club.

After I watched him chuckle to himself and nod his head, I cleared my throat.

"Back of the line."

"But you don't understand," I said, putting on my best naïve girl from Kansas voice, "Sierra said I could have a job here."

"Sierra?" The guy snorted. "That nutcase? Sure as shit ain't no one listening to her personnel recommendations."

I didn't like the way he talked about my sister, just like I didn't appreciate Alkemy's ridiculously high standards. To be fair, the next thirty women in line had as much fabric covering their combined bodies as I did alone, but I'd like to think I still stacked up. Then again, I'd been through the wringer today without a shower, so that was probably a dubious assumption on my part.

The bouncer smiled at the next group of girls, enjoying the sad amount of power afforded by his little fiefdom.

"Well, can I talk to her at least?" I batted my eyelashes.

The bouncer glanced at us in between stamping hands. "Nah."

"What do you mean, *nah?*"

Kai leaned over and said, "We should go to the back."

I swatted him away and put my hands on my hips, waiting for the bouncer to explain. He ushered in the next wave of tramps, then turned and looked at me through his stupid little eyes.

"You can go to the back of the line, then when you come up here, I'm gonna say *nah* to you and friggin' Thor here again."

"I don't think you understand," I said, my voice taking on a growl. But it was hard to sound menacing when you're not even five-six and the guy you're talking to is six-four, two eighty.

He just laughed. Adding injury to insult, the quintet of nearby girls joined in, too, like I was a pathetic piece of street trash that had wandered up for a handout.

I slipped my hand in my pocket, feeling the Reaper's Switch. One swipe, and this prick would know—

Kai brushed past and bent over to speak in the bouncer's ear. The guy's expression went from confident to ashen within a couple seconds. He quickly waved us through, stamping our hands like we were radioactive.

I gave him a wide grin and said, "I guess that's a *yes.*"

"Whatever, bitch."

I yanked the stupid stud out of his flabby ear as I strolled by, and he screamed.

Kai shot me a look and I shrugged. "He was rude."

"I thought we were trying to fly under the radar."

"Oh, relax, *Thor*." I nudged him in the ribs as we got in another short line to enter the actual club. Judging from the room-shaking thumps coming from the doors ahead, the place was already popping off. "What'd you say to him, anyway?"

Kai looked embarrassed about that, as if it was actually an insult. "I said that I knew about his rap sheet, and wouldn't bust him for his little side business."

"He has a side business?" I asked.

"He's a creep, Eden," Kai said. "I played the odds."

Who'd have thunk it—Kai Taylor, con man extraordinaire. What a poker face. Maybe I had a couple things to learn from an honest man, after all.

I'd have to brush the rust off my skills just to keep up.

In my defense, things *were* a lot easier when half of your ass was hanging out, though. Get me back here with a shower and pair of pumps, and we'd have gotten in without incident.

That was my story and I was sticking to it.

We flashed our stamps to yet another bouncer to gain entrance to Alkemy. He opened the door with a smirk, like we didn't know what we were getting into. Pumping bass and distorted vocals greeted us as Pandora's Box opened before our eyes.

In truth, Alkemy was little more than a massive dance floor covered by a sea of grinding bodies. The dance floor was flanked on either side by long bar areas. At the back was a stage, above which hung a darkened glass-enclosed balcony.

The club smelled like perfume and sweet sweat, and more than a little tinge of emptiness. You'd think loneliness doesn't have a scent, but it does.

And this place was drenched in it.

The DJ stopped his set, and the aural assault briefly abated. Even in the absence of music, however, the people on the floor didn't stop their sweaty gyrations.

I pressed my lips almost to Kai's ear and said, "It's not love, it's alchemy."

He nodded, receiving the message loud and clear. There was nothing special about this club. The interior was trimmed in black and stainless steel, giving it a modern and hip underground aesthetic. But that didn't explain the line around the block. *That* could only be explained by a secret ingredient—a little *actual* alchemy. Dangerous magic was afoot here. And my sister was at the center of it all, since alchemy demanded souls.

My stomach turned. Selling arcana kits to teenage entrepreneurs. Harvesting souls to create love potions. Could she be a murderer, too?

I led Kai through the dancing throng, keeping toward the bar, which was less crowded than the amorous dance floor. I knocked into a couple wrapped around each another like two gummy bears smashed together at the bottom of the bag. They barely even noticed my interruption. Their lips were locked again before I could even offer an apologetic nod.

To the left of the DJ's stage, I saw an open archway surrounded by velvet ropes. I guess the upstairs was for VIPs only. Luckily, we had the ultimate pass: an FBI badge.

After some more jockeying, I reached the ropes. A thick

guy in a black t-shirt stood between us and answers. I craned my neck around the DJ's stage to look through the rat's nest of wires. There were two doors on the opposite side. One looked like a fire exit, but the other was an unguarded stairwell.

That might've been an easier bet. I tried to turn around, but the music started again, and the crowd formed an impenetrable mass of swaying bodies.

That left us to deal with one final gatekeeper. Dropping Sierra's name hadn't worked before—the first bouncer had dismissed her entirely. But she *was* valuable enough to keep around—which meant maybe her name could work in a different context.

I approached the bouncer and, screaming to be heard over the corkscrewing bass, I yelled, "Sierra sent us upstairs to get the delivery."

"Sierra?" From his look, this seemed plausible. At least this guy wasn't laughing.

"Wants us to pick up a package for the boss, yeah."

The guy stared at me, then Kai. He glanced down at Kai's tattooed arm and broad shoulders, and must've decided that we looked like the disreputable kind of people Sierra might send for a pickup. He unclipped the velvet rope and gruffly nodded toward the stairs.

I tried to keep cool, but it was like the first time I'd snuck into a club with a fake ID.

Still had it.

About halfway up, near the first landing where the second flight switch backed, I felt an arm on my elbow.

"*What?*" I could see the VIP area from here. The closed door beckoned to me.

"If this goes bad..." Kai looked like he wanted to turn around, but his sworn duty to the FBI wouldn't let him.

"It'll be fine."

"How do you know?"

I waved him off, pretending I couldn't hear. It wasn't much of a lie. The stairs offered some protection from the constant bass drops, but anyone who went to a club to have a conversation was embarking on a quest more difficult than keeping the ring from Sauron.

Of course, the truth was, I had no clue what would happen. I hadn't talked to my sister in four years. She hadn't told me she'd come to Atheas. And she certainly hadn't told me about her new job. All I had was hope.

So, before hesitation could swallow me whole, I sprinted up the stairs and barged through the door. And then I stopped dead.

As VIP rooms went, it was middle of the road. Two leather sofas, a glass table, the royalty-like view of the undulating dance floor below. Dim lights that hid the kisses, groping, and cocaine bumps that otherwise would lurk in plain sight.

None of that surprised me.

What did, however, was the woman with the platinum blonde hair standing alone in her leather pants, surveying the partying masses. I could sense a collection of souls in the room—harvested souls. But more than that, I could taste one soul in particular.

A Reaper's. Uncloaked for the first time.

And I did not like what I tasted.

Sierra turned, a small glass jar clutched in her hands. Her big blue eyes grew wide. But before I could say a word, my sister pulled the fire alarm and raced out the opposite exit.

39

I wanted to chase Sierra.

Started to chase her.

But before I could, a strong hand grasped my shoulder. I turned, fist clenched, but Kai calmly shook his head.

"Not now." Kai's mellow baritone cut beneath the din of the wailing alarm.

"Let me go."

He did.

We stared at one another as, down on the dance floor below, the kaleidoscopic pulse of the fire alarm dueled against the DJ's light show. It was difficult to tell which was winning—the crowd had thinned, but many revelers were still caught in an alchemical trance.

Kai rifled through the VIP room, but there was little besides empty champagne bottles and melted ice.

"Good thing we didn't try to catch Sierra," I said, acid dripping from my voice.

"Rash actions won't clear your name."

"Whatever you say, Zen master." I could still taste Sierra's soul on my tongue. Vanilla mixed with a sharply unpleasant flavor that I tried to ignore.

The music cut off, as did the alarm, sending the clubbers into a semi-confused daze.

"Looks like something's happening down there." Before Kai could protest, I headed down the opposite stairwell.

I emerged in a roped-off section near the dance floor. A door stood nearby, a glowing exit sign flickering above.

Unfortunately, it was also blocked by a certain warlock with a serious stick up his ass.

"My dear girl, I would say it is a surprise to see you causing this mess," Moreland said, his willowy form shambling forward and ducking beneath the ropes, "but, alas, you always have your nose where it does not belong."

I instinctively reached for the Reaper's Switch, but Moreland sent a burst of flame soaring over my shoulder before I could even touch my jeans. The warlock flashed his yellow teeth, his dead eyes boring into me with frigid indifference.

Motive and reality crashed together in a lightning bolt of realization.

"You," I said. "It was you all along." He'd have known who Roan Kelly was. As Aldric's Head of Intelligence, he could've had eyes on my villa—which would explain how he'd ambushed Roan right outside. And if I took the fall, then his new Reaper—my sister, no less—would grant him a monopoly in the soul trade.

I hadn't seen it before, but it was obvious: Moreland was more ambitious than a mere number two. He wanted his own pie, and Aldric was never going to give him that. Building his own alchemical bakery, then, demanded a little ingenuity.

"Do not act so surprised, dear girl." Oh yeah—no surprise at all, finding Aldric's right-hand man at a club clearly competing against the vampire warlord's holdings. A boss who he still called Master. "Framing you was a true delight."

Totally unsurprising.

Definitely saw it coming.

Moreland raised his hand suddenly, a blazing, white-hot inferno spinning around his pale fingers. I turned slightly, seeing that Kai had raised his service weapon.

"Put it down," I said in a low steady voice.

"I can't do that, Eden." Kai didn't sound scared. Just doing his job. Goddamnit, why couldn't he have a little cowardice in his body? That would be useful for self-preservation in a time like this.

"Listen to the girl, my handsome friend. You have no dog in this race."

"Last chance." Kai's calm voice was stern. I'd listen to it. But then, I was still human—mostly. Moreland was a big shit sandwich of sociopath, warlock, and asshole, garnished with a thousand years of murder and terror, which meant he had no conscience and didn't scare easily.

I stepped between him and Kai. It was the only way to save Kai's life. Even if it meant dying myself. Clearly Sierra could handle herself these days—even if that meant throwing morality to the wind.

"You will die for him?"

"When you put it like that, I'm not so sure," I said, silently hoping that Kai would get the message and put down the gun. Sure, there was still a good chance Moreland would roast us both anyway. But there was a non-zero chance, if we surrendered, that the warlock would try to rope us into some scheme to dispatch Aldric. That would buy us time, which right now, was quickly ticking toward the end of our days.

"Your wake of destruction grows." The slightest glimmer flickered in the warlock's dead eyes. "It is a special sort of gift."

"I didn't ask for this."

"There is always a choice, dear girl." The fiery ball grew bigger. "And you made yours in the back of that car four years ago."

"When did you make yours, then?" I asked.

"When I saw a better opportunity." Instead of burning me into cinders, Moreland swiped with his hand. A sharp burst of wind flung me against the DJ's stage. My neck snapped backward like a crash test dummy as I hit the short metal supports. Woozy and stunned, I heard what sounded like a gunshot, followed by a stifled gag.

"Kai..." I croaked the name out, using what little air was left in my lungs. It didn't matter. Moreland was probably wearing the poor bastard's head as a hat, getting ready to parade it in front of me before he ended my life.

Yet another casualty on my watch.

I gritted my teeth, and briefly thought of Cross's sacrifice inside the treasure room. Two was too many deaths for one day. I coaxed myself into a sitting position and blinked, trying to orient my brain. The exit sign blurred orange, but Moreland was nowhere to be seen.

Then I heard Kai say, "You should have stepped aside."

Head swimming, I looked up, trying to process things. No large tattooed corpse tumbled next to me, no pleas for mercy.

Well, that wasn't true. But the pleas were coming from

Moreland, who burbled something incoherent out of my field of view.

"Can you get the door, Eden?" Kai knelt next to me and offered his hand. His expression was placid, although his eyes were filled with mild concern. I guess this was a test to make sure I wasn't bleeding out internally.

I got up somewhat unsteadily, but limped underneath the velvet rope and got to the exit. Sunlight streamed inside the club. Kai stood over the ancient warlock, who was still whimpering in the dingy corner nearby. There was a growing crimson stain around the warlock's tailored dress shirt. The agent's gun was trained firmly at Moreland's pale head.

"You can't kill me." Moreland tried to sneer, but his lips involuntarily twisted in pain rather than derision. "Do you know who I am?"

Kai didn't react. With his free hand, he brushed a few strands of long hair away from his face. I could see the tattoos glowing in the dim light. He had sigils hidden amongst them. The spear was alight, containing a magic I hadn't seen before. A sort of protective, gentle power that also contained a remarkable ferocity.

Instead of pulling the trigger, Kai dragged the warlock up by the shirt collar, then threw the injured man over his strong shoulder.

Still holding the door, I said, "What the hell are you doing?"

"Bringing him in." Kai ducked so that he didn't knock Moreland's slack body against the frame. I would've bounced that bastard's head off every column and wall from here to the field office. But then, I was still a little wound up about the whole him killing me thing.

Then him trying to frame me. Some people you just can't win over, you know?

I followed Kai down the back alley that filtered into the main street. There was a crowd still waiting outside Alkemy, clearly upset about the disturbance. I didn't blame them. Whatever Moreland was spiking the drinks with, the soul fragments gave them an addictive buzz.

The crowd barely paid us notice, despite the bleeding man hoisted over Kai's shoulder. The agent set the warlock down on the pavement as he fished out his keys.

"Tell me what you did to my sister." I knelt next to Moreland. "Tell me, you goddamn—"

"*Eden*." Kai finally spoke again. "You can't interrogate him now. He's injured."

"Yes, listen to your handler, Eden—" A terrible scream cut Moreland's taunt short as I jabbed my fingers into the gunshot wound perforating his belly.

I felt myself being lifted away, my legs kicking over nothing as blood dripped from my fingers. Everyone outside was now staring at me. Worth it. I think Moreland was shedding actual tears near the sedan's wheel well.

Kai set me down near the car's back door and glared at me. For him, that must've qualified as seething rage. "A conviction will be difficult enough already with the prime suspect present during the arrest."

"I was thinking concrete boots and a little trip out to sea was more appropriate."

Kai didn't find my joke amusing. He lifted a single finger, as if to say *cool it*, then turned his attention to the sputtering Moreland. I opened the sedan's back door, resisting the urge to inflict more pain on the man who had destroyed my world. The warlock slumped into the back seat and closed his eyes, his pale face turning a snowy type of ashen I'd only seen in corpses.

I could only hope the bastard would die before due process got ahold of him.

Protocol. This was why I didn't work with the FBI. Right before I'd dropped out of high school, a recruiter had visited our class. Singled me out to talk after—said I'd make a hell of a profiler. That I could read people, see the stories written across their faces. I knew that already, since I'd been studying for a few years by that point. But I wasn't a fan of paperwork, or making shit money, so I'd flipped him the bird.

Somehow, this all felt like some weird version of an alternate future, like one of those movies where the main character got to see the road untaken. And man, this path *sucked*. I silently seethed in the passenger seat as the engine roared to life. Kai cut the sedan through the crowd, which had returned to complaining about the interrupted party. The club zombies barely got out of our way.

We were around the corner, heading for what I presumed was headquarters, when I felt a tap against my seat.

Turning, I found Moreland's yellow, jagged teeth staring back at me. So the bastard hadn't died. And his color had returned.

"You should have listened to the girl," the warlock said. His dead eyes stared at me with what for him must've been insane glee. "For there is no cure for a rabid dog."

Kai reached for his service weapon. His tattoos glowed.

But the back door was already flapping open, and Moreland was tumbling out of the car, rolling along the road before either of us could stop him. Kai slammed on the brakes and backed up, but the warlock was up and sprinting, using the last of his magical energy to send the sedan careening off course.

We spun out and hit a fire hydrant, water spraying over the hood.

By the time Kai got out and looked around, the unpleasant truth had already settled in.

Moreland was in the wind.

40

BUT OUR RABID DOG HAD LEFT CLUES IN THE BACK OF the sedan. A business card, to be exact, emblazoned with the name Soul Enterprises, which would have meant nothing except for the neon pink font that screamed one man and one man only.

"We need to have a chat with the mayor," I said, handing the card back to Kai.

The agent looked up the street, which was largely abandoned, since it was the tail end of the workday. "I'm not sure, Eden."

"They're working together," I said, slamming the back door. "What's not to get?"

I wiped what felt like water from my cheek, but turned out to be Moreland's blood. Catching sight of myself in the side mirror, I saw what looked like a feral lunatic. No wonder I hadn't gotten into Alkemy. The gushing hydrant had subsided to a steady kind of stream that flooded the street. My shoes made a splashing noise with each step as I went to get back in the car.

"I'm sorry." Kai shook his head. "Look what happened."

Here my only ally was ready to throw in the towel because he didn't have clearance from on high.

"Let me ask you something," I said, letting my fingers slip away from the cool metal. "You think your superiors gathered all that information in my file through *legal* means?"

Kai's throat pulsed as he swallowed, but the agent didn't answer. He knew I had a point, but he still believed in justice and the badge and doing things by the book, and all that crap everyone swore to abide by, but then realized— once they hit the dirty reality of life—would never really fly. Otherwise criminals would rule the asylum, flinging shit at everyone's life.

"The system has checks and balances." Kai pressed his hands against the dented chassis, looking like he was trying to push the car over. Given the ass-kicking he'd handed Moreland, I wouldn't bet against him being able to. "Someone has to be the balance, even if it's not easy."

"So the mayor, Moreland, whoever else is out there, they all go free?" I still hadn't told him about the mayor's murderous proclivities, but we could get to that bridge if we needed to cross it. The way I looked at the situation, the mayor—and my sister—could skate with their soul harvesting business if he just told me where to find Moreland.

Unless Mayor Cambridge had been in on Roan's murder, too, in which case I was jamming my Reaper's Switch straight up his creepy foot loving ass.

"I didn't say these choices were easy," Kai said. "Only necessary."

"Well," I said. "Moreland's liable to die out there if we don't find him." I raised my eyebrow and suppressed the urge to smirk. "*That* has to be against protocol."

Kai's brow furrowed in supreme annoyance at my infallible logic. But it was true: if Moreland died out there, that would present all sorts of issues for the type of guy who filled out every box on the report. I mean, he could've just fudged a little bit—adjusting for Moreland's unparalleled ability to be an incredible asshole—but that wasn't his style. Career ending demerits, or whatever the Feds handed out, would rain down upon his beautiful, flowing hair.

"Then we'll find the warlock." Kai's hands slid off the top of the car. "Does that work for you?"

"I'll let you know after we talk to the mayor."

41

IT WAS THE KICKOFF TO CAMPAIGN SEASON, AND someone had forgotten to tell me. As the sedan pulled up to the ritzy cul-de-sac, I saw that the mayor's front lawn was covered in a crowd of excited people in board shorts and sandals, enjoying drinks made from actual pineapples. It was about as chintzy as you could get—full-on political cheese, complete with Firewalk Fundraiser banners draped all over his pink mansion like this was a going out of business sale. If I had a say in things, it damn well might be just that. Would-be donors danced barefoot across a pit of glowing coals, falling into the arms of their drunken and overly impressed colleagues waiting on the other side.

I shared a look with Kai before we got out of the car. Bad eighties pop music that should have been put out to pasture decades ago blasted from loudspeakers set up near the stairs. The slightly older crowd was loving it, reliving songs from their youth in cocktail-fueled nostalgia. I weaved through the crowd of poorly dancing forty-somethings, finding Mayor Stefan Cambridge chatting to a woman who had gotten one too many facelifts in her pursuit of the fountain of youth.

Not waiting for their conversation to conclude, I simply cut in and said, "We need to talk."

"Eden. Have you met the amazing Miss—"

"Cut the bullshit, killer. I'm not in the mood."

His friendly grin stayed super-glued in place, but his eyes turned cold. Yeah, yeah, we had a secret. I wasn't going to spill it to all the people risking third-degree burns trying to feel better about their lack of actual courage. Unless he insisted on doing the down-home, aww shucks routine around me. That might've been too much to take, after I'd helped him bury a headless corpse in the backyard, not two hundred yards away.

Stefan gave the plastic woman an apologetic smile. "I'm sorry, honey, but this is urgent."

The woman didn't seem bothered at all. She gave him a big, drunken hug, then stumbled off to join the festivities by the fire hazard. Once she was gone, the mayor looked between Kai and me and shook his bald, gleaming head.

"I thought we had an agreement, Reaper." There was the smooth, featureless voice that I knew so well. "Let us talk inside."

He gestured toward the polished concrete stairs. The blood from when I'd been here last had been scrubbed clean, leaving no trace of his misdeeds. Kai and I took the lead, filtering past the pulsing loudspeakers. The massive two-story front doors were open, welcoming anyone inside the sprawling mansion. After we were all inside the doors slammed shut behind us.

I gave Stefan a funny look.

He shook his head. "Merely a security feature."

"I see." I took the business card from my pocket and waved it in his face. "You've been busy."

Stefan glanced down each wing of the house. Satisfied no one was listening, he paced around the massive foyer. "Is it a crime to be a businessman?"

"We only want Moreland," Kai said, speaking for the first time.

"The name doesn't ring a bell."

"Cut the shit," I said.

"Do I need my lawyer here?" A tad of that *aww shucks* was coming back, and it was making my blood boil. I didn't care that he was running a side business with my sister's help that encroached on my gig. But I did care that he'd gotten my little sister involved in the first place—and was now preventing us from tracking down Moreland.

"You can have counsel present if you want, Mayor Cambridge," Kai said. "But we'd prefer if this was a quick visit."

Cambridge. The name was as fake as his manufactured accent. I had to admit one thing: the mayor had balls. Declaring war on Aldric from the shadows with his own soul harvesting operation. Stepping into the public eye with a secret like his. I could appreciate the audaciousness of that con, even if it made my skin crawl.

"I would think that would be for the best, wouldn't it?" Stefan smiled at me, and I lost it.

I leapt at him before Kai could stop me, bowling the mayor over into one of the curved marble staircases. We collapsed with a dull, echoing *thud* against the hard floor. The mayor was a lot bigger, but I'd caught him off guard. Perched atop him, with my knees digging into his chest, I looked down with wild eyes.

"Tell us where Moreland is."

"My, my, how aggressive." Stefan made no display of resisting. Even though he was of average build, he still had sixty pounds on me. And I thought it strange that he refused to cast any spells—after all, he was a rather potent warlock, if his soul's signature was anything to go by. Instead, he allowed his bald head to slump against the cold ground in defeat.

"I'll show you aggressive," I said, reaching toward my pocket.

"If you're upset about your sister, you should know something." He looked me dead in the eye. "She came to me."

"Bullshit." But my rebuke sounded less than certain. Confused by his lack of fight and what he'd just said, I hesitated for a critical moment. A strong hand settled on my shoulder.

"Eden." Kai sounded concerned, like I'd lost it. Maybe he was right. I turned to look at him, which is when it happened. Quick as lightning, Stefan's arm came up, holding a needle. It plunged into Kai's wrist with a pneumatic hiss. Surprise registered in the agent's eyes, and he stumbled backward, reaching for his service weapon.

He didn't make it. Kai was out on his feet before he crashed to the ground.

Stefan flipped me with ease, pinning me down by my wrists. Amusement danced in his eyes, like this was all a game. Pure fear sluiced through my veins. It had all been a con—a game of possum to trick me into over aggression. He had read the situation and arranged the dominoes accordingly.

All he'd needed to do was tip the first one by inviting us inside.

"It would be preferable if Moreland did not go to jail."

The cold, featureless voice returned, sliding past my ears like glass. "You understand. Bad for business. He's one of our best clients."

As a response, I spit in his face.

His joy didn't go away. Stefan hoisted me over his shoulder.

I kicked and clawed.

"I will be forced to use a sedative if you do not go peacefully."

"Fuck off." I bit him in the ear. Not a second later, I felt a needle nip through my skin.

The world went fuzzy.

Then it winked away like a television in a power outage.

42

Someone shook me awake. I punched blindly into the fuzzy darkness, and the same person caught my wrist.

"It's me," Kai said, by way of explanation. His tattooed arm held mine, my knuckles only inches from his jaw. He released his grip slowly, and I retracted my arm.

"What happened?"

"Drugged and kidnapped." The way he said it, we might as well have been out for ice cream or ticking a box on a list of errands. No fear, just pragmatic calm. This was the situation, such as it was.

I didn't share his stoic approach to the whole thing. The last few moments came rushing back—Stefan Cambridge leering at me in amusement. Goddamn, if I could jam my Reaper's Switch into his neck...

Our prison was dimly lit and smelled musty. Chunks of dirt crumbled beneath my fingertips as I rubbed them over the unfinished floor.

We were underground, in a tight cellar.

My head almost touched the ceiling as I stood. From the single, flickering bulb, I could see drag marks in the red soil.

Kai had a long streak of dirt along his back, and the tips of his black hair were covered in dust.

The cellar was narrow, no more than six feet wide. It extended about twenty feet in each direction, making it feel like a tunnel without an exit. Actually, that was wrong—up ahead, near the flickering bulb, there was a vault grade steel door. I approached it and pounded against the thick metal. My fists barely even made a sound.

No one would hear us die down here.

I walked the other way, past Kai. Lining the narrow room were shelves stocked with apothecarial jars. When I paused to examine the contents, however, I found that these weren't the healing herbs an apothecarial warlock might have. No. These were the kind of supplies an alchemist would have.

I unleashed a bitter snort at how on-the-nose Alkemy's name had been. Alchemy was the process of turning non-magical items into ones of magical power. It was dangerous and outlawed—the Department of Supernatural Affairs hunted alchemists like Salem had once hunted witches. That didn't stop some people from dabbling, creating their own homebrew concoctions in hopes of gaining powers. Most simply poisoned themselves or melted off their hands. From these supplies, however, it was clear that Stefan was one of the rare individuals who had mastered his craft.

He, my sister, and Moreland enjoyed a symbiotic sort of relationship. She reaped the souls, he brewed the love potions, and Moreland provided security and a millennium of guidance for the fledgling operation.

Maybe it was time to accept that the Sierra I'd once known wasn't the one who existed now.

I ran my fingers over the concrete back wall, finding no cracks in the surface. What I did find, however, was faded blood. I dropped down, spotting a message scrawled with a hairpin or paper clip. SAVE ME FROM THIS MADMAN.

The row of skulls in the garden shed flashed through my mind, and I realized with a sickened feeling that no one had come to save whoever was down here before. Stefan held his victims prisoner before finally decapitating them. I didn't know what pathological allure that sequence of events held, but then again, I wasn't a serial killer.

But, as the prisoner, I was less than thrilled by the prospect of experiencing it.

Dejected, I returned to Kai and slumped down across from him, a small cloud of dust whipping through the air as I settled in.

"Well, this didn't go as planned," I said in the silent still-ness, lacking any more eloquent observations.

"I suppose not." Kai smiled grimly. "But there are worse fates."

"Being locked up in a serial killer's root cellar is pretty close to rock bottom, man."

Kai's brow furrowed slightly, but he didn't answer. After a long silence, I said, "Fine. I caught the mayor burying bodies in the backyard, but didn't tell you."

"Why?"

"I might have been roped into burying one with him."

Kai brushed red dust from his hair. "I see."

"That's all you have to say?"

"I can see why you'd be loath to share that particular information with me."

"Nothing gets to you, does it?"

"That's true for no man." Kai patted his pockets. His service weapon was gone—naturally—but he'd been left with his phone. My heart soared when he raised the device up, but then it crashed when he shook his head. "No service."

"Guess that'd be too much to ask for." I put a finger in my shirt collar and stretched it out. The place was beginning to feel claustrophobic, and it was getting hard to breathe.

Kai, in a cool voice, said, "A vacuum seal keeps the wares fresh."

I did *not* like the sound of that—because it meant Stefan was slowly suffocating us by sucking the air out of the room. What an ignominious end to this whole affair. We'd solved the case and had Moreland in our grasp. But instead of glory—or revenge—we were going to die alone in a musty basement for our troubles.

As a final check, I patted down my own pockets. Empty. I felt a small pang of emptiness as I realized he'd taken the Reaper's Switch. Not that it made much sense to leave me down here with it.

Just as I was about to give into fate, Kai rose and began scanning the myriad jars lining the shelves. I watched him for a few minutes as he pulled things down and muttered to himself. Finally I said, "What are you doing?"

"Many years ago, when I lived on Oahu, my mother passed down to me what her mother had once taught her."

"You're talking about your sigils?"

"No. That was a gift from my father, given to me after he died." Kai didn't expand on this point, and it didn't seem like the time to go digging for details. But I was curious. His soul was clearly human, if slightly augmented by outside forces. Unless it was all some sort of scam, like Stefan cloaking himself as a powerful warlock—while actually being an alchemist.

My head was all kinds of fucked up. None of my

instincts were right. That was a bad place to be in, not being able to trust your senses.

I quieted the doubts in my head by looking at Kai. Here was a trustworthy man if I'd ever laid eyes on one. A man with secrets? Certainly—just the same as any other.

But could I be sure?

I said, "What was your mother?"

"Just a woman who believed in her son." Kai, by this point, was cradling so many jars that he had to put some of them down in the red dust before me. I recognized none of the labels. The glasses clinked together in the hollow stillness. After skimming the long shelves once more, he returned with one final ingredient.

This one I recognized.

I picked up the jar carefully. "You're not really considering this."

The faded masking tape read REAPER'S WILLOW in neat print. In times of emergency, when a Reaper's Switch wasn't present, the thorny plant could be used for soul harvesting.

I'd never had occasion to use it.

Until now.

The pungent smell of what could best be described as supercharged cinnamon flooded the tight space. I coughed and covered my nose with my t-shirt, eyes tearing from the sharp scent. Kai barely blinked as he mixed the ingredients in the jar's lid, measuring them out in pinches with a steady eye. When he was finished kneading the ingredients, he was left with a tiny pile of sawdust-colored powder.

"The Reaper's Willow, if you would."

I wrapped both hands around the glass. "You can't be serious."

"Unless you have a key to the door, I would suggest you hurry."

"You can't slice off part of your soul," I said, addressing the massive elephant sucking up all the oxygen in the room. "You have no idea what that will do."

"Who said anything about my soul?"

My pulse rose to a hammering crescendo until I realized he was joking. After running through the alternatives—and quickly realizing there were none—I handed him the jar.

"Thank you, Eden." He set the jar down and began unbuttoning his oxford shirt. "When I begin to shake, you must reach above my heart and extract a shard of my soul. And then shove that up my nose."

He pointed to the sawdust concoction.

"Oh, is that all?"

"I cannot do this without you. Only a Reaper can harvest souls." He gave me a kind look. "Just not too much, please."

"I'll try my best," I said, watching as he scratched himself with the willow's sharp thorn right above his heart. Blood dripped down his muscular chest from the deep cut, and I felt a slight bout of nausea coming on. That was new. I'd never been squeamish about this whole reaping thing, morbid as it was when you stopped to reflect. But I'd also never taken a shard of a living person's soul—Lucille notwithstanding. And I wasn't sure she really counted.

Kai put the thorny plant into one of the empty lids. The agent used his phone as a makeshift pestle, grinding the Reaper's Willow into dust as the air constricted around us. I slowed my breathing and tried to channel some of his preternatural calm. It didn't really work. My thoughts drifted from our predicament, then to Cross's, who was probably dead in the treasure tunnel. And, of course, Moreland, who was likely healing himself right now, and Stefan, who was glad-handing next to the firewalk somewhere above.

Actually, I didn't know where we were. Maybe he kept his supplies—like his trophy skulls—near the house. Or maybe we were stashed off the grid, where no one would ever think to look.

"Remember, when I begin to shake." A light sweat covered Kai's brow, and his breathing was shallow. His natural tan complexion was unusually pale, and a vein throbbed in his forehead. He checked the cut in his chest with a probing finger, working the digit into the wound to widen it a little more. I heard a soft groan escape from his clenched teeth.

"What are you," I said in awe as he removed his bloodied finger and exhaled.

"Just a man, Eden." With a blank look of determination, he took the lid full of ground-up Reaper's Willow and shotgunned the entire mountain of powder in one gulp. His thick neck worked overtime, trying to down it without any water. Almost immediately, his body began to shake.

I leapt into action, trying to get a hold on him. But he weighed about two-twenty of solid muscle, built like some sort of combination between a linebacker and Greek god—and by shake, he'd actually meant violently thrash. The shelving trembled as his shoulders bashed against the metal, even though it was bolted into the earthen walls.

I tried to plunge my fingers into the wound, but his head snapped forward like it'd been shot from a rifle, connecting solidly with my chest. What little air I'd managed to force into my lungs ejected into the musty cellar. Rasping, I dropped to my hands and knees, trying to will myself forward. Kai continued spasming, his foot kicking over the sawdust mixture as I dug my fingers into the hard dirt.

I heaved myself forward, landing on top of him as he bucked like a prized rodeo steer. One hand clutching his arm just to hang on, I aimed the other one at the bleeding wound in his chest. Then I jabbed my fingers in, feeling his warm flesh. The shaking grew more violent, probably from the pain, but I dug deeper. My thumb brushed up against his soul, the energy coursing through my skin.

His soul had sharp edges, sharper than I'd imagined. But it also felt smooth and inviting, like a pleasant stone. I torqued my wrist like I was revving a bike, and I felt a shard snap off in my hand. Kai let out a thunderous groan that filled the entire root cellar.

"Sorry." I yanked my hand out and let go, rolling to the side to avoid his thrashing arms. Between my bloody fingers, I clutched a swirling shard, light and darkness intertwined around each other. Not quite what I'd expected, but then, it was hard to really know anyone—right?

His movements dampened, and I felt myself getting lightheaded. I slipped the shard into my pocket and looked for the lid. The powder was gone, having been overturned during the chaos. But I spotted a small pile of it in the red dust. Beggars couldn't be choosers, and I took a large pinch of it, red dust and all, and shoved it right up his nose.

For a moment, nothing happened. His arms quivered.

Then Kai unleashed a massive sneeze, and his eyes flared open. He took a giant gulp of air, like he'd just come to the surface after being held down by a wave. For the first time since I'd met him, the agent looked scared and confused. Then his gaze settled on me and the calmness returned.

I had that effect on people, apparently.

Kai looked for his shirt. I dug it out from halfway beneath the shelf and handed it to him.

He glanced at his bleeding chest wound before buttoning his shirt up. "You got it?"

I nodded and pulled it out. "What now?" He still hadn't covered *why* we needed a soul shard in the first place.

He cocked his head at the soul, like he was staring at his own reflection in the mirror for the first time ever. There was no surprise in his expression, just a deep understanding and acceptance. With a wince, he tried to stand, but was still too weak from the ordeal to do so.

With a slightly embarrassed expression, he nodded toward the steel door. "Can you get the jar with the black powder?"

"What's it called?"

"It's unmarked."

My head swam, breathing more carbon dioxide than oxygen at this point. I steadied myself on the shelf, pulling myself along like a person caught in a windstorm. Near the metal door were a row of tipped over jars. I fumbled through them, trying to read the masking tape labels in the dim light. Eventually my heavy fingers found the unmarked jar.

Clutching it in both hands, I stumbled back to Kai and dropped to my knees. I held the glass out like I was offering him the Holy Grail. With substantial effort, he raised his right arm and took the jar from my grasp. He struggled with the lid, eventually getting it free. Then he slipped the white-and-black swirled soul shard into the jar and tightened the lid back on.

"You're going to want to cover your ears."

"Why—"

Kai chucked the jar against the metal door, and everything exploded in a sea of white light.

When the dust cleared, a smoldering hole sat where the door had once been. My ears rang from the explosion as oxygen flooded the narrow space, flushing out the stale air.

Kai turned to me, and I saw him mouth the words more than I heard them.

"Because it's about to get loud."

43

THE SOUL SHARD HAD ACTED AS A CATALYST FOR THE gunpowder Stefan had stored in the tight cellar. Good thing Kai had a few hidden talents—like powerful sigils and ancient crafting recipes—hidden behind that attractive jaw. Otherwise, we'd have both kicked it.

Outside the ruined door, there was a small ladder—about eight feet high—that led to a hatch. I scurried up first and tried the lock. To my minor surprise, it opened immediately. Guess there was no point in keeping this bolted down, since it was impossible to escape the actual cellar. Or so Stefan likely thought.

I peeked out from the hatch, smelling fresh cut grass, craft beer, and grilled beef. The sun was just beginning to set in an orange fuchsia burst, casting a tropical glow over a familiar place. Stefan's front yard, and just to the right, the large, wide, polished concrete steps. A large tree blocked my view of the festivities, but I could hear the bad pop music and drunken donors just fine.

I reached up and touched the top of the hatch. It was covered in sod. This guy got a charge out of doing everything in plain sight. The thrill made his hobby all the more exciting. I scurried outside, lying belly down on the grass. The tree shielded me from view. Kai joined me a few seconds later.

He said, "Unbelievable."

"Took the words right out of my mouth."

"This ends now." He swept the long, dark hair out of his eyes. "I'm sorry I didn't see it sooner."

"You have nothing to be sorry about," I said, looking into his calm gaze. But he seemed a little less gentle and a whole lot more dangerous. Shaving a piece off your soul will do that. The side effects, from what I'd heard, were unpredictable. Take too much, and a person could completely lose themselves.

"Sometimes the right way is the wrong way." Kai rose from the ground, stretching his broad shoulders wide like a viper about to strike. I scrambled to join him, but he was already marching toward the party with long, determined strides that left me far behind. Emerging from behind the tree, I saw him come up behind Stefan and grab the murderous alchemist by the throat.

Then the agent threw the mayor into the nearby equipment table. The music stuttered and skipped, finally groaning to a sad, sputtering halt. Nervous chatter erupted from the crowd of donors. Some people grabbed their phones to tape the incident, while others backed away, ready to leave. I hurried to the would-be videographers and snatched the phones. They were too stunned to notice.

One soccer mom wouldn't give hers up. "This is an abuse of power."

"You're right about that, ma'am," I said, then boxed her in the ear. She shrieked and let the device loose. I took the opportunity to drop it into the grass and then mash it into a silicon pulp with my sneaker.

Behind me, I heard a crack. It didn't sound like plastic. Judging from the mayor's screaming, it had been bone.

I turned to find Kai dragging the mayor by the shirt toward the street. Stefan's arm dangled uselessly by his side. Every time they hit a bump, the mayor would scream in pain. Satisfied that we wouldn't suddenly be trending on social media, I rushed after Kai.

He had his boot positioned over Stefan's head. Any vestige of the old Kai had vanished, repossessed by what seemed like a demon. The mayor babbled and prayed for his life—an ironic moment, to be sure, but one I couldn't fully appreciate when Kai was about to join him down a dark hole of no return.

"This isn't who you are."

"I thought following the rules was the answer," Kai said. "But now, I'm thinking that everything is just a little broken, no matter what you do."

Christ. This soul-losing business had hit him harder than I'd expected. I held up my hands and approached. "We need to get out of here."

"Not before he pays for his crimes."

"Oh, he'll get his," I said, looking at the blood-slicked bald head quivering on the pavement. "He'll have to live with his urges and never give in again."

"Why's that?"

"Because he doesn't want to die," I said, kneeling next to the shaking serial killer. There were no down-home politician put-ons or automaton-esque speeches. Just a sick man, a very sick man, who was now out of commission. "Do you want to die, mayor?"

"No!" Stefan's response was a screech.

"Then explain to the good people here what you did."

"I've done nothing! You're insane—"

Kai's boot ground his face against the gravel, and the mayor screamed.

"I don't have time for this," I said. "Repent."

"The bodies are in the backyard." He sniffled, practically drowning in his own snot. "And they weren't all bad people, either."

"I know." I pushed down the memory of filling the hole. At least that guy hadn't been a peach. Not that I could have done anything. Resist, and I would've just ended up in Stefan's root cellar earlier. But the mere association, even under duress, was something I'd just have to live with.

"And Moreland."

"He has a—a hideout."

"*Where?*"

"In the northeast." Stefan babbled an approximate location. From the geographical landmarks he spat out, it wasn't terribly far from Aldric's floating house on the ocean. Guess Stefan wasn't the only one who liked doing risky things right under people's noses. Aldric's very own right-hand man liked doing it, too.

I tugged at Kai's shirtsleeve. "Let's go."

"Our weapons."

I glanced at the sedan parked in the cul-de-sac. There really wasn't time, but I couldn't leave my Reaper's Switch here. The Feds would descend on this garish property like flies once they heard about the mayor's exploits, and the blade was liable to get lost in the bureaucratic shuffle.

"You heard the man," I said.

"In the tool shed."

Not this shit again. I glanced back at the partygoers. Those who had stuck around the Firewalk Fundraiser were still watching in rapt horror. From the glint on their dinner plates, they were using actual silverware. I sprinted back to the yard and plucked the first steak knife I could find off a skinny man's plate. Then I returned and placed the serrated edge against Stefan's thumb.

"What are you—"

I drove the steak knife down with the full weight of my front foot. There was a snap of bone breaking as I felt the blade cut through to the pavement. Blood dribbled along the perfect white lines beneath my sneaker. I pulled my foot away, and saw the thumb lying by itself.

I grabbed the digit and dashed to the house. Two minutes later, I was back with the Reaper's Switch and Kai's Glock 22—carried by one of the donors, since it would've seared my hands.

The agent lingered by the sobbing, broken mayor.

The donor handed him the pistol and scurried off.

"We need to wrap this up," I said.

Kai stared at the mayor for what seemed like an eternity.

I held my breath, eyes fixated on the gun.

Then the agent headed for the car, and I breathed a sigh of relief.

At least a shred of his former self remained.

But we'd see how much survived after the day was through.

44

THE GOVERNMENT SEDAN WOBBLED AND GROANED OVER the poorly maintained road. Finally, an axle snapped, and my side of the car dropped to the asphalt, grinding to an ear-splitting halt. Toucans squawked with displeasure. We were beyond the edge of civilization, having passed both Healing Paws Vet Clinic and the turn to Aldric's private on-the-water getaway miles ago. If those two places were off the beaten path, then Moreland's digs were off the grid entirely. Then again, no one chose to live at the base of a snowy mountain on paradise.

No one, that is, except an ancient warlock with an equally chilly heart and plenty to hide.

I slammed my shoulder into the door, and the twisted metal groaned in protest. A sharp kick was enough to open it about half a foot. I squeezed out, thankful for my slight figure, and shivered. We were still in the jungle, but the hint of frost hung in the air. The snow-capped peak—taller than Everest, if you could believe it—devoured the immediate horizon.

The beginnings of a moon shone above the road. Out

here, near Mount Danube—so named for the river near which Aldric had almost died—the treetops weren't as lush or thick. I joined Kai on the other side of the car. He was typing on his phone.

"What's that about?"

"I told Rayna where we are. I'm not sure if she's on my side, but she should be partially on yours, if you're part of their grand plan." Kai's features darkened. The spear sigil on his forearm glowed, casting a blue tint over the rest of his tattoos. Either he was afraid we weren't going to make it by ourselves, or he was afraid of what he might do.

Perhaps both.

My own phone buzzed like an angry hornet in my pocket. I was surprised the thing still worked. I glanced at the caller ID, but the screen was still a garbled mess of symbols. Nonetheless, I had a good idea of who was calling.

I answered the call with a friendly, "Hi."

"This is not what we agreed to." Aldric's icy voice cut across the crappy connection like a cold blade.

"You got your seven souls before noon."

"Do not try my patience."

"Ready for the big reveal?"

"Your life hangs by a thread, Eden."

I told him about the banyan tree, then said, "You're welcome."

"What's out there?"

"Telling you would ruin the surprise," I said.

"This had better be worth my while, Eden."

"For both our sakes, I hope that's true," I said before slipping the phone back in my pocket.

Kai gave me a look, but didn't ask who it was. From all I'd told him, he could probably guess.

The mossy road sprawling out in front of us looked like

it had been abandoned after a post-apocalyptic earthquake. Large slabs of asphalt jutted up from the ruined ground, like a giant had hurled a bunch of massive, crumbling discuses into the earth. We wove our way through the wreckage, following what looked like an ATV's tracks—fresh, judging by the indentations in the thick moss.

"Moreland is out here." I touched a red stain in one of the tracks, feeling a wintery chill rustle my hair. He was still bleeding. "Somewhere."

"Very helpful."

I slid over a downed banana tree blocking the road and glanced at my de facto partner. A little snark. I'd have to keep an eye on him. We'd narrowly avoided having Stefan's spinal fluid leaking all over the perfect cul-de-sac. To be clear, I had no qualms about seeing Moreland's guts staining the perfect snow. But with backup arriving, and goddesses-knew-what-else lurking at the base of mountain, I really needed the wise, controlled Kai. Not some loose cannon.

The agent didn't return my gaze. His pistol was out, ready to fire. The man who had been prepared to take Moreland in hours before—even if it hadn't been the right move—had apparently scrapped that idea completely. It wasn't just his damaged soul. I could taste it a little more, now. He'd been keeping some dark shit down before.

We all had secrets.

Some of them were more dangerous than others.

I wondered what Sierra had felt in my soul in the VIP room—if she could taste what the last four years had done to me. Was Reaping only from the dead—and keeping to the outskirts of Aldric's enterprise—enough to save me from the darkness? Or was the fact that I *hadn't* stepped into the actual arena the real source of the jaded cynicism that draped over my life like a cloak?

Flurries swirled in the chilled air. My sneakers slipped a little on the rough terrain. Patches of ice fought the moss for control of the abandoned road. We'd traveled about a mile from the sedan, and the trees were now turning into sparse, spindly versions impersonations of their former selves. Ahead, they stopped completely, the road disappeared, and the landscape was completely blanketed by snow.

The little hairs on my bare arms rose as I shivered. The blue sky framing Mount Danube was slowing ceding to a gray, foggy mess that meant only one thing: a storm was coming up here, too.

"Lucille," I shouted, my voice swallowed by a howling wind. "Where are you?"

The wind only roared louder in response. My shoes crunched in the soft, fresh snow. Multiple sets of additional footprints—and blood—graced the perfect white landscape. Across the blank, snowy expanse, tucked behind a craggy rock outcropping at the mountain's base, I spied a thin tendril of smoke snaking into the sky. The blood trail and footprints headed the same way Stefan's directions led.

I circled over to Kai. Frost crystals clung to his long hair and eyelashes. He barely acknowledged my presence. He'd seen the smoke on the horizon, and was marching forward with single-minded determination.

"You sure we shouldn't wait for backup?"

"No time," Kai said, moving ahead with longer strides. I hurried to keep pace in the now ankle-deep snow.

I tried to rub some feeling back into my numb arms, failing miserably. The temperature had dropped from a pleasant tropical balm to a freezing winter in a manner of minutes. I suspected Lucille had a little to do with that—normally, the base of the mountain was a little chilly, but not covered in frost. That meant Moreland had stumbled out here *after* the goddess had already arrived.

Which meant she'd figured out his alchemical scheme a little before we had.

"We're walking into a trap," I said, screaming to be heard over the storm. "Lucille is already here."

"Then we'll deal with her, too."

"I don't think you understand." We weren't far from the smoke, now. Ahead, there was a clump of disturbed snow—like someone had been tackled and pressed into the powder. It was heavily bloodied, mixed with dirt. "*Look.*"

Kai paused and looked, but not at the powder. At me. I felt his blank gaze trace over my face. "I'm okay, Eden. You don't have to worry."

"Bullshit." I knew a lie when I heard one. "You need to pull it together."

Kai swept the ice from his hair. "Perhaps I've found that your approach is best."

"Yeah, just look at the great results." But he was already walking past the muddied snow, intent on ignoring any warning signs that got in the way of his objective.

Kai made his way around the craggy rock first. The mountain loomed so tall above that, with the swirling gray storm, it was now impossible to see the peak. I didn't know what to expect as I trudged dutifully toward the smoke. But I heard Kai say *damn* which didn't fill me with confidence.

As I rounded the rock, I found a small one-story log cabin puffing smoke. It was tucked in between two rocky formations that jutted from the mountain's base and surrounded the building like two bookends. There was a body out front—torn to bits, missing both arms. Kai was already heading for the cabin's open door.

I paused next to Moreland, whose dead black eyes were

now really dead. The gunshot wound had soaked his business casual shirt through with blood, but that wasn't what had killed him. From the blood spatter gracing the snow, the involuntary removal of his arms had been the finishing blow. The warlock looked mean and angry, even in death. Resisting the urge to kick the corpse, I instead flicked out the Reaper's Switch and took his soul.

It was gross and gelatinous, almost like raw sewage. I caught the whiff of desolation and ash that I'd had to endure for four years. But, riding on the whipping wind, I caught something else, too: a darker soul, if that was possible, soaked in bourbon.

Lucille was *inside*.

I heard a mighty groan come from the cabin—deep, and filled with pain. My pulse churned as I slid the soul into my pocket and headed for the wooden door. It thumped against the log exterior as the wind picked up. Teeth chattering, I entered the small structure.

Lucille sat in a handcrafted chair in the corner on the right side, by a roaring fire. There was a matching wooden table—barely large enough to seat two people—in the room's center. Otherwise, the cabin was entirely empty, save for a glass cabinet that took up the entirety of the opposite wall. It was filled, floor-to-ceiling, with neatly organized souls in small, clear plastic boxes. One of Lucille's DSA bureaucrats —this one a wolf instead of a demon—restrained Kai next to the cabinets. It didn't look necessary. He was frozen in place, suffering the same fate as Cross had in the Boundless Jungle.

"Shut the door, would you Eden?" I caught a better glimpse of Lucille's face. There was a pink scar on her cheek about the size of a casino chip where the magical coin had burned her face. She wore the plain clothes of an office drone. The straw-colored braid hung down in her lap, touching a pair of dark slacks that would look at home in any department store.

I was about to oblige her request when the door shut on its own with a mighty *thud*. When I glanced back at Lucille, she wore a mirthless smile. She didn't need me to close the door. Hopefully she needed me for something, otherwise I'd be dead.

"Sit down, would you?" Lucille gestured at the other chair next to the center table. I did as I was told, sitting at the table, watching her sit alone next to the fire, like a queen on a throne. Silence settled over the cabin. With the storm whipping outside and the fire crackling, it would have been relaxing had there not been a vengeful goddess involved.

I drummed my fingers on the table and said, "Well, this is an unpleasant surprise."

"For one of us." The goddess reached down and threw a log on the fire, sending a shower of sparking embers up the chimney. "I must really thank you, Eden."

"Oh, I'm sure it's nothing," I said.

"The Department of Supernatural Affairs had been looking for this alchemist for some time. Always starting new businesses, always slipping in just as we were about to punish him." Lucile crossed her leg and clasped her hands together. "The gods and goddesses in the Elysian Fields were beginning to grow quite concerned."

"You're still in contact?"

"Only when they dislike how I am handling matters, it seems." Lucille waved her plain hand, as if that was normally not an issue. "But you solved my little problem."

"Don't really see how I'm involved."

"After you...caught me off guard in the forest, I had men sent to your house with orders to follow you. I wanted to see if you would lead me to your little stash of troublesome coins. Instead, you led us to Moreland." Lucille spread her arms out wide, gesturing at the cabin. "And he led us to the heart of his operation."

"He's not an alchemist," I said, probing whether she knew about the mayor's true identity.

"No matter. He was the bankroll and the mastermind. Without its head, the rest of the snake will perish." Lucille stood sharply, and I jumped. The goddess glided over on her sensible shoes and leaned against my table. "And now, the question is, what to do with the snake before me?"

She snapped her fingers at her henchman. The were-wolf came over and removed a familiar piece of parchment from his back pocket. I glanced back at Kai. I could see in his eyes that he was awake and desperately trying to move. His magic had been powerful enough to get the drop on Moreland, but had little to offer against a goddess's powers. That didn't bode well for our chances of survival.

Lucille unraveled the ancient document, gauging my reaction. I didn't really have one, other than surprise. It was the glyph-cipher I'd dropped in the jungle. I hadn't had the opportunity to actually examine it, but I could now see Latin writing in a neat, cursive hand graced the parchment, with symbols glowing beneath the text.

"It's a glyph-cipher," Lucille said, by way of explanation. "A favorite of treasure hunters for centuries."

"Have you shown this to Cross?" I asked, trying to feel out whether he was still alive.

"That man proves as slippery as ever, little Reaper." Lucille tapped on the document. "I was hoping you might assist me in tracking him down."

I breathed a little easier. Cross wasn't dead—hopefully. Magnus's wide broadcast on the radio had drawn too much attention to the area, causing Lucille's minions to retreat. It wasn't a matter of power. She could have killed all the treasure seekers easily. Rather, it was a matter of exposure—because even a goddess had to answer to someone. And, in this case, her bosses were the pantheon of *other* deities who had banished her to Earth. Poke that bear too hard, and she could find herself in an even more ignominious bureaucratic position. Or dead.

I smiled, and she slammed her fist upon the table. "Need I remind you of your transgressions? You have killed, and you have wielded weapons. Your sister's life hangs by the faintest of cosmic threads."

My smile immediately faded and my voice turned into a low growl. "You don't touch her."

"That depends on what you say next." Lucille picked up the parchment by its edge. "Give me what I want, and perhaps there will be mercy."

"I'm not giving you shit."

Lucille nodded over my shoulder. I snapped my neck around just in time to see Kai briefly unfreeze, and the werewolf punch him in the gut. The FBI agent wheezed and fell to the floor before being frozen again mid-gasp.

"Neat trick," I said, but my sarcasm sounded hollow even to me.

"Thank you."

"The whole time-stoppage thing doesn't really gel with the rain goddess thing," I said.

"Each celestial being has a power entirely their own." Lucille's plain face lit up with delight, the fire glinting off the small stud in her nose. "I chose what could inflict the most agony upon my enemies."

"Delightful," I said.

"That is what we call leverage, Eden." Lucille waved

the treasure map in front of my nose like a dog owner would a treat before their canine companion. Annoyance crawled over my skin like fire ants, but I had to admit—however begrudgingly—that she held all the cards.

"What can I possibly give a goddess?" I asked, summoning all the deference I could muster. Hopefully the act would work.

Lucille took the bait. Flattery was hard to deflect, even for a powerful being. "Two small favors."

"And you'll let my sister live?"

"We shall see, should you behave yourself."

"Anything," I said, putting breathy desperation into my tone. "But the agent lives, too."

Lucille rolled up the parchment in her hands, like she was considering my offer. It was all a ruse. She'd already decided that I was the sole ticket to what she sought. This was just to make sure the balance of power stayed in her court.

I added to the illusion by sinking into the seat, shoulders slumped, with a worried wince on my face.

Finally, Lucille said, "I suppose that is something we can discuss."

I broke into a huge smile and said, "Thank you," as my thoughts screamed, *I'm gonna get you, bitch.*

"It's really nothing," Lucille said, trying to keep from beaming. No one had worshipped her like this in years. It must've been a pain in the ass being a goddess on Earth, only to be forced to keep it secret to keep the peace. Quite frankly, it was incredible that someone with her ego had managed to do so. No doubt her powerful overlords in the Elysian Fields had driven home the importance of keeping a low profile.

"What can I get for you?"

The fire went out, and a biting cold seeped into the room. A little bit of theatrics before the big reveal.

"The piece of me you took," Lucille said. "And the treasure hunter."

I resisted the urge to smile. Instead, I said, "That can be arranged."

Yes, it could.

Hell, if I was lucky, I might just get rid of every noose on my neck by the end of the night.

"Then put your little pen knife on the table," Lucille said, watching me like a lioness as I removed the Reaper's Switch from my jeans. "And let's get started."

Oh, yes, Lucille, I thought. *Let's finish this for good.*

45

IF I'D BEEN EXPECTING FOR A GODDESS TO RIDE AROUND on dragons, or teleport at will, I was disappointed. Either Lucille's powers had more limits than I'd thought, or she was playing things close to the vest. A temporarily mobile Kai and I were ushered into a disappointingly bland minivan. We enjoyed the entire backseat to ourselves, while Lucille rode shotgun and her werewolf associate drove.

The automobile rumbled across the dirt, branches and flowers scraping against the paint as we bounced onto the main road. It'd been tucked away in the jungle, hidden from prying eyes, which was why we'd missed it on the drive over. We'd passed the government sedan with the busted-up axle on the way.

It was full-on night, now, and I had plenty to think about as the car headed southeast, to the banyan tree where I'd stashed the goddess's soul shard. I had little confidence in Lucille upholding her end of our tenuous bargain. The second she had her soul and Cross in her hands, my sister, Kai, and I were all dead.

"You okay?" I kept my voice low as I addressed Kai. On

the outside he didn't look much worse for wear, but his reaction was sluggish, like he'd been drugged.

He blinked twice and said, "Not so good, Eden."

"Any idea what she's doing?"

"Temporal vortex," Kai said, the words slow and enunciated almost syllable-by-syllable. "Manipulating time and space on a very small, specific scale."

Luckily her powers had limits. I assumed that was why the stoppage effect was more of an exaggerated pause, where the victim's eyes could still move and certain limbs would continue moving through space—albeit at a glacial pace. That, and it didn't work on me. Whatever allowed me to be a Reaper also granted me immunity from such tricks.

Still, that was powerful magic. Not that I needed further confirmation of her power. She'd brought my sister back to life, after all. The absurdity of it all—and how things were about to end—made me laugh.

Both Kai and Lucille gave me odd glances, but only the goddess spoke. "I see little humor in your situation, Eden."

"Then at least we share that," I said, amid halting bursts of laughter. Even Lucille's furrowed stare couldn't get me to stop. Nope—everything was just too chaotic and random.

Rip off the rich, get dead.

Keep a low profile on the beach, get framed.

Follow protocol, get kidnapped.

Never give up, get fucked again.

I'd have wallowed in despair, but it was like the universe had been sending me a message all this time, and I just hadn't been listening. And now, with the scales seemingly tipped back in my favor—as the van barreled toward a crash course with Aldric at the banyan tree—I was just wondering how I was going to wind up clutching the short straw again.

Lucille threw up her hands and turned around. Well, at least I had one hidden talent: I was inscrutable to the goddess of rain herself. That had to count for something.

I finally collected myself, regaining a small shred of the confidence I'd felt in the cabin. She was going exactly where I needed her to. In the meantime, I just needed to keep it together.

I rested my chin on the plastic door and stared at the passing scenery. On the way, we passed a nondescript sedan that looked government issue. Rayna must've come out to back up her actual partner. The sedan braked behind us, clearly not expecting to encounter another car in the hinterlands. Our werewolf driver accelerated, though, and the sedan was out of sight before it could pick up our tail.

The rest of the ride was as uneventful and tranquil as a girl could expect for a trip to the gallows. Finally, after miles of jungle and backcountry roads, we ran out of road. We'd arrived, and my heart thumped in anticipation like I was about to go on stage for the biggest performance of my life. Too bad I didn't have anything to offer that would prevent this particular crowd from voting me off the island.

I glanced out the front windshield and saw a half dozen black SUVs belonging to Aldric. They were empty. Beyond that, I caught a glimpse of the edge of Dale's Rum Hut. It looked closed for the night—or due to inclement weather. Thunder crackled as I stepped outside.

"In case you forgot, little Reaper." Lucille eyed the phalanx of SUVs with suspicion. "Everything you love will die if you attempt to deceive me again."

"Dale makes a killer tequila shot," I said. "His drinks are in high demand."

She wasn't buying that explanation, and neither was her werewolf associate. He racked Kai's Glock, and his eyes began to glow red at the edges. Too bad Aldric couldn't have parked in the bushes. It was a cold day in hell when I was rooting for the vampire to come out ahead.

Kai and I led the way across the tranquil beach. The Rum Hut sat still, the radio dormant on top of the bar. What I wouldn't do for a stiff drink. Up the beach, about a mile, I could see high-powered lanterns—the kind you saw at construction sites—and torches.

"Jesus, the hole's not that deep," I said. But Aldric knew my history, and he'd assumed I had some trick up my sleeve. Unfortunately, he'd overestimated me, bringing way too much personnel and equipment, which, in a cruel twist of irony, was making his survival more unlikely since it screamed that he was here.

Lucille yanked my arm sharply, spinning me around. "What is your game?" Despite her unthreatening frame, her grip felt like it was about to crush my arm.

"Nothing."

"No more lies." She squeezed tighter, and I buckled to the sand in pain.

"Don't do that." Kai stepped forward to help, but was blasted backward by a sharp, rumbling burst of wind. He disappeared into the foliage at the end of the beach, and the gun-toting werewolf went to retrieve him.

Lucille's braid swished back and forth as she stared down at me. Shouts came from up the beach. So much for a surprise confrontation. Now, everyone knew about everyone else, and I was officially screwed.

Through stinging tears of pain I said, "Aldric has your soul."

She released my arm, and I crumpled to the ground. Maybe I shouldn't have been so thankful her magic didn't work on me. The physical beatings still hurt plenty, and she'd barely made an effort. In the distance, over the rollicking waves, a huge lightning bolt sizzled in the sky, lingering longer than any natural weather formation.

Yup. She could kick my ass *and* still bend the elements to her whim at the same time. This was why you didn't betray gods. On the other hand, I wouldn't be here at all had I allowed that wolf to kill me. The very definition of a catch-22. So, in a way, I'd been playing with house money all week.

They always say that, but when you lose your stack of house money, it still hurts like a son of a bitch.

I rubbed my bruised arm and got slowly to my feet. Off in the grass, the werewolf dragged Kai back to the sand. The searchlights winked out up the beach.

"I can call him," I said, reaching for my cell phone. "He'll probably be amenable to a deal."

"It will be my pleasure to kill him." Lucille cracked her knuckles like she'd been waiting for a good excuse. Not sure why she couldn't have done it before—neither she nor the DSA struck me as terribly concerned with due process. Maybe Aldric was like one of those parasitic critters in an ecosystem that fucked everything up, but was nonetheless a necessity. Like Wall Street traders who claimed they were making the market more efficient.

"I can really call—"

Lucille slapped the device from my hands, sending it skittering across the perfect sand. "I will handle this." She placed two fingers in her mouth and whistled. The werewolf immediately dropped Kai and began a rapid—and painful looking—transformation. When it was done, he trotted over to Lucille's side and sat down like a loyal dog. The beast was pure black and had a row of spikes studding his back from neck to tail like sinewy shark fins.

"Good boy, Fenrir." Lucille patted her wolf and it growled with loyal satisfaction.

If I'd stood a nonexistent chance against Lucille, how had the odds shifted now that I knew she had the mythical wolf of Norse legend at her beck and call? It was hard to imagine subzero probabilities of success, but I think I might have been staring them dead in the face.

Lucille pointed to the jungle, and the beast disappeared. She turned to me with a bright smile.

"Don't go anywhere, little Reaper. This will only take a moment."

There was a shriek in the jungle, followed by gunfire. Snarls erupted, punctuated by brief muzzle flashes. Then there was a loud whine, and one of the spikes hurtled through the brisk stormy air and landed right at Lucille's feet.

"You were saying?" I asked, watching the blood seep into the tan, moonlit sand. Aldric might have been an underdog, but underestimating him was still a grave mistake. Fenrir had learned that the hard way. Lucille, for her part, seemed like she was in a state of shock. She stared at the piece of bloodied cartilage, struggling to process how her mythical wolf had failed to dismantle Aldric limb-from-limb. I wanted to say *Roman Empire, bitch*, but now was not the time for taunts.

Instead, I needed to kick-start things. I backed up so that I was side-by-side with her.

With a gentle, caring hand, I patted her on the back. "I think your friend needs a little help."

There was a yip, followed by a pitiful whine that sounded like a helpless puppy. It almost got my heartstrings going, too, until I remember who the sound belonged to: a four-hundred-pound engine of annihilation and, most likely, rabies.

Lucille stared at the spike, tears in her eyes. "I've had him since...since..."

I would've been surprised, but you know what they say. Even a certain infamous dictator loved his dogs. And this crazy bitch was no different, even if her treasured companion was more of a monster. I gave her a firm push with my hand, slipping my other into her back pocket. It touched the wrinkled parchment of the glyph-cipher, which I snared with a clean lift.

It was folded and inside my own pocket before she even reacted. "You're right, Eden."

There was a tremendous clap of thunder, then she sprinted into the forest with nimble grace, headed straight for Fenrir's pained cries. I didn't wait for the aftermath. I had a good idea what that would be, anyway, and had every expectation that the fight would be short and decisive. I picked up the injured wolf's spike, which felt like a giant gummy bear made of sinew, and then went to check on my ally.

Kai was on his side, knocked unconscious by the wind blast. After pocketing the spike—which some subconscious voice told me could be useful—I shook the agent's body, which felt like touching a warm statue. He didn't stir. The service pistol lay nearby, along with the shreds of Fenrir's clothes from the mythical wolf's sudden transformation. I didn't try to pick it up; instead, I kicked it closer to the FBI agent, since he was the only one of us who could use it. I rose from the grass and tried tugging Kai by the boot. Instead of him moving, I ended up ass-down on the ground, holding his shoe.

A tree cracked in the jungle as leaves swirled in the sky from some sort of miniature cyclone.

Guess Aldric was doing better than I'd thought. That luck couldn't last, though.

I yanked the glyph-cipher out of my back pocket and started digging at the edge of the jungle. You know what you do when you're a squirrel in a land of lions? You bury a lot of acorns for a fucking rainy day. I shoved the map into the damp soil, hoping that the magical enchantments would preserve it from worms and enterprising jungle critters. Then I tossed the dirt back on top and covered it in leaves.

After checking once more on Kai, who was still out cold, I began sprinting up the beach, toward the soul shard's location. To my left, the forest bent and crackled, intermittent thunderclaps and whines scoring a pitched battle. I heard neither Aldric nor Lucille cry out, so I couldn't tell who was winning.

My lungs burning, I hit the dig site a few minutes later. The funny thing about a long stretch of beach is that it's the opposite of your car's mirrors—all objects are much farther than they appear. Despite the passing minutes, however, the battle showed no signs of abating. A small fire had broken out from Lucille's repeated lightning strikes, judging by the smoke trailing up from the forest.

The searchlights were set up in a wide ring. Holes dotted the beach—some of them near trees, others in the sand. I could see why there had been haphazard confusion —the banyan tree under which they'd dug hadn't been the correct one. I spotted mine in the darkness, about two hundred yards up the beach, its massive canopy looming.

I hurried to the large tree and dropped to my knees before the knotty bark. Maybe it did have mystical powers, all things considered, if it had protected the soul from falling into Aldric's hands. I plunged my fingers into the soil, finding the soul shard without too much trouble. Its dark energy buzzed up my arm like an unpleasant and particularly infectious virus. I briefly tasted the faint burn of whiskey on my tongue before I slipped it into my pocket.

A plan formed in my mind. It wasn't much of one, but it was my only shot at not ending the night in a pinewood box. That was enough right then, so I willed my tired legs back to the dig site and got to work. The battle continued in the forest, although it was less feverish than before. The thunderclaps came less often, and the leaves didn't gust above the treetops with as much intensity. Even immortal goddesses and ancient vampires succumbed to fatigue, apparently.

I didn't have that luxury. My arms felt like jelly as I dragged the high-powered lamps across the sand, toward the edge of the tide. There were eight of them, which I arranged to focus on a very specific area of the beach. Then I jammed the soul shard into the sand and flipped the switch on the generator. A blinding glow cut through the dimness, causing me to shield my eyes.

That would do.

Then I walked to the edge of the water and pulled out Fenrir's severed spike, staring out at the sea as I awaited the battle's final verdict.

"I am trying to think of reasons to refrain from terminating your employment contract," a tired, but still authoritative voice said behind me, "but I am admittedly finding them difficult to generate."

I didn't turn. Hell, my body barely reacted. It was funny how, once you resign yourself to the inevitable and just accept the roll of the dice—instead of fighting, fighting, fighting—how liberating it all felt. The wind rustled through my hair and I held out my arms, almost believing that I could take flight.

I heard Aldric try to switch off the generator. He cursed, flicking the switch back and forth. *"Eden."*

It took him a little longer than his top speed, but he was at my throat in a few quick steps. His cold, slender fingers wrapped around my neck.

I didn't react, even as my windpipe closed.

"What have you done, Eden?"

"If you stop choking me, maybe I'll tell you."

His fingers relaxed, but his hand stayed put. "You lied to me."

"You didn't know where to dig, you dumb fuck." A small bolt of lightning crashed over a wave breaking far out to sea. "That's on you."

"Do not test me, Eden." His fingers twitched, eager to be rid of me. Luckily, he was a businessman, so revenge and annoyance were tempered by financial prudence. Reapers—even problematic ones—didn't grow on trees. And, if we were being frank, any fracture in our working relationship was his fault. His recruiting and motivational tactics weren't exactly winning any managerial awards.

"Aren't you curious what it is? Just a little?"

"My patience is razor thin." His fangs clicked out—the first time I'd ever heard that happen—and his head suddenly loomed over my shoulder, so I could see his hawkish green eyes in my peripheral vision.

As scare tactics went, I'm sure it had made many people throughout history shit their pants and give in. But I was all out of fucks to give, so I simply raised my eyebrow and said, "It's a goddess's soul shard."

Aldric retreated from my personal space. I thanked myself for having a juicy enough carrot to dangle, then watched in horror as my brief victory disappeared. The generator soared overhead, landing in the sea with a sputtering crash.

Turning around, I found Aldric wearing a maniacal grin. "There is an easy solution to all problems, Eden."

Shit.

"That is *my* soul!" Lucille's melodious voice roared around us, like the sea itself was having a word. I glanced up at the trees just in time to see the bedraggled goddess dive from the top of a tall palm and land atop Aldric, who was clutching the soul shard like it was the most precious object in existence. I could see that her forearms were covered in pink, scorching welts, not unlike what had happened when I had thrown Drake's treasure at her face.

The two tumbled in the sand. Lucille threw Aldric back, ripping the soul shard from his grasp. She looked briefly satisfied until he popped to his feet and hurled a handful of metallic-looking dust at her face. Up the beach about a hundred yards, I watched Fenrir limp from the foliage and collapse in a bloody heap. The moonlit glinted off the raw crimson patch on his back where the spike had simply been ripped off clean.

This wasn't quite the outcome I'd have bet on, but maybe having no clear winner was better than what I expected.

"Enough." My calm voice made both ancient beings cock their heads in confusion at me. Neither looked inclined to listen, so I made my pitch in a hurry. "I have things you both want."

"I have my soul back," Lucille said. "What more could you give me?"

"But you don't have this." I pulled the sinewy spike

from my pocket and then gestured to the ocean. "It'll be gone forever."

"You wouldn't." Good. We were skipping the whole *I don't care about that* bullshit I had been hoping to avoid. Her gaze looked plaintive. "Please, don't."

"Eden has nothing I desire," Aldric said, brushing off his ruined suit like it would make some sort of difference. "She's a defective toy."

"Gee, you know all the right things to say to a girl," I replied. "Too bad you're wrong, dumbass."

I let the insult hang on the stiff breeze. Aldric looked inclined to rip my throat out. But he also was curious about what I might have to offer.

"I have something you desire very much. A stash of hundreds of souls. And I have something you both desire."

"Which is?" Aldric asked with great suspicion.

"The name of your competitor."

"The one peddling alchemical drinks is dead," Lucille said. "You speak lies, little Reaper."

"Yeah, well, you don't have the guy who actually made them." I shrugged and dangled the piece of Fenrir's flesh over the ocean. "You know, the guy who you've been chasing all around, but have never caught? So, if you asshats would rather kill me—"

"Only if you bring me the rival Reaper and the thieves," Aldric said.

"And agree to a new trial for your repeated violations," Lucille said.

Tired as I was, I almost accepted their shitty terms. But I was done being pushed around.

I held all the cards.

I'd bet my life on it.

So I took a step closer to the ocean and said, "I don't think you two understand how leverage works."

"I'll kill your sister and the agent and the treasure hunter," Lucille said.

"No, you won't." I reared back like I was preparing to hurl the spike into the rough sea, and the goddess visibly trembled. "Feel that, bitch? That's true love."

She glowered, but didn't respond. Aldric also looked furious, but had nothing to say. Confident that I now had control of the floor, all I needed to do was stick the landing. I could've asked for the moon and pushed my luck. But instead, I just wanted to reset the game board.

I turned to Lucille and said, "You will stop hunting Cross." I held up my hand before she could protest. "You will not harm my sister or the agent. In return, we'll resume the terms of our old agreement. No weapons, no killing."

She looked about ready to shake her head, so I threw in the kicker. "And you get your own Reaper. The DSA could use one, I presume."

"You knew the Reaper's identity all this time?" A vein bulged in Aldric's lean neck. Anger cut across his sharp features.

"And you," I said, addressing him like a misbehaving child, which I enjoyed far too much, "You will not harm my sister, nor those who stole thirteen million in gold bullion from your vault."

"Why would I harm your sister? She's already dead."

"Because she's the rival Reaper making my performance look so terrible." I relished the ancient vampire's reaction to that truth bomb. It was sweet to see his own plan—four years in the making—return to bite him in the ass. Maybe if Moreland hadn't been a murderous asshole, this storm could've been avoided. Oh well. No going back.

"These terms are not acceptable," Aldric said, and took a step forward. Lucille took a step toward him.

The goddess said, "I do not know where you acquired objects imbued with deicide arcana, but a continued battle is in neither of our interests."

"Nor is agreeing to these terms."

"I didn't tell you the best part, jackass," I said, striding up the dark beach until I was nose-to-nose with him. "I'll keep delivering seven souls a week to you. Forever."

His emerald eyes lit up with surprise. "You would do that for me to spare these pitiful humans?"

"It's a yes or no question."

Aldric extended a hand. "It is a deal."

I looked at his hand, then at the goddess's face. Lucille looked hesitant, her braid swishing in the breeze. One of her hands searched the back pocket of her slacks for the glyph-cipher as she eyed me with suspicion.

I matched her stare with a cool poker face.

"You have taken the glyph-cipher, little Reaper."

"Look behind you." She followed my finger to the smoking jungle, where a quarter of the nearby trees had been stripped of their leaves. "Think you could've lost it, I don't know, somewhere else?"

She reflected on my explanation, then sighed. It was hard to deny that the lengthy skirmish could have knocked something loose. She extended her hand.

"I do, however, believe you have something of *mine* that was taken by force." I tapped my sneaker against the perfect sand to show that I was impatient. Her lips curled up in a sour expression, and she reached into her pocket to get the Reaper's Switch.

The duct-taped handle had never felt so good in my

hand. I flicked it out, just to make sure everything was intact.

Lucille kept her hand out, clearly expecting me to grasp it. I looked at the goddess's and warlord's dirt-covered hands, but didn't extend my own.

"Forgive me if your promises aren't exactly gold." I grinned—the smug expression of someone who had prevailed against the odds—and added, "But I think we have a solution that will keep everyone on their best behavior."

Thirty minutes later, Agnes Willsprout was trotting across the storm-torn beach in her expensive heels with a contract in tow.

One hour—and one bloody thumb later—and I was sitting at the empty Rum Hut, nursing a tequila on the rocks as I looked at a copy of the magically-binding contract I'd just signed.

Being back to square one had never felt so damn good.

46

I HITCHED A RIDE BACK TO THE SERVICE ROAD, AND then I willed myself up the beach to the villa. Khan bitched at me about the lack of adequate food—whiskey was a poor source of nutrition for a cat, apparently—but I paid him no heed, falling into a deep sleep on the worn leather couch.

Saturday morning rolled around, and I was awakened by a deep knock at the door. Scrambling over the scratched hardwood in the same sandy, sweat-stained clothes I'd slept in, I glanced through the peephole to see who was outside.

Kai. He'd been gone when we'd walked back up the beach. How he'd managed that was hard to say, considering the ass kicking he'd absorbed from Lucille.

I threw open the deadbolt.

"How'd you survive?" he asked.

"I could ask you the same question."

"Rayna tracked my phone when she passed the van."

"She didn't send backup for me?"

"By the time she'd called in backup at the hospital, the beach was empty. Save for a couple broken searchlights." Kai held up his arm, which had a hospital band around it.

When he stepped inside, I could see that he was moving slowly. Guess getting slammed by a goddess's wind spell will do that.

"Probably lucky for everyone involved," I said.

Kai nodded and limped toward the kitchen. He grabbed the whiskey and poured himself a healthy cup. He sipped it, then looked embarrassed. "I should have asked."

"Glad you're back to your old self."

"Closer than I'd like." A faint darkness danced in his calm eyes, then vanished. The spear sigil branding him as a warrior glowed for a miss-it-if-you-blink shred of a moment. "Thought I'd come by to tell you what's going on."

I glanced at the digital clock on the microwave. It was eleven. A lot could have happened since I'd gone to sleep. I pulled up a stool next to the polished limestone island and took the whiskey cup from him. After a long drink, I slid it back.

"You should really get some snacks," Kai said.

"This is what I have been telling the stupid human," Khan said from the living room.

"File your complaints in the customer service box." I flipped him off. "Tell me what's up."

He ran down the highlights. The FBI had gone to the Mayor Stefan Cambridge's mansion to make an arrest for our kidnapping and illegal detainment. Apparently, the mayor's activities hadn't actually come as much of a surprise to the Feds. Truth was, he'd been an informant for some time. That bit about my talking to gods in the file? Yup, that'd come courtesy of Stefan Cambridge. And here I'd thought we'd had an understanding. But when the Feds had dangled the electric chair over his head, the serial killer had started snitching on everyone.

He'd gotten his in the end, though. Instead of making an

arrest, the Feds had found Stefan Cambridge's headless body in the backyard, lined up next to twenty-four similarly headless skeletons and a matching number of graves. It was hard to tell whether Lucille or Aldric had gotten to the alchemist first. They'd probably drawn straws for the honor.

After that, the FBI had retrieved Moreland's armless—and headless—corpse from the melting frost around his cabin. No one could quite explain the empty glass cabinet, but the murder's MO seemed like a close enough fit to the prolific mayor's that everyone had been comfortable calling Moreland victim number twenty-five.

Alkemy had officially been shut down due to public safety violations, but Sierra hadn't been found or implicated in the whole operation.

And Rayna, off the record, had explained to Kai why—when he had asked—she had helped to steal the money from Aldric. One motive was obvious: Aldric was an asshole. But the other was more troubling: Drake's true treasure was a long-lost cache of artifacts imbued with the power of deicide arcana—that is, god-killing magic. The coin had been a tiny taste of the power contained within the cache. The real power lay within the Sword of Damocles, which could topple a god—or even an entire pantheon—with its strength. It had been created as a check against wanton abuse of power, should humanity's rulers get too comfortable surrounded by the trappings of their celestial kingdoms.

Good thing I'd buried that glyph-cipher.

It dawned on me, standing there, that Moreland wouldn't do his own dirty work at his new gig. Sure, he *could* have done the wetwork, but that had been his job for Aldric going on a thousand years.

So while he'd ordered the hit on Roan, someone else

had been the triggerman. My first thought was James. He clearly worked for Moreland—snappy dresser, dumb enough to do his duties without asking any questions.

He'd spun a story about receiving a phone call to plant the gun. It had rung true for a reason: it contained a kernel of truth. All the best lies did. Except it hadn't been Cross who had called him.

I just didn't know who.

Maybe I could get James's phone records to see who had called for the frame job.

Kai drank the last of the whiskey and put the mug down with a light—but still decisive—clink.

I said, "I never knew bureaucracy moved this fast."

"Our branch of the FBI is a little different." Kai batted the mug between his strong fingers. "It has to be, given the island."

"When you guys tossed Stefan's mansion, you didn't find anything about him killing a blade sorceress, did you?" I still didn't understand if Doris had been a random victim, or simply gotten in the way.

"He actually kept a diary." Kai looked completely disgusted.

"What'd it say?"

"Something about how a woman had been hired to kill him by some kid he was blackmailing."

"Renard?" I asked.

"Yeah, that's it," Kai said. "Why?"

I recalled the kid's words to Sierra. *The guy you work for, he has them.* By them, Renard must've meant his mom and sister. His spreadsheet had started six months ago— about the same time Alkemy had opened. The hundred grand on his spreadsheet must've been what he "owed" the mayor as ransom.

"You find anything about two hostages?" I asked.

"Yeah. There was another note in there. Written in a different hand."

"That makes no sense," I said.

"We found a mom and her teenage daughter in a room beneath that shed." Kai shook his head, and I could see that he'd encountered the skulls, too. They left an impression. Not a good one. "It'll be a long road for them both, but—"

"They were alive?" To think I'd been right above them. Renard Martin's family probably could've heard my conversation with Stefan. That made my blood boil and crawl at the same time.

"Brought them back to their house about an hour ago." Kai stared at the whiskey, and then finished it. "Damnedest thing though, Eden."

"What's that?"

"There was a note in the journal, beneath the info about their location." Kai's calm eyes looked up at me, but I could see it shook him. "I'm sorry I wasn't braver."

I bit my lip.

I knew who had killed Stefan Cambridge. It'd been neither Aldric nor Lucille.

Because Sierra had gotten to the mayor first.

I switched gears to the still unresolved murder that had dogged me for the entire week. "You guys confirm Moreland killed Roan Kelly?"

The skin around Kai's eyes bunched up, and he looked away. "That's actually why I came."

"Bad news?"

"I have to take you in. Trial's being pushed up."

"But Moreland—"

"He's dead. And no physical evidence links him to the murder."

I let that sink in. After everything, I was still going to end up behind bars.

But, for now, I was still free, so I said, "How about one last favor?"

"I don't know, Eden—"

"Fuck protocol for once."

The agent finished the whiskey and wiped his chin.

Then Kai Taylor looked me dead in the eye and said, "One hour."

I said, "That's all I need."

And if it wasn't, that was all I was gonna get.

47

Looking up James's phone records turned out to be a bust. Most of his calls were to Moreland—who had indeed been his employer—and his father. Nothing unexpected. It was conceivable that the call to plant the gun had come in on the tattoo shop's line, or some designated pay phone. It was also plausible that I was grasping at straws, and there had been no call. In that case, James was the killer—or we had no leads on the real murderer, which amounted to the same thing. Zero evidence, Eden hangs out behind bars for a long time.

In my book, I'd file that outcome under "suboptimal."

We pulled into the cracked parking lot outside Lion-hawk Ink. At noon, the neon sign didn't throw the same sort of light over the faded asphalt. In the daylight, the entire strip mall seemed like a relic from a past age. The nail salon and laundromat still didn't look like they were open.

"I'm due back at the Getaway in thirty, Eden," Kai said as we got out, the unspoken subtext clear. I had thirty minutes to crack this case, otherwise it was straight to jail. I wondered if Aldric would still shell out for Agnes to represent me in court.

"The Getaway?"

"It's what we call the office," Kai said. "You know, because it's a hotel."

"Sure. Got it. Clever." My mind was focused on other things. How would I get James to talk? Kai had done me a solid and pinged the guy's phone, so we at least knew the fixer was inside. But he hadn't talked last time, and now that his boss was dead, he had even less of a reason to spill any incriminating details. I'm sure most people thought that Aldric was responsible for killing Moreland. If that's what he thought, then opening up to me would only paint a target on the back of his nice suit.

No, I needed a different tactic.

"Just go with me," I said as we walked toward the tattoo parlor. No one was inside, save for the staff. That was good. "Follow my lead."

Kai said, "Should I be worried?"

"I'll let you know." I swung the door open with a big flourish, causing the bell to rattle loudly. Darius looked at me from behind the counter and set down his sandwich. Mick barely looked up from his silver case over by the vinyl chairs.

"I'd say your return is welcome, Miss Hunter, but we both know that'd be a lie."

"We're here to arrest your son." I glanced around the shop, taking in the four empty chairs and the wall of tattoo designs. "Where is he?"

"James isn't here."

"We know he's here," I said, nodding at Kai. "He killed that guy outside my house and set me up."

"Did he, now?"

"His prints are on the murder weapon," I said. "Forensic analysis is a real bitch."

I sensed tension from Darius, so I turned to the were-wolf and wagged my finger at him. He placed his elbows down on the stickered countertop and kept a watchdog-like gaze on me. I smiled, then returned my attention to Mick's craggy face. The old man showed no signs of cracking, although his sigil-covered knuckles were glowing a faint shade of blue. That was funny. I thought they were only activated when he was inking someone. But perhaps the magic had other uses as well.

"Something on your mind, Mick?" I asked. "You seem a little...less sanguine than usual."

"I don't know what that means, Miss Hunter. Some of us didn't go to college."

"That makes two of us," I said. "You know what I think, actually?"

"I can't wait to hear." His rough voice contained a bit of an edge that I hadn't heard previously. Good. I was rattling him. A few more minutes, and maybe he'd reveal something he shouldn't.

"I think I'm feeling a little vengeful. A little pissed off." I came closer, taking measured steps across the dirty plastic floor. I slid into the vinyl seat next to him, my jeans squeaking against the worn material. "And maybe I'm thinking the FBI's version of justice is a little bit tame for someone who tried to ruin my life."

"What did you have in mind instead?" Now his voice was quiet, his good eye cast at the floor, while his scarred socket seemed to stay fixed on me.

"Maybe I call Aldric. Tell him your son tried to elimi-nate one of his prime investments." I drummed my fingers on the metal case on the tray table before him. "You heard what happened to Moreland, I presume? And then there was Mayor Cambridge..."

I let out a whistle between my teeth as if to say *well, shiiiiiit.*

The fluorescent box store style lights buzzed. Mick's chest heaved in and out, his breaths loud and nervous. "You bitch."

"Just a phone call away," I said with deadly sincerity.

"You don't even care." Mick stood suddenly, the sigils on his knuckles glowing a white-hot shade of blue. "Just wreck things like a hurricane, and never look back."

The safety clicked off Kai's service weapon, and I heard Darius growl. Things were heating up. Good. Maybe James would emerge from hiding in the back room and confess. Mick stared at me with a wild eye, his fist balled tightly around a tattoo needle. It gleamed like a tiny scalpel.

"If this is about the eye—"

"Of course, you bitch. It was always about the eye." His remaining eye blazed with intense fury, any calmness gone. Now, instead of his mess of hair making him look like an aging bad boy, he looked like a meth-addled mad scientist on the verge of blowing up a city.

I didn't feel good about being the city in this metaphor.

"What was about the eye?" I asked as innocently as possible, just to press his buttons.

"I killed your stupid boyfriend after Moreland told me who he was. He suggested I do it to solidify a new partnership between us. But I didn't need to do that. I just wanted to make you suffer." A crazed smile crept over Mick's wrinkled face. "And then, I thought, after I'd run away, there was a way to make things even worse for you. So I called my son, and he planted the gun."

Well, that was certainly unexpected. I hadn't even

considered Mick a suspect. But he checked all the boxes: great motive, knew where I lived, could have discovered my association with Roan through Aldric's network.

"And what about your old friend Aldric?"

The ink master laughed bitterly. "Do you know how long I trained and studied? And that vampire bastard still treated me like disposable dogshit all these years."

"What about the cash?" I asked, recalling the banded twenties in the duffel bag allegedly given to James as payment for framing me.

"My cut from Moreland," Mick said. "More than that prick Aldric ever threw my way."

"Interesting," I said, keeping an eye on his fist. He was about five feet away, but with a quick lunge, he could jab me in the eye—or worse. Busting him only to die would be the very definition of a Pyrrhic victory.

"*Interesting?*" Mick laughed bitterly. "It was genius."

"Until you just told it to an FBI agent. Very genius up until that point." I shot him a look like I wasn't impressed. "And Moreland pulled all your strings the whole time, if we're really getting technical about it."

"It doesn't matter what you say." Mick shook his glowing fist at me. "You finally suffered for stealing my eye." His mouth opened wide, the smile threatening to overrun his craggy face entirely. "And Aldric suffered as he watched his precious investment spiral out of control."

Mick rushed forward, rearing back to strike.

Kai's gun barked. The ink master collapsed to the ground.

Transforming claws clicked against the counter. The gun roared again, and a body crashed to the dirty floor.

I spun to find Darius, maybe an eighth shifted into a

wolf, staring lifelessly at the ceiling. A single gunshot wound ran through his head.

Sometimes primal instincts got you killed.

The murderer, however, remained very much alive.

"You're like a plague." Mick spit on my shoes, or at least tried to. "Eden? More like *Devil*."

"Oh, don't talk like that." I knelt next to him, watching the blood seep from his shoulder. Perfect shot—incapacitating him, but no risk of death. A dead body wouldn't do a whole lot of good for clearing my name. "You might hurt a girl's feelings."

"You'll get what's coming to you. One day."

"We all do in the end." I rose and watched Kai cuff him. As the agent led the bleeding man to the door, I said, "One question."

"She has a question." Mick sneered, his lips torn between pain and hatred.

"How'd you burn Roan?" His screams had occurred *prior* to the two kill shots. He'd had scorch marks on his skin. It could've been from the hot barrel of the .45, but somehow I didn't think that was the case.

Instead of answering, Mick held up his faintly glowing fingers. The sigils. The heat and pain that I had felt when getting the lantern tattoo four years ago had been energy channeled from them. It stood to reason that, when that power wasn't transferred through the tip of a needle, it had to dissipate in other ways.

Kai put Mick outside on the sidewalk's curb, then reentered the tattoo shop. In a low voice, his lips close to my ear, so close I could smell his woody aftershave, almost feel his stubble on my skin, he said, "I don't think you should be here when the ambulance arrives."

"I'm pretty sure James is still hiding like a bitch in the back room."

He leaned back, his dark hair briefly covering his calm eyes before he swept it away. "Then we're on the same page, Eden Hunter."

"Don't get used to it," I said with a quick wink. Then I exited the shop, bell ringing merrily behind me as I headed home.

48

I saw Dante Cross's Porsche parked on the service road near the banana tree. That meant Lucille had kept up her end of the bargain—not that I was surprised. Violating magically binding contracts tended to have bad consequences. Besides, she was presumably happy with her haul: a Reaper of her own, the fragment of her blackened soul returned, and Stefan's head separated from his body. Even if the latter had been Sierra's doing, it cleared a thorny problem from the DSA's plate.

Of course, had she known Cross and his crew planned to unearth a god-killing sword, she probably would have reconsidered granting the treasure hunter amnesty. For now, however, the immortal man would see another day in paradise.

Spotting his sun-bleached messy hair up the black sand beach, I waved at him. He gave me a nod, his hair blowing in the pleasant afternoon breeze. A loose t-shirt billowed around his bronzed arms, and he walked barefoot, his shoes located safely on the dry part of the sand. After all the storms yesterday, there wasn't even a hint of a cloud on the blue horizon. His golden-flecked eyes glittered as I approached.

"I received two visits today," Cross said, poking at the wet sand with his toes. For someone who had lived for almost five hundred years, he seemed quite content with the simple act. When your life hangs briefly by the thinnest of threads, tiny pleasures take on more significance. "I suppose I owe you my life, Eden."

"Don't mention it."

"You could have left my name out of Aldric's mouth."

"Sure, if you wanted to end up hanging from a banana tree one day." Better for Aldric to know and forgive him for the gold heist—or bury it deep—than for him to discover the responsible parties a year from now and fly off the handle.

"Both Lucille and Aldric said you have the agreement in writing."

"Magically binding."

He winked slyly. "Remind me not to cross you."

"Hard to forget when I saved your ass."

"If I do recall, Eden, I saved you down in the caves."

"Technically, you brought me into your five-hundred-year feud," I said. "By the way, about that."

"Yes?" His eyes shimmered as he waited for my question.

"What the hell did you need *me* for?"

"What else?" Cross said. "You're a Reaper who has Lucille's ear." The corner of his lip turned in a sort of grin. "Well, used to. I don't think she likes you after what happened."

"Probably not," I said, wiping a bead of sweat off my hot skin. "What's being a Reaper got to do with it?"

"The Sword of Damocles is but a larger Reaper's

Switch. Which means only a Reaper can wield it." Cross tilted his head and nodded. "Well, one difference."

There was a long silence during which the waves gently crashed over the shore. Finally, I said, "Well, you gonna tell me or what?"

"It destroys the soul so that the deity can never return. True death."

"So I couldn't kill her with my Switch?"

"That you even cleaved a tiny fragment of her soul away shows that you're a very special Reaper indeed." Cross gave me a sly wink, then added, "Of course, I hear your sister is better."

I shoved him gently. "I'm sure Lucille will appreciate this display of loyalty after whatever she's done for you."

"Lucille granted me immortality," Cross said, answering the implied question. "But..."

"But?"

"You know Lucille. Everything comes with a trial attached."

"Is that why she has to go?"

"She's a danger to the world."

Not sure I bought that. A danger to me and Cross, maybe, since we'd screwed her over and yanked her chain one time too many. But the world at large? She couldn't even leave the borders of the island. It was like a large prison where she was both warden and inmate.

"I'm more curious about who you had to kill for the ingredients." Goddess or no helping you out, Cross's brand of immortality could only be purchased with the full soul of a family member or lover.

"The only person I've ever loved." He looked almost wistfully out at the perfect vista, his devil-may-care guard dropped completely. His fingers were rubbing across his carefully maintained designer stubble as if they were searching for answers. "But that might be a story for another time."

A wave crashed on the dark shore, the tide soaking my low-tops in salty foam. I watched a brown pelican dive into the water like a jackhammer and return with a glistening fish. Cross crouched and skimmed his fingers across the foam residue coating the wet sand.

"Then tell me your trial."

He glanced up at me, the friendly smile returning. "Oh, that's easy." He hopped up. "I was supposed to stop treasure hunting."

"How long did that stick?"

"Less than two months." Cross shook the water from his tan fingers and stretched out his shoulders, revealing the hard V in his lean torso. From the way he arched his back, it was intentional. Probably worked on all the girls. Not this one, though. "Worst two months of my life."

"And when was that?"

"1580."

"You're fucking insane."

"It only made it more exciting." Cross tipped an invisible hat. "I believe there's someone waiting for you at the house."

"Who?"

"Platinum hair, long legs for days, lips to—"

"That's my sister."

"Oh, I know," he said, giving me a cocky wave. "But I like your look better."

I bit my lip hard to prevent from blushing like a teenager.

"Say," I said as he looked ready to leave, "how'd you meet Roan and everyone, anyway?"

"They all came to the shop for supplies, just like you." Cross gazed at the perfect horizon. "And, eventually, I started to piece together a team who could crack the map."

"But you didn't let them downstairs."

"They just took my word that it was shit down there, Eden. You should try it some time."

"Sometimes you just gotta discover the truth for yourself."

Cross nodded and winked before picking up his shoes and walking away, back toward the service road. I watched him for a moment and shook my head. I could've told him about the recovered glyph-cipher, but I'd have to feel him out a little more. A little voice in my head said, *yeah, you'd like that*, and I rolled my eyes at my baser instincts. That was a dumpster fire waiting to happen. He'd already gotten me almost killed at least twice.

With a foreign mixture of trepidation and excitement, I raced across the black sand to see Sierra for the first time in four years. I saw her hair, glimmering in the perfect sun, before I saw the rest of her. Heart slamming against my bruised ribs, a thin sweat trickling down my brow, I slowed down and tried to walk as casually as possible toward the marble steps.

My sister was wearing a white summer dress—cut well above the knee, of course—with a black leather bag slung over her shoulder and simple black heels that, naturally, complemented the outfit perfectly. Not practical for the beach, but such mere trivialities had never stood in the way of her fashion sense. Besides, I'd never seen someone so adept on heels. It was a rare skill indeed, one that clearly wasn't genetic. I wore sneakers for a reason.

A faint breeze brought her familiar smell—subtle, hints of vanilla shampoo and little else—and a wave of nostalgic memories. At least she wasn't hiding from me anymore. I tamped down the memory floodgates and instead focused on the other thing on my tongue: her soul. It wasn't as damaged as I'd worried, hadn't been corrupted beyond repair. Hints of the party girl and social butterfly remained. But she had lost her way over the past months, and that had left a mark. Whether that was permanent, or could be fixed with time, like Kai's, remained to be seen.

She glanced up but didn't say anything. I wondered if she too was sizing me up, feeling the changes the last four years had wrought.

She looked over her shoulder, at the villa's winding stairs. "Not bad, E."

"It's all right."

"You could use a carpet."

I raised my eyebrow. Her big blue eyes looked back at me—those big blue eyes I'd seen take down just about every guy in her path, much to my teenage annoyance and jealousy—with a look like *come on*.

"You broke in."

"That's barely even a lock." Yes, only to her did two locks and a deadbolt qualify as pitiful security. I understood what the bouncer had meant by *nutcase*. She had always played by her own rules, pulling the occasional batshit stunt just because. And most everyone just forgave her after she batted her eyelashes a couple times and turned on the fake waterworks.

"How'd Khan take your unannounced visit?"

"Ooh, he's a sweetie."

I wondered if I'd somehow acquired another cat and not noticed. "The one that looks like a skunk?"

"I patted him on the belly and he purred the whole time."

Sierra even had the magic touch when it came to ornery animals. Either that, or she was lying, and Khan had tried to decapitate her. I mulled it over and shrugged. Everyone loved her. That was her gift.

She leaned back against the marble staircase, wind blowing through her hair like she was on one of those shampoo commercials. "So I guess I have you to thank for ripping me off. Twice."

"Well, you almost got me killed, so that should make us about even."

A flash of her perfect smile came, then it was gone. "So, who's the guy?"

"What guy?"

"The hot one." She puckered her full lips, which were covered in her trademark pink lip gloss. "Like, *really* hot."

"Cross?" I rolled my eyes, even if she had a point. "I call him the jackass who almost got me killed."

"Speaking of jackasses." Sierra rose with effortless elegance, and her heart-shaped chin puckered into a scowl. "What the fuck, E?"

Her hand shot into the bag and retrieved a piece of paper. She balled it up and threw it at me. I didn't really need to pick it up to see what this was about.

"I take it Lucille paid you a visit earlier."

"You signed me up to be that bitch's servant." Sierra wrinkled her nose. "Not cool."

"I don't suppose the goddess explained how that arrangement came about, did she?"

"Goddess?" Sierra looked at me like I was insane.

Yes, I suppose a fair amount of backstory was necessary. But first, I needed to clear the air about something else.

"Renard Martin." The name hung on the salty breeze like an accusation.

"I killed that prick Stefan for that." Sierra gnawed on her lip, her eyes tearing up. "I wanted to...I just...I just couldn't."

"Why's that," I said, my tone hard as diamond.

"Because Stefan threatened *you*." A tear came down her perfect cheek and she sniffled. "He said he knew something about you that would get you killed. That if I even approached you, talked to you, anything..." She shook her head and looked up at the cloudless sky. "I couldn't be responsible for that."

"What'd he want with the kid?"

"Distribution of his stupid arcana kits." Sierra sighed, her shoulders shaking slightly. "The kid's a natural, Eden."

"I noticed," I said. Silence lingered over the winding marble staircase. "The mayor said you came to him."

She nodded, but didn't respond. Finally, she said, "But I didn't sign up for that."

"How long?" I asked.

"A little more than six months," Sierra replied, bowing her head in shame. "I wanted to talk to you, E. So bad."

"And before?"

"The last thing I remember is New Orleans."

That struck me as a lie. I'd heard her voice on the other end of the line four years ago, the night I'd asked Lucille to bring her back from the dead.

But I wasn't going to press.

Not when I'd just gotten her back.

I brushed away my anger and gestured up the winding marble stairs. "I hope you like shitty coffee."

"Why's that, E?"

"Because we have lost time to make up for." I walked past, then paused. Turning around, I clasped her in my arms and whispered, "Don't you ever die on me again."

I felt a little hitch in her breath as she tried to keep the tears from flowing again. Me? That was nothing but the dry breeze irritating my eyes.

And if anyone tells you otherwise, they're running a con.

END OF BOOK 1

BOOK 2: Eden Hunter returns in *Soul Fire* to investigate who killed a phoenix's guardian—and why.

TAP HERE to get *Soul Fire* (Book 2)

Made in the USA
Coppell, TX
24 September 2023

21971497R00225